GRAVE
INSTINCT

GRAVE INSTINCT

ROBERT W. WALKER

BERKLEY BOOKS, NEW YORK

B

A Berkley Book
Published by The Berkley Publishing Group
A division of Penguin Group (USA) Inc.
375 Hudson Street
New York, New York 10014

This book is an original publication of The Berkley Publishing Group.

First edition: September 2003

Visit the author's website at
www.RobertWWalker.com

Library of Congress Cataloging-in-Publication Data

Walker, Robert W. (Robert Wayne), 1948–
    Grave instinct / Robert W. Walker.
        p.   cm.
    ISBN 0-425-19170-2
    1. Coran, Jessica (Fictitious character)—Fiction.   2. Medical
examiners (Law)—Fiction.   3. Serial murders—Fiction.   4.
Cannibalism—Fiction.   I. Title.

PS3573.A425385G73   2003
813'.54—dc21

                                          2003051814

PRINTED IN THE UNITED STATES OF AMERICA

10   9   8   7   6   5   4   3   2   1

ACKNOWLEDGMENTS

This is to acknowledge the extremely important contributions (too many to enumerate) to this novel and indeed the entire *Instinct* series by Lara Robbins, aka the Copyeditor.

I would also like to acknowledge the nonfiction opus entitled *The Beast Within* by Benjamin Walker, a volume filled with delightfully arcane and esoteric information that I have drawn on in the penning of this work. Mr. Walker's research puts into perspective mankind's wobbly often embattled relationship with the human body, mind and soul. Given what mankind has attributed to the human monster over the eons, it is little wonder we have begun to raise a larger and larger crop of sociopaths and psychos like Grant Kenyon. . . .

PROLOGUE

Groveland Memorial Cemetery, Morristown, New Jersey
August 16, 1990

WORKING quietly, Daryl Thomas Cahil had dug into the cemetery earth for several hours while the windswept night played about the headstone he had located.

AMIEE LEE PHEIFFER
BELOVED DAUGHTER 1983–1990

He again sank the spade into the dirt, finally gaining a response—a greeting between metal and concrete. At last, he'd found the little crypt. A concrete vault concealing the coffin, a slab-stone top over all.

"All right . . . good . . ." he congratulated himself from the bottom of the grave he'd spent the early-morning hours reopening. Glancing at his dirtied watch, he read 4:02 A.M. Less than an hour and the cemetery superintendent would be driving up to unlatch the rusted old gates. Still, it was enough time to gain the prize buried here, which he had come to claim as his.

Daryl had to dig out earth alongside the vault to create

space enough to force the concrete lid aside, just enough to get at the coffin. He worked to clear the lid of remaining soil as a light sprinkle began to add to his problems. He needn't remove the lid entirely, only partially, enough to climb in and open the coffin lid.

Spade tip against stone tablet clattered more than once, making him wince. Finally, he tossed up the spade to the level earth, fearful it was making too much noise now against the outer stone coffin.

The cemetery stood amid a half-mile-long quad of neighborhood homes, homes he would just as soon leave undisturbed. He could not afford waking so much as a dog.

He got down on all fours.

He clawed away at the dirt lying over the small coffin.

He imagined what lay inside, what he had come for, his goal.

He felt his pulse quicken, his heart pound.

He felt cold and hot at the same time. And the cold rain only added to the chills following the sweats.

His brain calmed him, talking soothingly to him, saying, *"Once you have it and you consume it . . . you will know a tranquility and enlightenment like none other."*

He kept digging and clawing the dirt away from the lid. Soon Daryl Thomas Cahil reached up over the lip of the grave to locate the crowbar. As he felt for it, he also felt that the temperature in the grave was far cooler than that overhead at ground level. Stretching for the crowbar, he heard the night sounds of the graveyard—leaves rustling along the ground, scurrying in unison with small vermin; dead branches scratching at tombstones; a haunting *whirr* of the city's electric current coursing through the silence.

His hand found the crowbar and his handheld, battery-operated bone saw. He brought both into the pit with him. With the crowbar held firm, he pried open the small stone lid, the noise of his rending the stone from its moorings sent up a soft scraping sound like muted barking and crackling.

A dog somewhere the other side of the cemetery walls barked its reply. Daryl cursed under his breath. He had come a long way to find Groveland—a quiet old cemetery protected by a high wall on all four sides, its entire length and breadth. And he had spent many days and nights waiting to learn of a suitable burial in the papers. He had even listened for the weather report, and he expected the wind to soon turn to storm, rain and possibly thunder and lightning.

This was not his first grave-robbing foray, and the newspaper in Newark had made so much of his earlier raids that he'd had to come to Morristown for a fresh start. In Newark over the past year, he had earned a reputation in the press as the New Jersey Ghoul.

The lid moved slowly under his bleeding hands now. He had finally made enough space to crawl through to get at the coffin inside. The actual coffin lid came open easily once he located the latch, and there she lay as if in slumber, a little princess. Blood from his bruised and cut hands dripped onto the child's virginal white taffeta dress.

Overhead, he heard the low rumble of approaching thunder, and the light sprinkle turned to full raindrops that found him even below the concrete lid inside the vault. "I only need your head, dearie," he said to the corpse in her ballet outfit. The papers said she'd been buried in her favorite dancing outfit, that she'd been a beauty-pageant child, and he could see why. But he was little interested in her appearance, her name or who she'd been in life—only that her brain was intact. "I only want your head," he confided as he brought the battery-operated handheld saw to her throat.

The thunder would help mask the noise from the saw, but even as he turned it on, light flooded into the chasm of the vault and men and dogs descended into the pit and onto the stone lid, the dogs barking wildly. Daryl saw guns pointing and heard voices shouting for him to drop the saw and to come out with his hands in the air.

He instead desperately turned to the dead girl and began cutting her head off until a powerful blow struck him unconscious, and he fell across his dead victim, whose head had been halfway severed.

"My God, we got the Ghoul, Mac! It's him, the one they've been troubling with for a year in Newark. It's gotta be the Ghoul."

"If it ain't him, this one'll do for now. Cuff 'im and drag his ass outta here. Get 'im up to ground level."

Pulled and yanked aboveground, Daryl Thomas Cahil watched as lights in the windows from all the surrounding houses came on in a flurry of activity. "Turn your lights on the girl! Illumination. You can see I only wanted a piece of her," he shouted.

Daryl pulled loose from a uniformed cop's grasp and dove headlong back into the pit, shouting, "I must have her brain! I must have it now!"

Again Mac Strand and his Morristown police officers dragged the ghoulish offender from the child's disturbed grave.

ONE

Beware lest you lose the substance by grasping at the shadow.

— AESOP, 6TH CENTURY B.C.

Duval County, Jacksonville, Florida
June 6, 2003

GRANT Kenyon grabbed his head in his hands and pleaded, "Stop asking me to kill. Stop making me kill." Grant sat upright in the lonely Jax-Town Motel bed in his empty room, catching glimpses of his mirror reflection as if it were someone else. "It is someone else. Sure," he said aloud to himself, yet if he worked at it, he recognized something in the twisted image—the boyish face, the sad and deep-set eyes. But here in the semidark, there was something else going on. . . . *Nothing fit*—not his features, not his manner and not this place so far from his wife, Emily, and little Hildy. Staring into the looking glass, he felt that the real Grant Kenyon had fallen into it and metamorphosed into what he now saw. "It's really not me, this guy in the mirror. It's some other force that has hold of me."

He lifted the beer and toasted to the uncanny image toasting back, and he hated what he saw.

He clawed his way to a standing position and, once sure

of his footing, Grant bellowed and charged at the reflected image now moving toward him—*that other entity*—and they nearly collided where they met, face-to-face. "What the hell do you want from me?" he asked the stranger in the mirror.

"Just do what you're told," replied the other.

"Leave me, now! I don't want this . . . this kind of life . . . this possession of me by . . . by you."

His reflected image in the half-light showed an irregular brow, eyes too close together, a crooked nose larger on one side than the other, a sad set of dark eyes, a mouth in perpetual downturn. *Do I feel as bad as I look?* he wondered.

"I've grown 350 percent since your ancestors crawled out of the muck, Grant," his reflection said, as if it had a brain independent of his.

Grant beat a fist on the bureau top and glared at his Hydelike reflection. "Damn you, how many times're you going to tell me that? How fucking many times? I am pleading with you, my insistent brain, to never repeat that goddamn number again."

"Three hundred fifty," it replied.

"I've heard it all before."

"Your simian ancestors discovered that eating the brains of their enemies increased their mental capacity," the reflection said. *"Read about all the folk remedies of the Chinese, Tibetans, Hindus and Arabs."*

"I know . . . I've heard you say it a thousand times. I know man's brain is a stimulant, an aphrodisiac, a medicine to expand the powers of rational mind."

The man in the mirror grimly replied, *"Then you know why we're doing what you're doing."*

"I'm not doing a damn thing. You . . . you're doing it," he replied to his reflection. "And I won't allow it again! Not once more. I forbid—"

"Not once more. Not once more," mocked his mind of the distorted image. Then the voice turned deadly serious. *"What are you saying, Grant?"*

"I'm saying, don't lie to me. It's not working. I know it's a twisted obsession, a morbid craving that—"

"Me? Lie? But me is you and you is me, Grant."

"All that crap about your being somehow special, the descendent of all the prophets, all the philosophers, all the teachers, the wise men and the great spiritual leaders since time began."

"How then do you account for me, Grant? The most highly organized material substance on Earth—the human brain?"

"You're just an organ, an electrochemical factory."

"Nonsense! I am the great raveled knot, the—"

"I've heard it all be—"

"—world has ever known. I am the enchanted loom, the giant—"

"I don't want to hear it!" Grant tore out tufts of his hair, hoping the self-inflicted pain would blot out the voice inside the *him* inside the mirror. It failed to help.

"Within this 'chemical factory,' as you call me, are the secrets of the universe. I . . . you . . . us . . . we have the blood of kings running through our veins, Grant. The molecules of Plato and Aristotle. We . . . us . . . we're on the verge of complete enlightenment, on the verge of becoming pure energy, Grant. You must understand that?"

"So hang in there?" he scoffed at his reflection. He then violently shook his head, while his reflection maintained calm. Staring directly at his own forehead, he said, "Mind . . . mind you are so damn repetitive, so please, I'm begging you. Shut off! Piss off!"

For a brief second, his brain was silent. Then it said to him, *"I need nourishing until the metamorphosis comes, Grant."*

"I ought to just kill you."

"I am you, Grant, and you are I, and we are what we are."

"We are what we are?" Grant asked.

"So you must feed me."

Grant thought of the taste of the gray brain matter he had already fed on. He had tried it in casserole form, even in Hamburger Helper to mask the taste. "Feed you . . . from the brains of virtuous young women."

"As virtuous as we can find. Now feed me."

"But it's murder, what you've made me do."

"God doth work in mysterious ways indeed. His wonders to perform."

"Now you're claiming to be God? At least it's a new approach."

"God is in the over mind, the cosmic mind, Dr. Grant."

"What more can you possibly want from me? Already I've taken two lives, two souls for you."

"It's not enough."

"It's not? Well, tell me, what is enough with you? Three, six, nine, nine hundred?"

"We are seeking out the over mind, the cosmic being here, Grant. No one said it was going to be easy!"

Someone next door pounded loudly on the wall. The clock flipped to 1:35 A.M. Some teens or children raced down the hallway en route to or from the pool, even this late. Their racing shadows slowed to peep beneath his door.

"So you want me to dissect another person for her brain. . . . Why not dead children like Daryl Cahil did in Newark and Morristown in '89 and '90? You sure he wasn't on the right track?"

"No dead bodies. We tried that, remember, at your morgue? As for children . . . too much uncontrolled thought and nervous, directionless energy, and you don't need that."

"No . . . that's a certainty."

"Young women are pliable, their minds energetic and well mod-

ulated and, Grant, don't tell me you get no satisfaction out of it. You may be able to lie to your ego, but you can't lie to me, Grant old boy."

"How can I derive pleasure from it? I have no conscious memory of it happening until you fill me in. You got a name?"

"It's 'Phillip' if it helps, and I have enough conscious memory of the feedings for both of us, Grant, so no guilt afterward."

"But none of this . . . it's not normal."

"Normal is as normal does. What's normal, Grant? What's normal enough?"

"For me or for you, you mean?"

"For anyone. Look, just accept it, and get on with it. If you can't face yourself, Grant, then I'll do it for you. A nice compromise for that tiresome phrase, 'To thine own self,' all that . . ."

He turned to the bed, his reflection doing the same with the reflected bed in the mirror. Each curled up in opposite dimensions, each wary of the other, but Grant in this world could not move away from his brain sitting atop his head. He momentarily wondered if the guy in the mirror could escape his brain. Then he wondered what he meant by "his brain." Was it sensible to say that his mirror image was carrying his brain as well as his features? Or was the mirror-man's brain separate from his own?

"No more thoughts of getting rid of us. OK, Dr. Grant? All that's behind us, right?" His brain spoke now from the coiled recesses and fissures of the cerebral cortex.

"No . . . no such thoughts."

"I know. . . . I've been monitoring."

A knock at the door. The food from a carry-out deli that specialized in giving the customer what he wanted. Grant prayed the delivery boy was a boy and not a girl. He got up, found his wallet and opened the door on a pimply-faced young man with a dour and sleepy look. They exchanged food for money, and Grant returned to bed with the food and drink, giving silent thanks for the specialty order—a cheese, egg and brains calzone and a bottle of V8 juice.

"Brain food," he muttered and bit into the calzone.

Kansas City Public Library
The following day

THE nineteen-year-old community college student had nowhere but the library to work on her paper, since the computer center was closed on Sundays. She had set up everything she needed and had begun surfing the World Wide Web for information on the brain and functions of the mind for her term paper assignment. She logged on to something dealing with the cosmic mind, the strangest Web page she had ever come across. She forgot about her term paper and simply read:

> *The flesh, blood and body of man is nothing to the brain which houses the soul.*

"That's beautiful," she said aloud. She read on:

> *As the great thinkers and poets of all time have pointed out time and again—the beauty of the soul lies in the mind. The brain stem, the medulla oblongata, the pons Varolii, the reticular formation, the cerebellum, the cranial and trigeminal nerves, all these masterful works control every movement of the body down to the twitch. The tenth cranial nerve alone controls the ear, neck, lungs, heart and abdominal viscera. It controls breath and digestion, all at the direction of the mind.*
>
> *Man's brain is larger than that of ten prehistoric reptiles that measured one hundred feet long but whose brains were the size of*

walnuts. According to evolutionists, man's brain began growing at an unprecedented rate one million years ago. Strangely, the mind of man is, a million years later, still trying to determine its own power and energy, and the source of that energy. Many cannibalistic tribes reported to eat the brains of their enemies killed in battle claim they have touched on that power, glimpsed it, as a result of brain-feeding. If you are interested in knowing more about the mystery of the collective universal soul inherent in the brain, read on. . . .

The student hesitated, unsure she wanted to read on. There seemed to be something ominous about this information. Still, it was intriguing, and if there was something to it—that cannibals had some sort of insight into the very deepest inner workings of the universe through a recognition of the soul housed in the human brain—then perhaps she ought to write her paper on that. But who would believe it?

She paused her hand over the keys, trying to decide whether to move on to some information more in keeping with an encyclopedia or to continue on this strange Web page. Either way, time was running out. That paper and Mrs. Weston weren't going to wait. Maybe the safe and conservative road was best, after all.

But her eyes, unlike her fingers, weren't poised. They read on. . . .

TWO

*When armies are mobilized and issues joined, the
man who is sorry over the fact will win.*

—LAO-TZU, 6TH CENTURY B.C.

FBI Headquarters, Quantico, Virginia
The following day

IT *feels like a war being staged,* thought Dr. Jessica Coran,
medical examiner for the FBI, and she was fearful of how
long and hard this battle might be. For now the human
frenetic energy from activity and tension in the hallways as
people made their way to the debriefing room rang like free-
flowing electrical current. Everyone sensed something big
was on the horizon, but so far only a handful of people knew
precisely what that big item might be. Jessica and Dr. John
Thorpe, her closest associate at the lab, were among the
select few on a hastily put together psychological profiling
team to deal with two back-to-back killings, which might
be a kill spree that ends abruptly or the beginning of a serial
killer's career that spans years—like none Jessica had ever
seen before. In these two mutilation murders, the attacker
had used medical knowledge to literally open his victims
from scalp to ears and across the forehead at the eyebrow
line, creating a surgically precise window on the forebrain.

From there the victims' brains had literally been ripped from them. Speculation ran rampant as to why.

Some conjectured that he turned the brains into mementos of the kills, preserving each and so reliving the crimes over and over. Others in the profiling group said that he might be drying them out, pounding them into a fine powder in order to smoke the brains. Still others thought he might be bathing in the awful prize of his murder, turning them to oil as an aphrodisiac to rub onto his body. No one knew for certain just what use the monster made of the gray matter, and thus far no connection had been made between his two victims other than they were both chosen to die in a hideous manner—the vault protecting their brains cut into while they were yet alive.

Together Jessica and J.T. made their way to the meeting called by Chief Eriq Santiva. Jessica and J.T. had seen the autopsy results on the two victims only in passing and only via paper and photos. They had been on standby to drop whatever they were doing and report to Quantico's D-30, the largest, state-of-the-art debriefing room in the building. They were to come with anything they had on the Anna Gleason and Miriam McCloud cases—two cases so striking in similarity, they were immediately linked to one offender. The brutal killer called to mind no one Jessica had ever dealt with in the past, for his ghoulish need proved as horrific as any brutality that she had encountered in her career as a medical examiner and FBI agent. This particular monster wanted only one thing of his victims—their brains.

He took nothing else from them . . . nothing but their lives.

J.T. stopped at a bay of coin-operated machines for a Snickers and a cup of coffee, complaining of the date he'd missed the night before. "Sandy's already got some hare-

brained notion that I'm seeing someone else. This is going
to kill our relationship."

Jessica frowned and shook her head. "I'm not so sure you
two are a good match, anyway, John."

John Thorpe, in wire-rim glasses, still retained his boyish
features and a shock of hair habitually covered his forehead.
"Whataya mean? Not right for each other?"

"You're a scientist, she's a Presbyterian minister."

"So?"

"Seems a bit unusual."

"She is that. . . ."

Jessica asked him to get her a cup of black coffee as well,
and then she hustled Thorpe onward. The two old friends
and colleagues hurried for the arena-sized debriefing room.

"You look as if you're going to church yourself," he commented on her appearance. Jessica wore her auburn hair at
shoulder length, complimenting her heart-shaped face and
piercing hazel eyes. She had removed her lab coat to display
her well-cut, gray-green suit.

"You liar," she replied. "I must look like hell in winter."

"Not at all . . ."

She had been busy on other pending cases when this bizarre case had surfaced. Santiva had the unit locked down
in a room for hours the night before in an effort to come up
with some ideas about the killer, to develop a profile, and
to create a rudimentary victim profile as well. Eriq believed
time was of the essence, that the killer would strike again,
and after seeing the evidence photos, Jessica agreed. As a
result, she hadn't gotten much sleep. Despite this, she
wanted to look her best since this was a major case, and
since the computer visual linkups went to every field office
in the country.

Chief Eriq Santiva had already gaveled the meeting to

order and had quickly informed everyone why they'd assembled. "No expense will be spared to catch this butcher," he said, fists clenched, as Jessica and J.T. entered and quietly found their seats alongside the podium.

Eriq frowned at them but kept talking. "Headquarters is insisting, people, that every state field office east of the Mississippi be here today in person." This was met with some boisterous cheers. The Cuban-American Santira now waved down the crowd and again spoke into the microphone, thanking everyone profusely for hustling to get to Quantico. "You'll notice," he continued, "the distinct absence of reporters. This is not a briefing for the press, and I want a lid kept on this case. Nothing goes to the press unless it goes through me first. Any leaks, you deal with me!"

Everyone murmured approval over this.

"I'm sure by now the rumor mill has given you some idea of the problem child we're here to talk about, ladies and gentlemen. This death in Richmond—" Eriq paused to focus on the slide photo of the victim in profile, the side of her head cleaned of blood by the medical man who'd autopsied her in Richmond, Virginia. Even cleaned, the gaping hole only hinted at the size of the entire hole left in this woman's head. Although this was a mere third of the wound, the black emptiness of it proved terrifying to stare at, but stare everyone did. The wholly unusual nature of the crime displayed on the large screen over Jessica's shoulder made the room gasp in a collective venting of horror. The next photo displayed the frontal shot of the victim, and her wound—a missing forehead and scalp where the skull had been splayed open across the frontal lobe area.

The collective gasp turned into a collective, disjointed moan, followed by chattering confusion. They had all heard of the case, heard that the victim's brain had been "stolen" from its cranial cradle, but here were numerous shots being shown of the cleaned opening for autopsy. No one had expected this precise an incision. A good portion of the agents in the room had looked for a messy, cracked skull with a huge chasm atop the cranium, the results of a brutal attack from overhead. Most had expected to see the results of a killer's having ripped and torn apart the crown in a passionate, insatiable animal fashion to get at the brain below. As Jessica, J.T. and the unit had learned the night before— and the reason she'd gotten no sleep—nothing could be further from the truth.

Instead, what stared back at the assembled agents was a huge dark cavity where the victim's forehead and forebrain ought to be. The empty open skull was proof of a dispassionate, deliberate animal at work, a thinking animal.

"And then in Winston-Salem—" continued Eriq, swallowing hard as another mechanical *pulop* signaled a new slide had rotated into the viewfinder and was now projected against the screening wall. It proved a slide of such similarity that many took it to be the same victim now held in time against the large screen, her eyes mercifully closed, looking for all the world to be in an angelic repose if not for the satanic wound above the eyes—a rearview-mirror-sized hole in the head.

For a moment, even Jessica, where she turned in her seat to look over her shoulder, thought it the same victim, Anna Gleason. But no, this slide showed Miriam McCloud, victim number two. The ages were close and there were striking physical similarities in the two women; but it was the sameness of their wounds, like a fulcrum for the eyes, that drew the most attention.

The deaths had occurred within days of each other, and the authorities in North Carolina did not immediately know of the earlier such slaying in Richmond, Virginia. As a result, the two autopsies were done independent of the other. Only later did someone put the two cases together when a routine program on an FBI computer flagged them as being the same MO. Jessica knew when or if a third such body surfaced that she and J.T. wanted to autopsy the body themselves. Reading the entire case files on the first and second victims, viewing the autopsy photos and speaking with the doctors who had performed the autopsies, had all been helpful, but Jessica knew it was no substitute for firsthand knowledge.

Still, with the autopsy results in hand, she had spent many hours attempting to understand what kind of mind could conceive of such a crime. Trying to find reason in a mad hatter's reasoning. The two questions on everyone's mind remained: What is he doing with the brain matter; and why is he performing these deadly operations?

Behavioral psychologists in the Behavioral Science Unit working to profile the killer kept coming back to a simple case of brain cannibalism. She recalled the words of Dr. Linda Pearlman, a member of the team: "Everyone wants a ready answer to what the madman is doing with the gray matter. Everyone feels it *must* be for consumption, that this craving is an appetite for cranial matter. For now, since we really know nothing to the contrary, we're best served by simply agreeing with the common notion . . . at least until we learn otherwise."

"What does he hope to get from consuming the brains, if that is what he's doing with them?" J.T. asked Pearlman, who sat beside him.

Jessica stated, "For all we know, given what we see on the streets nowadays, he could be using them as dashboard ornaments."

"Throughout history, all cannibalistic tribes removed the heart and the brains of an enemy," Pearlman replied, her glasses shimmering on the end of her nose.

"But this guy's just into the brain."

Pearlman put her glasses on the table, rubbed her eyes and added, "Cannibals fed on the heart, believing it the seat of courage, and the brain for its wisdom and power as a force within the fierce enemy derived from a divine source. In consuming these parts, the heart-eater and the brain-eater believes he can take on the courage and wisdom of a fierce enemy and see into the invisible universal energy of a psychic cosmic mind that binds all matter as one."

"Here I always thought the cannibal saw the consumption of such parts as a gesture to affirm the life of the enemy, giving him renewed life inside the victor's own body and mind," said J.T.

"That's the common thinking."

"I know it's primitive thinking, but given our collective unconscious—that the memories of our eldest ancestors still reside in our genetic makeup—well, it has a certain passionate power to it, doesn't it?" asked Jessica. "Kind of a quid pro quo?"

"You could say that, yes. The two reasons do not necessarily negate one another—search for the universal mind and granting respect to one's enemies, or victims in this case."

"A tough sell to the crowd," said J.T.

Jessica believed that to put forth a formal stand on the killer's rationale so early in the investigation could harm the case more than help. Still, she had to convey to the assembled agents the majority opinion, and everyone had conceded that Dr. Pearlman's had made more sense than any of the other theories that had been put forth.

The open void of the massive but clearly surgical wound

to Miriam McCloud's head had now brought on a deep silence that filled the room. All the agents present pondered the image and their individual response to it.

Santiva finally broke the silence. "I can't tell you how dangerous this . . . this *brain-hunter* is, people. And he is working Richmond, our backyard. We have to stop him before he strikes again, if he hasn't already done so. Both victims we know of were dumped in poorly secured watery graves, and found less than forty-eight hours after they were killed."

"This is so . . . so gross." Someone moaned in response to the slide. Santiva meant to shock his audience.

"Dr. Coran and Dr. Thorpe will fill you in on what we have so far," said Santiva.

J.T. took the lead, championing Dr. Pearlman's notion for why the killer "stole and presumably consumed the quote 'enemy,' victim that is."

Jessica took her cue from J.T. She pushed her seat back and stood to add, "What we have so far, unfortunately, amounts to very little since the offender has been extremely careful to leave no trace of himself. Now as to the incision, *and* what it tells us about our man . . . This maniac literally carved out a major surgical incision from the scalp, beginning direct center of the scalp or fore crown, here."

She used a light pointer against the picture of Miriam McCloud's remains, still up on the screen wall, to indicate where the incision began. As she did so, she noticed a strange marred area on the screen wall, and mentally noted that someone ought to get the screen surface fixed or replaced, since it was a so-called high-tech solution to using a pull-down screen—the wall itself had been treated with a finish made for perfect screening of videos and slides. The marred area in this slide was directly inside the dark hole at the victim's forehead, so it hardly showed. Jessica ignored it and continued. "The killer *did* leave a *little* something for us to decipher."

J.T. picked it up, adding, "This guy operates like a surgeon. He clears the area where he cuts off any hair, shaving back the scalp and temple areas as well as the eyebrows." J.T.'s light pointer followed his discussion of the giant missing cranial area, all round the wound. "It's the way he works, ladies and gentlemen, that tells us something about him."

"Chemical anaylsis tells us these red flecks are residue of red marker," added Jessica, pointing with her laser light to the faint red dots showing up like mini-bloodstains along the cut lines of the bone.

"And from the depth on the right and left sides of his lines—assuming the killer and not an accomplice made the lines—we can hazard a guess that the killer is left-handed or ambidextrous."

"How did you get that?" asked a young agent.

"Handwriting analysis tells us that the more pressure applied along a constant line from left to right indicates this, rather than the other way around. Perhaps more important, after marking the incision lines, he next sliced into the flesh in the exact same order, side to side from the midpoint to each ear. The pressure again tells us something." She demonstrated with her laser beam. "Along the crown, then the lower trapdoor cuts, as we M.E.'s call them, from each ear and back to center, ending right between and above the eyes. This creates a kind of door at the forehead and crown, from which the brain is lifted. And again, indications show a left-handed person at work, even our computers blessed this much."

"What kind of blade did he use?" asked an agent at the rear.

"He begins with a scalpel of the type we use in autopsies," interjected J.T. "The scalpel cuts also indicate a tendency toward more depth on the left side. Then he followed with a bone cutter, a small but powerful circular saw of the sort we use in the autopsy room every day."

"Wouldn't that . . . don't those things make a hell of a noise?"

J.T. nodded. "That they do, particularly when hitting bone."

"The final result of the madman's bone saw, ladies and gentlemen," Jessica said, "was to create an incision going across the forehead above the eyes, thus removing the brow and bone covering the frontal lobe. Once exposed in this manner, well, it becomes relatively easy to reach into the cavity and pluck out the still-attached brain with forceps."

J.T. added, "And since our man is not interested in any other organ or any other body part, *time itself* apparently— or hunger for his object—is of the essence for him. Get into the cranial cavity, get the brain, eat it or pack it away, and get rid of the body. In and out."

"This frontal assault on the victim is a medical procedure," said Jessica, pushing back a strand of hair. "One that allows him to gain access to the entire brain in a relatively short period of time."

"Just reach in and remove the brain," commented someone seated in the front row. "You suppose he takes time to weigh it and bag it like you guys in the lab do?"

"This identical incision is done in autopsies, yes," said Jessica. "But we always put the brain back—at least most of it."

Again the audience contemplated the slide along with this information. A collective, quiet gasp went about the room.

"Get that slide turned off," Santiva sent out the order. The female civilian aide manning the projector responded by hitting the wrong button, going back two slides to the original slide, showing Anna Gleason's horrendous wound in profile view. Then it ran to Gleason's frontal view, and again Jessica saw the flaw in the screen, a tear, she thought, at exactly or near the same spot, buried in the shadow of the dark cavity. Then the slide disappeared and the lights went up, and the screen wall appeared fine. It must have been something on the print slide, she concluded.

Eriq thanked Jessica and J.T. for their "invaluable input," which gave rise to a feeling of hives in Jessica. She knew they had nothing.

"Any additional photos of the two crime scenes or autopsy information, contact the two jurisdictions, or come by our ready room located down the hall from here."

A questioning hand slowly snaked up. "Agent Quinton?" asked Santiva. "What is it?"

"Has VICAP been searched for similar crimes nationwide?" The agent referred to the FBI's main computer file for the Violent Criminal Apprehension Program.

"VICAP and every other program we have is in full function on the question. We didn't stop at nationwide. We went worldwide. If this guy has struck before, using the same methods, we will learn about it—when and where. We're praying, of course, that there haven't been any such previous cases sitting in cold case files somewhere out there, but that's why all of you here and on linkups have been notified. Look at your cold cases for any that have not been CAPed. Who knows, it could uncover a lead."

"One thing we do know about the killer," Jessica added from her seat, "he's thorough and competent with his tools."

"Can you elaborate on that, Dr. Coran?" asked Quinton.

"In both cases, he has lost or left only minuscule brain tissue from his victims. He wants it—his prize—intact, brain stem and all," Jessica replied. "However, as for leaving anything of *himself*, sorry. He's crafty and neat about what he brings with him and what he takes away."

"As neat as a surgeon, you mean?"

"We don't want to lock down on that just yet, but yes, he could be a medical professional," said J.T. "If not, he may have some medical training. Certainly, his tools would suggest that."

"It's a fairly educated assumption," added Santiva, "given his precision with the tools, and it fits with what little we have on the offender."

Jessica said, "Unfortunately, there've always been a lot of Jack-the-Rippers among the medical profession. Equally unfortunate, we have only one possible witness, and her testimony is vague at best. A Viki Rollins claims to have seen a man force a woman into a van at gunpoint in Richmond. No crime scenes exist, as we suspect he's using a van. So no clues other than those left on the victim—meaning what he did to her, I'm afraid. There is no fingerprint evidence, no DNA, no complete profile of the lunatic monster, so . . ."

"We have a *psych* team on the case as we speak," Santiva assured his audience.

Jessica added, "We suspect he's a white male in his mid thirties—and we're pretty much agreed that this doesn't look like the work of an erratic kill-spree murderer, due to his behavior here, just methodical as hell. He will blend in as if invisible, just a normal-looking guy. No maniac eyes or Neanderthal brow. More like the neighbor next door."

"Will he be wearing suspenders?" asked Quinton from the floor.

Everyone laughed at this.

"Most assuredly, Quint," said Santiva.

J.T. added, "At the moment, profiling of the victims may be our best bet, although we're still compiling more on the young women each day."

Jessica agreed with J.T.'s assessment. "Our victim profile that's coming around to you in flyer form has obvious gaps. After reading it, if anyone finds any associations or patterns and similarities between the victims, please let us hear from you. We've pretty much used up all the information forwarded thus far on the young women."

Agents seeing the victim profile began to consult one another and a general clamor, fueled by concern, demonstrated their discomfort. The victim profile fit nearly every young adult female in the country, down to their favorite rock groups—Outta Sink, Buglebeee Blow and Rag Bushy. This only punctuated the youth of the victims.

"Admittedly, it isn't much," said Santiva, getting the doctors off the hook, "but at the moment, it's all we have. As noted, the killer is mobile—working out of a dark blue or black van, according to information gleaned from a near-abduction case in Fayetteville, North Carolina."

"With victim one in Richmond, two in Winston-Salem, North Carolina, and a possible later attempt in Fayetteville, North Carolina," said Jessica. "This indicates that he has been roughly on a southerly course down the length of I-95."

"Another I-95 killer with a new twist?" asked Quinton from the floor.

"After Fayetteville we can only assume he's on a southerly course—perhaps toward Georgia, possibly Florida," replied Jessica. "If he stays his course."

"The dates of discovery bear this out." Santiva looked beyond the audience again and called out, "Henrietta, the map."

Lights went out and a map of the southeast states appeared, marked at the two cities where the victims had died. "If not Georgia or Florida, he's likely to show up in Tennessee, going southwest from Winston-Salem instead of straight down I-95 as predicted."

Jessica added, "This . . . this brain-snatching bastard made his first kill within shouting distance of us, gentlemen, ladies, which means one of two things: He is either oblivious to us, or he is spitting in our faces."

An undertow of anger erupted from the crowd, a low growl of collective derision.

"What's this ghoul really doing with their brains?" asked one agent near the front.

"Who knows, Birch?" replied Santiva. "Maybe he's making love to them, maybe he's freezing them for laboratory study, maybe the creep thinks they make good doorstops the way you use books, Birch. Who knows?"

This brought on some much-needed laughter.

"Maybe he's doing like that guy in that old black-and-white sci-fi movie, the one where the doctor puts human brains into animals, chickens and goats and such," said Agent Quinton.

More laughter followed.

"Weren't there some Nazi war crimes involving brain removal and study?" asked a female agent midway back. "I seem to recall reading about it."

"Yeah, maybe Hitler's risen from the grave thanks to cloning," said another agent.

"Why don't you look into that, Mort?" said another.

"All kidding aside, Agent Sydney, since you brought it up, find out what you can about Nazi evisceration experiments, will you. Who knows, maybe our killer is a neo-Nazi with a plan to indoctrinate us all by stealing our minds."

More discussion followed and questions were hurled at Santiva now, and Jessica thought of her lifelong career as a manhunter. During her decade-long career as a medical examiner for the FBI, Dr. Jessica Coran had encountered the strange, the bizarre, the heart-wrenching and the gruesome. The monsters had come in all sizes and myriad forms, but now her sleep was disturbed by a killer who wanted something so out of the ordinary that it surprised even her. He killed to possess that single prize. The idea alone unnerved Jessica. Everyone held some object or place or attribute near and dear, but how many felt their very organ of will and mind and soul was up for grabs by some maniacal beast anxious to rip it from them? Carried within and protected by the skull lay this three-pound gift of God and nature, and now it was threatened by a monster who wanted to take it.

Precisely why he wanted it remained a mystery, but want it he did, and now two young victims had fallen into his hands.

Why did he want it? Was it a mad craving or a twisted fantasy that had revealed some magical potent power or elixir made from grinding the brain and beating it in a mixer to be consumed? Or did he like it solid and raw? All speculation. No one knew. No evidence collected thus far had pointed to what motivated him to kill others for the only *sentient* organ in the body.

Jessica had, in the course of doing autopsies since her first medical training in forensics, removed a lot of gray matter in her searches for cause of death. She had seen the brain destroyed by all manner of disease, toxins and slow poisons like alcohol. She had seen the results of massive trauma to the brain from highway accidents to dining-room murders. The dead brain itself always felt the same to her—inert matter with no life force left—a three-pound misshapen dodo bird shot down, lying wingless, earthbound, not so much as a feathery flutter of a nerve.

The fully developed brain always looked and weighed the same—three pounds, give or take. But looks deceive. Jessica knew from her readings and experience that no two brains were exactly the same, no more so than human fingerprints. In some distant future, she imagined a time when a John or Jane Doe might be "recognized" and given an identity through a brain-print or brain map. The brain in its infinite folds and fissures has a unique pattern all its own, not unlike any two mountain ranges or glaciers, no matter the outward appearance. Still, some brains were put to better or weightier use than others, so if not in scale, in *power* the brains differed. Was there something in this fact of individuality that had prompted him to murder?

She and J.T., along with her significant other, Richard Sharpe, had discussed these very issues the night before. But they had come to no meaningful conclusions. In fact, they had come away as confused as before.

"If this brain chef is killing in order to feed on brain food," said Richard, "if you will, then why cannibalize young teens who have amassed little or no knowledge of the world beyond rap music? If, of course, you are doing this deed for the reason put forth by aboriginal tribes and primitive peoples the world over. That is, to take on the qualities and intellect of the man or woman's brain you consume," Richard said as he packed for a diplomatic mission to China to shore up the extradition proceedings to bring a suspected terrorist prisoner back to the States.

"Good question," replied J.T., sipping at his wine.

"Suppose he's not doing it for reasons put forth by primitives," said Jessica. "Suppose he's answering to a different, perhaps more personal calling."

"You mean perhaps his dead mother is telling him to do it?" Richard stared at her for a response.

"Something like that, yes."

J.T. nervously laughed. Richard continued to pack. His plane would soon be leaving from the Quantico airstrip. The evening quickly ground to a halt, and she shooed J.T. out and then drove Richard to the airstrip where they had only a short time to embrace and say goodbye.

"I may not be here when you call. I may be in the field," she'd told him. "If you can't reach me here, use the cell number."

"Jess, why must Santiva always send you out on the worst, most awful crimes the FBI has to offer?"

"You mean like the time he sent me to London? Where I met you? Habit, I'd say."

"Yes, London, but also where you damned near got killed. Just be careful while I'm gone." He kissed her and again they embraced. She had remained there, waving until the six-passenger jet transport took off.

Santiva's meeting now at a close, people filed out. Jessica lagged behind. She picked up all her notes and thought about how helpless they were in the face of the random violence brought about by spree and serial killers. When and where the Brain Thief might strike again must wait until it happened. Unless they could find a miracle in all the thousands upon thousands of tips already flooding in on who the Brain Thief was. "He's everyone's neighbor or lover," as J.T. had put it.

In the now empty room, Jessica looked up at the wall where the slides had been. The blankness felt like a challenge they would not soon or easily overcome. It made up a clear metaphor for the case—not so much as a clue on the smooth surface of the manila wall.

"Would you like to see the slides again?" asked a female voice from the back of the room.

"Oh, Henrietta, it's you. I thought I was alone," she replied. Henrietta was Eriq's technical assistant. "No, thanks to seeing the slides again. Maybe another time."

"Just putting all of this stuff in a safe place," said the technician. "You people, you've got to catch this SOB fast, Dr. Coran, before he butchers someone else's little girl. That's what he is, a butcher, not a doctor, not like you. He kills people; you save people."

Jessica thanked Henrietta for the vote of confidence and quickly left. And though part of her did want to see the slides again, another part did not.

STILL hiding in his Jacksonville, Florida, motel room, Grant Kenyon assessed his situation: thirty-nine years of age, facing forty, and somehow his life had been turned over to this insidious other self that he found his body, mind and soul contracted to—his damnable brain. A thinking organism living within him and fighting him for dominance; a thing telling him even as a child to consume brain matter. He had fed on small animals in this way as a child, working his way up to larger animals, and he had fed on the brains of medical cadavers when in medical school. No one had ever discovered that he'd had anything to do with the two missing brains there. Another kid, accused of pulling off a fraternity stunt, was expelled but no one had pointed a finger at Kenyon. In later years, he had fed on several fresher dead brains in the hospital morgue where he worked after earning his degree. None of it involved murder, no more so than the Jersey Ghoul, Daryl Thomas Cahil, had murdered his victims in '89 and '90.

Now all that had changed—gone was any semblance of concern for where he got the brains. His mind now insisted he take them while they were still warm. Now he committed murder in the name of this craving, and for such a leap, his brain had had to concoct a perfect rationalization about glimpsing into the cosmic mind, one he'd first learned of from Daryl Thomas Cahil. Kenyon had followed the man's case from his first grave snatching to his apprehension, incarceration and release from prison. Using a fail-safe system with a firewall, he had remained in touch with Cahil from the moment he discovered the man had a website called Isle of Brain, which Cahil had begun in prison. The website had toned down over the years, preaching the use of symbolic tools such as animal brains instead of human brains to reach the cosmic over mind, but anyone reading between the lines knew that this was Cahil's only way to remain free to communicate. Even so, he had animal-rights activists working diligently to shut him down.

Cahil had abdicated the thrown of the brain-master, and Grant Kenyon's other brain had latched on to it, promising itself that it would surpass anything Cahil had ever attempted.

Still, a relatively new development had come—an aberration as if out of nowhere. His other mind/brain wanted to bond with him over this obsessive craving for the *living*, warm brain. He had already killed and consumed such. At least his altered self had, but to do so, it had had to collaborate with the part of his mind that premeditated selecting and attacking a victim. The uncontrollable urge belonged to the *other within*, while organization and carrying out of the specifics belonged to *him*. Highly unlikely that anyone but himself would or could see the distinction, save perhaps a competent shrink like those who had found some redeeming quality in Daryl Thomas Cahil.

Grant didn't know where the original obsession plaguing him had come from, what its roots might be—whether genetically based or something that had occurred at an extremely early moment in his life. Perhaps it'd begun in the womb inside his forming brain, perhaps just after. He didn't know how deeply the fixation extended, or how long it would go on; nor did he begin to understand the need to consume human brain matter. Yet the necessity—according to the one within, calling himself by Grant's father's name as some kind of cruel joke—grew more powerful and insistent with each feeding. And as the need grew, he felt more and more of his own identity waning, flickering like the last moments of a candle until soon it would be extinguished, consumed by Phillip altogether.

The words of an old professor somehow filtered through to Grant Kenyon. "Our present understanding of the brain leaves us in the dark, and we may as well say the encephalon is filled with cotton wadding as anything else."

Since then, as a medical man, Dr. Grant Kenyon had learned that the brain had no parallel, and that it was a supernatural organ that bridged the gap between physical and psychical realms. "Look at what it's done to me," he said to the empty room, his now-distant reflection winking at him in the dark created by the closed drapes. "The bastard thing's got me on a scavenger hunt for immortality."

"I've told you, Grant. I'm not seeking immortality for you or for me," Phillip replied.

"What then? What *do* you want?"

The man in the mirror across the room shook his head as if disappointed in Grant. *"The cortex is equipotential. . . ."* he said.

"What do you mean?" asked Grant.

"Capable of learning and operating under unique and unfore-

*seen—often unimaginable—circumstances doubling and quadru-
pling its capacity for memory and storage. Don't you see? Anything
can happen."*

"It—you learn exponentially?"

*"Every new generation is evidence of this. There is no end to the
wisdom to be gained when we finally locate the perimeters of—"*

"Stop it! Stop it! Enough! Goddamn you."

"—perimeters of the mind in this inner solar system."

At what price? Dr. Grant Kenyon asked himself, silence
filling him. But his brain had to have the last word. *"At any
price, Doctor . . . at any price."*

Kenyon knew only that there was one merciful element
to his bloodletting and cannibalizing of brains. He had no
conscious memory of it, only what the other within him
wished to tell him; he had to be informed of it after the fact,
like an amnesia patient after a train wreck. He was *aware* of
planning it, even executing the initial phases of abduction,
but the actual murder? The taking of the victim's brain?
No, he had no conscious memory of killing young women
for what Phillip prized. Perhaps, he reasoned, this partition
his mind had created between his victim and himself was
the only way he could accomplish the task. Still, Phillip
made sure that Grant always heard about it. His brain told
him about it afterward like a story read to him from a book.

Grant knew he had killed three times now; Phillip had
relayed the details in unfailing and excruciating minutia—
every detail. But his mind did not replay these details in the
ordinary sense of memories. He got no visual images other
than what he imagined *after* hearing it rendered in words.
Only then could he feel, hear, smell, taste and see the "pictured" killings and feedings.

At first he could not be made to believe the images real;
not part of his memory. Yet, it was real—the simultaneous
attack on all his senses proved it so. It had in fact happened;

he had to believe his brain was telling the truth. After all, his brain must know, and it was the only explanation for the dried gray crumbs of brain matter he had found in his van alongside the bloodied tools he remembered gathering up for Phillip. At times he would stop long enough to clean his tools and the rear of his van. He'd left nothing behind at his home in Holyoke, New Jersey, nothing but Emily and the baby, Hildy. Once Phillip had killed their first victim in Richmond, Grant had not dared go back home. Instead, he'd gone to a gun show and he'd purchased a shotgun and a .38 snub-nosed Smith & Wesson.

The first killing in Richmond signaled the end of one life, and the beginning of his new existence. He had taken that first life, had taken the prize and run away. Knowing that Phillip would never be satisfied with only one such meal, he knew he had to at least protect his family by putting distance between Phillip and them.

Wishing to rest his mind, he clicked on the television and *Oprah* gave way to the local Jacksonville station, an advertisement for a local watering hole called The Stacked Deck where the young could find gaiety in the pounding music overlooking the ocean. Phillip insisted that Grant write the name of the place and the address down. They'd go hunting tonight. Last night, before settling in, they had scoured the area for a safe dumping ground for Phillip's third victim. After locating an abandoned place along the St. John's River, they had scoured the bus station for a victim without result. Prior to that, they had scouted out the local library where Phillip insisted on checking Cahil's website to see if he'd received the strip of brain matter Phillip'd sent to his mentor—to prove there was nothing like the real thing *and* to implicate Cahil should a time come when he needed a scapegoat.

"Time we roll, boy." Phillip's order spiraled through his brain. *"Enough wasted time."*

Grant stood and stuffed his pockets with his keys, wallet and loose change. From the door, he looked back at the mirror and, from the angle at which he stood, there was no one in the mirror.

Outside, Grant and Phillip found the waiting van rigged with all that they needed to subdue and gut a victim of her brain. They drove away from the Jax-Town Motel and into the Jacksonville night.

Public library, Fayetteville, North Carolina
July 5, 2003

THE keystroke took her to the Internet, and from there she typed in the website address and opened it. She began her much-needed transfusion of knowledge—information on the inner workings of the human mind. It was a subject that held a never-ending fascination for Juliet Sims. Besides, she had met many weird and wacky people in the chat rooms to discuss the "ultimate" subject—how the mind worked. One of them, she had set up a date with. He was on his way to Florida, he had said, and could stop over in Fayetteville, to meet her, if she liked. The meet had been arranged. She'd planned to sneak out because it was late, and she had to rely on a Greyhound Bus to get her to downtown Fayetteville from home, and it all would have worked out if her father hadn't caught her. She was embarrassed now and somewhat fearful of contacting her computer pal to let him know what had happened. She had stewed for a few days now, trying to come up with a better reason than the truth. She had concocted a story about a lightning strike and a flood at the house, but it could be checked. Then she came up with a story about how her parents abused her and sometimes when they got real angry, they'd lock her to a bedpost in the attic. Yeah, that would work. She logged on to the Isle of Brain site.

Chicago Public Library, North Ravenswood Branch
Same time

MARK Alex Ziotrope had gone to the search engine and keyed in the words "brain" and "mind." His screen immediately filled with possible trails to follow. He'd been given an assignment by Dr. Stephens to locate and report on some unusual facet of the mind-body relationship. It was punishment for having missed an exam because of basketball, an away game. He loosened his tight jeans at the belt, unbuttoned them and eased off on the fly, breathing a little easier. He had come back to this assignment several times now, and each time he found it excruciatingly boring. He had pleaded with crotchety old Stephens to allow him another area of inquiry, but the old professor would not hear of it. So here he was. He chose a selection entitled "Origins of the Brain and Nervous System." His screen filled with an encyclopedic tale that read:

> As the central part of the nervous system, the brain is the most highly organized substance on Earth. Lying within the protective helmet of bone, it is distinct from the body, which is built in vertebral fashion—soft tissue covering a bone structure. The head is built in crustacean fashion—bone covering soft tissue, like a crab. Some have called the human brain the giant crab.

"Hmmm . . . like old Doc Stephens himself," Mark muttered. He put the stuff about its being like a crab in his notes, along with the line about its being the most heavily ordered stuff on Earth. He read on:

> The brain consists of the forebrain or cerebrum, the interbrain or thalamus and the hypothalamus, the midbrain, consisting of the brain stem, that is medulla and pons, and the hindbrain or cerebellum.

Beyond bored out of his mind, Mark decided to bail and locate another site. When the new list came up, he skimmed it and liked the one called Isle of Brain. He'd hit on it before, and he found it a lot less stuffy and pretentious—and a lot more readable. The Webmaster was an ex con who'd managed to get himself released from a facility for the criminally insane. Mark thought that was cool. Not even Manson could get himself released from prison. This dude had to be sharp.

The site was far less scientific, far more philosophical and speculative, and Dr. Stephens had wanted something unusual, not generally known about the brain in the report. The Isle site was unusual, its master believing that the brain was altogether a separate dimension in which lived the cosmic mind.

Reacquainting himself with the site, Mark went to the welcome page to get the vital information—Mr. Cahil's full name and the name of the prison he had spent almost twelve years in. Cahil had begun the site while in the Pennsylvania Federal Penitentiary for the Criminally Insane, yet here he was on the outside and running a website. Cahil, convicted of a string of ghoulish grave robberies in Newark and in Morristown, New Jersey, between 1989 and 1990, openly talked about this fact and his crime—grave robbing for the brains of children, and in particular one strip of tissue in the brains that he fed on, believing it gave him some sort of eternal life and put him in touch with the "cosmic mind."

"This ought to rock Stephens. *This* is my report," Mark said aloud, drawing the attention of a librarian who looked over at him and put a finger to her lips. He nodded and quietly considered his choices. He could play up the fact that anyone. And that anyone, even a kid like him of an *impressionable age*, could log on to Cahil's website and become a disciple to the prophet for the cosmic mind, a con. Mark read:

Cosmic consciousness or the cosmic mind—also called "cosmic psyche"—is the extrasensory-spiritual element in the cosmic ether. It is all pervasive as it coexists and merges with matter, and is the source of all mental power and vigor—or psychic energy—which constitutes all knowledge and awareness that all objects and elements share in a universal mind.

The human mind is fed from this great cosmic mind, a limitless reservoir. The human mind is part of and channeled into the vast mind, and the area of its operation in you and me is a kind of supra-consciousness that lies dormant in us—unless we choose to awaken it!

In other words, in every man, there is a region where all—all—can be known.

The site then went into a sales pitch for "symbolic" brain tissue to be consumed by serious seekers of truth and the cosmic intelligence. It all sounded crazy to Mark, but he found the pitch and the product as curious as the site itself, and he knew he had to include it in his report. Maybe he'd contact the Newark and Morristown newspapers for accounts of Cahil's crimes, add some pictures. Fact is, if he purchased the product Cahil sold as "substitute" gray matter to be cooked and consumed, he'd have something for show-and-tell.

Mark breathed in deeply and sent off an E-mail of thanks to the webmaster, expressing appreciation for his insight into the natural power of the human brain. He added that it would make a great report for his college project. He then logged off, stood and returned his little number card to the information desk, where the librarian—pencil nose and sunken cheeks red with embarrassment—quietly suggested he zip up his fly. With apologies he did so.

"You do realize you can be expelled from ever using our facilities if you can not abide by our rules, young man." She pointed to a sign that read:

No Pornographic Surfing!
Anyone breaking this rule will lose library privileges.

"But . . . I only needed to loosen my pants, ma'am, a bad stomach. I was doing a boring research paper on the brain, honest. No porno stuff. Look at my notes, if you don't believe me."

She glanced at what he held up and told him to be on his way. She then glanced at a report on the most popular sites being visited by patrons of the library. One that was coming up a lot nowadays among the young demographic was the website called Isle of Brain that the young man had listed in his notes. She decided she had to find time to review this site herself. The public library detested censorship of any kind; however, times had changed dramatically.

"What was all that about?" asked the head librarian

who'd watched the exchange between the desk librarian and Mark.

"I don't know yet. Says he was on this site." She pointed to the one she'd highlighted with yellow marker on her list. "But he was playing with himself over there."

The head librarian bit her lip and shook her head. "People want to build a bomb, they log on to bombs.com. People want to murder someone, they go to palladin.com for a how-to manual on assassination. Porn's gotten so rampant on the Net that you can trip into it without knowing it. So, what is this Isle of Brain business?"

"Not sure. I'll get on it soon as I find the time."

"Do that, and let me know what you find, Gladys."

OUTSIDE, young Mark breathed in a deep mouthful of fresh air, free of stuffy and decaying books. He said a kindly good-bye to the library and walked calmly toward his car, secure—*for the moment at least*—in the knowledge he and his own brain were in sync with the hunt for the cosmic mind—for his report. He rested his notebook on the top of his car as he worked the key to open the door. He laughed, recalling how anyone with the courage and determination can find the cosmic soul and tap into it by *symbolically* eating some weird-shaped gray *noodles* that were supposed to represent the piece of brain tissue called "the real stuff," and thereby no harm would come to animals or other living beings in the pursuit of one's ultimate quest for a glimpse into the *universal* mind—God's mind.

Cahil's site also *sold* weird clay-molded brains that the customer could break open, and within them a cache of oddly shaped, crosslike noodles rested on an island within. Cahil shipped these to buyers, who in turn fished out the noodles, boiled them one at a time, and ate them in lieu of eating the real thing that was supposed to house the soul of a living creature.

"Weird shit . . . unusual? Sick, man . . . this is sick. Yeah, Dr. Stephens is going to love this." Mark slipped into his car and drove away with his notes.

THREE

Often an entire city has suffered because of an evil man.

—HESIOD, 800 B.C.

Duval County, Jacksonville, Florida
July 7, 2003

LESS than an hour before a fantastic sunset had settled over the city of Jacksonville, but a river of clouds had poured in from the ocean and blotted out everything. The grim darkness had come on like an approaching army. Next came a light silver drizzle, the sort that warned of worse to come. The night sky masked the gray clouds of earlier, now creating a black blotter of the Heavens with only the occasional star winking through.

"No stargazing tonight." The hefty black officer named Lamar Plummer shoved his white partner while they sat eating a fast-food dinner in their cruiser. He had been talking about the beautiful sunset before, speaking of it in reverential tones, saying that only God could paint a sky like that. Sipping coffee and chewing on burritos, Duval County sheriff's deputies Wayne Bierdsley and Lamar Plummer groaned in unison as the police band announced a 911 call on a ten-26-cardiac/drowning/asphyxiation. They had just begun a meal break—but the call was for Venetia Wharf on the St. John's River, less than a mile away. Bierdsley tossed his burrito aside and picked up, radioing in a ten-4, adding, "Cruiser 44. We're on it."

"Whoa, damn it, Wayne," muttered Plummer as the car pulled from the curb and coffee spilled over his lap. "Jesus."

"You're always complaining, Plummer."

"Whataya mean? This stuff's hot as hell."

"You just got through saying you were bored out of your gourd, so we get a homicide call and you're pissed?"

"Just get me there in one piece. Where'd you learn how to drive?"

When they arrived, they found a rank old fisherman arguing with a uniformed harbormaster, who wanted the man and his shrimp boat out of the restricted area. "Abrams, you take that thing off twenty yards, the other side of the fence. Cops can find you there as well as here."

"Damn you, fool. Are you deaf? I've got an emergency here, a dead woman caught up in our nets."

Climbing from their cruiser, the two sheriff's deputies laughed to see the two old men standing pipe to pipe, fists clenched. A third man, well dressed and stepping from one of the yachts joined them, shoulder to shoulder with the harbormaster, curious about Abrams's catch.

The well-dressed man said, "I'm Jervis Swantor. That's my boat there. Can I be of any service? What's the emergency?"

Other yachts-people living on their ships were now gathering outside, having been awakened by all the noise: men arguing, police sirens approaching and uniformed men in boots pounding down the seasoned planks.

"Dead girl's body come up in my fishing net, and when I saw what'd been done to her . . . I called nine-one-one. The poor thing's been robbed of her brain! Can you imagine that? A hole cut clean through her head, here!" He indicated his forehead with his finger. "I screamed bloody murder, I did. And this old fool wants me to take her back out and come in proper on the other side, but now the deputies are here, they can give the orders, Mr. Harbormaster Blowhard."

"Mr. Abrams?" started Bierdsley.

"Captain, son . . . Captain."

"That shrimper's where the body is?" asked Plummer, rushing ahead, Bierdsley following. Their boots beat an anthem as they rushed down the wooden platform ahead of Captain Abrams to where he'd illegally put his dilapidated shrimp boat in, nose first.

A strident warning from the old fisherman trailed the two Duval County deputies down the ramp to the old man's vessel: "Prepare yourselves for the worst most *horriblest* thing I ever seen in this life. Prepare!"

"Can I help here?" asked the lone yachtsman who had rushed out to try to get a look at the dead body. "I'm Jervis Swantor, boat owners' association, and we all pay dearly to use these spots. What's happened?"

"I told you what happened!" Abrams shouted at the man.

It was the one truly dark spot along the wharf where missing lights added to the overcast sky. "Looks like she's beyond help," muttered Lamar Plummer, the beefy black deputy.

Bierdsley, a moderately sized, plump white man, stood beside Plummer, still on the wharf. From where they stood, they saw the mermaidlike figure caught up in the shrimper's netting. "Yeah, looks bad, and now it's getting crowded. Civilians starting to gather. We'll need back up just to keep them at bay." He turned to Swantor and asked him to back off. Bierdsley and Plummer had seen floaters before. They imagined it was a suicide, so what was the old man ranting about? Some massive hole in the head? In the dark, they saw nothing of a bullet wound.

"Let's see what kind of package the old man's got caught up in his net," Bierdsley calmly said to Plummer as they boarded the bobbing boat.

Getting shakily aboard himself, Plummer asked no one in particular, "Is this boat tied secure? It's bouncing like a cork." At the same time, Plummer pounded his flashlight in an effort to improve the beam. "Fucking Eveready."

Behind them, they saw Jacksonville police cruisers lining up, their strobe lights challenging one another. "We beat the Jax boys this time," said Lamar, laughing. Off to one side of the harbor, the well-to-do yachts-people huddled. Swantor promised the crowd that he'd get to the bottom of this hullabaloo for them all.

The old fisherman had scurried down behind them now, storming off from the harbormaster, and he warned again, "I'm telling you two, it's one awful, awful sight."

"Floaters always are," agreed Bierdsley. "Worst kinda things happen to a body that's been in water too long."

"Not to worry, old man," Plummer assured the captain, his black face becoming all smile as he winked at Bierdsley.

The deputies rocked on their boots aboard the fishing vessel, and from where they stood in their brown uniforms, they could see the broad expanse of US-295 where the bridge spanned the river, and they could see the Jacksonville Naval Air Station. In the opposite direction a patient skyline awaited the eye. A beautiful blue-lit city on the waters of the St. John's River.

Captain Abrams's boat was like any of a hundred others along the Florida coastal waters, plying a trade in the fresh fish markets that lined up to buy their goods.

Going aft, the two deputies closed the distance between themselves and the body.

She lay in a curled position, her form seemingly cut into the square pieces of a gingham cloth due to netting she lay in. A few of the fish inside the net with the body remained fresh enough to flop from side to side. Obvious to the deputies, the fisherman's crew had worked to salvage what they could of the most profitable fish—red fin and grouper—leaving some pockets of cod and halibut in the net with the dead girl.

Lamar Plummer ignored the odors and went to his knees beside the crumpled body and net. "Least she's all in one piece and still has her skin, so she's not been in the water for too very long."

Dark shadow obliterated the face. Wayne Bierdsley moved in closer and stared at the girl's drenched form; her dress had the look of a shrink-wrapped shroud, the net was like an oversized shawl. Then his eyes fell on the dark concave black portion of the white head. In the darkness of shadow, with only the harbor lights on, he didn't know what he was looking at or what to make of it when something strange happened. It must be a hallucination, Bierdsley thought a moment before Plummer said, "Jesus, Joseph and Mary . . . She's got a third eye, and it's looking right at us."

Bierdsley saw the eye at the center of shadow along the dead girl's forehead a moment before it disappeared, and for a nanosecond he believed in the supernatural and in mermaids. Then he saw a silver-looking reflection replace the eye. Finally, he located and flipped on his flashlight, placing the beam to the dead girl's forehead. As he did so, he found himself in a graceless motion going to his knees opposite his partner, "Jesus . . ." escaping his lips.

Both officers gasped in response. The dark blotch was

indeed a large cavity the size and length of her forehead; in fact, what ought to be her forehead stood out as a void, and inside the void another dying fish struggled for air in a losing battle. It made Bierdsley wonder what kind of fight the young woman had put up. Now in its death throes, the small cod began to blow out its gills, wink wide and flutter.

"G'damn old man was right. That is a big sum-bitchin' hole," Lamar said. "I thought he was talking gunshot. Ain't never seen anything like this, Wayne."

"It'd take a cannon to make a hold that big; besides, it's too damn neat around the edges for a gun blast. OK, we gotta get that fish out of the cavity," Bierdsley insisted.

"Now wait a minute. It's not our job to go fishing inside somebody's splayed open head for no fish."

"Captain Abrams!" shouted Bierdsley.

"Yes?" Abrams had been standing alongside the deputies the entire time. "What can I do you for?"

"You got something I can use to spear a fish? Maybe something like clamps?" Bierdsley didn't want to place his hand inside the hole. "How the hell's there room enough for a fish inside her head anyway?"

"Wayne, you're messin' round with the crime scene when you tamper with shit. You know that, so let the damn fish be."

"Close-range sawed-off shotgun, maybe?" asked a man who'd gotten down to the boat before a single Jacksonville cop had. "I come to find out what happened, relay the news to the rest of the people tied-to here."

Plummer and Bierdsley exchanged a look of exasperation. "We told you, Mr. Swantor, to get back of that police line and stay there. You can't help here."

A Jacksonville policeman tugged the curious yachtsman back. "You believe that guy?" asked Bierdsley.

"Some guys with money think they can get away with anything."

Another Jacksonville cop came aboard and looked over the body from a safe distance, remaining in a standing position. "You guys need help?" he asked.

"No . . . something's just weird here." Bierdsley hunkered down closer, and he leaned in over the body, flashing the beam ahead.

Lamar added, "She's been cut open somehow like a goddamn can opener was put to her head. Cut clean through the bone."

The Jacksonville officer pulled out another flashlight and the beam somehow motivated the fish in the victim's head to dart out, which caused the officers to all jolt back and laugh at themselves all at once. Their laughter ceased as they stared at what the lights now revealed.

The forehead was indeed gone, so too was the crown, which had been shaved of hair. A large, half-conical-shaped doorway had been removed from the top of the eyebrows toward each ear and up and over the crown. The cut had gone through the cranial bone. It had created a kind of open trapdoor large enough for a small hand to enter.

Lamar moaned to the dark sky overhead. "Lord God in Heaven."

Captain Abrams, a Georgia-born fisherman, added, "May God forgive us all."

"It's worse," said Bierdsley. "Take a look inside the hole."

Lamar fearfully did so.

Bierdsley knew he was near gagging. "Whoever did this, he . . . he took her brain."

"What the fuck for?" asked the Jacksonville cop.

Bierdsley muttered, "Sick fuck."

More city cops arrived boat side, asking if the deputies

needed any help. Lamar was doubled over the keel, puking into the St. John's, garnering laughter from men who had not viewed the body. Bierdsley invited the others aboard to have a closer look. Soon there were several men joining Lamar Plummer in polluting the river.

Word had spread, and next came the sheriff of Duval County, Lorena Combs. She stood tall and sleek in her uniform among the men, and even after looking over the corpse, she held in her dinner. "On the quick, I want this crime scene secured. No one on the boat or near the body until I say otherwise."

"But, Sheriff," complained Captain Abrams, "the harbormaster wants me outta this slip. Me, I gotta get my boat back out to sea. Can't lose another day. Can't you just take the dear little thing off my boat and off my hands?"

"Take some time off, my friend. Your boat is a crime scene, Captain, and it could be a while. FBI's going to want to see this."

"But . . . but . . ."

"Until I say otherwise."

He scrunched his face up at her and gnawed on his pipe. She simply walked back to her squad car and asked dispatch to put her through to Quantico—FBI Headquarters. As she did so, she saw the harbormaster and a fellow on his arm trying desperately to get closer to the crime scene, rubbernecking as they approached.

"Christ, do we sell tickets next?" She shouted orders to her men to get all civilians, including journalists, back.

Quantico, Virginia
The same night

JESSICA Coran downed her cup of coffee as she worked late into the night, pushing through her office door with her free hand, and thinking about the telephone call she'd had from Richard. He had called from the plane, still en route to China. She smiled with the memory of his voice in her ear.

Stepping into her office, pushing errant curls from her eyes, she instantly realized someone was seated in the semi-darkened room, deep in shadow. She looked up to see Eriq Santiva, her boss. For a long moment they glared at one another like adversaries in a duel. Her highlighted auburn hair contrasted sharply with the white lab coat she wore over her clothes. She pushed past the dark-featured Cuban-American to take a seat behind her desk. She was angry with him for having sent her live-in lover, Richard Sharpe, on another overseas assignment. Somehow Richard's impeccable credentials were always at the center of Eriq's decision-making lately.

Eriq stood and paced the room before he again settled into a chair, this time opposite her. She'd just come from an autopsy, her hazel eyes tired and weary. She hadn't expected to find her superior waiting here in her office, impatient for the results of the autopsy, but here he was.

"Aren't you getting tired of playing gofer for Senator Lowenthal?" she bluntly asked him.

"I resent that, Jess."

"I resent my office being used this way, Eriq. If Lowenthal were not a senator, this case would have never crossed my desk, let alone yours."

"Sometimes, Jess, you have to play ball with these guys. Like it or not, the FBI is mired in politics."

"Politics has no business in decisions regarding scientific investigation. We established that years and years ago."

"Politics aside, the man is a friend of mine, and he's distraught over his daughter's death, after all, and he wanted the best—you."

"Eriq, it's an easy spot. Any pathologist in any hospital in the country could have—"

"But they didn't at Bethesda! They took it on the doctor's word that his wife had developed complications from some sort of food poisoning."

"Yeah, right, food poisoning by strychnine. Something her husband doctor would know all about."

"Then you found the murder weapon?"

"My protocol will be complete by tomorrow. You can fetch it for the senator then."

"That'll be fine, Jess."

"The wife was killed by person or persons unknown, by use of ingested strychnine poisoning. Not very creative on the husband's part if he did it. Hair and fiber aren't much use since they shared the same space before their estrangement. With no struggle, she left us little to work with."

"At least we know it wasn't some mysterious disease or food poisoning that killed her."

"The senator will have to pursue it with local police now."

"Of course, you're right."

"Appears a fairly straightforward murder of one's spouse, as the senator suspected."

"I suspected as much, too. If you'd ever met this creep . . ."

"Just, please, next time someone puts the screws to you, Eriq, at least talk to me first and level with me. Maybe put someone else on it. I have a backlog of work that would sink an elephant."

"You always told me that any murder is worth your time."

She took in a deep breath, realizing he was right but not wishing to give in. "That was a long time ago, before the rash of maniacs out there crossing jurisdictions and filleting people, and those crimes need our attention and expertise. Hell . . . some new psycho every other week, Eriq. Out there raping, torturing and now cutting open people's heads for their gray matter . . ."

"I'm afraid there's been a third, Jess."

"When? Where?"

"In Jacksonville, Florida."

"Right on the Georgia-Florida line, just as we predicted."

"Just got the call. It's the real reason I'm here."

"Christ, when did you get the news?"

"Just got the call while you were in autopsy. I called down; they said you were nearly finished, so I let you finish. I know how you hate to be interrupted during an autopsy."

"Yeah, especially one involving *pol-a-tics!*"

Ignoring her dig, Eriq said, "As you know, we put a call out on the law-enforcement hotline for anything to do with victims missing any or all of their brains in a surgical manner?"

"Yes, go on."

"And we suspected he'd show up in South Georgia or North Florida."

"I guess you want me down there?"

"You're our logical choice, along with J.T." Jessica had visited the Richmond authorities to get a firsthand account of what they thought of the Brain Thief, as their local papers painted the killer. J.T. had done likewise in Winston-Salem. J.T. had also interviewed a young woman nearly abducted in Fayetteville, learning only that the would-be offender there drove a dark blue van. Little had come of their efforts to find patterns or evidence that might help form conclusions about the killer.

"Bring back as much photographic evidence as you did on the previous cases. Jess, higher-ups think that you should be devoting all your time to this case."

"Figures." Fatigue whispered in her ear, saying, *Run away!*

"And, by the way, your telephone is going to ring right about now." Eriq looked at his watch and pointed to the phone.

The telephone indeed interrupted them, and Jessica answered. "Dr. Coran. Can I help you?"

"I certainly hope so," replied a female voice at the other end. "I'm Sheriff Combs of Jacksonville. I guess your Chief Santiva's informed you of our situation here. I had just seen your request in passing yesterday, and now this . . . sad business here, and sad to say you people were right. The Skull-digger has come to the Sunshine State."

"Skull-digger? Is that what he's being called now?"

"That's what Winston-Salem's calling him."

"Guess I'm out of the loop. Has the body there in Florida been disturbed?"

"Secured at this point, and if you can come right away, we'll hold off disturbing it any further than it's already been disturbed by my officers. They turned the body for some unaccountable reason; I guess to see if there was any other violence done to the back of the skull."

"Was there?"

"No, the only other notable item was the restraint marks."

"Hands, feet, throat and temples?"

"Hands and feet certainly. Throat and temples . . . I'm not so sure. How does he restrain the victim by her temples?"

"We suspect a viselike head restraint."

"My God."

"I'm taking a chopper out immediately. Hold on everything."

"Might have trouble keeping Bulldog Koening off."

"Who would be?"

"Dr. Ira Koening. Our city M.E. Good, stubborn and tenacious man, but he's been backed up due to health problems. Still, he wanted the case when he heard of its uniqueness."

"I've met Ira at a number of conventions. I agree, he's a good man. Tell him I look forward to working with him."

"Will do. I told him we intended to get FBI assistance, and that you'd be using lab space at the FDLE."

"Florida Department of Law Enforcement has labs in Jacksonville now?"

"We're progressing."

"Tell me what you have so far."

"A big nothing. Nothing but questions, I'm afraid. The victim's not giving up any clues. Not yet. But she was wearing an expensive summer dress, appears young—perhaps eighteen, nineteen. Not dressed provocatively, not likely a prostitute, no reason we can see that she should have attracted such violence. Then again, who would?"

"Was she sexually assaulted?"

"Hard to tell. She came up out of the water in a fisherman's net in a dress, but that's as far as we've gotten. Wanted your input before anyone else got to the scene."

"I'll be there by daybreak."

"Once the press gets this, and they will, there's going to be an outcry here for vigilante justice if we don't find some answers," Combs told Jessica.

"Anything else you can tell me relative to the body?"

Combs described the details of the discovery of the

body and redundantly spoke about the missing organ. She sounded frazzled. She sounded young for such a position. This was likely the single worst case she had ever caught. She repeated herself on everything, ending with, "Press is going to have a field day with this shit."

"Yours is the third such victim that we know of, all young women. And I don't think this creep's going to go away anytime soon."

"Is he killing women who look alike? Can we warn women with the same general appearance?"

"Fact is, there's some superficial likeness between the first two victims, physically, I mean. But as to anything else—likes, dislikes, community involvement, economics—no. But they were both white and young and brunette. One was attending a flight-attendant school, the other was a nursing student. Anna Gleason was twenty-one; Miriam McCloud was twenty-two."

"That appears to square with the new victim," said Combs.

"Still, they differ in the details enough to make us suspect that they could be randomly selected—chance and opportunity murders—but we're not certain at this point, so we're ruling nothing out."

"If they are randomly selected, that will make it all the harder to find this creep."

Jessica sighed deeply and said, "We've run the details of the other two crimes through the historical files of the VICAP system, to see if anything remotely like this has ever come up before. Cases involving people's brains being smashed in, cut into with knives, pitchforks and axes, but nothing like the kind of thing we're seeing here."

Jessica recalled the first instance of a body that was missing its brain that VICAP had isolated. It had been in Normal, Illinois, in the 1920s. The body had been dumped in a river there. The killer had been a quiet farmer up until the day he murdered his wife and removed her brain and ate it for supper one night. At his execution, he gave a strange statement: " 'I done it to please the voice inside my head that pleaded it be done until I could not stand it no more.' " It had been his ailing wife's voice, he claimed. He died in the electric chair.

Jessica told Combs, "These recent killings are serial in nature; either he feels he must kill the same thing over and over, or he feels he cannot get it right, so he keeps coming back for another try, or he simply likes it so much he can't give it up."

"Like an addiction."

"Sometimes it's more than that. Sometimes it's the only way they can get their twisted, sexual gratification."

"Through such horrid violence to another person?"

"Yes . . . afraid so."

"This guy kills in Richmond and Winston-Salem, and makes an attempt in Fayetteville, and now here. So, he gets around."

"We suspect he may be a working as a deliveryman using a van, dark blue, but then again, anyone having a reason to travel the southeast could be him."

Jessica said goodbye to Combs and looked up at Santiva.

"Hey, it's your kind of case, Jess."

"Death of a third victim from this brain-hunter," she muttered, her hands racing to her temples.

"Jess, I've seen brains caved in, I've seen brain knifings, but I've never seen one stolen. Look, I'll put a helicopter on standby for you. Get out of here and get packed."

"The crimes in North Carolina and Virginia began what? A month ago now? I wonder why he slowed down, and what lured him to Jacksonville, Florida."

"Anyone's guess at this point. Like I said, a helicopter will be waiting for you. Pack and get out there. I'll say good night, and Jess, be careful. You know firsthand that there're a lot of sharks inhabiting Florida waters."

FOUR

Marriott Hotel, Savannah, Georgia
Same night

H E located the computer terminal in the hotel and went onto the Internet in search of the words that would encourage him to continue on his quest. Like an addict, he quickly found the site he wanted. It read:

> While we have separate bodies, we have a singular mind. Every individual shares in this universal mind or soul. The result of even touching slightly on this cosmic mind is an illumination and understanding so profound and mystical, as cited by St. Thomas Aquinas before his death in 1274. Comparing it, he declared all his learning a mere "straw." Mystic Jacob Boehme wrote: "The gate opened to me . . . so that I saw and knew more than if I had been many years at a university."
>
> It is a sharing, my friends, in the inexhaustible spring of eternity.

He read it, breathed it in, this confirmation that, despite the horror of his actions, he was doing the right thing. This was no simple rationalization. These were facts. Cahil's words were essentially correct, all but his having wrongly fed on the days-old dead in his grave raids rather than the living—and, of course, the foolish notion that a single small island of tissue deep within the medulla oblongata alone held the soul, could also be dismissed as wrongheadedness.

Grant Kenyon and Phillip knew better. The brain to be consumed had to be minutes fresh, not days old. And the entire brain had to be consumed, not a small shred of Cahil's ridiculous gray noodle. Grant had argued this with anyone logging on to Cahil's website who cared to listen.

Cahil had robbed those graves thirteen years ago *not* for the whole brain but for a two-inch-long finger-sized sliver of it. Such a piece of tissue could not possibly house all of the cosmic mind or soul of an individual, to act as the funnel for the cosmic river to enter the brain. Besides, why take chances? Consume everything, his own mind consistently told him.

Still, it was good to know all of Cahil's thoughts on the subject in order to implicate Cahil as the so-called Skull-digger. To this end, Grant Kenyon had used Cahil's beliefs against him. Still, fortified with Cahil's encouraging words, Kenyon logged off, signed off on the computer use with a fake ID and returned the key to the desk.

It was time to acquire more of the C-mind, the cosmic soul, the most profound excitement, and that awe-inspiring power that his other self required of him and fed on. Promises had been made; a deal between him and his brain had been struck: that if he stepped up his hunting, and Phillip could feed faster, the final prize was realized sooner.

He asked the desk clerk where he could find some action.

The man's confused expression asked, *What kind of action?* Grant said, "Where're the clubs around here? You know, music, dancing, women?"

"Oh, well, there are a number of strips."

"Can you show me on a map?"

"Most certainly."

Outside Savannah, Georgia
2 A.M., July 8, 2003

ALL that the completely possessed Dr. Grant Kenyon—as Phillip—wanted was the girl's brain, nothing more. They—the authorities—could have the rest.

And so Phillip the Cosmic Seeker—as his brain sometimes called itself—would feed.

He switched on the tensor lamp directed at his fourth victim's cranium. The light blinded her as she struggled for consciousness and blinked in disorientated fervor. He began the operation by shaving the area of the scalp, backing off her hairline. He whispered, "So as to make the cut as clean as possible."

She moaned in response, her body somehow aware of him atop her, independently squirming against her restraints there in the back of the van. Next he shaved her eyebrows with a battery-operated shaver followed by a razor. They must come off completely. He didn't want any hairs adhering to the brain when he removed it.

The Demoral was enough to keep her groggy, but she was coming around, feeling the pressure of the razor against her scalp and eyebrows. More forceful now, she continued to struggle against her bonds a struggle that only excited the Cosmic Seeker. She had no power against the handcuffs around her wrists and ankles, which Phillip had instructed

Grant to install in his van—along with the surgical leather strap that held her head in place at the throat and temples.

He had driven out to Picketville, an area of little population, and parked in a wooded area near the train tracks. No one for a mile or so. No one to hear her struggle or her screams when he chose to take the gag away and click on the handheld rotary bone saw.

Grant had no trouble performing the operation. After all, it was a procedure he'd performed on cadavers at the morgue. He had studied the pathology books and had been placed in charge of the morgue when old Graham Dobson had died. Since then, four years ago, Grant had opened up and examined some thirty brains, most of which he'd put back, but many he'd consumed. He had become proficient while at Mt. Holyoke Memorial Hospital at opening and closing the cranium in the manner he now performed on the living. It was a procedure he watched closely during his medical training. He recalled the excitement of wanting to know precisely how each incision was made in order to create a large enough frontal window from which to take hold of and remove the brain—to pluck it free of its prison. The medical books, his pathology instructor and the old hospital pathologist had made it look easy, but he had known even after doing it several times now on a living subject that it was never easy or without problem. The brain could be stubbornly anchored, especially in the living.

He removed the gag and said, "Now, this is just a razor. I just finished shaving your head. Necessary, Winona, before I cut it open."

Winona Miller screamed in response. He glanced at the tape recorder set up earlier by Phillip to catch all the sound effects—in order to prove to Grant that he had actually done this hideous deed again.

"I have to search your brain for answers. I want to share

with you all my sight, dear girl, and you will come to know who you really are. I know your soul is in there, inside your head."

"What . . . what do you . . . want from me?"

"Your memory, your DNA and your cosmic mind."

"What?"

"Now, I have to mark where the cuts will go," he said, replacing the razor with a red marker. The soft kiss of the marker made her tremble even more than the razor had. She started screaming and pleading for her life.

"I don't wanna die. I don't wanna die. I don't wanna die. . . ."

"I don't so much want your life as your brain. It's the only reason we're here, Winona."

She screamed in response.

He breathed in her terror; it made Phillip feel powerful to make her scream. Her screams penetrated the van walls and echoed out into the night, but they were far from anyone who could hear.

"Time to cut," he said as he began the incision with the scalpel. Her screams heightened at the scalpel's kiss, which brought the blood. Outside, a train screamed by as if on cue, drowning her out. Then she fainted. He eased back on his knees vulturelike, then he continued with the operation.

He hadn't known whether he could perform the operation on a living person that first time, back in Richmond, Virginia; but now, with his fourth victim in his complete power, held as she was to the van floor, it certainly presented itself as the thing to do again, to add to his collection. Why he wanted her brain in his hands, or what he might do with it, once he had it removed, he had not known the first time he had severed a living, still-pulsating brain from a person. But now he knew that his own brain wanted them. "Don't you understand, Winona?" he asked. "Your power source will join with mine. I know it's in there somewhere." He caressed her head, her hair, her brow. "You're never going to be alone. You'll be with the rest of us. We'll all be one. . . ." he told her even though she'd swooned into unconsciousness. "Too bad I can't hold it up to your eyes for you to see before your last breath. Maybe then you'd believe me."

Phillip had taught Grant well. He was coming to accept what he was. As he worked the handheld, relatively small electric bone cutter, the saw wheel whirred and screeched. The sound lulled him into the thought of how he had entrapped her, using her own childish naïveté against her.

Grant had been cruising by a residential home in south Georgia when he had spotted Winona getting into a car with a young man. He had followed as she and the boyfriend went to a dance spot called Sandman's. On the dance floor, he got close enough to see it in her eyes, that she was one of *them*—the virtuous chosen. She smiled at him, and he nodded casually. Having a beer at the bar, he watched and waited, patient and vigilant. He soon realized that the couple was not getting along. When she bolted from the dance floor and her boyfriend followed, so did Phillip.

The girl and her boyfriend appeared to be in their early twenties as they stood arguing in the dimly lit parking lot.

He stayed at a safe distance to watch their argument escalate while other couples politely ignored the discord and passed by—the comings and goings of any nightclub. Phillip saw many underage teens playing at being older, and he worried about looking too out of place here, too old for the general clientele.

Then he saw the girl storm off alone down the street and away from the club, leaving her vulnerable. He watched her boyfriend rush to his car, peel off and go right past her, slowing only to call her a bitch, not stopping.

Returning to his van, Phillip—or the thing Grant had become—followed her progress. Phillip got into his van and made his way toward his prey.

She had been drinking heavily at the club. Now she was hitchhiking for a ride home. He closed the distance between them, and in a moment he stopped alongside the young woman. "Need a lift?" he asked, smiling wide.

At first she held back, but then she half stumbled to the window, slurring her words as she spoke. "How far you going down Turnbull Boulevard?"

"As far as you need me to, darlin'. You came off a pretty bad scene back there at Sandman's."

"You saw that?" she asked.

"Bad scene," he repeated. "Been there, done that more than I care to say. Guess we all have. But it'll look better to you in the morning. Look, I'd be happy to get you home."

She stopped to stare at him intently, studying his features.

"I'm just a little wasted," he added, "but not so much I can't drive."

He wasn't entirely a stranger to her. "Didn't I see you inside Sandman's?" she asked. "I thought you must work there or maybe own the place."

"No, wish I was an owner. I just go there sometimes. So, yeah, you did see me inside. I know I saw you."

She looked over his dark van, a look of uncertainty coloring her features. She was pretty, he thought, in a Southern suburban prissy girl way.

"Come on. I've got the ride and the time and something to help with your pain."

"No way. You sound dangerous. Besides, you're too old for me."

"Whoa, that hurt. But maybe a little experience and danger . . . maybe that's what you need about now. Forget that loser. I promise, I'll be nothing but a gentleman—until you get to know me, of course."

She hesitated, trying to ponder exactly what that implied. "A gentleman until I get to know you, hmmm . . . Well, it is a long way, and my folks'd kill me if they knew I was out here alone. I thought that jerk was going to come crawling, but that didn't happen."

"Where do you live?"

"The Heights."

"Coincidence, so do I. Come on. I won't bite."

"You don't sound like you're from around here, and my mother always says never to talk to strangers."

"Your mother's right, and so are you. No, I'm from up North. Just moved here to get work."

"Whereabouts up North?"

"New Jersey."

"What's your name?"

"Phillip"—he was not lying—"what's yours?"

"Not sure I should tell you," she teased. "Listen, Phillip, you got any weed or anything that might cheer a girl up?"

He nodded and smiled. "You're not one of those undercover narcs now are you, baby?"

She laughed at this.

"Sure thing," he assured her. "Plenty enough for both of us. Plenty."

She didn't answer, her mind contemplating him and his offer. She hesitated but placed a hand on the door handle and then cranked it down, opening the door and cursorily checking the cab from the door to be certain everything was normal. She glanced into the dark void of the empty rear. She could not make out anything there but a toolbox and some discarded boxes.

"No backseats?" she asked.

"I have to keep the back for my work, you know—supplies and stuff," he said.

"Supplies of what?"

"Just stuff I have to cart around." He gave a thought to the concealed .38 below his seat and the shotgun in the rear. These were for emergency use only.

"What, like tools? You a mechanic, a carpenter, an electrician, what?"

"Yeah, an electrician," he lied.

"You work with your hands, then." She gave him a coy smile and he returned it.

"What's your name?" he asked again.

"Winona."

Mimicking her Georgia accent, he replied, "That's a right pretty name, Wiii-no-naaa."

"Why thank you, Mr. Phillips." Calling him "mister" reinforced her earlier remark that she found him too old for her liking, but she was interested in getting high.

She got into the van, inspected the door for anything strange, making certain she could open it before she closed it. "With all the weird shit going around in the world today, you can't be too careful." She relaxed, accepting the ride by getting into the front seat and instantly putting out a hand, asking, "So . . . what've you got to smoke or pop?"

"Sure . . . sure . . ." He fumbled with a joint, lit it, and dropped it into her lap. While she fought to retrieve the burning thing, her high-pitched voice telegraphing her distress, he suddenly plunged a needle into her forearm, saying, "Meet Mr. Demoral, Winona."

At the same instant, her boyfriend's car raced by again, the burning rubber indicating his anger. He'd gone around the block and watched to see how easy a pick up she'd be. At the same instant her boyfriend sped by, Winona raised the mace she'd been clutching to Phillip's eyes, burning him only a little before he tore it away.

He pulled the door closed and drove off. At a safe distance away from the club as the Demoral began to work its magic, he stopped the van and dragged her back into the rear, hand-cuffing her into position.

She pleaded with him not to rape her. He promised that he would not do anything of the kind. "I told you I was a gentleman, a *gentle*man. I'm only interested in your mind, Winona."

He'd remained true to his word as the saw now bit into her scalp. He liked to start at the top and work his way to each side at the ears, run to the base of each ear and then return to the midpoint between the eyes at the eyebrow line. Dr. Grant knew it was the neatest, most efficient way to handle the job with the least amount of bone shrapnel and blood. He didn't particularly care to have blood everywhere.

Jacksonville, Florida
4:25 A.M., same night

THE helicopter descended over the gleaming Jacksonville cityscape, its surrounding waters reflecting the buildings, many lit with colorful pink and pale purple lights, turning the skyline into a *Wizard of Oz* setting. The pilot pointed at the police strobe lights below and said that he would put the chopper down as close to the scene as possible. That meant landing atop a small, weedy little plateau of pitted earth along the riverbank, a dusty sandlot for parking near the Venetia Warf. The dirt-and-sand parking lot looked at odds with the surrounding sheen of concrete high-rises, huge bridges and blacktop everywhere else.

While the new sun played hide-and-seek with the morning clouds, the pilot brought them down. Once the skids had settled and the chopper sat firm, Jessica took her medical bag and rushed out, crouching below the blades. J.T. followed. They then waved off the pilot and made their way to the waiting party of two uniformed people and one man in a gray suit.

"Dr. Coran, so glad you could come." Lorena Combs shook Jessica's hand. "I'm Sheriff Lorena Combs, Duval County." Combs had a gazellelike grace about her, and a firm grip as she next shook J.T.'s outstretched hand. She then introduced the Quantico team to George Sheay, the heavyset chief of police in Jacksonville. The FBI's agent in charge, Henry Cutter, a tall man with a misshapen nose, stepped forward and introduced himself as well, telling them, "You can count on our full involvement and all the help we can offer, Dr. Coran, Dr. Thorpe. Sorry to take you away from home and family."

J.T. was a bachelor, and Jessica shrugged Cutter's remark off, even as she gave thought to Richard Sharpe, who'd called from Korea during a stopover on his way to consult on the Beijing extradition case. "Where's the corpse?" Jessica asked.

Combs indicated the way and escorted Jessica to where the body still lay on the boat. With the onset of morning, traffic on the bridge nearby had increased and motorists were hearing about the victim over radio waves as they passed the wharves. The helicopter landing had also alerted people that something odd was going on at the wharf. A nearby sightseeing tour group chugged off on a river excursion, passengers pointing to the activity at the death boat. Jessica saw that they were surrounded by small businesses catering to weekend fishermen and tourists, but that the body was on a boat along one of the wharves filled with expensive yachts. Amid the yachts squatted the rusty old shrimping vessel. On the other side of a chain-link fence, a second wharf was lined with professional fishing boats and shrimp boats. "Community of yachtsmen are pissed off because the shrimp boat dared to dock in their little territory," Combs mentioned.

While equipped with motors for maneuverability and chase, some of the relatively small shrimp boats also maintained backup sails. Though most of the rigging, Jessica realized as she approached, was actually nets strung about the boats—in serious need of disentanglement. Most of the shrimpers had already set out for an area where they could go from the St. John's River to the ocean. Those remaining were chugging and sputtering badly while at idle; some were under repair, while the one in question, squatted among a bevy of beautiful yachts, dead silent. This boat was littered with almost as much yellow police caution tape as rigging and netting.

An elderly, thin-faced man used a sea cap in his hand to punctuate his shouting at stationary police guards on the dock beside his boat. "What in God's creation is taking so long? I shoulda just threw the body back into the St. John's when it come up!"

"Since the fish population has declined, the shrimpers usually go out twice a day, twilight and dusk," said Combs in Jessica's ear. "Owner-operator of the boat being held is pissed off that we haven't released his vessel."

As Jessica and J.T. walked toward the boat, their shoes slapping the boards, Jessica read the name painted across the wooden rear: *Uneven Odds.* As she neared the boat, she studied the screeching seagulls all around and overhead, and aside from their footfalls on the boardwalk, she heard a playful sound like melodic chimes. It was the boat's rigging just overhead, the ropes in the wind tapping out a tune over the body, as if playing a hymn for the dead girl.

Sheriff Lorena Combs said, "Boat captain says he picked her up about a mile north of here. I've got men combing that area for anything unusual, trying to determine exactly where she may have been dumped into the river."

"Shot in the dark, huh? Any luck identifying her?"

"Possibly. We put missing persons on it, and they're bringing over a couple to have a look."

Jessica exchanged a look with J.T. No one wanted to break such news to the family in a normal death, let alone a mutilation death, and yet they had to have a positive ID. The two previous victims had been identified and put to rest, so those parents, family and friends at least had the closure of a burial. "Part of the killer's MO has been to take with him anything that might help officials identify the victim," J.T. said to Combs.

Combs replied, "Worst part of the job. I told the *possible* parents that it would be easier on them after we got her to the morgue, that they could view the body through a window, but they're adamant and on their way here."

"Determining where she entered the water might well be of help in the investigation," Jessica said, changing the subject. "Might locate some tire prints, some cigarette butts."

"We can only hope."

They now stood on the dock, high over the boat captain in the hull. Abrams's clothes marked him as a working crewman as well.

"Dr. Coran, Dr. Thorpe, meet Captain Abrams."

"Permission to come aboard, sir?" Jessica asked the skipper.

He laughed in response. "You know how many people have come and gone here? You're the first to ask permission."

"So, may we?"

He returned his cap to his head. "Why not? Permission

granted. I'm going to find a drink." He stormed off to his pilothouse.

Jessica noticed the tarp someone had positioned over the body, and now she and J.T. went toward it. J.T grabbed hold of the tarp and pulled it down to the victim's chest area. Jessica went to her knees beside the dead girl and tore the cover away entirely. She found the body now just as it had been described to her—as having been rolled. The victim lay on her stomach, no visible sign of injury. "Help me turn her, carefully."

J.T. did so as the others held back. When the body was fully turned, Jessica heard Police Chief Sheay, standing well back, moan and say, "My God, Cutter. Do you see what this butcher did to her?"

"Gentlemen," said J.T., "this is surely the third such victim found in this horrid condition within a month. But it's not a butcher's job he's done on them."

"What do you mean?" asked Chief Sheay.

"The cutting open of the skull, the manner in which it's been done here . . . this is no amateur at work. He's highly skilled with a scalpel and bone saw."

Jessica let them know she agreed with J.T. "Scalpel, bone saw, forceps. The killer had all the right tools for his ends."

"Forceps?" asked Combs.

"He had to have used forceps to snatch hold of the brain and remove it through the front like this," Jessica explained. "It's as if he's trained to do it or has seen it done. It only happens on autopsies. Brain implants or brain surgery usually leaves only an oval in the affected area."

"But this guy wants the entire brain," said Combs.

"Why?" asked Sheay, handkerchief covering his nostrils and mouth.

"To eat it, to weigh it, to dissect it?" asked Special Agent

Henry Cutter. "We don't pretend to know why, Chief. Even the FBI's never seen this kind of thing before."

"If we knew why, it might help us find him," said J.T. "But we honestly can only guess at his motives."

Jessica added, "Our earlier examinations have shown that he uses a surgical saw, rotary style from the findings we've seen. Makes clear striations against the bone. If we could locate this guy and his saw, we could nail him on the saw markings to the skulls alone."

"How do the other victims compare to this one? Physically, I mean," asked Cutter, stepping closer, wincing at the wound.

"Approximate size and shape, hair color difference, color of eyes no match." Jessica bent down and stared into the eyes to determine an answer to her own question. "Blue. The others had brown and hazel eyes."

"So he isn't too picky. Not in search of a specific type with blue eyes, brunette hair, size, weight?" pressed the hawk-nosed Cutter.

"It appears his only interest is what lies inside their skulls," replied Jessica. "None of the previous victims were raped either. Tests are likely to show the same here, I suspect." She examined the eyes more closely for any telltale signs of strangulation—the minuscule red dots of hemorrhaging in the eyes. She found none. She next felt about the exterior of the throat for any damage there, and other than the now-familiar restraint marks at the throat and temples, where the head had been held in place by some elaborate restraint, she found nothing of particular note, certainly no merciful sign of strangulation. "J.T., that medical head strap you brought," she said, hand out. J.T. obliged, handing the strap to her.

She fitted it about the neck and head of the deceased. It

matched perfectly against the head restraint marks left on the girl. "That tears it. This guy knows medical supplies, John."

"And no signs of strangulation?" asked J.T.

"None."

"Like the others."

The two M.E.s knew that this indicated a death that came with the shock of having one's skull split open by a bone cutter.

Agent Cutter asked, "Any sign of drug use in your earlier victims?"

"The only significant amount found in either was the drug Demoral."

"Demoral?"

"Used mainly as a sedative and muscle relaxant," said J.T.

"Found in both prior victims, and no apparent injury to any other part of the body. We've determined that they all died while alive—while under this madman's scalpel and saw."

"That's what the autopsies show?" Combs's obvious empathy for the victims showed in her eyes now.

"Afraid so. This guy works methodically. We've found residue of red marker. He maps out the cut just after shaving the hair away from the crown and eyebrows. His first incision is with the scalpel, after which he brings the bone saw to bear along the scalpel lines. We've determined that he is left-handed from the angle of the pressure he brings to bear on the marker."

"And he'll strike again?"

"If he can, yes."

Combs hesitated. "Strange, all so strange . . ."

The case was indeed strange, Jessica thought. "It fits no pattern I've ever seen in all my years as a forensic scientist."

Jessica examined the bruised wrists and ankles, noting that they appeared to have been caused by handcuffs. J.T. concurred.

"Well then . . . if her head and limbs were restrained . . ." Combs's light brown eyes grew dim.

"Then we know the killer has mapped out his every move," said J.T.

Jessica said, "Be clear on one thing, people. It's not enough that the bastard kill her. He wanted her to know what he was doing, wanted her conscious. He wanted her brain still palpitating when he got to it."

"So if he's eating it, he wants it fresh and warm," added J.T.

"And he's into torture as well as murder." Combs almost choked on her deep sigh. "You have no doubt of that?"

"None."

A policeman escorted a well-dressed couple to the crime scene. They were in search of their missing daughter. The couple clung to one another as if for breath and life. Supporting one another like a pair of beams that had fallen over, the father introduced himself and his wife as the Mannings. He looked as shattered and fearful as she.

Finally, they mustered the courage to come close enough for a look. The sight of the victim caused her to faint, and he fell to his knees holding her. "It's Amanda. . . . It's our little girl!" moaned the tearful father. "My God, what have they done to her?"

Combs got the parents up and off the boat with the help of uniformed officers. The sad processional going from wharf to street level was heartrending to watch. Like two children in the dark, the parents stumbled the entire way.

"Jane Doe has a name now," said J.T.

"Amanda . . . Amanda Manning," replied Jessica, who

stepped away from the body long enough to breathe in the air coming over the river.

"They'll want the body released as soon as possible, Dr. Coran," said Combs upon her return.

"Yes, certainly. We'll do all we can to accommodate Amanda's parents."

Jessica and J.T. returned to the body and began the work of gathering microscopic data in vials and on slides. Jessica studied the fine features of a young woman barely out of her teens, a dimpled cheek and a lovely curvature to the face and eyes, accentuated by a slim nose. All of it and the girl's life marred by the missing forehead and empty skull, marred by a madman's twisted and awful designs.

Just then a shaft of sunlight illuminated the dark cavity of Amanda's empty cranium, and Jessica stared into that well, as if studying it might release some answer to the mystery.

"Well . . . let's get the morgue involved," said J.T, about to wave on the attendants.

Combs agreed, adding, "Amanda will be waiting for you at the FDLE morgue, Dr. Coran."

"Wait . . . There's something else here," Jessica said, her eyes widening as the other two started away. "Something inside her skull."

J.T. and Combs got down close to see what Jessica referred to. J.T. fully expected Jessica had found some small crustacean had taken up residence inside the empty skull. "What is it?" he asked, his nose bristling with the odor of dead fish ground into the boards of the old boat.

"It's etched inside the back wall of the cranium . . . some sort of mark or . . . or symbol, I think," said Jessica. "Must be something the killer *intentionally* left behind. He's trying to tell us something."

J.T. crouched in closer and his knees popped as he looked

into the space of the empty skull and at the back wall. Seeing the mark, he added, "Definitely not of nature's doing."

Combs bent even closer in over the body. "What is it?"

"A . . . a circle sitting atop a cross." Jessica drew the sign on a small yellow pad fetched from her case. She held it up to them, and everyone studied the strange glyph.

"Looks like some kind of religious cross or other icon. But in this context . . . What does it mean?" asked Combs.

"I'm not sure."

The boat captain, Abrams, had reappeared and was studying the sign on the pad. "The upright line like the number one represents upright man, the horizontal line crossing it represents the horizon, while the circle atop the vertical and horizontal represents God."

"Was this symbol found on the other two victims?" asked Combs.

"Unless they missed it . . . I mean it was nowhere on the protocols. Maybe it was missed."

"The sign wasn't on the other two," said J.T. "I read the reports, too."

"Can you go back, take another look?" asked Combs.

"Both of them have since been buried," J.T explained.

Jessica sighed heavily and shook her head. "I'm certain the attending M.E. would have seen it if it was there."

"What do you think it means?"

"Who can say? Perhaps that he's doing this out of some holy crusade only he understands."

"Sonofabitch is so twisted he thinks God approves of what he's doing?" Combs had to move away. She went toward the front of the boat and stared across the river at the teeming city coming to life, morning rush hour in full swing now, an army of cars passing over the 295 overpass. Jessica joined her there.

"You OK, Sheriff?"

"No . . . are you?"

"No . . . not really. Hell of a number this guy did on her." On the outside, Jessica knew she presented the picture of calm, but inside she shivered each time she looked back at the corpse's head.

Combs lit up a cigarette and offered one to Jessica, who waved off. They both fell silent a moment, each with her own thoughts until Combs said, "You think you've seen it all, then something like this comes along. Blows your mind."

"Yeah . . . I know . . . I know the feeling." After a moment, Jessica added, "Agent Cutter wants to set up a joint task force—state, county, city and federal involvement."

"I already told Cutter fine. I have no jurisdictional ego battles in my department. Whatever works . . . whatever gets us this . . . this creature."

"Murder still gets the chair in Florida, right?" asked Jessica, the wind coming off the river playing havoc with her auburn hair.

"It's too good for this guy, but it's the best we can do. What he really ought to face—"

"I know," concurred Jessica.

"—is the kind of torture he put his victims through. God, can you imagine having your head cut open while you're alive?"

"And under no anesthesia," Jessica added. "As for the parents, they don't need to know the details until and unless they insist."

Combs nodded and took another long pull on her cigarette. Jessica returned to the body to finish her preliminary examination. Everyone had fallen silent. Jessica spoke to J.T. "Imagine Amanda Manning when she was filled with life and love, J.T., filled with tenderness, pity, heartache, sorrow, contentment, jealousy, frustration, shame, despair, pride, triumph, hatred, rage, accomplishment."

"*Anima,*" said J.T., summing it up. "Her anima was taken along with her organ. I know."

"All her noisy, boisterous, excitable, passionate, determined, anxious self—stolen in one night of horror."

"Now it's all gone," added Combs, standing nearby.

J.T. had been sketching out the scene on a pad to indicate precisely where the body was in relation to objects around it. He sadly noted that since they were on a boat, there really were no fixed objects unless the boat was tied down permanently.

"Do your best with what we've got, J.T."

Jessica took scrapings from beneath the victim's nails. Combs asked, "Do you think that Amanda ripped some skin or blood from her assailant?"

"I wouldn't count on it, but only time and tests will tell," Jessica replied. "You can wave in those ambulance attendants now, if you will, Sheriff."

FIVE

The descent to Hades is the same from every place.

—ANAXAGORAS, 428 B.C.

Evening, the following day

JESSICA found her room at the Ocean View Inn on Jacksonville Beach perfect not because of the spectacular view of the Atlantic, but because it had a bed. Exhausted, she kicked off her shoes and fell into the bed's soft comforter fully clothed, wanting only to lay there a moment and relax and rest her eyes.

Jessica had found the stiff, proper Agent Henry Cutter to be a man of his word, determined to rid Jacksonville and the state of Florida of this ghoulish fiend the press had been calling Skull-digger. Cutter had spent the day debriefing his command and putting them on the street in pursuit of leads. Such activity went on as Jessica spent the day doing a thorough autopsy of Amanda "Mandy" Manning to confirm what she expected to find. She and J.T. believed beyond any doubt it was the work of the same man who had struck in Richmond and in Winston-Salem. Her report to Cutter and the FDLE read that Amanda had not been sexually abused, in keeping with previous victims. Their final judgment: trauma by bone saw to the cranium, causing hemorrhagic shock and eventual death.

While the autopsy earlier that day went as smoothly as could be expected, given the extent and nature of the crime, Jessica had to make the difficult call of violating young Amanda Manning once again—and at the head—because Jessica wanted the portion of the back wall of the interior skull carrying the only message left for them by the killer. She wanted it removed and preserved for study under the largest microscope she could find. There might well be clues within the clue, she had told Combs, Cutter and the others.

Cutter balked at the idea, saying a high-resolution photograph would do just as well. Combs agreed and said, "The girl's been violated enough."

"No, it's too important. It needs microscopic analysis," Jessica countered. "It could save lives."

"You're talking about mutilating what's left of the skull, Dr. Coran, and for what?" asked Cutter. "An artifact that may well prove useless in the investigation?"

"Take it up with Chief Santiva. I'm taking the 'artifact,' as you call it."

"To add to your collection?" Combs asked, her eyes narrowed.

"What the hell does that mean?" Jessica stood eye to eye with the sheriff.

"We're not backwoods people here, Dr. Coran. We know your reputation for taking on the weirdest cases in recent history. In fact, such cases have built your reputation."

"Listen, Sheriff Combs, you asked me in on the case, remember?"

"As a courtesy and only because you had an APB out on this guy's MO," Combs shot back.

"I'm taking the bone fragment."

"Not before I have a chance to talk to Santiva," replied Cutter, intervening. "I'm the special agent in charge here, Dr. Coran."

It was their first argument, and it didn't bode well. Cutter and Combs stormed out.

"Lotta emotion flying, Jessica," said J.T. "So . . . I guess we wait until we hear back from Cutter? Meanwhile, somebody's got to explain the delay to the parents. They want the body released ASAP."

Jessica didn't hesitate. "I'll need your assistance, John, and get us a couple of attendants to turn Amanda facedown."

"Are you sure, Jess?"

"It's too important to bury with her, especially if it has already been buried with two other victims." She went to the phone, contacted Santiva and informed him of the disagreement, telling him, "You've got to stand with me on this one, Eriq, no matter what arguments Cutter or Combs may feed you."

Eriq proved more curious about the mark inside the cranial cavity than in the disagreement about how to proceed with it. "Why haven't we seen it before? What did you say it looks like?"

"We're going ahead with the cut, Eriq. I'll be sending it to HQ for analysis if I'm not sent packing, in which case, I'll personally bring it to you."

With the help of attendants, they turned Amanda. Jessica pleading with them to be careful not to create a coroner's snap—a broken neck from careless handling. After the attendants left, Jessica assured J.T., "I'll make the cut as small as possible."

"We can replace the piece with a Bonemide," he suggested. Bonemide was the newest product in a line of concretelike, yet elastic, molding materials designed to replace bone parts. The white finish of earlier products was now replaced by a bone-gray that could easily be cosmetically enhanced to match any cadaver's bone coloration perfectly.

It had first found use in dental offices for making casts of teeth.

J.T. added, "I've already created a replacement part for both the forehead and scalp." He held the cast up for her appraisal.

"You're a genius, John. Do whatever you can to patch her up."

"Working on a latex skin covering. She won't look beautiful, but she'll at least look intact, *if* no one looks too closely."

"As for the interior cut, no one should be looking for it . . . whereas the wound to the forehead, by the time her parents arrange a funeral, will likely be front-page news."

"And how long before the cross inside the skull is front-page news?"

"We've got to swear everyone here to secrecy. We need this kept in-house, John."

"Between us and the killer."

They both knew the value of that detail being kept under wraps. Anyone apprehended or confessing to the crime would have to know of the strange cross left behind and in what location on the body. That way, they could quickly dispense with any of the hundreds of false confessions bound to come from across the nation.

Jessica lifted the bone saw and was taking a deep breath when Dr. Ira Koening appeared. "Put the saw down," he said.

Jessica expected a fight, but instead, the quiet little white-haired man examined the find he'd heard news of. "Combs told me about it. This is extraordinary indeed, Dr. Coran . . . Dr. Thorpe." He saw that they had readied surgical scissors and shaving equipment, a red marker and a set of scalpels and sponges. A Bonemide kit sat prepared nearby.

"I see you've already decided to go ahead with the procedure, Dr. Coran," said the Jacksonville M.E. "But you know, Doctors," Koening continued, "the best way to proceed is with a guided laser cutter."

"It would take days to get one down here from Quantico," said J.T.

Such precision instruments were extremely expensive and rarely available. "Are you saying that you have one available, sir?" asked Jessica.

"My office does not, *but* the FDLE has recently acquired one, state-of-the-art."

"With a precision guided laser, we can calculate the depth of the cut to encompass *only* the bone, and we can do it straight through the already existing hole in the forehead," said Ira Koening.

"That way we remove only the bone, no skin . . . no hair loss at the site," added J.T., "and I can reconstruct the bone loss from the inside wall."

"Nobody would ever know it was ever tampered with, whereas with your primitive bone saw, there's no hiding the fact," added Koening.

"Where is it? Do we need a damned requisition form?" asked Jessica.

"I've already taken the liberty of ordering the laser be brought to you, Dr. Coran, but it will take ten or fifteen minutes. Paper and tape, you know. So . . . shall we find a cup of coffee? Take a break while awaiting the instrument?"

As they relaxed over pastries and coffee in the office turned over to Jessica, Dr. Koening said, "I'll do the cutting, Dr. Coran. That way no one can blame you. It is, after all, my jurisdiction, and I agree with you that it needs to come out for close microscopic inspection."

"I think I speak for both of us," J.T. said, raising his cup as a toast, "when I say that we happily concede the chore, and our sincere thanks."

Koening returned the gesture and drank from his cup.

Jessica sighed. "I really didn't want to use that awful bone cutter on her or go through the same ritual her killer followed, Dr. Koening. Thanks for alerting us. It didn't occur to me that a laser cutter would be within reach."

"It's not every city the size of Jacksonville that has a precision guided laser. It came with a new influx of governmental dollars since Nine-Eleven."

They then returned to the autopsy room where Amanda's remains awaited them alongside the laser, a robotic-looking tool chest on wheels, a square version of R2D2 from *Star Wars*, with multiple swivel arms. Dr. Ira, as he asked them to call him, went immediately to work, as the other two suited-up doctors looked on. Ira had obviously handled the laser before. In a matter of minutes, with no noise whatsoever, no markers or scalpels, he had removed the silver dollar–shaped bone fragment with the design etched in it. The laser mechanism had a long needlelike arm with a catch basin at its tip, which Ira had positioned to catch the thick chip of bone, and the procedure was complete. It had taken only two and a quarter minutes. It would take J.T. an hour to reconstruct the inner wall.

"An excellent job . . . perfectly done. My compliments, Dr. Ira," said Jessica.

"It's hardly my accomplishment. Our thanks to science, Dr. Coran. With the explosion in medical technology, I imagine a time when someone will invent a mechanism that will record and play back our dreams!"

"I've never heard of that one, Doctor," replied Jessica, "but you're probably right."

"They'll turn the human mind into a DVD player." He

laughed lightly at his own words. "Of course, we won't be around to see the day . . . but perhaps that's as it should be. . . ."

Jessica looked overhead. In the viewing gallery, she saw Combs and Cutter. The two appeared all right with the compromise that Dr. Ira had worked out by using the laser.

Later in the day, with the bone chip secured in a polyethylene bag, Jessica had arranged for print copies of the sign left by the killer to be made and distributed. The information was also sent to Quantico for dissemination there. The unusual symbol and its placement might lead to something tangible.

She still had to await toxicology and serology reports, but she imagined they would find the same as in the earlier cases—high levels of Demoral, nothing more.

How many people in the state were using Demoral as a sleep aid, she wondered. The killer used it to induce compliance until his victim's own shock mechanisms kicked in. Shock as a merciful savior come to rescue her with the first screaming touch of the bone saw, and the smell of her own skull being cut as she lay helplessly strapped down, her head, hands and legs in restraints.

Jessica must get her thoughts off the awful details of the case for a time, to ease her mind and rest her brain. Easier said than done at nightfall in the Ocean View Inn, she quietly determined. Still, she willed the case away and continued willing it away, searching the eternal blue-green sea in her mind's eye for peace and comfort from where she stood on the fourteenth floor balcony.

When the phone rang, she came in from the pleasingly warm, salt-filled ocean breeze, lifted the phone and brought it onto the bed with her, but she couldn't bring herself to lift the receiver. Instead, she closed her eyes and allowed it to ring on while her thoughts continued where she and

Richard languidly existed among stars lying amid the depths of the ocean in a dream world, until consciousness suddenly told her that a telephone wasn't part of her dream state. The phone remained insistent, floating just above her lap in the ocean water, and just out of Richard's reach. It continued to ring, and still her eyes remained closed, yet she saw all the coral colors of the sea and the beautiful creatures of the deep.

Eyes still closed, wondering how many precious minutes she'd been asleep, it occurred to her that the call might be from Richard in China—*in the real world.* She bolted upright and lifted the receiver, saying into the phone, "Yes? Yes? Who is it?"

The phone kept ringing but no one was on the other end. She abruptly hung up, but the ringing continued. She finally realized it was her cell phone, tucked in her pocket. She tore it out and again asked, "Who is it?"

A woman's voice answered. "Never mind who it is. I have information regarding the Skull-digger." The voice proved grating on Jessica's nerves, running the length of her spine like fingernails against a chalkboard.

"Who is this?" she repeated. "How did you get this number?"

"Shut up and listen."

Jessica caught her breath and did as told.

"I know who the Skull-digger is, and he will not stop until you people put him away again."

"Again?" Crank call, Jessica thought. She checked the time. Just after midnight. Must be a full moon. But how did the woman get her cell number?

"I owe a debt, and I want to pay it in full," said the strident voice on the other end. "I know it's him."

"You can file a formal complaint with your local law-enforcement—"

"Shut up, you stupid bitch! His name is Daryl Cahil. He lives in Morristown, New Jersey, after being run out of Newark—nobody wants a ghoul in their town, and that's what Daryl is, a *ghoul*. He was put away as the New Jersey Ghoul by the local authorities but they're working *with* him now! They arranged for his release just this year!"

"The Jersey Ghoul?"

"The sonofabitch once tried to cut my head open for my brain, so I should know he's the one you're after."

"He threatened to cut out your brain? Is he your husband or your boyfriend?"

Jessica remained calm and skeptical, having heard this scenario many times now from confessors and accusers who'd come forth for official absolution of their sins—the usual crowd that only wanted to make something of themselves, even if it was a reputation for mass murder or for having shared a bed with one. Both accusers and confessors had shown up at Jacksonville PD, at the FDLE, at the Sheriff's Office, as well as at the doorstep of every law-enforcement agency in the southeast and across the nation. And now somehow one had gotten hold of her private number.

"He used to do children, for God's sake!" shouted the woman. "I was at his trial, which they closed to the press and cameras out of respect for the grieving parents. I know he took their heads in order to eat their brains."

"He murdered children?"

"Robbed them of their brains, I tell you. He dug up dead children out of their graves . . . for their brains."

Jessica tried to picture the image, but it was too awful to contemplate. "Look, ma'am, the Skull-digger kills young women in their early twenties, and he hasn't robbed any graves so far as we know, so perhaps—"

The woman's cracking voice interrupted. "I once thought him innocent by reason of insanity, you know? Morbid obsession, you know? And that he was redeemed, cured, after all, when . . . when they released him."

"Who are *they* and from where did they release this man—what did you say his name was? And while we're at it, do you have a name and an address?"

"Never mind me. My name's to be kept out of it. I'm of no consequence, and besides, I don't intend on becoming tomorrow's *deadline*. . . . Get it, 'deadline' instead of 'headline'?"

Jessica imagined the caller would like nothing better than notoriety, that this alone prompted her call. She must have worked extremely hard and acted extremely well to have gotten Jessica's cell number. Still, Jessica decided it was best to placate the woman, get her off the phone, get back to sleep and change her number tomorrow.

"All right, does he have a name and address where we can find him, ma'am?"

"Daryl Thomas Cahil, 153 Orchard Row, Morristown, New Jersey. Now, what're you people going to do about it—*him*, I mean?"

Jessica gave the woman a final shot at her fifteen minutes of fame. "And what is *your* name and current address, ma'am?"

"No way . . . he'll find me."

Jessica took a deep breath, blinked sleepily and asked, "Do you have a place to go? To get away from him tonight?" She assumed it was a case of battered-woman syndrome.

"I left him when he threatened me, and no sooner'n I left, he did it to somebody else! I read about the killings in Virginia and North Carolina, and then I saw the news coming out of Florida about that poor girl down there. I tell you, it's Daryl's work."

"OK, all right . . . if you know this man's secrets . . . if you know he's the killer, what private message has he sent to us, Ms. Ahhh . . . ?"

"Private message?" She sounded utterly confused.

"Can you tell me what it is and where it's located on the Florida victim's body?"

The caller, faced with this question, abruptly hung up, and Jessica said, "Just as I suspected." She knew her phone had logged the caller's number, and a glance showed it to be a New Jersey exchange. She'd look into it further to-morrow, she told herself. While statistics and common sense told her it was just a nuisance call, a small portion of her mind asked *What if?* The killer profile did have him living with a woman, maintaining a semblance of normalcy, while undergoing some recent traumatic event in his life. Still, with so many "sightings" of the Brain Thief across the southeast, why go looking for the killer in New Jersey? It was sometimes impossible to separate those tips worthy of attention and those merely hallucinatory, or separating out-right fantasy and lies from legitimate leads.

Since the voice on the phone had not proven her case well, Jessica returned to her night's sleep. However, as she lay there, she wondered about the grave-robbing remarks, how this Cahil character had supposedly stolen brain matter from the graves of children. She thought it just ghoulish enough to be true as opposed to some macabre film or horror novel. Maybe it did bear some looking into . . .

UNABLE to sleep, the strange phone call reverberating in her head, despite her attempts to dislodge it, Jessica rang Chief Eriq Santiva at home. "What've we got in the way of interesting hits on VICAP, Chief? Anything we might like to investigate in connection with the brain takings?"

"What time is it?"

"Just past one A.M. Sorry to bother you so late, but I'm afraid this creep is only going to escalate his attacks." She looked down at her rumpled clothing and realized she hadn't eaten since lunch. She'd been asleep for several hours when the strange call had disturbed her. "What do we have, Eriq?"

"Nothing strong or I would've called you."

"Yeah, of course you would have. Sorry."

"Something bothering you, Jess? Aside from what you found on the inside of the Manning girl's head today?"

She described the unusual call, and he listened attentively. Eriq then said, "I do recall something about a guy on a yearlong grave-robbing spree. Nineteen eighty-nine to ninety, I believe. They called him 'the Ghoul' or 'the New Jersey Ghoul.' Caught digging up kids and making off with their heads."

"How many graves did he disturb?"

"Four, I think . . . Yeah, four graves, four heads . . . never recovered . . . A fifth one, he was caught in a seven-year-old's desecrated grave. Sick sonofabitch was put away in an asylum as I recall. All handled by the Jersey authorities with local bureau help, but Quantico was never involved, either directly or indirectly."

"I suppose there's a logical reason as to why it didn't come up on the VICAP search?"

"Nature of the search question, maybe. We were looking for brain thefts, brain consumptions, brain batterings, not decapitated kids. A lot depends on what the locals did with the information, and as I said, Jersey wasn't keen on our involvement at the time. Consequently, even the local bureau wasn't kept abreast, so maybe it never got to VICAP at all, and if it did . . . like I say, likely under beheadings or grave robberies."

"Thirteen years ago I had my hands full with being the new medical examiner in Washington, D.C."

"Long before I became Division Chief. Look, I'll find out more about the case, get back to you."

"The caller wouldn't give any identification on herself, but here's the name and address of the guy she informed on: Daryl Thomas Cahil at 153 Orchard Row, Morristown, New Jersey. That might help you."

"You mean this nutcase is on the outside?"

"The woman claimed he'd been released from someplace."

"Yeah, well, I know he was put away, but I didn't know he was out on the street. I'll look into it. You think there could be some connection with the brain thefts?" Eriq's voice gave way to a hope. "I mean, can we get so lucky? As it is, we have zip."

"Let's just say it's a rock that bears looking under. And if he is located, I want to interrogate him about the sign left inside Amanda Manning's skull."

"Excellent find, Jess. It will help us separate the wheat from the chaff." Santiva yawned into the phone. "I'll look under that rock first thing tomorrow."

Pittsburgh Pennsylvania University, dorm room
Same night

THE Net user, Washington Williams, was caught up in the sheer detail of information and photos of the brain provided by the website he was on. A medical student, he had a great deal to learn, and he had to memorize it by *yesterday*. His weary, swollen eyes scanned the information as his pen and pad began to create what was beginning to take shape as a self-directed quiz.

The page before him was from Encarta and it read:

Included in the limbic (border) system are the amygdala (almond-shaped), associated with the primitive emotions of fear and aggressiveness, or fight and attack necessary for survival; and the hippocampus, also in the temporal lobe, having to do with memory formation.

The extension of the upper end of the spinal cord, about the size of the little finger, is the brain stem, lying at the base of the skull cavity. Regarded as part of the midbrain, it is some five hundred million years old. It is here that the switchover of nerves takes place, giving control of the right side of the body to the left side of the brain and vice versa.

The upper end of the spinal cord passes through the foramen magnum (large opening), the hole in the floor of the skull, and ends in the medulla oblongata, a prolongation of the spinal cord. The medulla oblongata is . . .

The medical student's pen slid from his fingers as he lolled into sleep.

July 11, 2003

THE day after the strange call on her cell phone had passed uneventfully for Jessica, but on the day after that, she accompanied Lorena Combs to Amanda Manning's funeral. The Jax-town police and Combs's office positioned plain-clothes detectives and cameras at every angle, some mingling in with the crowd of mourners. Anyone and everyone attending was put on videotape.

The funeral over, Jessica and Combs poured over the photographic surveillance of the funeral, searching for any likely suspects to the girl's murder. Often, out of a sense of guilt and remorse—or a perverted sort of pride in their work—a killer showed up at his victim's funeral, *unable* to keep away. Some did it out of a sense of pride at having gone undetected, a final flip of the bird to officialdom, society, the church, the family, the parents and the victim.

Similar tapes had been made at the funerals in Richmond and Winston-Salem. But no one had looked out of place, nervous or anxious beyond the grieving loved ones. There were no loners holding back behind nearby trees or tombstones.

J.T. arranged for a member of the family, an uncle, to review the tapes with them as well. Ted Manning picked out any faces that didn't belong, and he was accurate with all the undercover officers, male and female. Then he hit on one face in the crowd he could not recognize, a blurred profile shot of a man standing at the center of the crowd, left of the coffin.

J.T. had the shot blown up, and still the Mannings did not recognize the man, but Sheriff Combs did, coming out of her seat. "I know that face. He was at the marina the night the body surfaced. He was supposedly off one of the yachts, and he got pushy with my men, real interested in what had happened."

They detoured back to the Venetia Warf and located the harbormaster, who instantly identified the man in the picture as Mr. Swantor, and he pointed out the man's large yacht. Welcoming them aboard, Swantor showed them gracious hospitality, sitting them down topside, offering them drinks. Combs agreed to lemonade and Jessica thought that sounded refreshing. She expected him to call out to a servant or a wife to fetch the drinks, but Swantor did the dubious honors himself. Jessica thought him overeager to please the authorities, as was reported the night of Captain Abrams's gruesome discovery. Still, while this could point to a hidden agenda, it could also say that Swantor was civic-minded or downright lonely and starved for attention.

"So . . . sir . . . tell us," asked Combs, "what was your purpose in attending the Manning girl's funeral?"

"You people . . . you are so clever. How did you know I was there? Never mind, I'm sure you don't dare reveal your sources or methods to a civilian."

Jessica set aside her lemonade. "Will you please answer the question, Mr. Swantor?"

He took a deep breath. "Because I felt awful about what had happened to the Mannings and thought it the only thing I could do under the circumstances, you know, to represent the yachts-people. None of whom," he added apologetically, "could make the funeral, although I made it my business that each should know when and where it would be held. Short of that, I set up a collection, you know, for everyone to chip in something for the parents, called the local TV news channel and asked to form a fund in memory of the dead girl. They said they'd get back to me on it, but haven't so far. So far, I've collected five hundred dollars from guess who?"

Swantor had just set himself up as the exception to the thoughtless well-off people residing on the yachts surrounding them. He was a tall, strong-looking man, robust from the sun on his face and arms, with the pontification of a pacing, fully displaying peacock. Lorena Combs complimented him on his generosity and concern. He blew it off with a suave wave of the hand, saying, "Look . . . let me show you two ladies the rest of the boat, belowdecks! Ladies . . . ahhh, Sheriff, Doctor?" He gestured with both hands for them to follow him as he backed down the steps to the cabin below.

He was expansive in showing them his beloved yacht, opening every nook and cranny for them to fawn over. His yacht was magnificent, state-of-the-art and fully equipped with the latest in nautical equipment. Jessica noticed the computer aboard, and he freely talked about its capacity.

"The damn thing can practically run the ship on its own.

Hardly needs me. It can detect objects in its path! Warns me fifty to a hundred yards in advance, depending on the size of the obstruction."

Jessica saw a separate computer with a large screen and a movie camera attached to it.

"Where is Mrs. Swantor?" asked Lorena.

"Oh . . . no . . . I'm quite alone aboard," he explained. "Mrs. Swantor . . . Lara and I . . . well, we divorced some months back. Still adjusting to the new life. Not easy, I can tell you. Maybe the trip to Cancun will help. Plan on going there soon."

After talking to Swantor, they walked down the wharf back toward their unmarked Sheriff's Office vehicle.

Combs said, "Satisfied with Swantor's good intentions?"

"Maybe . . . maybe not."

"Same here. I always get the creeps when somebody's in such heat to get near the body. And this guy did it two or three times when she was on the shrimp boat, and then he goes to the funeral."

"But we've got nothing on him." While Jessica felt some unnamable nagging sensation at the base of her skull creep down her spine, she knew they had nothing but gut instincts to go on. Not enough for a next step. "I just don't like the guy."

At the end of the dock ramp, Jessica suggested, "Lorena, I think you should do a thorough background check on our Mr. Jervis Swantor."

B ACK at the Duval County Sheriff's Office, Jessica spent time with the first officers on the Manning scene to get their first impressions of the condition of the body, but she also really wanted to know what they had thought of Mr. Swantor. Both officers thought him strange and overbearing that night. Officers Plummer and Bierdsley were leaving as Lorena Combs came into the temporary office given to Jessica. She had the background check in hand. "It's *Dr.* Jervis Swantor, retired GP."

"Doctor? That makes him even more likable."

"Maybe that explains why he thought he could help that night, assuming he thought the victim in need of medical attention."

"So, why didn't he tell Plummer or Bierdsley or any of the other officers that he was a doctor?"

"I can't say. All we know for certain is that he was very interested in getting a good look at the dead girl, as if he wanted to know precisely how she died."

"What else did you find out?"

"The check revealed a run-in with the law that involved a messy domestic dispute, sometime before his divorce. It got a little violent," said Combs.

"How so?"

"He had roped her to a tree and was threatening her with a meat cleaver the size of Rhode Island when the police arrived."

"Where did this occur?"

"Someplace called Grand Isle, Louisiana, where they lived at the time."

"And Swantor's also a doctor. Wonder why he was so modest about that," asked Jessica, scanning Combs's report.

"Well . . . he's not a surgeon. Aren't surgeons the big-headed ones?"

"Heavily invested in computer and tech stocks, but his picks all went south right before his marriage did."

Jessica called Santiva and, putting him on speakerphone with Lorena and herself, asked that he have Swantor's name run through the VICAP program. In a half hour, Santiva phoned with the news.

"We ran his name and his record reflects the single domestic disturbance warrant, that's all. How good does this guy look to you for the Skull-digger?"

"Only so-so. He's not a surgeon, and he doesn't drive a van. Though we've only assumed that since our shaky near-victim eyewitness in Fayetteville put him in a van, and then *we* outfitted that van with restraints and tools as his killing ground, based on the autopsy findings. Suppose the killer drove a rental van to his *boat*, and the *boat* was the site of the restraints and the killing ground?"

"But you said you had a thorough look all over his yacht, and he gave you the grand tour without your having to ask."

"Suppose he reserves another boat for his butchery?"

"Sounds like you're reaching, Jess."

Jessica exchanged a look with Lorena. "It occurred to me, yes, but—"

Eriq cut her off. "You said the guy is or was a general practitioner. Would he *know* how to make those cuts we've called—what was it—precise, professional, surgical? Although, I suppose, he could learn to cut a hole like that from one of those god-awful pathology books of yours, couldn't he?"

"I suppose his good intentions act might actually be genuinely motivated out of a concern about the Mannings and the girl. He even talked about getting a fund started in the girl's name.

"Could be he's one of those rare individuals we seldom see, Jess, a good, caring, wanna-be-helpful, OK person? So rare, we forget that we've ever seen one."

"Maybe you're right."

Lorena piped in, "It's just that both Jessica and I got the same vibes off him. Maybe he's not the Skull-digger, but he's got something strange about him. I've put a watch on him."

"Maybe he is just a pompous ass . . . makes himself feel better by setting himself up as a spokesperson for the rest of the community on the wharf," said Jessica.

Lorena added, "He claimed he was representing them someway, but the neighbors are pretty much in agreement they didn't grant him any such authority, and most see him as a self-important mini-potentate out there at the wharf, and he's only been docked there for a week!"

Jessica said, "If he's been plying the coast prior to tying up at Jacksonville . . . Well, it just points out that if he *isn't* the killer, then maybe he is in someway trawling for victims as an accomplice."

"Don't tell me, the ex-wife is the killer," Santiva's tone gave the remark a less than serious tweek. "And he's going to blow both their covers out of a curiosity over something he already knows has happened?"

"All right . . . We're just saying that he may bear watching," suggested Combs.

"What about this Daryl Cahil character, Eriq? Anything you find useful there?"

"Are you kidding? He's a gold mine, Jessica. He could well be our man."

"Based on?"

"Based on timing."

"*Timing?*"

"The creep was released a few months ago, after almost twelve years in the detention center. These brain theft crimes began after his release, and Richmond's not that far from Morristown."

"Released from where?" she asked while Combs's tall body leaned in an effort to hear more about this possible break in the case.

"From the Federal Penitentiary for the Criminally Insane in Pennsylvania. I think you know the facility," Eriq replied.

Jessica indeed knew the Pennsylvania facility well. She had placed some of its most notorious inmates there. She had also interviewed more than 160 lunatic killers at the facility in an effort to learn how a sociopath became a sociopathic *killer*, and what their thinking was like, and how they lured victims, and in some cases where bodies that had been missing for years might be found. But she recalled nothing about Cahil. Perhaps due to his not having actually murdered anyone.

"You're telling us this guy's resumed his previous behavior *after* being released?" asked Combs. "What a surprise. Released after twelve years?" she asked. "What happened? Overturned on appeal? Some technicality of arrest or seizure? What? And who is this guy, and why's his record got you so excited?"

"Slow down, Sheriff Combs," replied Eriq. "The guy's been on psychoactive drugs for twelve years, and he was a model prisoner, got religion, all of it, the whole nine—"

"I get the picture, but—"

"Been in the facility since late 1990. He was the head shrink's model project; that's why you never heard of him. He was a test case for a theory of rehabilitation that Dr. Jack Deitze was championing, and he didn't believe that FBI access and studies about sociopaths fit Daryl Cahil's particular aberration, because he hadn't actually *murdered* anyone. Remember, he fed off dead people he dug up."

"Then he was at the facility while I was doing my study, and now . . . only a few months before the Skull-digger shows up in Richmond, Dr. Deitze proclaims Daryl cured and releases him? Coupled with the call naming him—"

Jessica had told Combs about the call, but she'd characterized it before as a crank call.

Eriq said, "Maybe 'cured' isn't exactly the right word."

"You mean, it's most likely that his cure and release all had to do with the *success* of Dr. Deitze's study, I presume."

Combs added, "Must be an impressive particularized case study—*cured* of grave robbing tendencies."

Jessica shook her head. "No . . . cured of feeding on the brains of *dead children*."

Combs, hearing this, winced and swallowed hard. This was the first time she'd heard of Cahil's crimes.

Jessica continued, "Truth is, since this particular loon didn't actually murder anyone, it's unlikely he'd start now."

"So? Sounds like his crimes've gone well beyond murder, if you ask me."

"I agree," said Eriq from about six hundred miles away, "but now we have to deal with what's in front of us. He's free and it's a good bet that Daryl has *graduated* to murdering young women. All Deitze cured him of was the effort of digging for his victims.

"Nothing solid just yet, and authorities checking the address you gave me say it appears abandoned. No dark vans sitting outside."

"Well, if Cahil is committing murders with his van down here, it's highly unlikely he'll have a van sitting outside his home," Jessica pointed out wryly. "Penn state's federal pen," she repeated, again giving thought to the facility and her history with it. "They're building a reputation for hiring the worst damned shrinks I've ever come across."

"I know the irony's not lost on you, Jess."

Jessica explained for Lorena's benefit, "Same facility that housed Mad Matthew Matisak, who so ingratiated himself with Dr. Gabriel Arnold that the doctor let his guard down and paid the ultimate price. His foolishness also allowed the way for Matisak's escape."

"An escape that left a wide swath of murder across the nation, from Pennsylvania to Oklahoma and Louisiana," added Santiva.

"Now Dr. Jack Deitze has fallen under the spell of this maniac Cahil," Jessica said. "Setting him free."

"Deitze wants to meet with us, Jess. He says he has proof that Cahil could not have committed the Skull-digger killings. Can you get back soon to see him? Maybe stopover in Pennsylvania on your way back home? I could meet you there, perhaps?"

"I suppose, although I don't relish visiting that place."

"Soon as you wrap up there, we'll make arrangements."

Another office phone rang, and Combs went to that line, picking up and listening intently to someone on the other end. Combs hung up and interrupted the conference call by saying, "Jessica, Chief Santiva, that call I just took. News of a brainless body found in a farmer's field outside Savannah, Georgia, only about a hundred and forty miles from Jacksonville."

"Did you hear that, Eriq?"

"I did."

"I've gotta go to Savannah."

"Good luck and keep me apprised. I'm going to keep digging into the Cahil lead from here," he replied before hanging up.

Combs said, "I can get you to Savannah. My patrol car'll get you there as fast as anything else might."

"I'm sure you have friends in Georgia, and I'm sure to bristle a few hairs there. I'd welcome your company and assistance, Sheriff."

"I know I've allowed myself to become emotionally involved in the Manning girl's murder, Jessica, but I still want to do everything I can to help catch this snake."

"And cut off his head?"

"You think my anger's a bad thing?"

"I'm not the one to tell you that becoming emotionally involved in the Manning case is a bad thing. I'm too highly invested in this case myself to point any fingers."

Lorena bit her lower lip and slipped on her gun and trooper hat. Jessica called the FDLE in search of John Thorpe. Unable to locate him, she left word at the lab regarding what had occurred, and that she'd call him from her cell phone. Together, she and Combs rushed for the waiting cruiser in the underground lot.

COMBS drove the cruiser herself. The two law-enforcement women talked the entire way, learning that they enjoyed many of the same leisure activities, including swimming, diving and flying. They had even visited some of the same vacation spots over the years. They talked about the beauty of Florida's underwater state park, the John Pennekamp Coral Reef State Park.

Strobe lights ahead alerted Jessica and Lorena that they were at the location outside Savannah, Georgia, where the victim awaited them. Along the way, Jessica had reached J.T., who had agreed to remain in Jacksonville to tie up the loose ends there and to await the outcome of the tests they had run on Amanda Manning.

Lorena pulled off the gravel road they had been on for the past mile or so, within a foot of thick trees and brush, but while they saw three Georgia State Patrol cars parked to form an oddly shaped triangle, nose to tail like circling wagons, there was no one around to greet them. No one in sight.

It was still daylight, but the woods seemed eerily still. No birds in the trees, no sounds of life whatsoever, not even insect life. A cloud-filled sky and a darkening horizon threatened rain, while the tops of tall pines began to rock in a developing wind, creating a welcomed noise. Then came a rolling thunder from the distance.

"Where is everybody?" Jessica wondered aloud.

"Kind of creepy. Like a B horror movie," commented Combs. "Let's go see if we can find these *crackers*."

As they exited the car, Jessica and Lorena heard someone coming through the dense wood alongside them. Lorena fingered her holster but remained calm. From the trees came a uniformed deputy. "That you, Combs? Dr. Coran?" he asked.

"It's us, Milt," replied Combs.

"You look as sweet as ever, Lorena," replied Milton Stoffel, extending a hand, his smile cheerful and reassuring. "Sorry we have to meet under such awful circumstances, Dr. Coran, but I guess you meet a lot of people under . . . Well, I won't say worse conditions, but similar conditions."

Jessica extended her hand, reading his nameplate as they shook. Lorena had told her all about Stoffel's call to her office on the trip up to Georgia.

"Unfortunately, Senior Deputy Stoffel," Jessica replied to him, "you're only too right about meeting me. Most people would rather see Jack Kevorkian coming their way than to see me."

Stoffel laughed at this. "Ol' Dr. Death? Hell, you're a sight prettier."

"Most of the people I meet are engaged in their work when I meet them, and most I meet deal with death daily."

He nodded knowingly. "We know about the case in Jaxtown, but we just never expected it to happen here. But we do have *some* good news for you, Dr. Coran, Lorena."

"Oh, and what's that?" asked Combs.

"Killer left something of himself behind this time."

Jessica instantly wondered if the deputy had found the

mark inside the victim's skull. She exchanged a look with Combs, and Lorena instantly asked, "What've you got, Milt?"

He led them cautiously to the triangular center of the three patrol cars, and Jessica saw the marker where a tire print was clearly visible. "Could be the killer's," commented Stoffel. "Didn't want to lose it before we got a cast made."

The two women stared at the tire treads in the soft red earth of a bare spot alongside the road, encircled by the patrol cars. Another state trooper came through the thicket and said, "I'm on it, boss. Just have to get the kit from my cruiser."

"Thanks, Wil," replied Stoffel, "and don't forget the shoe prints."

"I'm on it! I'll do the shoe prints first."

"You've got shoe prints, too?" asked Jessica.

"We do. It's why I have to lead you in and outta the crime scene. So far, they're intact and untouched."

Jessica clenched her medical bag to her chest. "I want to see the shoe prints."

He led Jessica and Combs to the shoe prints, again a sparse area giving way to soft red clay. "Photos've already been taken of the tire and shoe prints."

The shoe impressions were clear and easily read, like giant fingerprints against the earth, the wild swirls and eddies of the pattern indicating a unique design and wear. As a result of design and wear, no two shoe prints were the same. The prints isolated by Stoffel showed a man going into the field and coming out. "We'll need an impressions expert to be sure, but my guess," said Jessica, "he weighs between one hundred and seventy and one hundred and ninety pounds. I'm going by the shoe prints pointing away from the body, not toward it."

"I calculated him somewhere in there, too, if not heavier,"

said Stoffel. "Ground's soft here, so he made quite an impression, especially going in . . . carrying her weight, we speculate."

Jessica examined the prints with more care. "Given the size of the foot, we can calculate him at between five-eight and six feet tall."

"How do you figure that?" asked Stoffel.

"There's a definite logic to assumptions about the size and weight. Body parts correspond and align with one another in surprising harmony. A foot this size indicates a tall man wearing casual shoes—sneakers."

"Now all we need is for the guy to come in with his shoes," said Combs.

Stoffel said, "Figure he couldn't get through the thicket in his vehicle, and maybe . . . just maybe he took the clearing under last night's moon to be a body of water, so he come through the trees, expecting to dump her in a pond or a lake that isn't here. Tells us he doesn't know the area so well."

"So we got lucky with the tire prints and the shoe impressions," said Combs.

"It's something, Lorena. This guy's left so little behind because he's always dumped them in water before now," replied Jessica.

"In Jax-Town, the St. John's runs north, so the body traveled upstream to Venetia Wharf. We couldn't locate the actual entry point, every possibility was littered with tire marks. During the day, those places are busy parks, but at night they're pretty well empty."

"Lotta these old dirt roads look alike," Stoffel added, "but still . . . Savannah's not that far away. There's water everywhere going east. If he wanted to stow her body in water, he coulda just gone east of I-95 for a ways. Hell, the tide comes in over there and you got instant lakes surrounding you."

"And if the tide's out at the time?"

"Has been dry."

Jessica shook her head. "He must've simply run out of time. He's on the road again, likely I-95 but who knows."

"Maybe he's going back to where he came from to begin with, north toward home, maybe?" suggested Combs. "New Jersey, maybe?"

They carefully stepped around the shoe prints just as the officer named Wil showed up with the plaster of paris mixture that would make the impressions permanent and portable.

As Jessica and Lorena were led through the final thicket, Stoffel said, "The crime against young Winona here . . . Well, it's the worst ever thing I've seen on the job aside from a motorcyclist we once had to get a crane for."

"A crane?"

"To get his headless torso from the top of a pine tree out on County 345A. Fool had to have been hitting 110 when he left the rise at Three Forks. Had sixty or seventy lacerations, his clothes and most all of his skin'd been peeled and was hanging like bloody garland. Some of the officers on scene tried shaking the tree, but that only dislodged the head, which hit one of the officers on the skull and sent him in with a concussion. It took a crane and a lot of effort to peel the rest of the motorcyclist down from that tree."

Deputy Stoffel spit out tobacco and pulled back the last of the branches and brush. They stepped into a farmer's open field where a tractor and discs sat idle some ten yards from the body of a young woman lying amid a field of decaying and turned under cornstalks. Neat rows of furrows led up to the body where the discs had turned under the dead stalks, weeds and earth, but the other side of the tractor looked like a burned out jungle. The heat and the rotting stalks, whipping now in the growing evening wind, sent up an odor of plant decay. When the killer had left the body, he would have been looking at a field of picked over, dead stalks, several miles of them. He likely did not expect the body to be discovered for some time.

In the distance, Jessica saw a white farmhouse with a green roof, little specks of movement and activity telling her that children were at play there.

"We've already been up to the house; everything's all right there. Nobody being held hostage. No one being harbored or taken in," said Stoffel.

"The girl . . . you know her name."

"Winona Miller, yes."

"Does she belong to the house up there?" Jessica pointed.

"Oh, no . . . no, that's the Pratt place. What happened was old Lyle Pratt come up on the body in the dark of early this morning."

Jessica imagined the old man's fright and his proximity in time and space to the killer.

Stoffel continued speaking. "Winona Miller, the dead girl, is—was—a native of Savannah, and I'm told a good kid, normal kid. . . . You know, typical fun-loving, free-spirited, happy kid. Lived in Savannah with her aunt and uncle, dealing with the usual teen angst and rebellion."

"And her parents?"

"They live in the city, too, but they had all agreed on a trial period with the girl at her aunt's place. Parents filed a missing persons report with Savannah PD after being told that Winona had failed to come home from a date."

"A date?" asked Jessica. "What about the boyfriend?"

"Boyfriend has been grilled, but he appears to be of little

help. Last saw her out his rearview mirror getting into a dark van, possibly navy blue, possibly black."

"Wait . . . the boyfriend saw something?" asked Jessica.

"We got very little from Nathan. He's shook up pretty bad. Blaming himself for her disappearance. Don't know what he's going to do with the truth."

"I'll want to talk to this Nathan, right away," insisted Jessica.

Combs agreed. "He's the only eyewitness of any sort that we have except for the girl in Fayetteville who may or may not have come across the killer's path. She also said the van was dark blue."

"We already canvassed the club where her boyfriend left her in the parking lot. According to Nathan, they'd had a fight, an argument, he says, over her using too many drugs and mixing them with alcohol."

"Toxicology can verify or refute that," said Jessica.

"Like I said, she was a good kid at heart, but a mixed up kid, too. She might've been using pills or sniffing this or that," Stoffel said, "but no tracks on her. Still, I know it'll take an autopsy to tell for certain."

"Even if she were using drugs, that's no reason to wind up dead and having your g'damn head cut open and your g'damn brains stolen," shouted a younger deputy who'd stood watch over the body. The anger in his thick-throated attempt to keep from losing complete control was understandable. His nameplate read Hayes. "She was basically a good kid, and she didn't have any *real* enemies, not a one."

Beyond her addictions, Jessica guessed in silence.

"You suppose she was without a care beyond school grades, makeup and make-out woes?" Combs cynically asked Jessica.

Stoffel put a hand on the younger deputy's shoulder and

said, "Jeff here was the first trooper to arrive to secure the scene. It's been a shock. He knows the family and has volunteered to break it to them. Fact is, Jeff's married to the victim's cousin, so I've OK'd his talking to them. So far, all they know is their daughter's missing. There's been no press on it, yet. So, if you don't mind, I'll let Jeff go over to Savannah to break the news to the parents."

"No objections," Jessica said.

No one envied the young man his awful chore. Hayes disappeared into the brush, going back toward the squad cars. The thick brush and trees hid the road and the cars from view, even more so where Jessica squatted beside the body.

It had grown dusky, the sky darkening with clouds. Jessica dug out a flashlight and filled the open brain cavity with light, looking for the sign left on the previous victim.

"Is it there?" asked Combs, dropping to her knees alongside the body, opposite Jessica.

"Is what there?" asked Stoffel, inching closer.

At first Jessica had trouble finding it, but then it came into focus. The circle atop the horizontal and perpendicular lines forming a cross of sorts, roughly scratched into the bone at the back of the skull. As Jessica stared at it, a realization hit her, and Lorena saw it.

"What is it, Jessica?"

"I just remembered something that might be important. Several weeks ago at Quantico we were shown slides of the first two victims, and I noticed some imperfection on the screen in the grainy blowups. At least, I thought it was the screen. Santiva was impressing the hideous nature of the crimes on his agents. The photos of the violence done to each of the first two victims were external, but looking back now . . ."

"The marks were present?"

"Perhaps when one or more of the shots was taken, maybe the flash revealed some indication of the mark. But I'll have to verify that."

"What is it?" asked Stoffel, staring over Jessica's shoulder. "Some cult ritual thing?"

"It's a sign of some sort, a *signature* the killer leaves behind," explained Combs. "The mark is absolute proof it's the same killer. Milt, this is strictly *taboo*. Nobody outside law enforcement can know. It could be the Holy Grail to solving the case."

"No one but the three of us knows at this point, Deputy Stoffel," Jessica added, lying to him. "If it leaks out, it can't be used effectively when and if we ever get this monster into an interrogation room."

"Understood."

"I've got to call Quantico, have an associate take a closer look at the photos of the first victims. I may have been staring at this evidence and simply missed it altogether in the photo array."

"You wouldn't have been looking for it at the time," countered Combs. "No one who autopsied the bodies reported it; obviously, no one saw it."

"It must mean something to the killer, a kind of cryptic code of his intent or motive." Jessica got on her cellular phone and contacted headquarters. Unable to get Eriq on the line, she opted for Jere Anderson, a young female assistant in the lab, who asked cheerily, "How're you, Dr. Coran? We miss you around here."

"Same here, Jere. Look, I need your help. I need you to review those slides Henrietta Wyans has of the two brain cases. The ones used at the briefing last month."

"Anything you need . . . anything I can do, sure," Jere replied. "Shoot."

Jessica told Jere specifically what to look for in the slides and exactly where she must focus on the wounds to the victims.

She told the young assistant about her suspicion that the mark might have been on the previous victims, but that it had been missed during the autopsies.

"Are you going to order exhumations on—"

"No, no! The families have been through enough." In her mind's ear she heard J.T.'s voice repeating what he'd said earlier in the day: *We're not going to get a court order to disinter two bodies on a hunch, Jessica.*

"No, no digging up anybody, Jere," she repeated, "but I do want a fine-tooth exam of the photo evidence—the blowup slides."

"Right . . . right, for corroboration that the mark was left inside the skulls of the other two."

"If you can't establish both, then one. I'm eighty percent certain I saw something on at least one of the slides."

"OK, Dr. Coran. I'm on it."

"Jere, it may be nothing, a wild goose chase but we have to—"

"Doctor, I'll chase this one for you. No problem. We all want to see this creep go away, and if there's any slight chance I can help from this end, of course, I will."

"Thanks, Jere, and in case I miss you, report your findings to Chief Santiva as soon as possible."

"Understood." After goodbyes, they broke contact.

Jessica then went to work gathering blood, tissue, fiber and hair samples.

Combs, watching Jessica work, asked, "I doubt seriously if anyone in the Savannah area has a laser-guided scalpel, Jessica."

"No . . . not necessary since we have the one bone fragment. We'll just make sure this one photographs clearly."

Combs was kneeling beside Winona's body now. Insect activity—ants in particular—had already become a problem, especially around the large wound to the head—the single most obvious sign that this was the work of the same killer who had so recently struck in Jacksonville.

"Let me have another look at this thing," said Stoffel, placing on a pair of glasses and kneeling in toward the body. After a moment, he asked, "What do you think this mark means, Dr. Coran? Looks awfully strange indeed."

Jessica asked Stoffel for his pen and pad. The deputy obliged, and she quickly drew the sign of the etched cross.

"Ain't that the Lutheran cross?" asked Stoffel.

"Right now . . . we're unsure what it means, Deputy. It could be important to the killer or simply left behind to throw us off."

Combs, still on one knee across the body from Jessica, asked, "How? How did he lure her in? How did he find her, and how did he target her?"

"You could ask that of all his victims," replied Jessica. "At the moment, we don't know. Nothing specifically links the victims. Other than their ages and the horrible nature of their deaths, they have little in common."

"Yeah, they all got their brains sucked out, and they all got this mark put on them," replied a solemn Stoffel, stabbing the crude drawing of the cross on the pad.

SIX

Evils draw men together.

—ARISTOTLE, QUOTING A PROVERB

Public library, Savannah, Georgia
July 12, 2003

NURSE Susan Thorn aspired to be a doctor. She had been taking classes part time, and to maximize her time, she had taken to the Internet for help. In her anatomy class, she had arrived at the frightfully difficult chapter on the human brain, and she had to know everything she could about it before the exam. Signing on to the computer as Twisted-Nurse, she had been cruising for information for sometime now.

She'd seen some weird stuff on the Net, but there was one website in particular that spoke of the cosmic soul being housed in the brain. Some of the talk on the site had gotten into cannibalizing animal and human brains, which she chalked up to juveniles at play on the Web. While the site had at first promised to be useful, not long into it, she decided it must be for comic-book readers. She logged off and soon found something more professional, and from there Susan Thorn began taking notes from what she read:

The medulla oblongata serves as the organ of communication between the spinal cord and the rest of the body. In the embryonic state, it is called the brain bag—the centers that govern such autonomic functions as breathing, heartbeat, regulation of blood vessels, body temperature and certain reflexes of swallowing.

This is more like it, Susan told herself. Still, something about the other site nagged, like a little cyber voice, calling her back. She held firm to her initial conviction, however, stayed with her study, and read on:

Projecting a little in front of the medulla is a wide band of nervous tissue forming a bridge over the two halves of the cerebellum called the pons Varolii. This along with the medulla forms the brain stem.

In the brain stem lies a network of nerves known as the reticular formation—millions of neurons in a matrix of fibers, from which long branches are sent out to every part of the body. Thus, it participates in every neural function; so it coordinates and filters information in the brain.

It is the center of arousal and wakefulness, regulating awareness. Anything that might put the reticular formation out of action would result in coma or death. Lying longitudinal along the brain stem is the raphe system, active during sleep. Anything destroying the raphe system results in chronic insomnia.

Susan came back to herself, thinking about her aunt Naomi's insomnia, wondering if her smoking interfered with her raphe system. "Maybe she needs to cannibalize somebody else's brain to recover," she muttered to herself, thinking of the foolish information floating around on that first Web page she had cursorily visited.

Since the news of the Brain Thief had been aired on TV, everyone was hoaxing in one manner or another, and the Web was filled with lunatics who professed responsibility for the killings. Word had it that the FBI was inundated with such fools. "Got brains?" asked one Internet site.

Savannah Police Department
Same morning

"You don't understand. I had too much to drink. I get mean when I drink, but I'd never hurt anyone, 'specially my sweet Winona," Nathan Campbell told them, his brown eyes wide and bloodshot. "I picked a fight with her. Wanted to test her, you know. See if she really meant all those things she said. I wouldn't do that kind of thing if I was sober."

Campbell was several years older than Winona, and their relationship had been stormy. Jessica saw instantly that Nathan Campbell was in a state of exhaustion and mental anguish. He blamed himself for his girlfriend's death. Agitated, no words of solace could calm him or dissuade him from his belief. The end result: It proved difficult to get relevant information out of him.

"Can you tell us the make and model of the van?"

"I think it was a Dodge, maybe a Plymouth, maybe late '90s, but I couldn't swear to that." This corroborated info from the near-abducted woman in Fayetteville, North Carolina.

"Did you see anything at all of the driver?"

"Older guy I think. White, I think. Didn't recognize him, but didn't really get a good look at him, either. Pretty sure he wasn't one of our crowd or a regular at the club . . . at least, I don't think so."

"Did Winona act as if she knew him?"

"I can't say but maybe . . . maybe she did act that way, I mean. I first saw her alone where I left her. I'd gotten so mad I fuckin' drove off . . . but I was just going round the block—throw a scare into her, you know."

"So, you drove around the block and then what?" pressed Jessica.

"By the time I came back around, she was being chummy with this guy, flirting through the passenger window like a cheap hooker."

"What did you see of the driver?"

"I didn't get a decent look. Like I said, his van didn't look familiar, but she acted friendly like maybe *she* knew him. But I thought that was for my benefit, you know— that she knew I'd come around the corner and was playing me, you know. That's when I kept going the second time. Time I drove back again, the van was gone and so was she."

"You think she could have known him?" Combs asked again.

"I thought she was doing it all for my benefit, to teach me a lesson, you know. I thought for sure she'd get back out of the van as soon as I disappeared, and that I'd just come back for her again. I'd been drinking, not thinking so clear, you know? I got pissed off again. I went home think- ing it was over for sure between us, and I slept it off. Next thing I know, the cops're knocking at my house and my parents are waking me up."

"Did you happen to notice the van's plates? In state, out of state?"

"I didn't see 'em. Damn me . . ."

"Did Winona ever talk about meeting anyone on the

computer?" asked Combs, who had a team working that avenue of inquiry.

"No . . . no, she said people that did that were sick fucks."

"Did she spend a lot of time on the Internet?" persisted Lorena.

"Nah, she wasn't like addicted to it or anything. Why?"

"Just part of routine questioning these days, Mr. Campbell."

"Is that how the sonofabitch works?" he asked.

"We're exploring that notion."

Sheriff Combs had already pressed the local deputy related to the victim, Jeff, to confiscate Winona's computer. Amanda Manning's parents had turned over her computer to Combs as well, and leads had been made and investigated regarding men who had propositioned Amanda over the Internet. So far, none had panned out.

When they had discussed this line of inquiry, Jessica was guardedly enthusiastic, but she had suggested, "Watch for any crossing of the same guy in contact with both victims. If we have probable cause, then we can get the Net server to open its files."

"It'd help if Richmond and Winston-Salem would share what they have along these lines. You think some high-ranking SOB with the FBI could get on them to confiscate and examine the computer tracks of the other two victims?"

"I've already asked Santiva to push for it, Lorena."

"Who knows . . . maybe we'll get lucky."

Combs volunteered to go through all of Winona's E-mail to see if anyone had contacted her for a meeting on or around the time of her murder. She would also attempt to find any matchups with correspondence between the two young women—Winona and Amanda—as well as anyone writing to them both.

Here in Savannah's largest police station, Jessica felt the

weight of the case on her shoulders. She stepped away from Campbell and his weak-to-useless testimony. "We still have little to go on."

Combs countered, "We've got more than we had. The tire prints, two and a half shoe prints. We know for a fact now that the killer leaves a mark on his victims."

"Yeah . . . his final statement of power and ownership. The marking likely makes the bastard feel good, that he holds sway over his victim even after death. I can't tell you how many times I've heard such killers profess a belief in an afterlife that'll reunite them with their victims—that they will be *connected* throughout eternity."

"Madness begets fantasy."

"Mad Matthew Matisak himself had such plans for me," Jessica confessed.

"You'll have to tell me about it sometime."

"On the way back to your town."

"Well, while we have little to go on, it is a good deal more than the Skull-digger's left anyone before now."

Campbell asked, "Can I go now? I gotta go see Winona's folks. Try to explain."

"I'd caution you away from them for a while, Nathan," Jessica suggested. She and Sheriff Combs had gone to the Miller home earlier in the day to question the barely functioning, distraught parents to no avail and to confiscate the computer and all of Winona's disks. They found a typical young girl's bedroom, filled with stuffed animals, rock CDs, posters, makeup and mirrors. Jessica's gaze had fallen on a sculpture of an angel on the girl's nightstand. Winona was not quite out of her teens yet. "If the victims have any one thing in common, I'd call it innocence," Jessica had confided as Lorena lifted the angel statue and stared at it.

Nathan Campbell now nodded at Jessica's advice to keep his distance from the parents for the time being, but she sensed he would not heed her words. "Maybe you're right," he said without conviction.

"You might want to get some professional help too, Nathan. You're free to go. Your parents are waiting outside."

Campbell stood, thanked them and left in a dejected state, his shoes having been confiscated and replaced by prison booties.

"What now?" asked Combs of Jessica in the empty interrogation room.

"Boyd's having Campbell's shoes and his tire treads checked against the casts. But Nathan doesn't strike me as a vicious killer."

Just then Jessica's cell phone rang and she dug it out of her pocket. "Coran," she said into the phone, "how can I help you?"

A strange, strident male voice replied, "Don't believe a word of the lies my woman has told you."

"Who is this, please?"

"I'm not the Skull-digger. I'm cured of all that a long time ago. Just don't waste your time coming after me."

"Who is this?"

"You focus all your efforts on the right man. Not me." The phone went dead.

Jessica went into the answered calls in her phone log and punched SEND for a dial back, and though it rang, no one picked up. Her phone displayed a number with a 609 area code. A different number but still a New Jersey exchange— the Atlantic City area of New Jersey.

"What was that all about?" asked Combs.

"Not sure, but I may just follow up on a lead that'll take me to New Jersey."

"Want to tell me about it?"

"I've got to alert Eriq about this call I just got."

"Go right ahead. Then maybe we can get a bite to eat, a cup of coffee," suggested Combs, looking tired.

Jessica again caught Eriq and put him on the speaker-phone. "The creep may have called me."

"What creep? Cahil?"

"None other. He didn't identify himself, but he pleaded with me not to listen to the woman who'd fingered him. He's got my cell number now. The number he called from was an Atlantic City exchange." She read the number off to him. "Maybe it'll help to pinpoint his location."

"What'd he say, exactly?"

"He's concerned I'd be wasting my time on him, that he's not the Skull-digger."

"If it's from a pay phone, we'll check surrounding area hotels. If it's from a phone he owns, we've got the bastard, and this time no one's going to let him out of his cage ever again," said Eriq. "Oh, and we're running down leads on the wife-*slash*-girlfriend as well."

"Maybe the wife's already dead, and he took my number off her body."

"I've made arrangements with Deitze for us to see him at two P.M. tomorrow afternoon. Can you make that?"

"Make it four if you can."

Eriq had an incoming call. "Let me know of any new—"

"Will do!"

He hung up and Jessica did likewise. She looked over to Lorena and said, "I'm with you. Let's go get something to eat and drink."

PEOPLE milled about the corner restaurant called Savannah Sal's in downtown Savannah, just off the historic section of the city where tourists flocked. Jessica watched the crowd, trying to get her mind to relax from the case. She watched people try the patience of those behind the counter as they stared at an overhead quick-order menu; she saw others picking up their orders and complaining about this or that. Still others searched for their parties, while a few urgently sought the bathrooms. A number of people sat reading newspapers, while one or two worked on their laptops, one of them laughing at something on his screen, the other grimly silent. The average clientele appeared to be of college age, and countless textbooks were stacked and flung across tables and on seats. Some of the young people looked hungover.

Jessica and Lorena had coffee while awaiting a waiter to find them in Sal's more formal dining section. Jessica rested her head in her hands, complaining of her lack of sleep.

"I know what you mean," agreed Lorena.

Jessica excused herself and snatched out her cell phone and contacted J.T. back in Jacksonville. She informed him, "We've got an identical killing up here, John, down to the skull etching on the inside. But he left tracks this time."

"Footprints?"

"Shoe prints and tire marks." Jessica quickly brought J.T. up to date on both the Cahil angle and that she had to be in Pennsylvania the following day to meet with Jack Deitze. "I need you to get all the evidence gathered on the Manning girl, including the bone fragment, up to Quantico ASAP."

Their drinks arrived with hot rolls and butter. "Thanks, John. I gotta go now."

For a brief time, the two women remained quiet, each trying to cut the edge of her hunger. Combs broke the silence. "So, anything else you can tell me about this Cahil guy?"

"He hit a number of cemeteries in New Jersey as a modern-day grave robber, a *ghoul*—the old expression aptly fits here, Lorena. Hasn't been a recorded case of actual grave robbery—as opposed to grave vandalism—in the U.S. since."

"The New Jersey Ghoul, yeah, I remember now. Saw a segment on *Ripley's Believe It or Not* that highlighted his questionable accomplishment as the last of the ghouls."

"Apprehended in 1990 in a Morristown cemetery with a bone saw. He cut the heads off and took them with him. Left the graves wide open."

"1990, yeah . . . I was still in high school at the time, but I recall the case. Something about necrophilia, that he robbed the graves of their heads and used them as sex objects. A real sick freak."

"I don't know too much about the man's motivations." Jessica wanted to change the subject, so she asked, "How old are you, Lorena? You must be the youngest female sheriff in the South, or the country for that matter."

"Democrats thought a woman running for office would fail, but we surprised them. I got the black vote and the Indian vote and a good chunk of the white vote." Lorena stirred back to the case. "So, how does grave robbing and brain snatching go together?"

"I'm not sure, and I'm not sure that Cahil won't lead to another dead end. If I hadn't gotten those two calls, we probably wouldn't even be looking at the guy."

"So, you don't think anything'll come of it?"

"Maybe, maybe not. I'll know more after I talk with Dr. Deitze."

"The clown who authorized Cahil's release? Good luck."

The waiter returned with two hot steaming plates, Jessica's a roast beef dinner and Lorena's a vegetarian lasagna. Jessica glanced at the décor as she ate, studying the walls covered with historical items supposedly out of old Savannah's past: old soda pop and cigar signs, buckets, milk pails, rusty traps, harnesses, an entire plowshare heavy enough to kill someone should it fall. Combs, following Jessica's gaze, said, "All items no one in his right mind would hang above a plate of food anywhere but in a restaurant."

Jessica laughed in response, and Combs joined her.

"I still have no idea how someone like Cahil could get my private number."

Combs said, "Doesn't take much these days with computer access to everyone you know on the planet, Jess. Remember the Theresa Saldana stalking murder attempt?"

"The actress who survived—what was it?—seven or eight knife wounds?"

"Yeah, that's it. Her attacker told police that a hundred dollars to a private eye gave him the family address." Combs allowed the fact to sink in. "And nowadays with the damn Internet it's easy enough to get information on your own. Cut out the middleman to get names, addresses, phone numbers."

"But I'm very careful with that number."

"The celebrity stalker told Saldana that he was a production assistant for Martin Scorsese, and wanted to know if she would look at a script for 'Marty.' Now, maybe you didn't get a call from Scorsese, Jess, but you did get one from a resourceful lady in a day and age when you don't have to be all that resourceful to electronically get reams of information on what you want."

"I know you're right. I guess I just want to hold on to the illusion that I have some privacy left."

They continued their meal. Then Combs asked, "What next?"

"I want to be on hand at the Miller girl's autopsy. From there, I find a bed, get a good night's sleep and tomorrow get myself up to Philadelphia and the penitentiary."

"I'll be heading back to Jax-town, but I'll keep you apprised of anything useful we might find on the Net searches, if you'll part with that number of yours."

"Why don't you steal it, if it's so damned easy to do?" Jessica joked.

"How do you know I haven't already?"

Jessica wrote out the number on a pad and gave it to Combs. "I want to thank you, Lorena, for all your help and hospitality. Sorry you've got that long drive alone."

"Not in the least. Just doing my job."

Pennsylvania Federal Penitentiary for the Criminally Insane, outskirts of Philadelphia
4:15 P.M., JULY 13, 2003

ERIQ had failed to show up, leaving Jessica on her own to deal with Dr. Johnathan "Jack" Deitze. Furious, she had telephoned Santiva only to learn that he'd gone to Atlantic City, New Jersey, on a lead in the Skull-digger case. She pictured his search there motivated out of a sense of desperation. He must have a great deal of pressure on his back at the moment to stand her up and leave her alone with Deitze. She told Henrietta in no uncertain terms that her boss was to get in touch with her as soon as possible. Henrietta conveyed the last of Eriq's message to Jessica: "You are to meet a Detective Maxwell Strand at the penitentiary. The two of you can interview Dr. Deitze."

"Strand? I don't know any Strand."

"He'll be looking for you."

The facility was a gleaming new and sleek structure back in the '70s when it'd been built, but its age was beginning to show in small ways, from poor windows to cracks in the tiled floors leading through the massive lobby where a pair of security guards walked her through a tired metal detector. A man in a suit watched her give up her two guns and come through the detector with unusual interest, and he asked, "Dr. Coran? Dr. Jessica Coran?"

"Yes."

The tall, stout man with thin gray hair looked too old to be a working police detective. "I'm Strand."

"Are you with the Philly police?"

"No . . . Retiring Morristown PD in a couple of months. I worked the Cahil case with my partner. We apprehended Cahil in the act."

"What more can you tell me about our target?"

"Nobody knows more about him than I do, but Deitze will tell you he does."

She sensed there was no love lost between the cop and the shrink. "So, fill me in."

"Full name is Daryl Thomas Cahil, aka the Ghoul, age thirty-six. Apprehended in Morristown after things became too hot in Newark for him. Caught red-handed in the dis-interred grave of a child named Amiee Lee Pheiffer by my partner, Reed, and me. Cahil was only twenty-three at the time."

"How much does he weigh?"

"Kinda slight from his photo, which I've sent copies of to your boss, who's likely forwarded it on to every law-enforcement agency in the southeast by now. Weighs maybe 155 maybe 160."

"Did you send a picture of him at twenty-three years of age?"

"No, I've kept him under surveillance since his release, up until a few weeks ago. I had a bout with some trouble that put me in the hospital. But the photo's current." He slid a photo from a file he carried. Jessica looked at the sunken-faced, small man in the picture. He didn't look large enough for the image she'd had of the Skull-digger. His weight, he's got to weigh more, she was thinking of the prints found in Georgia.

"Height?"

"Five-ten."

She told him of the shoe print find at the latest murder scene. "It's from a guy who's at least 175 to 180, possibly one hundred and ninety pounds, Detective Strand."

"Prints at a crime scene can be unreliable."

"The officer in charge was very thorough and professional. And Cahil can't have changed his foot size or his height, so . . . Then there's the thing about how leopards don't change their spots."

"You mean a ghoul can't graduate to live prey?"

"He dealt in dead bodies, not live ones, right? Like his height and weight, his MO and his fantasy aren't likely to change."

"Unless it has developed into something else. Hell, he had nearly thirteen years to tweak it."

"Our current ghoul *makes* dead bodies; he doesn't dig them up. Other than the brain theft, there's not a lot of similarities here between what Cahil was convicted for, and what the Skull-digger has done."

"But that's just it. Cahil lost more than twelve years. He's now making up for lost time. He could well be the Skull-digger, still in search of this 'island' thing, this 'real thing.' "

She had no idea what he meant, but she asked, "Then why isn't he in custody, Detective?"

"He will be as soon as we can locate him. Place is under surveillance at the moment and an order for his arrest has been issued. I took the liberty and asked your field operatives in Jersey to haul him in on suspicion, just to see if he was there, but he's not, which tells me he's elsewhere."

"Where is 'elsewhere'?"

"Possibly in Atlantic City, as your mysterious phone calls suggest."

"Santiva told you about the calls?"

He nodded.

She knew the way to Deitze's office; it had been Gabe Arnold's before Matisak had hooked him up to a dialysis machine in the infirmary and drained him of every ounce of blood. Jessica hadn't returned here in almost nine years, and she'd forgotten about the constant wail of madmen behind these walls. Fortunately, she needn't go through lockup for her purposes today. Her groundbreaking study on socio- paths, done here back in the early '90s, had become required reading at the FBI Academy.

Strand struggled to keep pace, a bad leg plaguing him. She slowed in response.

"Can you verify that he's actually been out of town, and if so do his vacations coincide with the killings?"

"Neighbors verify that he's *been* out of town, but no one can say where or for how long. He's a recluse, and he timed his disappearance to coincide with my operation and hos- pital stay."

"Was he living with anyone in Morristown?"

"I've seen a woman come and go, but it's him . . . one of his personality manifestations."

"He's schizophrenic?"

"Multiple personalities. So, in a sense, yes. A woman re- sides there with him. I suspect the first call you got, the female caller, was this manifestation. So, you can stop wor- rying about her safety."

"He has no wife? No girlfriend who lives elsewhere, maybe out of town, maybe down the street or in Atlantic City?"

"None. He has no interest in anything smacking of nor- mal, Dr. Coran."

Jessica imagined the pressure Eriq must have been under

from both above and from this man to place someone—
anyone—in custody for the Skull-digger's heinous crimes. "I
want to believe this is the guy as much as you do, Detective—that we're closing in on the bastard, but I have to be
careful."

"Are you preaching the book to me?" he asked and then
laughed.

"I'm sorry. I've been down a lot of dead ends recently."

"I'm sure you have."

One of the guards at the greeting desk must have called
up to Deitze's office because he stood outside the door, waving her forward while telling Detective Strand that he would
speak only to Dr. Coran.

The two men glared so hard at one another that Jessica
feared each would be turned to stone. Obviously, they had
some bad history between them. "I'll speak to Dr. Coran
alone or not at all, Strand," declared Deitze.

Strand whispered in her ear, "Watch him. He's a liar."

Jessica had met Deitze at various law-enforcement functions, but they had never spent any time together, and what
little she knew of him, she didn't care for. He was an overbearing, self-aggrandizing sort who, she believed, would sell
his mother for a chance to be published in a major medical
journal.

The first thing he extended to her was his published paper on Cahil's treatment, and secondly, his sweaty hand.
"The paper is on Cahil, although I used a fictitious name. If
you will, Dr. Coran, read it thoroughly, you will find Cahil
harmless and incapable of the skullduggery and butchery of
this so-called Brain Thief who takes human life. If Cahil is
involved at all, it is only peripherally and not of his own
choosing."

"What do you mean by that?" she asked.

"Let's retire to my office. I have coffee. This will take
time."

As she entered his office, she apologized for Santiva's absence. He replied, "Hardly a problem . . . much better for medical people to understand one another before we go off to others with our theories, wouldn't you say?"

She wondered if what he said was meant as a slap of sorts. She wondered how much Santiva had told him about her suspicions of Cahil. "I suppose so, yes."

"Can I pour you coffee?"

"Black, please."

He poured for them both. "Take the time to read the report."

She did so, asking questions as she went. "Cahil admitted to *why* he robbed the graves of five children? Says here it had nothing to do with the tabloid speculations about necrophilia."

"Cahil was not sexually motivated whatsoever to attack his dead victims, no. He wasn't in it to create sex objects of his victims, no. All balderdash."

"I was within these walls on several occasions while he was incarcerated, doing my own study, as you recall, Dr. Deitze, just before you took over as Chief of Psychiatry here. Neither Dr. Arnold nor you thought him of interest to my study, yet he harbored these antisocial behaviors? Why was he kept from me?"

"Hardly kept from you. He was kept in isolation."

"And you two worked with him."

"Yes, before Arnold's unfortunate end . . . yes."

"I see."

"Cahil was never a candidate for your study because he had not actually murdered anyone."

"Necrophilia was the sensationalized story, yes. Page one of the tabloids. So, what's the real story?"

"He cut off the heads in order to take them to a *safe* place where he could do what he wanted with them. To take his time."

"The safe place being his basement at home?"

"With a stopover at his place of work, a butcher's shop, where—"

"Where he could damn well take his time with the victim's head, I'm sure."

"Yes . . . but it was in order to take his time with his true intended prize, the brains of the dead children, Dr. Coran."

"Ghoulish, all right . . . and what did he do with the gray stuff? Breakfast, lunch and dinner?"

"Not exactly, no."

"Blended it in the mixer and drank it with his Ovaltine?"

"If you'll just listen, Doctor."

"Bathed in it?"

"No."

"What then?"

"To gain his freedom, he had to describe his crimes in detail. He had to give a complete elocution."

"Dr. Deitze, what the hell did Cahil use the brain matter for?"

Deitze cleared his throat, sipped at his now-tepid coffee and replied, "The man sincerely believed it would place him in touch with something he called the eternal cosmic mind."

"Then he did consume it?"

"Not all of it, or so he professed in open court. Said it was just a small island of tissue he really cut the head open for."

"Small island of tissue?"

"Discarded the rest of the brain. But to get at this small dab of brain matter, he had to cut deep into the center to pluck it out."

"Island of tissue?"

"Deep at the center, something of an island. Called it the Real Island at his elocution. No one knew what he was talking about, least of all me."

"You were at the trial?"

"I found him fascinating; I asked to be put on his case, and Dr. Arnold arranged everything and set me up for the case study. I was not long out of psychiatric study at Stanford."

"Tell me more."

Deitze had an overlarge face, uncannily wrinkled with worry lines for one so young. Perhaps this single case was meant as his crowning achievement, and it had taken its toll on him. "It was assumed this object Cahil sought was some imaginary prize, part of his warped fantasy. But later on, during incarceration, I began to listen more closely to Cahil. I dug through old texts and esoteric books on the brain, and I made a stunning discovery. This 'Real Island' he spoke of, it was spelled R-h-e-i-l after its discoverer, a Dr. Rheil in the late eighteenth century. Cahil wasn't talking about some fiction his mind had concocted but a real—that is tangible—piece of brain matter, Dr. Coran."

"I've never heard of this Rheil Island, Dr. Deitze. Is there a formal, medical term for this brain part?"

"Just Rheil. Rheil dissected hundreds of brains during his lifetime, but only stumbled on his so-called island late in his life. Said it was located in the deepest recesses of the medulla oblongata.

"The midbrain. Cahil claimed in perfect lunatic fashion how the *soul* resided there, which had been Rheil's eighteenth-century speculation. Cahil said that in consuming this portion of the children's brains, that he meant to consume the *souls* of these children in order to be more powerful and in touch with something he called the cosmic mind."

"Christ save us all."

"I'm only telling you what he told the court, and details he filled in later as I worked with him. At any costs, Cahil had stumbled onto the esoteric teachings of the likely demented Dr. Benjamin Artemus Rheil, and he twisted what Dr. Rheil had to say about the Island of Rheil. My own study into Rheil and his work shows there's next to nothing remaining of the man or his theories, and others have simply chalked up his island as a leftover from our primitive brains. But in Cahil's mind, this small portion paradoxically holds all our spiritual being within, and when you die, you go to this island to await your next journey or voyage or incarnation."

"You mean purgatory is all in the mind?"

"Strange thing is that Cahil would draw pictures of it over and over again."

"Purgatory?"

"No, no, the island itself, and it is roughly similar in appearance to a cross that signifies upright man, the horizon, and the godhead."

"Do you have any of his drawings?" asked Jessica.

"I do . . . and it coincides with the etchings you located on the dead women killed by the Skull-digger. Your chief sent me the image and asked if it meant anything to me."

"Strange coincidence, I admit, but you said you could prove that Cahil is not the killer. It looks the opposite to me, Doctor."

"Cahil is being set up. Someone is using him. He's accepted my therapy as his cure, to replace the object of his desire—which violates human morality and all the laws of decency known to mankind—with something *acceptable*. He now consumes a symbolic diet like many of us consume the host and the body of Christ with the wine and the wafer."

"And you think he's remained on his diet since leaving here, Doctor? We all know how many patients go off their meds after leaving here, and we are speaking of a symbolic gesture here, something far more difficult to absorb than a psychoactive pill."

"I know he's remained true to his new path."

"You want to bet the lives of more young women on that assumption?"

"It's not . . . I mean, yes."

"Tell me, Dr. Deitze, what did this guy do with the children's leftover heads and the portions of brain he didn't want?"

"Cahil had been a butcher on the outside. After warming to me, he told me that he ground up and fed the rest of the remaining gray matter, along with the heads, to his dogs."

"I see . . . mixed it all together with the usual bonemeal from his little *chop shop* of horrors. I'm sure the animals went mad for it."

Deitze stood up and wandered to his window, looking down on the courtyard below where the less dangerous patients were allowed an hour a day.

Jessica was getting messages from the man's body language. "Has Cahil been in touch with you, Dr. Deitze?"

He hesitated a hair. "No . . . and I've lost track of him. He's disappeared from the home and job we placed him in."

"Morristown? Where did he work?"

"Babyland Furnishings."

"My God . . . you placed him in a job involving children?"

"He is cured, I tell you, and he is not your killer."

"Dr. Deitze . . . Jack . . . it's one thing to do a case study and put forth a theory of rehab never before tried, but it's foolish to maintain that we should not take a close look at this guy, unless you have some irrefutable evidence that he is innocent."

Jessica thought of their initial profile of the killer, and she asked, "And if he's disappeared from where he was placed, that only points up the fact he's roving. Possibly roaming the coast from Jersey to Florida."

"I know Cahil is cured of feeding on—"

"On the *real* thing? Look, we're not excluding other leads, but the mark left on the victims is identical to this man's drawings of his Rheil tissue. You won't mind if I take one or two of his drawings with me, will you?"

"No . . . go right ahead. But I wish to caution you about Maxwell Strand. He only wants one thing: to see Cahil killed."

"These drawings are more than coincidence, Doctor. They're quite compelling. As for Strand, I'm sure I understand his biases."

"Read the rehabilitation paper in its entirety, Dr. Coran," he called after her as she left.

Strand had waited on a hallway bench. He stood and came alongside her. She wanted to get out of this building full of horrors and bad memories.

"Did he feed you that line about how he's cured Cahil of his cravings for cannibalizing brains?"

"He told me about it, yes, along with the story of how Cahil only wanted a small portion of the brains of his victims."

"Yeah . . . the Rheil tissue."

"You know about that?"

"I was there at his elocution, and I've read Dr. Blowhard's case study. I told you, I'm an expert on Daryl Thomas Cahil."

"Then tell me," she asked, slowing her pace so that he might keep up. "Where do these sickos come up with their fantastic rationalizations?"

"Adolf Hitler rationalized genocide right along with Osama bin Laden."

"So they place him in Morristown and provide him with

a job at a kid's store? I can't shake this inconceivable idiocy."

He countered sharply. "But it made a warped kind of sense—*bureaucratic nonsense.*"

"How crazy *is* the system?"

"Has this harmless job by day, and cracking open and feeding on young women's brains by night," said Strand.

Jessica felt an urgency to find and put Cahil behind bars for the sake of his next victim. Something about Cahil's working around children convinced her that maybe she ought to be pursuing this man exclusively and full throttle.

They passed the security check, waved to the guards and were out the door. Jessica breathed in great breaths of air. Strand, at her side, said, "Santiva told me about what you found in the victim's heads, that picture of the Rheil cross. It corresponds with the pictures that Cahil drew while in prison, and the one he has up on his website."

"Website? Whataya mean, website?"

"Don't you know? It's all in Deitze's case study, part of his rehab program for poor little misunderstood Cahil. While he was incarcerated, Cahil was set up with a computer and was given access to the Internet as part of his *therapy.*"

"You're kidding."

"Read the report Deitze gave you. It's all there."

"Damn . . ." She thought of Lorena combing through the computer trails for any connections between or among the Manning girl and the other victims. Could it be Cahil's website? If so, it was a connection that could not be ignored.

Still, Jessica heard her father's voice caution her as they left the prison for the parking lot. *Careful, Jess, what at first appears suspicious coincidence is often only a disguised version of wishful thinking.*

"You coming back to Morristown with me?"

"I had no such plans, no." Jessica was taken aback by the question.

"Santiva and his agents are closing in on Cahil in Atlantic City. I can feel it. Your boss said something about getting his best forensic people to go over the man's dwelling. Search warrants are in the works. I'm working closely with your field operatives in Jersey."

"If you don't mind, Detective Strand, I think I'll wait for orders before I go racing off to Morristown."

He nodded, took her hand, shook it firmly and left her at her rental car. Jessica wondered who was stranger, Strand or Deitze, and she opted for the latter. She felt anxious now to get to her hotel room in Philadelphia and look over Deitze's paper for information on this website of Cahil's. She hoped it would be the noose that would slide around the killer's throat. She thought she now knew what Deitze had been holding back. And yet he had handed it to her and asked her to read the paper in its entirety—and she would.

She opened the door to the rental, a strange feeling coming over her. She looked up to where Deitze's office window reflected the fading sunlight back at her, and the man was standing there in the orange glow, staring out at her. She climbed inside the car, tossing the case study on the seat next to her.

She revved up the car, barked its tires in reverse and rushed to the gate, wanting to get off the grounds.

SEVEN

In the one hand he is carrying a stone, while he shows the bread in the other.

—TITUS MACCIUS PLAUTUS, 184 B.C.

Wichita, Kansas
Same time

WANDA Rae Hamilton ran her fourteen-year-old fingers over the keyboard at the Wichita Public Library, searching for religious meaning from the Internet. All her life her parents had pressed religion on her, and she wanted to know what the rest of the world thought about it. She thought she might write a book on it one day.

However, the articles she had found so far proved boring until she put in "mind" and "soul" as her keywords. Suddenly the screen was alive with choices. She made her selection and the screen filled with:

> Spirit or soul is like God, androgynous, without a sexual element and so in a class by itself, and it cannot be derived from any other field of knowledge. The soul has preexisted, having had its beginning in God, before its earthly and bodily time. It is the God-element within man. It rules over the earthly body as the nucleus or inmost center of man's being.

"This rules," muttered Wanda Rae. She read on:

Some believe it resides in the heart, but most concur it resides in the brain at the center of the mind. Partaking of the brain leads to partaking of the soul, and to partake of the soul, one arrives at the cosmic soul.

To learn more about the mind inside your own body and its relationship to the soul therein, and the cosmic soul of the universe, read on. . . .

Wanda Rae Hamilton looked away from what she'd read, trying to digest it. Somehow, tearing her eyes away from the website felt like the right thing to do, that there was something underlying the seemingly benign exterior of the words that wanted to rob her of something . . . something she could not quite put her finger on but it was there, palpable even. Alive. And dangerous. Yet the words, while confusing, proved so tantalizing to her young mind. She wanted to understand it better. Perhaps by reading on:

The soul is the permanent ground, the continuing ent of each individual.

Wanda wrote down the strange word "ent," thinking she must look it up later. She read on:

The soul is restored and rejuvenated to true life only after death of the body, but it does not remain long; therefore, if one wishes to 'harvest' the soul, that is by inhaling and consuming another soul, one must do so quickly. When the individual dies there is that brief time—no one knows exactly how long this time period is—when a soul leaves a brain.

Aboriginal tribes who ate the brains of their enemies believed that this soul, once consumed—if still home within the human cortex of the brain—energizes and makes powerful the feeder, so that his soul benefits by glimpses of God, the most ecstatic of all feelings on the planet. . . .

Wanda again pulled her eyes from the text. She clicked back to the Web home page where she had come across this information. It was created by a man named Daryl Thomas Cahil. She wondered if it were true. It must be, she guessed, if it's on the Internet.

Public library, Chimera, Louisiana
Same time

Total, pure, transcendent, the cosmic mind is an ocean of light and objectivity opening onto the universe. Fed from this unseen source, the brain has a limitless potential, and it certainly exceeds the capacity of the nervous system. Men like Zoraster, Buddha, Muhammad, Jesus Christ, St. Paul, Lao-tzu, Shakespeare, Blake and Byron—sages, prophets and seers—have tapped the radiance of the cosmic ocean, but these are minds above the ordinary. The rest of us must take our share of the trickle from the cosmic spring.

Greater minds than ours know that the cosmic consciousness—the universal soul—has shown itself to men in heightened or altered states, in moments of high intensity as in the presence of death!

Do not hesitate to take that portion of the mind you have a right to.

The fifteen-year-old Chimera high-school student backed his chair away from the computer, puzzling out just what this guy in New Jersey was saying to him. The young man was a straight-A student and a member of the Key Club; he had a civic sense of duty. He had stumbled onto the website while looking for information on how the brain worked for a school paper.

"What's this guy saying?" he wondered aloud.

He returned to the keyboard and opened on a chat room. In the room, people were talking back and forth about *brains—and how to prepare them.* Some put forth recipes, and while it was ghoulish and it made the young man squirm in his seat, he imagined it all that brand of stupid humor reserved for the adolescent mind, a demographic that Rick Trewalen sometimes felt ashamed to be a part of. The words on the screen, however, became worse when he encountered a strange section of the site that spoke of the Skull-digger.

Some of the people in the chat room made the Skull-digger out to be a hero, someone capable of doing what the rest of them only dreamed about. While they fed on animal remains for their needs, he had tapped into something these nutcases referred to as the *Rheil* thing.

"Can't even spell 'real,' " the kid said to the computer.

He then went to a telephone and called Information for the closest FBI office. An agent named Sorrento asked young Rick if he could forward what he had on his screen to his office.

"Sure . . . sure, I can do that."

After performing the operation, Rick was drawn back to the screen. He wanted to see more. As disgusting as the site was, he felt a strange fascination with it.

When he finally became exhausted with the Web page, he checked to see if he had any incoming messages. A few keystrokes and he was staring at his message board. Two from friends, one from the Mail-Demon. This meant he'd keyed in some wrong digit in the message to the FBI. He'd have to try all over again, and pray he'd written the address correctly. But first, he decided to contact his two friends and clue them into the weird website he'd stumbled onto.

By the time Rick got back to attempting to contact the FBI, it had gotten extremely late. He'd do it tomorrow. He picked up the scrap of paper he had written down as the agent's E-mail and stuffed it into his jeans pocket, and after signing out, he rushed home on his bike.

New Bern, North Carolina
Same night

GRANT Kenyon felt a great frustration coming over Phillip, and a growing anger directed at him from Phillip. He could not effect a kill tonight, no matter how hard he tried. The only possible victim he'd been able to locate was an obvious street slut, hardly virtuous, his mind told him, hardly adequate. He'd gone hunting on his computer as well, contacting several local women, but in all cases they could not come out and play.

None of his powers of persuasion worked tonight.

So he had cruised every downtown bar and grill and nightclub. Nothing presented itself. No opportunity came. It simply wasn't meant to be, unless he got bold and forcibly abducted his prey. Phillip pushed him to do just that, the urge to feed outweighing all other considerations.

He grabbed a tire iron he kept beside the seat, got out of the van and approached a couple coming out of a movie theater. He quickly moved on the man, pounding one hard blow to the head, sending him reeling and falling against his car. At the same time, Grant grabbed the girl and yanked her toward his van. She kicked and screamed for help. Taking hold of her neck, he cut off her breathing and plunged the Demoral into her forearm. Attempting to pull open the van door and place her inside, he didn't anticipate her strength and resolve, as she kicked the door closed.

Another man came racing toward them, his hands raised, prepared to fight. Panicked, Grant pushed the girl into her would-be savior, and he rushed around the front of the van and got into it.

He'd left the motor running, and now he backed out, hitting the prone boyfriend and tearing off as the bystander helped the young woman to her feet.

He tore away, watching the result of his second failed attempt to abduct a North Carolina woman, first Fayetteville the month before, and now New Bern. Maybe I'll give up on this state, he told himself and Phillip, who was already berating him for failing to get what they'd come for.

Sometime later, miles from the failed attempt, Grant grew weary-eyed and fatigued. He found a Motel 8, pulled in and got a room. He parked his van against the wall, opened the rear and snatched out his wireless laptop computer.

In order to keep his computer tracks hidden, he often used public computers at libraries and hotels, but sometimes he opted for the convenience of his laptop. He felt an urge now to communicate with others of a like-mindedness tonight. He knew of several websites devoted to the brain. Some were quite technical, scientific, medical, while others were far from it, what one would call far out—ideas about the brain that predated any modern knowledge of its workings. Some were devoted to arcane beliefs, long since refuted by modern science. However one site, which he had followed since its inception created by Daryl Cahil from his asylum cell, agreed with Grant's belief that the brain was the seat of the soul.

Kenyon had chronicled Cahil's arrest, incarceration and recent release. It was on Cahil's website that Grant had learned about the Island of Dr. Benjamin Artemus Rheil. Cahil had put forth his idea along with a crude sketch of the two-inch island of tissue. He depicted it in a cross shape with a bulb atop it.

The idea that you needn't consume the entire brain to consume the soul, but rather simply consume this island of tissue had appealed to Grant. On the other hand, Phillip, who loved the taste of gray matter, remained fixedly unconvinced of Cahil's ideas. As a result, Phillip dictated feeding on the entire sword and sheath—soul and brain.

Still, Phillip also grew fascinated with Cahil's ideas. Grant argued with Phillip repeatedly over the issue, and to settle it, Grant had cut away at his and Phillip's first victim's brain until he found Anna Gleason's Island of Rheil and announced to Phillip, "Since you disbelieve Cahil's theory, I'm sending Anna Gleason's Rheil to Daryl. You can't mind that, can you?"

"Why should I?" Phillip had responded. *"It is not the site of the soul or the portal to the cosmic mind—to God or the God-force—as Cahil preaches. The brain itself is."*

"I will do it," Grant had held up the tissue to his eyes so that Phillip could see he meant what he said.

"Go right ahead," Phillip had dared Grant, who realized that the strange Cahil had caught Phillip's imagination. *"It'll be interesting to* test *Cahil's resolve to lick his habit by sending him a savory morsel. Of course, it has to be the island of tissue that Cahil so craves."*

And so it was sent overnight via UPS.

Grant had given a fictitious return address with no card or explanation. He just wanted Cahil to know that someone was listening and doing something about his theories. Just a one-time offer to share with Daryl to see what would come of his foolish notions about symbolically feeding on the cosmic mind, a trite and idiotic gesture.

It had started out for Grant as an attempt to maintain some sort of control over Phillip, to hold on to a shred of defiance. Phillip, on the other hand, saw this as an opportunity to implicate Cahil in the killings, should he need a stooge in the future.

Now settled in his hotel room, Grant and Phillip logged on to Cahil's website and entered the chat room, sharing brain recipes and small talk about brain functions with the cyber community—most of whom knew next to nothing about the brain. Still, he felt a great amusement at their foolish and often bizarre notions.

Remaining the most bizarre of all was Cahil's own "revelation" about the Island of Rheil, which he described in great detail, having eaten a number of them before being caught in that Morristown, New Jersey, cemetery. Cahil had even drawn a picture of it that detailed where in the brain it was located, curled and waiting deep in the midbrain. He described his criminal history of robbing dead children in their coffins of their Islands of Rheil. He claimed children were more potently endowed with the cosmic mind. He also bragged that he had "licked" his "horrible" habit, and now he only fed on the kind of animal brains found in tin cans on grocery shelves and representations of the island, using pasta of all things.

More than a month had gone by since Grant had shipped off that small portion of Anna Gleason's brain. Tonight Grant opened a news page of the website to find a computer *photograph* of the Island of Rheil. Cahil had placed the real thing on the Web. He had foolishly put it out there that he had a human Rheil in his possession, and that he wanted to share in what it actually looked like. Beside it, a six-inch ruler had been placed to give it scale. It did roughly resemble the cross he had drawn earlier.

Most cyber-folk looking at the image would likely think

it a hoax, reasoned Grant. Phillip concurred. But Cahil declared it the real thing, sent to him by a devotee—someone who had taken him at his word. He thanked the faceless benefactor.

Grant and Phillip keyed in the question,

Cahil, did you eat it?

They waited for a reply but it didn't come.

"He ate it," Phillip told Grant.

"You really think so?"

"I'm certain he could not have resisted. A leopard never changes its spots."

Public library, Florence, Illinois
Same night

At age sixty-four, James McPherson prided himself on being a lifelong learner. After retirement from the military, he had little to do to occupy himself, so he had determined to learn everything and anything he could from the world of books and now the world of the Internet.

He had become curious recently about how the brain worked and functioned, computers so often being likened to it. And he had a friend who had recently succumbed to Alzheimer's, and James was having trouble now with balance himself. While cross-checking, he had come upon information on the cerebellum at a curious website, and now he read up on this part of the brain:

> The cerebellum, or little brain, is also known geographically as the hindbrain. While not part of the brain stem, it is connected to the stem. It lies in the lower back part of the

skull and regulates equilibrium and coordination of muscular movement and balance in walking. Injury here creates a staggering gait, palsy and slurred speech.

"This shit may be helpful but it's written in such a boring manner," he told himself. "There has to be something more lively on the subject." He shook his head over this and surfed off toward another site.

He came across something on the "cosmic connection" of the mind, and this phraseology instantly caught his attention. Surfing through, he read:

Mind is the factor inherent in and underlying all things in the universe. In varying degrees, we find it present everywhere, even though some psychologists have denied its existence, dismissing **mind** as a mistake of language—that it was a semantical blunder to have put a name to it. Still, there exists a kind of psychic life that abides not only in mankind and animals but in plants, and in all (so-called) inanimate ents (units of existence) or entities. This leads us to ask about the universal ocean of consciousness from which our minds are mere drips . . .

"Drips indeed. Now *that's* interesting," McPherson said to the screen. "We're all a bunch of drips." His laughter caught the ear and the ire of a desk librarian, who now squinted vulturelike in his direction.

The Krandal family home, Calvert City, Iowa
Same evening

SEVENTEEN-YEAR-OLD Jill Krandal opened the website she had become fascinated with, logging on as Chixwhix. She had a soft drink and potato chips beside her, and she had settled in for a long party with others to chat about brainy matters on the Net. She hadn't logged on for a long time. She wanted to see if Surreal and Motormouth might be on-line tonight with their funny remarks about the brain—Got brains?

They all agreed that the Webmaster was weird, but that didn't matter. If he really ate cat and dog brains, and if he really did once steal brains from humans in their graves—*children*—who cared? If he was allowed to set up this website and talk about cannibalizing brains, then it must be all right, she reasoned.

Still, she knew her parents would put an end to it, if they knew. She just liked the chat room and topics provided there. She didn't take the Webmaster seriously, and she and her friends online guessed that he had a problem with telling the truth.

Her heart leapt when she made contact with Surreal. She keyed in:

CHIXWHIX: Surreal . . . How've you been? Whataya hear from Motormouth?

SURREAL: Hey there Chixie-wixie. Nothing from Motor, but lots from that guy who keeps hitting on me.

CHIXWHIX: What's he want?

SURREAL: Says he wants to get together.

CHIXWHIX: That Seeker guy? Don't even think about it. He hits on me, too.

SURREAL: Did he offer you a way out of Calvert City?

CHIXWHIX: Whataya mean?

SURREAL: He wants to send me a bus ticket, and it's tempting.

CHIXWHIX: Don't be a fool, Surreal.

SURREAL: I hate Lynchburg as much as you hate Iowa.

CHIXWHIX: A ticket to where?

SURREAL: He said anywhere I'd care to meet him.

CHIXWHIX: Don't do it, Surreal.

SURREAL: Wouldn't you do it? Use the ticket if he sent it to you?

In Calvert City, Jill stopped typing long enough to consider the question. Then she adamantly keyed in her reply:

CHIXWHIX: No, and you shouldn't either!

SURREAL: One way to get outta this hick town and away from my mom.

CHIXWHIX: You could be raped or murdered. Would that make you happy?

SURREAL: You've been watching too many repeats of UNSOLVED MYSTERIES. Don't worry. I'd be too chicken anyway.

CHIXWHIX: Promise?

SURREAL: All right already!

CHIXWHIX: Meantime, have you seen what Daryl the dickhead put on his news page?

SURREAL: No what?

CHIXWHIX: A photo of a G-D brain part!

SURREAL: I gotta go take a look. Be right back.

CHIXWHIX: I'll be waiting. Want to hear your reaction.

Canton, New York
Same night

DAVID Byrd, superintendent for the Canton Public Schools, pulled his glasses from his eyes and tried to fathom what he was reading on his computer screen. It did not make a lot of sense, but it sounded an alarm in his head. This trash he was looking at might entice young minds. He had been hearing about a strange fascination many of his students at Canton had developed over a computer website. Word of mouth had fueled like a brushfire, and Byrd had pried information out of a problem kid who wore dark clothes, bleached his hair and sported jewelry and a tattoo. As a result, Superintendent Byrd had stayed late at the office to take a look at the Web page.

The page was filled with strange and disjointed information on the workings of the human brain and its relationship to the more spiritual mind, and how to expand the power of one's own brain by *consuming* the brains of other "ents" or "units of creation"—from chickens and other animals and even plants that "dream as we do."

This immediately disturbed Byrd. He read on, wondering what steps he could take to bring an end to this frightening message board and newsletter, which even reported on the doings of the serial killer known as the Skull-digger the way others kept abreast of baseball and football players.

He scanned the reports and got to the Webmaster's explanation of why the Skull-digger fed on his victim's gray matter:

> The Skull-digger knows about the cosmic mind. There is a thing we call the universal soul, and a gradation of mind in nature determined by varying degrees of awareness. The Skull-digger is more aware than any of us that there is a potency of mind from atoms to galaxies, and that all units of creation lead us closer to touching God in the sense that we touch on the universal mind. Such a touch or a glimpse will infuse us with a transcendent mind-aura beyond anything we might dream.
>
> Mind even manifests itself in stone and other inanimate objects from particles to crystals and stars. Higher on the

mind scale, we come to the mind that dreams in plants and proto-biological ents like viruses and amoeba. Unlike the inanimate, these ents are characterized by a vital mind devoted to metabolism, growth, reproduction and decay.

Finally comes the mind we see in animals, operating by means of organized neuro-atomic elements through senses and instinct. These we can consume in a symbolic and sometimes a real sense. In doing so, we have an opportunity to glimpse into the universal cosmic mind from which all minds were formed.

Superintendent Byrd took a moment to gather his breath and sip his coffee, which had gone cold. He girded himself and read on:

In other words, your present awareness is only a narrow band in a vast galaxy of mind awareness. You must learn to expand it. You do this by various means, and the Skull-digger is at the farthest end of that scale. You don't have to go out and kill someone for his/her brain in order to expand your conscious awareness of the universal soul. There are safer routes. I know because I spent time in prison for stealing brain matter from graves, but—

Superintendent Byrd recoiled at this last statement. "These are the rantings of a lunatic," he said aloud. "I've got to expose this for what it is." He wondered how widespread this bizarre site had become. He wondered where he might start to voice his objections: local authorities? State or federal officials? Scrolling down, he realized the man's rantings went on for limitless pages. He saw the photo of the Island of Rheil, the supposed center of the soul of an animate being—no, a human being! And he scanned the discussion on what this tissue from the brain meant. It was all madness.

He determined to contact the local FBI and have their experts look at this.

He scrolled back to where he'd left off and read:

I've served my time, paid my debt to society, and now I seek that higher mind through the use of hunting and killing fair game, and consuming the Island of Rheil of the animal (deer, rabbit, etc.). A noble calling inherited from our ancestors, who were ignorant of the Island of Rheil, and so they barbarically consumed the entire brain. No, to consume the entire brain dulls the impact of what can be found in consuming only the island of the soul. . . .

Byrd keyed in the order to print the pages he'd just read. As his printer worked, he reached for his telephone. After being left on hold for fifteen minutes on a phone tree, frustrated, he told his story to a field agent in Syracuse, New York, the closest federal agency. The agent said he would look into it and get back to Byrd, that he and every agent in the FBI appreciated such tips in locating the Skull-digger.

"You misunderstand me. This guy is *applauding* the Skull-digger and spreading unsafe and insane information to children all over this and other countries through the Internet. It's sick propaganda directed at our children, Agent. No telling how long it's been going on, or how much irreparable damage has already been done. It's a kind of insidious, demoralizing—"

"We'll make it a priority, sir. I have the dot-com address you've supplied, sir."

"It's like nothing we've seen before. Likely a terrorist group behind it, I tell you. We must put an end to it for the sake of America's youth."

"I'll make it a priority, sir, I promise." The agent hung up.

Byrd stared at the phone and listened to the dial tone. He wondered if he ought to call the mayor's office, who would in turn call the governor, and maybe then he could get some assurances.

The wee hours of July 14, 2003

THE phone awakened Jessica from a sound sleep in her Philadelphia hotel room. It was just past midnight. She had somehow avoided any nightmares, willing herself to find comforting dreams instead. She'd gotten back to the room in Philly early, had eaten room-service food, showered and gone to bed with Jack Deitze's case study of Cahil. She found Deitze's rehabilitation effort and theories questionable, but she focused on what she could learn of Cahil. Amazingly, Strand was right; the former grave robber had begun a website from his isolation ward. Dr. Gabriel Arnold had given Deitze complete authority over Cahil's treatment, and Deitze believed Cahil would benefit greatly from communicating to the world about why he had done what he had and to seek alternative ways to reach the pinnacle of "faith" he so craved.

The hotel phone continued to ring. She hesitated lifting it off the cradle. As far as she knew, only Eriq and J.T. had the hotel number, and she had turned off her cell phone.

When she lifted the receiver, Eriq Santiva launched right in with, "We've apprehended Daryl Cahil."

"Where?"

"Where he called you from, Atlantic City, a phone booth near a motel he was at. Traced his whereabouts through a credit card number found in his house in Morristown."

She mentally calculated how long it would have taken Cahil to travel from southern Georgia to Atlantic City and back again to make those two calls. He could not have easily made it in the time allotted. "And the woman? His wife or girlfriend?"

"Negative. I'm ready to believe what Strand told us, that the female caller was Cahil himself. That part of him that wants to be caught, Jess. We've seen the syndrome before."

"All the same, maybe we should alert Atlantic City authorities that we'd be interested in any recent Jane Doe's."

"Count on it."

"Did they do a search of his van, the beach motel room, along with his Morristown house?"

"Nothing came of the room search. A quick search of his house was done by our men in Morristown, which turned up the credit card number. He wasn't driving a van—a rental sedan instead. No restraints or cutting tools found either."

"We need the tools, Eriq. We need the van."

"So far nothing of the sort. The searches have turned up nothing, but I'm still hopeful that a full forensic treatment will turn up something."

"How much time do we have on the search-and-seizure order at the Morristown location?"

"Another twelve hours and it's history."

"I want to see how this guy lives, what he surrounds himself with."

"We're having him transported to Quantico for interrogation, but Jess, the creep . . . he won't talk to anyone but you."

"Me? Why the . . . why me?"

"That's what he wants. Second to you, he'll only talk to Deitze, and none of us wants that, right?"

"Damn it, why me?" she repeated.

"Liked your whiskey voice, I guess. Come on, Jess, he knows your reputation, so he's going to play to that, and he knows you understand his *kind*."

"Lucky me. He's just yanking our chain. He wants another fifteen minutes of fame and publicity, Eriq, could be he's just cashing in on our case."

"He's the guy. The Ghoul is the Skull-digger."

"Eriq, you sound like Strand. You've already got this guy guilty without the evidence to back it."

"All right, just supposing Cahil isn't the Skull guy, he still may well give you some insight into what this latest ghoul is up to, why he's fixated on brain matter. Face it, Jess, with VICAP unable to provide us with anything, Cahil is a go."

She didn't care for the sound of so much missing—the van, the restraints, the murderous tools, the height and weight problem—yet the sign left at the crime scenes and the drawings done in prison pointed to Cahil. "Do you really think this could lead to a conviction, Eriq?"

"It's our best shot so far. I've arranged for a chopper to pick you up at the airport in Philly . . . to bring you home."

"With a detour to Morristown, have a look-see at what this creep calls home."

"All right. I'll meet you when you arrive at HQ. By the way, Jere Anderson asked me to pass along word that yes, the two earlier victims were tattooed with that cross you found in the skull. Only a small portion came up on the slides, but it's unmistakable under the microscope. Good work!"

"I've gotten hold of a pair of prison drawings that Cahil did. I'm going to forward them. Have our documents experts compare them to the bone etchings."

"We'll arrange it."

"Is Cahil left-handed?"

"Matter of fact, yes."

They said their goodbyes and Jessica stared up at the ceiling of the hotel room, the fan whirring overhead. She had earlier telephoned Lorena Combs and had left word about Daryl Cahil's website, asking if she could find any evidence that Manning or Miller had ever browsed or used the site. She dared hope they had found the monster, but not even a confession would put him away if they could not prove it.

EIGHT

If I cannot bend Heaven, I shall move Hell.

—VIRGIL, 70–19 B.C.

Home of Daryl Thomas Cahil, Morristown, New Jersey
July 14, 2003, several hours later

J.T. HAD flown in from Quantico to meet here there on Santiva's order. She also learned of an incident report coming out of New Bern, North Carolina, involving a white male in a dark blue van attacking a woman outside a movie theater. The victim had been stabbed with a syringe and her system showed signs of drugs administered to sedate her. The MO sounded eerily similar. Jessica had contacted New Bern police for any information on the type of drug used. Too soon to tell, she was told. She asked for a copy of any sketch of the attacker that might come out of the witness testimony. They promised to forward anything but were doubtful. With Cahil in custody, she again wondered if he had anything at all to do with the Skull-digger murders.

Now she was on the street where Daryl Thomas Cahil lived, staring at his house. From the outside, the small house at 153 Orchard Row in Morristown defied anyone to say it was any different from any other along the ragtag street, where even the trees looked in ill repair.

Surrounded by a broken-down chain-link fence with a gate resting on a single hinge, the house was penned in on each side by identical houses. Approaching close, Jessica and J.T. saw the dilapidated shingles, and the peeling paint, and the weathered boards. A rusted out lawn mower had been tucked—motor under—beneath the stairwell of a modest little porch area where two mildew-covered plastic chairs acted as obstacles before the doorway.

Max Strand accompanied Jessica and J.T. along with local FBI field agent Sam Owens. On their second meeting, Jessica found Strand a hefty, muscular man, round, rough-looking, not in the least frail for a man his age only recently out of surgery. Strand's face was a mask of experience, his eyes clearly having seen a lot of gruesome events in his years as a police detective. He appeared stoic and sad at the same time. Owens appeared Strand's opposite in every way. Cahil's residence had been kept a secret by the FBI who had moved him here from Newark. Strand had pulled a lot of strings to learn where in the city of Morristown the man resided.

After introductions were made, Jessica asked, "So, Strand, how do you like having Cahil back on your turf?"

"You don't understand. When he was relocated initially to Newark, I put in for a job there to be close by in the event he should resume his former habits. So, when he was relocated here, that solved the problem."

"If you were on him, how'd he disappear?"

"He was my obsession, not the department's. Like I told you in Philly, I've been in the hospital. Bypass operation."

She bit her lower lip and said, "Sorry. Hope all is—"

"He must've known I was down," Strand said of Cahil. "We're old adversaries. Frankly, I thought he was done with his old habits, since he's done absolutely nothing after being released other than play games on his computer."

"His computer?" asked J.T.

Strand told Thorpe about the computer site, ending with, "And while he goes on about his crimes as if they were the work of a Lord God doing what a god does, there's nothing he can be charged with, even if he is encouraging people to worship as he does."

"How do you mean 'worship'?" asked J.T.

"He's got some strange notions about gaining a glimpse of the cosmic mind—God—through feeding on brains."

"He's advocating cannibalizing other people to reach God?" asked J.T. "And he's free to do that?"

"I haven't plugged in to his site recently, but he's been careful not to be too specific about what kinds of brains his audience should be chewing on. He's opted for meat products in the local grocery freezer and canned goods for a while, but now he's into pasta."

"So he's untouchable?"

"The law has a long way to go to control the Web." Strand took a deep breath as they walked toward the house together. "Like I said, I'd begun to believe Cahil through with it, until I got word of the murders. They occurred just as I was incapacitated, and I had no access to a computer. No one but a lunatic who might log on could possibly find some sort of 'truth' in Daryl's rantings."

"How do you feel about him being on the loose now?"

Strand, stretching the full-length of his tall, rugged ex-marine frame, replied with squinting eyes and gnashing teeth. "How do you think I feel? This guy should've been put away for life. I knew he'd be at it again. Just figured it would be in another cemetery, not killing young people outright. That nuthouse they sent him to only graduated the lunatic to the real thing."

The absence of yellow police caution tape indicated that this was no crime scene, and that Owens was moving on the place with a light hand, likely having anticipated Cahil's return—before he had been apprehended in Atlantic City.

"We kinda tiptoed into the house carefully from the rear. Went in and got out quickly when we located an active credit card number," Owens said.

"Didn't trip over any bodies?" asked J.T.

"Found nothing extreme except the filth. Place is a pig-sty, so we decided we'd leave it until you experts arrived. Our guys wanted him apprehended. We thought he might just be down the block at a bar or store. Then we got word you were on your way, so we waited."

"And you drew straws to pull this return duty, Sam?" she asked.

His face told her it was true. No one wanted to revisit this horrible place. "Like I said, after we located the credit card number, we got out, hoping to surprise him on his return. When we got news he was picked up in another town, we ceased the stake out, had the lock repaired, gave the landlord a key and kept one for you."

She squinted, wondering what Owens and the earlier team had accomplished here. He must have read the question in her face.

Owens added, "Sorry, but we found no smoking gun to link him to the Digger killings."

"So, what you're saying is you were in and out. No evidence techs or high-tech searches done?" asked Jessica.

"That's about it. We didn't confiscate any of his belongings, nor did we disturb anything."

"Understood," replied Jessica, her hand out. "I'll take the key, Agent Owens."

"Back door," he repeated, handing her the shiny new key.

They followed a narrow and cluttered passageway alongside dirtied basement windows to the rear of the house. As Jessica turned the key in the lock, she wondered if this could indeed be the home of the Digger and/or an accomplice. Could Daryl be the Digger or a coconspirator?

Easing the door open, Jessica held back as the odors from inside assailed her. She steadied herself and pulled the door wide. It creaked and complained—groaned animal-like—as it came to a stop, fully open now to the outside world. A fetid odor combining vermin, stale air, pent-up mildew and rotting fruit wafted past her to attack Strand and J.T., while the young Morristown field agent coughed and covered his nose.

"Terrible in there," he muttered. "I warn you all again . . . watch your step. It's a rat's hole."

"We'll be careful," J.T. replied as he struggled with a pair of rubber gloves. Jessica had already slipped her gloves on, and she offered a pair from her valise to both Strand and the junior agent who had reluctantly entered behind the group.

"Somebody find a light switch," suggested Jessica.

J.T. did so, but the switch didn't work. "No lights. Sorry."

"We were here during daylight hours. Light wasn't a problem," said Owens. "Electric company must've shut it down."

"But the fridge is operating," replied Jessica, hearing the hum.

"Maybe on a generator," suggested Strand.

A single shaft of light from a streetlamp outside somehow penetrated the kitchen area they walked through. Jessica located her high-intensity penlight, and the others did likewise.

The bungalow's floors were completely covered in newspapers, magazines, books and clothing, scattered food containers—pizza and Chinese food boxes everywhere along with filthy towels and linens. Jessica's light explored the kitchen to the humming sound coming from the refrigerator. The small kitchenette reeked of stale odors. Food stains discolored every surface, including walls and ceiling, along with something the color of gray, the color of brain matter, making Jessica gasp. "Owens, your team didn't see this?"

Everyone stared at the end of her beam. "Looks like brain matter," said J.T.

"It's only clay," explained Owens.

"This some sort of sick departmental joke, Owens, meant to frighten us?" Jessica touched it with her gloved finger, found it sticky to the touch, clinging to her. Sniffing it, she decided Owens was telling the truth. "Clay," she repeated.

"This a joke, Owens?" repeated J.T.

"No, Dr. Thorpe, no. None of *us* in the bureau put the clay here. It's all over the place. He makes these weird-assed clay models of the brain, and he stuffs them with noodles. And look here." He opened a kitchen cabinet and his light revealed it stuffed with bags of green-gray noodles.

"He sells this shit on his Internet website," explained Max Strand. "Gets the noodles from a gourmet shop downtown."

Jessica ripped open one of the bags. The pasta was shaped in the form of crosses. "Deitze warned us about all this, but seeing it up close is something else."

They moved on toward the interior of the house.

Their lights revealed no furniture in the living room area, only a small TV and VCR, along with a makeshift chair of blankets where one might prop against a wall amid the squalor and stench.

"I don't get it," said Strand. "If he's got the fridge on a

generator, why aren't the lights hooked up to it?"

They ventured forward.

"Damn sure stinks in here," said J.T.

"Coming from a coroner, Dr. Thorpe," said Owens, "it must be true."

The few videocassettes Cahil had were copies of TV programs if the labels could be believed—*The Learning Channel: Brain Matters.* Another was entitled *This Is Joe's Brain*, and a third read *Realms of the Mind.*

Owens looked the titles over as well and muttered, "Looks like our boy is still fixated on one thing."

"Put these in an evidence bag for me, will you, Owens?"

"Sure thing, Dr. Coran."

As Owens alternately protected himself with a handkerchief over the nose and stuffed the cassettes into a large evidence bag, Strand returned. "No generator in the basement. Maybe a fuse blew, but I couldn't find any problems in the box."

"He must have the fridge on a generator located somewhere here," said Owens.

J.T. had wandered off alone, and suddenly he called out from deep in the house, shouting, "In here, Jess!"

The others instantly located J.T.'s flashlight. He had gone exploring through a hallway that led deeper into the nightmare. Along with streetlights that pierced the transparent newspaper-covered windows, the flashlights created an eerie ghostly glow flooding through the house, even as their eyes became accustomed. Careful of every step over the litter-strewn floor, they inched their way toward J.T.'s light, which led them toward a bedroom.

Strand slipped, almost lost his footing but righted himself. "Shit," he complained. "I think I slipped on some damn clay. I found maybe fifty of those clay brains in the basement workshop."

They reached J.T.'s location, and Jessica saw what had so excited him. In the bedroom with a makeshift tent of blankets, a green glowing light filtering through the tent. Cahil had covered over some furniture against the far wall. J.T. stood pointing at the light, saying, "Look, electricity."

The others now saw the green light filtering through the weave of the blanket. Removing the blanket, J.T. displayed a chair, a wooden desk and a state-of-the-art computer.

J.T. sat at the computer and said, "Here's his nerve center you were telling us about, Strand."

"Wait a minute, this thing's got juice," said Owens.

"Selective electricity," said Jessica. "Food and communication. From the fridge to the computer. It has to be a generator."

"Your earlier search didn't uncover the computer?" asked Strand of Owens.

"I guess it was missed. *I* didn't know it was in here."

"Don't tell me . . . you didn't get this far."

"Agent Donaldson found the credit card bill, and we got out. I just follow orders, and I wasn't in charge."

J.T. examined the computer hookup. "This is no wireless. He's got electricity in here from some source."

Jessica immediately went to the nearest wall receptacle and with her gloved hand, she stuck a scalpel deep into it. An electrical spark shot out, jabbing at her. "Sonofabitch. Just for the hell of it, Owens, try that lamp beside you."

Owens, sniffing at an ammonia stick that Jessica had handed him, tried the lamp with no result.

Jessica stepped to the lamp and put her hand below the shade, learning there was no bulb. "Hold on . . . wait a minute. Are we stumbling around in the dark because the bastard's too lazy to replace his bulbs?" she asked.

J.T. suggested, "Maybe he *abhors* light?"

"That would figure," said Strand, eyeballing Owens.

Owens, embarrassed by this turn of events, said, "I'll go back to that pantry in the kitchen, see if there're any bulbs."

After pushing aside books and papers on the desk J.T., with Strand and Jessica looking over his shoulder, went to work on the computer. "See what I can uncover here." With that, J.T. got comfortable and began a search. He was locked out; the machine asked for a code word.

"Three strikes and we're out," said J.T. "We're going to have to crack it at Quantico if we can't come up with the right code tonight."

Owens returned, saying, "No bulbs but cans and cans of this stuff." He held up a can of Hydar's animal brains and hash.

"Gets it from a specialty deli downtown, buys it by the case," said Strand, turning his attention back to J.T. and the computer. "Try 'brain food,' " said Strand.

"What?" asked J.T.

"It's a thing with him, brain food. These people who plug into his site swap brain-food recipes."

"Then the password could just as well be brain bran or brain clusters or brain cuisine," countered J.T.

"Just try it."

"Right . . . right."

Jessica stared across the filthy room at Owens. "Local FBI never gave Cahil serious consideration as a candidate for the Digger, right?"

"Ahhh, correct."

"Why not?"

He whispered, "Well . . . Strand there's been crying wolf for so long about this boob, that, well . . . nobody in the Morristown PD or the local bureau takes Strand seriously anymore. We all thought . . ."

"Spit it out, Owens."

"We thought it'd be a—*you know*—a kind of embarrassing joke once Chief Santiva was led down the primrose lane by Strand's obsession over Cahil."

"Embarrassing for Santiva, you mean. I see. Local joke becomes national headlines. Somebody in your department have it in for us?"

"Not you. Your boss, Santiva. Our SAC, Fromme. Over some beef a few years back."

"A perfect setup. Santiva doles out valuable man-hours, two M.E.'s and field operatives, and God knows how much in currency on a raid your boss believes is a waste of time. Is that about it?"

The preppy-looking Owens nodded. "What can I say? I work for an asshole. Fromme thought he'd let out enough rope for Santiva to hang himself with the bureau heads. The order was to leave everything intact, *for your eyes only*. Except I was told—ordered—to give Max a call to bring him in."

"I get the picture." Santiva had said on countless occasions that you could never divorce the FBI from politics. Jessica had briefly met Morristown's Special Agent in Charge Marcus Fromme. The man did have the look of a savagely ambitious politician.

"Fromme doesn't believe Cahil's the Digger. He wants to discredit Santiva, not you, Doctor."

"Should be interesting to see who wins this pissing contest."

"It was out of my control. When I heard they'd nabbed Cahil, and that you were on your way here, well . . . none of us could muster much enthusiasm . . . consensus was . . ."

"I get it, Owens. The picture comes clear now."

"From the get-go, as far as Fromme was concerned, we didn't have enough probable cause—a phone call to you from the girlfriend. That's all we were told. Fromme then told me to"—he brought it down to a whisper again—"rope in Max. We all know how Max feels about Cahil. Fromme even arranged for Strand's trip to see you in Philadelphia—at Quantico's expense. He thinks Max is a lunatic for Cahil, obsessed with him."

"So he throws Max in as another wrench in the works?"

Owens bit his lower lip and nodded. "Fromme was at Quantico when you all began the chase for the Skull-digger. He never looked under this rock because he never believed Cahil a *worthwhile* lead, you see."

Strand, overhearing snatches of the conversation, pulled away from his argument over the possible code word long enough to say, "What're you talking about, Owens? You idiots in the bureau think you're using me? You all know I am the authority on Cahil."

Jessica held up a hand to him. "It sounds like your case of the New Jersey Ghoul has taken on a life of its own, Detective Strand," said Jessica, "and for better or worse—the local field office is playing political hockey with our case."

Strand turned all of his glare toward Owens.

"Look, Max, every lawman in Morristown's got an opinion on the New Jersey Ghoul," pleaded Owens. "Most want him to go away and stay away, like it never happened. Like Fromme said in his debriefing, some people *embrace* the story as if it's a cult manifesto."

"Is that what Fromme thinks of me?" asked Strand.

"Hell, Max, first words outta your mouth when they wheeled you from the ICU were 'where's my laptop.' You wanted to check in with this weirdo's Web page."

"Does it make me crazy to see a guy get off after decapitating five children in their coffins? Yes, it makes me a little crazy, Owens."

"Just what Fromme counted on," said Jessica. "He's gambling . . . jockeying for some leverage to gain a better position on the ladder. Likely, he's not working alone. Someone either in D.C. or at Quantico who's after Eriq's head."

"I swear, I don't give a damn about any of it," said Owens. "Most of the men in the department would love nothing better than to be out from under Fromme's so-called leadership."

"Well, this setup ought to backfire in his ugly face," declared Strand, stepping back to J.T., who sat pensive, considering his options regarding the password. Owens slinked off a bit, grateful the confrontation had ended.

Jessica now flashed her light on articles and stacked books on the subject of the human brain. She lifted two of the titles and read them aloud: "*Mind and Universe, In the Likeness of God—A Study of the Spirit of the Brain. The Architecture of the Soul-Brain Conduit.*"

Jessica next lifted and opened a huge book entitled *Arcania of Mind and Magic* to its index and searched for the word "Rheil," and not finding it, she spelled it aloud, "R-H-E-I-L." Turning to the page, she found an ancient photograph of a Dr. Benjamin Artemus Rheil and a discussion of the man obsessed with the island of tissue he discovered during an autopsy of the brain of a diseased woman. After his discovery, he sought this phenomena of the brain out in every autopsy he performed to determine that it did indeed exist inside every human brain—a self-contained small sac of tissue, an island within the mind. Rheil found it slightly larger in the female than in the male, and he noted this as a strange paradox.

"Try this as a password, J.T.," she told him, holding out the book.

"Of course," said Strand. "Rheil. It's staring us in the face."

"Real?" asked J.T.

She spelled it out.

"Once he cut his deal with the prosecution, Cahil talked about Dr. Rheil during his elocution of the crime to the court."

J.T. keyed in the name Rheil.

Again he was denied access.

Strand suggested, "Isle of Brain. I-s-l-e-o-f-B-r-a-i-n. Do it."

"It's our last chance before a final lockout. Are you sure?" asked J.T.

"Are you sure, Strand?" Jessica asked, her face creased with doubt.

"It's how he referred to it back then, again and again."

"All right. Go for it, J.T."

"If it's wrong, we'll have to take it to the experts at Quantico." J.T. keyed it in and suddenly erupted. "*Bingo!* Our friendly neighborhood lunatic's website is coming up on the screen now."

J.T. scanned several lines off the master page, and then said, " 'Brain Matters—Home of the Soul and the Cosmic Mind'—his banner reads. We gotta confiscate all this, Jess." A comical character looking like a mad professor blipped on the screen, asking, "Got brains?"

"This guy's something else," Jessica said as the cartoon image came up on the screen.

"Do a search, Dr. Thorpe," said Max.

"Of what?"

"*Recipes*, you gotta see this."

"You're serious?"

"Absolutely."

J.T. keyed in the word. After fifteen seconds, he replied,

"Here we are. Chat room for brain recipes. Brain Kabob, Shrimp Creole and Brains, the ever-popular Brains and Eggs. And here's Brains and Legs—*poultry*. Damn, here's Beef Bullion Brains, Creamed Spinach is under a whole list of vegetarian brain casseroles, and it goes on. Someone here even sharing a recipe for Brain Brownies and Chocolate Moose."

"Forget about the recipes," said Jessica. "Key in 'island,' 'isle,' 'Rheil' . . . see what we have there."

Again J.T. typed into the search box.

"What is this island of the brain place?" asked Owens.

Now the ancient brain surgeon, Rheil, was depicted on the computer screen as well, along with the article Jessica had seen in the hefty book, scanned and lifted word for word, down to the photograph of Rheil.

"So this is what the man was searching for when he dug up all those graves," commented J.T.

"A bit of gray matter, real estate deep within the cortex." Jessica leaned in closer.

"I give you the Island of Rheil," Strand said. "Finally, someone is paying attention. Take a walk with a lunatic to an island in his mind."

Owens swallowed hard, regretting the odors going down his throat.

Jessica read aloud from the screen. " 'Rheil believed that this island of tissue supposedly housed the spirit since it had no apparent physical reason for being—or for being located at the core of the brain, at the geographic center of the cortex. He then concluded that it must have a *spiritual* reason for being there, since in his words, "all things unknowable must then be spiritual." ' " Jessica paused and then read the remaining short paragraphs devoted to the man.

"Daryl conveniently left out that the man's scientific

method was questionable to say the least," said Jessica. "The article he copied this from ended with a good deal of skepticism."

"Not included on Cahil's website meanderings," added Max. "Any disparagement surrounding Dr. Rheil's work and conclusions found no way into Daryl Cahil's thinking."

Jessica then lifted the book she'd discovered Rheil in and read on. " 'The drama and flare of Rheil's conclusions, according to contemporaries and colleagues, far outweighed any scientific reasoning or study of the Island of Rheil.' "

"Check out the footnote," said Strand, pointing. The book footnoted the fact that Rheil's work had been cut short by an untimely death from a brain fever. In his will, he asked that his own *island* be removed and preserved for scientific investigation. However, no one continued his study, only adding fuel to the mystery of his strange discovery.

Cahil's own editorializing on Rheil appeared fictitious, that the man not only removed and studied his "finds" but that he consumed them. He pointed out the robustness and content in the man's image at so advanced an age, claiming him more than a hundred years old in the photograph.

"Daryl *fixated* on this bogus nonsense," said Strand, "as he testified at his trial. It's what got to all the shrinks, his telling the court that he actually robbed graves from '89 to '90 for this *thing*—*why* he took his dead victim's heads off with him, *to dig this sac of tissue out of their brains*."

"Cahil's courtroom elocution—did it get any press?" asked Jessica.

"None. Courtroom was sealed from the press. Special arrangement agreed upon by prosecution, the defense and Judge Hiram Skinner. Nobody really wanted this business to fuel headlines for months. It was all so damned bizarre, and the court officials really did want to spare the families any more indignities and harm."

"So it takes on the proportions of a legend, shrouded in mystery," said Jessica in a near whisper.

"Hollywood wanted to make a film," replied Strand. "On any account, no details were released other than a few generalities labeling Cahil as a cannibal, and with the press shut out, all sorts of rampant reporting went on, especially in the tabloids, how he was a sex-lust murderer, which didn't apply, how he was a necrophiliac, you name it."

Jessica recalled how Lorena Combs, as a high-school student, had gotten the story.

Strand went on. "He replaced the boogeyman; hell, he *was* the boogeyman. Christ, before Cahil's activities, the dead could assume themselves safe in their graves, but not anymore. Imagine the parents of these departed children learning what had happened to their babies? Like I said, Judge Skinner, with the best of intentions, didn't allow cameras or reporters in the courtroom. Nobody but people directly involved in the prosecution and defense of the case, which included Drs. Gabriel Arnold and a young Jack Deitze on one side, me and my partner, along with Newark detectives on the other."

"So the trial transcripts and what Deitze has on him are the only record of his madness?"

"Until now. He's still thinking the same thoughts only now with live game."

"To get at this lump of brain tissue?" J.T. asked, clicking on an icon that opened on a sketch with a caption indicating it was a drawing of the Island of Rheil. "Here it is. Look familiar?" asked J.T.

It was the first time that J.T. had seen Cahil's drawing to compare it with what they had found inside the victims' skulls. "It does look like the cross," Jessica muttered into J.T.'s ear, "in a rough kind of way."

J.T. shook off a shiver and asked, "How mad can men get, Jess?"

"It would appear as mad as they wanna be."

J.T. clicked on an icon below the article. The computer screen now filled with a scanned *photograph* of something oddly shaped like a small filleted fish lying beside a six-inch ruler, measuring approximately two inches. It had the gray appearance of real brain tissue, bulbous at one end, cross shaped at the other. Below it read a caption: *Human Rheil, sent to me by the Seeker. May 3, 2003.*

"What the hell is that?" asked Owens, pointing to the screen.

Strand said, "A photograph of this Rheil thing from an *actual* brain."

"From one of the Skull-digger's victims," suggested J.T.

Jessica gasped and stared at the small strip of brain tissue. "This alone ought to put the man away for life."

Morristown, New Jersey
Early morning

"DARYL'S website is getting hits from all over the U.S. and the planet, Jess," J.T. told her.

"Can you trace them?"

"Which one? They're coming in at warp speed. We need more help and a focused target."

A light drizzle had begun around the dark little house vacated by Daryl Thomas Cahil. Jessica had seen that the man's computer was equipped with a digital camera. She asked J.T. to bring up the photographic image of the material Cahil had labeled as a real piece of human brain tissue. "I want another look at it."

Now she and Strand stood over J.T.'s shoulder, staring

fixedly at the fleshy-looking lump in the digitized computer image. The tissue resembled skin peeled and cut away from a raw chicken leg, except that it was gray, tinged with a blueness, J.T. explained, "The blue color is either from being cold, or it's an enhancement made by Cahil—to dramatize it more."

The tissue sample indeed had roughly the same shape as the cross found left inside the victims' skulls, a perpendicular feeder line, a horizontal connecting line and a bulbous top that was roughly circular in shape. More chilling than anything else was that Cahil represented it as the real thing, taken he told his subscribers, from a living human brain.

"The Internet," muttered J.T., "you just don't know what kind of crazoid thing is coming outta cyberspace next."

"Cut from someone's medulla oblongata."

A tired J.T. said, "It's been real, all right. . . ."

"What're you saying, that we all have this *tingler* inside us?" asked Owens, who'd hung back, clinging to an ammonia stick.

"Yes, we do," replied J.T.

Jessica closely examined the image. Thinking aloud, she said, "If the sonofabitch photographed it here and put it onto his system, is it possible that it's still around here someplace?"

"If he hasn't consumed it," countered Strand.

"If he left it here, he'd have put it on ice," suggested Jessica, recalling the hum of the refrigerator.

"In with the Miller Lite," joked J.T.

She rushed for the kitchen area and tore open the refrigerator in search of the small body part depicted in Daryl's photo. Nothing on the shelves other than a few bottles— olives, pickles, pickled beets and rotted vegetables and cheese. No other dairy products or cold drinks or juices, only a jug of water. She snatched open the freezer and began ferreting for something in the many foil-wrapped, un-marked items there.

"Find anything, Dr. Coran?" asked Agent Owens from behind her.

"Help me out here. Anything that looks suspiciously like . . . like . . ."

"Like a brain or a piece of a brain?"

The freezer compartment was stuffed with small items wrapped in newspaper, and Jessica feared the worse. "Any-thing that isn't chicken, pork, beef or fish, I'll want to ex-amine, no matter how small, you understand?"

"Mystery meat, I get it." He went to work with his gloved hands and talked as he did so. "Look, I'm sorry about the false pretenses of my superior, Dr. Coran."

"I accept your apology, Owens." She unwrapped a soup package. He found a bag of peas. They emptied their finds into the crowded sink.

"I'd just like you to know, I truly am sorry."

"Forget about it, Owens, until such a time as I need a favor." Jessica now unwrapped the intact brain of what ap-peared a small animal, likely a cat's brain. She placed it gently aside, as Owens gasped on unwrapping a slightly larger brain—most likely that of a dog. "My dear God," he repeatedly said. "My dear God."

"It's not human," she informed him.

Strand had entered the kitchen and, seeing this, he said, "I see you've located the neighborhood strays. Do you think they have this island of tissue thing in them, too?"

"They might, but let's stay focused on anything smack-ing of human brains."

Jessica told Owens, "Look through all these wrapped goodies, and cull any that look or even smell suspicious." Out of the corner of one eye, Jessica saw Strand going down into the basement.

Jessica called out to Strand, "Let me know if there're any freezers down there, Max."

"Gotcha," he called up.

STRAND's light shone on an ill-matched washer and dryer set that dominated the small basement—no freezers or locked storage areas, only an array of boxes, garden and house tools, a small workbench, grease-covered tools and parts, and grimy stone walls, but then he saw the stone wheel and small kiln where Daryl fired his clay brains. It was an elaborate set up of raw materials he'd put together, and on shelves behind it, an array of what appeared to be homemade clay pots, each distinct in one way or another, but these were no pots, but his wares. Some were painted bright colors, while some were left gray, to appear natural. Some were large, others small. Some intentionally stylized or misshapen, others realistic. All could be pried open from the top, and a small area inside left room for the pasta.

Strand moved closer to the finished products for a better look at what appeared a strange hobby even for Cahil. As he neared the clay creations, perhaps fifty in all, he shouted up, "Some hobby Cahil indulged in!"

He pulled out his camera and began taking photos. "Nobody's ever going to believe this."

Just then Strand heard Agent Owens shouting from overhead. He grabbed three of the brains to hand over to Dr. Coran, one painted, the other two neutral gray, and he rushed back up the stairs and into the kitchen area where he placed the clay brains on a countertop. One of the gray ones, having yet to be fired, suddenly crumbled under Strand's fingers. "Shit," he cursed.

John Thorpe, having raced from the bedroom, stood

alongside Jessica now. The two M.E.'s were busy examining the thing Owens had discovered in the tinfoil that lay thawing out on the counter. "What is it?" Max asked Jessica.

Owens, who stood aside, shaken by his find, said, "I think it's maybe a child's finger."

But Jessica turned and faced Max Strand, her blanched features solemn. "It's that thing he photographed for the Internet. That Island of Rheil tissue."

"The Rheil thing from the computer photo?" asked Strand. "You can nail his ass to the wall now for certain."

"You mean this little strip of gray matter is all Cahil fed on?" asked Owens.

"It would appear that he wasn't *quite* the cannibal everyone painted him," replied J.T., poking at the frozen finger-sized, fleshy cross of matter with a pen. "He just went in for this little delicacy."

"Whataya mean?" asked Strand, his calm broken. "The bastard cut off and discarded whole heads of dead children; fed them to his dogs, and he consumed human flesh—*brain tissue*."

J.T. raised his arms in defeat. "OK . . . OK . . . The man's a cannibal no matter how you slice it," he tried to joke.

"So . . . did this tissue come from a child's head or an adult's?" asked Owens.

"I couldn't hazard a guess except that it corresponds in size to what we read from the book on Rheil. Which means it's probably been taken from an adult brain," replied Jessica. She turned her eyes back to the counter and stared down at the tissue, icy blue with cold from its sleep inside the freezer and foil cocoon. "It hasn't been in the freezer for too long, probably a month or so."

"Right around the time the Digger killings began," commented J.T.

"We need the lab at Quantico, John," she replied. "We need to match the DNA from this to the victims. We need the brain-imaging program to take a look at this thing in a normal adult brain to make any determinations about its origin. Frankly, until this case, I'd never heard of this brain piece."

"Neither had I," replied J.T.

"What does it—what's its function? Why is it inside of us?" asked Owens.

"First one I've actually seen," said Strand. "I always took it for a hoax Cahil pulled on the court, the doctors and his legion of Web visitors. I never took it for a real item out of here." He pointed to his own skull. Then he parroted Owens's concern. "What is it inside our heads for?"

Jessica sensed the uneasiness both men felt on learning that something strange and remarkable had been inside their brains all their lives and they had not known it. She didn't know how to answer their questions.

J.T. broke the silence. "No one—and I mean no one— knows what it's in there for, kind of like the appendix in the body . . . a leftover from previous eons, likely quite as dormant as the appendix."

"The appendix," said Owens, nodding.

Strand said, "You mean it has no use anymore? That whatever it once functioned as has just sort of atrophied?"

"Something like that, yes."

"That's good enough for me," said Owens.

Strand bit his lower lip, gave it another thought and added, "Makes sense."

Jessica was glad for J.T.'s comparison as well. She could also now draw a bead on it and put the thing in proportion, she hoped. It was a theory at the opposite pole from that put forth by Daryl Cahil and Dr. Rheil himself. For them, the small organic cross of tissue was hardly dormant; for them, this thing comprised a *palace* for the soul. Jessica momentarily wondered at the depth to which Jack Deitze could have fallen under the spell of such a theory.

"Have we got enough now to get out of this goddamn hole?" asked Owens, anxious to get out of Cahil's world.

"I'm taking possession of this thing," said Jessica, preparing a formaldyhyde-filled vial and dropping the brain tissue into the vial. "But the man's computer's not going to fit in here," she indicated her valise. "We'll want any disks, any and all books with titles on the brain, especially any with markers in them. They'll be boxed and sent to Quantico. Can you—"

"I'll get some help down here," said Owens, anxious to make amends.

"If it's no bother. We could use some agents handy with lightbulbs."

Owens frowned at this. "I'll arrange for help."

"Strand," she said to Max, "you may want to canvass the backyard for any recently turned earth. We may still have a missing woman on our hands, and if this Rheil item doesn't match one of the victims we have, it could belong to Cahil's girlfriend. I noticed women's clothing in one of the closets."

"At his trial, I tell you, he spoke in a personality that was a woman. He's quite convincing because he's that rare case—a real schizophrenic. All the same, I'll take charge of a search out back. I need some air anyway."

Jessica, too, was ready to vacate the morbid sea of squalor and misdirected thought. But first she asked Strand, "Are these clay brains all you found in the basement?" She pointed to the three models of the brain, one cracked and broken, shards of it everywhere, the other two intact, one natural gray, the other painted half chartreuse, half psychedelic orange.

Strand demonstrated how the two parts of the brain were detached to reveal the pocket of space inside for the cache of noodles. "There's maybe forty-five or fifty of these things downstairs, with boxes, labels and packing material, but no freezers and nothing smacking of a new false wall or new concrete floor. I got no odor of decay or death, but we might want to get some dogs down there."

"Some hobby to pass the time with, huh?" said J.T., examining the wildly painted brain.

"More like a fixation," said Max.

"Yes, a fixation," Jessica agreed.

"One of the shrinks at Cahil's trial said he had never seen such an advanced case of hyper . . . hypro . . ."

" 'Hyperprosexia,' I think they call it," Jessica suggested.

Max nodded. "That's it." He went carefully toward the exit in search of air. Jessica followed in his wake. Just outside, Max lit up a cigarette and added, "Said even if Cahil could not be proved insane by reason of multiple-personality disorder, that he could easily be proved to have this hyperprosexia thing."

They looked to the sky for signs of stars, the moon, anything for some respite from this place. "As I remember it from the trial," Strand continued, "it had something to do with the sheer depth of his obsession with the brain. Course, at the time, I thought it all hogwash. But now . . . seeing that piece of brain tissue in there . . . this Rheil thing . . ."

"Hyperprosexia is a term for rigid, undeviating attention of a pathological intensity. It's considered a psychotic condition in which the mind takes hold of an idea with unshakable *fixity*. It certainly fits the Skull-digger's profile."

J.T. had followed them out, listening to their conversation. He added, "In layman's terms, it's a morbidly adhered to fixation, like monomania—*idée fixe* the French call it."

"Like I told them in '90," said Strand, inhaling deeply

from his cigarette. "If they ever let this guy out again, he'll go right back to what he did before. Looks like he's cooked it a little differently, but he's still after the same thing. He's only recently displayed the picture of it, I can tell you, or I'd have been on his ass in a flash."

"Which of his recent victims—murdered this time around—do you suppose this brain item came from?" asked J.T. "The girl in Virginia, North Carolina, Georgia or Florida?"

"Hopefully it's his last," said Jessica falling silent, thinking about the second near-abduction incident in New Bern, North Carolina, and trying to square it with the newly discovered evidence against Daryl Cahil. She thought of the female voice on the phone the night she had first heard of Cahil, the voice that had so pleaded for Jessica to take an interest in Daryl as the Digger. Had the first call actually been from Cahil himself while under the control of another personality? Could he be working with an accomplice? Or were both of the failed abductions the work of another man who had no bearing on their case?

Owens had gone out to his car to call for a team of evidence techs to get to the address. He returned now to the rear stairs where the others stood talking.

Jessica told Owens, "Dr. Thorpe will have the honor of overseeing the evidence collection from here on. Right, John?"

J.T. nodded his assent. "I know you need to get to Quantico, and picking through this mess . . . well, it'll take some time. I'll see to it that Cahil's computer will follow you. We're going to need some real experts to delve into the man's website, to determine just how nuts he and his cyberspace connections are. We'll bring in someone from the Cyber Squad and get a fix on anyone out there who has taken Cahil too seriously."

"What for?" asked Strand. "You can't charge them with anything. Hell, he's selling those brains through eBay and Amazon, along with his damned Rheil noodles."

"Agreed, but we may just want to put any of his more serious followers on a watch list," replied J.T.

"And remember, no one has yet proven that this creep Cahil is in fact the Digger," added Jessica. "If we learn there's still a killer at large, even though Cahil is in custody, then we *may* have someplace to start over. That's supposing Cahil has become master to some disciple out there."

J.T. contemplated the complexities of getting at Cahil's Web list. "We've got a lot of decisions to make. Do we go back six months, a year, two, three? It's all for nothing if we can't force the Internet server to give up the profiles of the people who've logged on. And we're bucking the ACLU here, known for fighting any infringement on Internet users, Jess."

"I thought servers didn't want profane garbage on the Net," said Owens, "that they monitored everything."

"Not Cahil's server. They've built a reputation as the bad boys of the Net. Anything goes. That way, they get sub-scribers," replied J.T.

"We'll need a fire-and-brimstone federal judge to get a warrant to open the thing up then," said Jessica. "I'm sure it won't be a problem for the FBI."

"The creep has been influencing a potential audience of billions," said J.T. "That's got to stop."

"Still, *good luck* getting the Net server to release the in-formation. It won't be easy. I've tried it myself," said Strand. "It'll take an act of God, Dr. Coran, not the FBI."

"Maybe if we can narrow it to people who keep coming back to the well, not to mention we'd like to know if any of the Digger's victims are among the subscribers to Cahil's site, then—"

"It's a catch-22, I tell you. Without that list, no court will give you a warrant, but you can't get that list without a damned warrant," Strand assured her. "Trust me. I've worn myself out pleading for it."

"You're dealing with local judges. We'll get our top echelon at Quantico on it," J.T. assured Strand.

"Owens, can you drive me to the airport?" Jessica asked.

"Of course." She detected a note of happy anticipation in his two-word response.

"I've got to hook up with Eriq Santiva and meet this guy Cahil, face-to-face."

"Wish I had ten minutes alone with him," commented Strand. "Or at very least help in his interrogation, but I'm not feeling so well, and doctors tell me I need another operation, so I'll be sticking close to home."

"Sorry to hear it. Your insights have been extremely helpful, Max."

"Just get the confession, Dr. Coran."

"Do you think you can get a confession out of him?" asked Owens.

"With this in my possession"—she held up the formaldehyde-filled vial in which the tissue found in Cahil's refrigerator floated—"we might have the leverage needed to shock him into confessing, yes." Making certain the cap was properly tightened, she placed it again inside her medical bag.

"Are you sure you can take that without it having been put through the chain of evidence process?" asked Owens.

"For once, the kid's right," added Strand. "You break chain of evidence nowadays and you'll get an O.J. result."

"I know you're right, Strand, but I need something to scale and gut this guy with, and this . . . this is perfect. So, since we conducted the search and seizure under a federal

warrant, I'm officially declaring all evidence goes directly to
Quantico. That makes our lab there responsible for the chain
of custody. We'll take everything but the dog and cat remains, and should a body be located here, you guys can
process it and ship it to Quantico."

"Leaving us with an animal-cruelty case against Cahil?"
asked Owens. "Thanks a heap."

Strand held back a laugh. "Let Fromme choke on that."

"Exactly." Jessica did laugh.

"A wise move, Dr. Coran. Do an old detective a favor.
Put that bastard away forever this time, will you?"

"I'll certainly do my best."

AFTER Jessica Coran got on a flight, leaving New Jersey
and the "estate of Rheil" as J.T. had jokingly referred to
Cahil's house, Owens and his men canvassed the place another time, while J.T. packed the computer for shipment.
Meanwhile, Max Strand oversaw the grid out back to determine if any fresh graves had been dug. Enlisted to help were
cadaver dogs. As the dogs worked, Strand wondered again
if dogs and other animals had this Island of Rheil in their
heads. He asked Owens what he thought of the notion, but
Owens said he'd just as soon not give it any more thought.

Strand felt a pull, a kind of fixation on the question. If
animals did not, it might prove interesting; if they did, it
might prove there could be some credence to the whole idea
of where the soul resided, and if not in this small cross of
tissue, then where?

With the search turning up nothing untoward in the
backyard, Strand said his goodbyes to everyone and walked
to his car. Earlier, when Owens was busy and J.T. was oc-
cupied, Strand had taken one of the cat brains from the

refrigerator. He now drove off with it beneath a coat on the passenger seat beside him. When he got to Ash Pine Park, only blocks away, he stopped the car and got out. He reached in and took hold of the cat brain. Discarding the foil wrapping, Strand held the fist-sized walnut-shaped organ over a water fountain, thawing it under the water. He next pulled out his Swiss Army knife and began hacking away at the little brain. He easily opened up the two hemispheres and began searching for the Rheil tissue inside the medulla oblongata. These many years of chasing Daryl had left him with some knowledge of where to cut.

He had for many years now monitored Daryl's website. He knew what the man's religion was; and he knew it to be insane. Still, he searched for the island of tissue in the animal brain, curious and wondering.

It was not a pretty autopsy, he told himself as he now cut deeper into the medulla oblongata and a tiny piece of material fell out and into the dirt and grass at Strand's foot. He tossed the rest of the dead brain into the bushes.

Slowly, reluctantly, fighting gravity the entire time, Strand went to his knees over where that small bit had fallen, attempting to find it in the grass, but the thing acted as if alive, hiding, camouflaged in the dry, brittle grass.

Then he saw it, but it wasn't large like the human one, only a fraction of the size. He reached for the thing, and a part of his brain said, *Consume it . . . consume it.*

He thought about it, thought how it would taste, how it would feel going down, what it might do to him, whether mad Daryl's claims were true or not. He wondered if it had magical powers or was as magical as one of the blades of grass. Either way, he knew that if he consumed it, the act itself would hold sway over him for the rest of his life. "It's only an animal part," he said aloud as the wind whipped by and he heard the flutter of trees overhead.

The park, an unsavory, broken down piece of real estate the city had for years vowed to clean up, was home to many transients on any given night. Strand searched about himself for his own safety. No one nearby, no one watching him. He didn't see the two figures crouching behind his car.

Strand now held the slippery item in two fingers and was about to consume it when the lead pipe came crashing down into his skull.

Two human vultures living in the seedy park had jumped Strand, leaving him bleeding to death as they tore into his pockets. One wanted to take the car, but the other located his ID and threw it at his companion, shouting, "My God, Danny, we've killed a freakin' cop! Forget the car. We gotta run, now!"

Quantico, Virginia
Same morning

JESSICA, having returned to Quantico, knew she had to immediately log in the evidence she had placed into a vial from Cahil's Morristown home. She hoped after seeing to the chain of evidence protocol that she might take a moment to drop by her office, look over the mail and say some hellos.

Chief Eriq Santiva met her on the helicopter pad when the FBI chopper landed. It was still early in the morning, and she had gotten little sleep on the chopper, and here he stood, obviously anxious for her to meet with Daryl Thomas Cahil. "Jessica, you look tired. Are you all right? Personally, I couldn't sleep on a chopper if my life depended on it. Was your detour to Morristown helpful?" came Eriq's volley of questions. "Why isn't Strand with you? He wanted to be here for the kill."

He had watched her climb tiredly from the chopper, her bag at her side. She immediately informed Eriq, "I have to log in evidence gathered at the crime scene in Georgia and at the Morristown location. Did the tire and shoe print casts arrive? Any news from Combs on the victims computer habits?" She finished with a yawn, realizing neither one of them had answers for the other, and then added, "My suitcase is in the chopper."

"It's taken care of, Jess. How'd it go in Morristown?" He took hold of her medical bag.

"That can't be out of my possession, Eriq," she argued.

"Can't be out of your sight, and it won't be until we get it inventoried."

They found the rooftop door and started down a flight of stairs to the elevator.

"Actually, it went quite well in both Philly and Morristown," she informed him. "We learned that Cahil has been operating a website since before leaving prison. One that advocates cannibalizing brains."

"Wait a minute, are you telling me that while behind bars, while in an asylum for the criminally insane, that Deitze allowed him to start up a website?"

"Began as a question-answer thing, information on the workings of the brain—his brain in particular. The brain's magical power and magnificence, all that. People asking him about his crime and him responding, all with Jack Deitze's consent."

"Really? Don't tell me, this is Deitze's idea of therapy?" asked an amazed Santiva.

"Before he left prison he had more than a hundred thousand hits," she informed Eriq. "Second only to Charlie Manson's many websites, you know, the ones attracting cult followings on college campuses and high schools across the nation."

They boarded the elevator, and she punched the button for subbasement-one, where evidence and lockup were located. Eriq breathed deeply, ending with a sigh. "Yeah . . . I knew about Manson, but not about Cahil on the Web."

"Manson's imprisoned for life but set free on the World Wide Web. . . . Jack Deitze thought it a good avenue of *release* for Cahil, a way to get his reticent patient to open up. Deitze's way was paved by our old friend Dr. Arnold. Deitze characterizes the website as *benign*."

"Benign?"

"Apparently, he hasn't logged on for a while." She stepped off the elevator ahead of him, turned and said, "Fact is, the website has been quite informative for our side. It may be enough to nail him. He plastered a photo of a human brain part onto it, and we found the piece he photographed in his freezer."

"And you have it with you?"

She slapped her valise. "Yes, I do."

"Then we can nail the bastard—and make no mistake about it, he's a disgusting piece of shit, Jess."

They had arrived at the evidence lockup, a huge room of locked cages with shelves floor to ceiling filled with file boxes and all manner of misshapen objects and items. It looked like the secret back rooms of a large museum.

"Cahil covers his behind with this veneer of symbolic feeding he goes on about," began Jessica, "but beneath it, he's advocating that people find some sort of immortality by consuming some mysterious swath of tissue inside the human brain. How else to get at it but through cannibalizing a victim? That's advocating murder."

Eriq nodded. "If the website is now promoting actually finding and feeding on brain tissue, and we can link him with the Digger killings, then we'll put him away again. This time, we'll get the death penalty."

"Yeah . . . now that he's infected countless others with his lunacy. That Jack Deitze had too much of Gabriel Arnold rub off on him. The man doesn't know what the hell he's released on the world. And probably will never acknowledge the harm he's caused."

After turning over all the labeled evidence and seeing each officially itemized, she signed off on it all. "I'm keeping hold of this item," she told the clerk. "It'll need special attention and preservation."

The clerk stared at what Jessica showed her but asked no more than the number of the label placed on the vial. "So noted," the clerk finished.

"I'm going to want this for interrogating the suspect as well," Jessica told Eriq. When the clerk held out a pen and a release form, Jessica gave the vial to Eriq. He stared more closely at its contents, his face contracting, his nose contorting a bit as he got a whiff of formaldehyde. Santiva swallowed hard and next held it up to the light and peered through the clear plastic at the island of tissue inside. "Some weird shit, Jess."

"It might well lead to a confession."

"Well, are you ready for a go at Cahil?"

"First, I really need a pit stop, Eriq. I need to stop at my office and kick back a moment."

"Kick back? This is no time to—"

"Eriq, I've been up and down the southeast, in and out of airplanes and choppers like a yo-yo for the past week, and I never got to sleep last night. I need to touch base with familiar surroundings, get grounded, OK?"

"All right . . . OK."

"Besides, I want to get an assistant working immediately on DNA from this thing," she added, taking the vial from him again. "We need to match it to DNA on file for the victims. If it's come from one of them, there's little question that we're on the right track. And I want photos taken of the thing before it deteriorates any further."

Reentering the elevator, she pushed the button for the eighteenth floor where her newly renovated offices and labs awaited. "Let me have another look at that thing," Eriq said, taking the vial and holding it up for another look against the light.

They rode up in silence, Eriq continuing to stare at the thing in the vial, strangely fascinated by it. When the elevator door opened, and Jessica stepped out ahead of him, he was still staring at the Island of Rheil.

"I'll take that back for the time being," she told him.

"Wonder why Cahil kept it in his freezer," he replied as he handed it over.

"Where else would he hoard it?"

"I mean . . . Why didn't he just eat it, you know? If it's what he pries out of his victim's brain . . ."

"Who knows what goes on inside such a head?" She unlocked her office and stood with the door ajar, the semidarkness within inviting.

Eriq added, "But if he's such an addict for this thing?"

She turned on him, asking, "How the hell should I know, Eriq? We're dealing with a psychotic with a morbid fixation. He doesn't have to make sense, now does he?"

"Easy, Jess. Just thinking aloud. I'll ask him when we get around to him."

Eriq followed her into her office. She had somehow escaped being seen by any of the lab personnel. She wanted to have some peace before any of the others came after her for one thing and another. Still, it felt good to be home. She buzzed Jere Anderson's desk and asked her to come to her office but to tell no one that she was in the building.

Jere entered, said a quick hello, and got her orders from Jessica. Jessica informed her junior staff member of what she needed done with the strange piece of brain matter in the vial. "Jere, you're in charge."

"Thank you for your confidence, Dr. Coran. I won't let you down."

"I'm sure you'll handle it in a professional manner, Jere. Now, I'm going to get some much-needed sleep in my office, and I don't want to be disturbed," she said for Eriq's sake as well as Jere's.

She skimmed through the messages and mail on her desk while Eriq waited in a high-backed cushioned chair. "That computer is being handled with care, right?" he asked her.

"J.T.'s seeing to it, along with everything gathered at Cahil's place, except material relative to an animal-cruelty case the field office will develop against the suspect."

"Animal case?"

"He had cat and dog brains in his freezer as well."

"Are you saying you stuck Marcus Fromme's people with an animal-cruelty case? That's rich . . . Very good . . . very good." He laughed and stood. It had been a long time since she'd heard Eriq laugh about anything, and it made her feel good.

She snatched up a blanket she kept in the office for such occasions and curled up on her couch, thinking Eriq was on his way out. "Give me an hour, maybe two?" she asked.

"I had copies of the *Washington Post* and the ever popular *Instigator* placed on your desk for your return, Jess. They're getting damn nosey and close on our heels."

She glanced up to see him holding the two newspapers side by side, photo arrays of all the victims, including Winona Miller in Georgia accompanied screaming headlines in both the tabloid and the legitimate paper. One read:

BONE SAW, SCALPEL USED BY SKULL-DIGGER
WHILE VICTIMS SUFFERED ALIVE

The other read:

Brain-Eating Bone Saw Slayer
Eludes FBI, Police

Jessica sat up, scanning the news accounts for any sign that they had knowledge of the cross found on the bodies or anything related to how small a section of the brain had actually been the killer's object. On both counts, the storytellers had nothing. She stood and went to her window, staring out over the Quantico grounds, lush with greenery. "At least the word isn't out on the cross or this Rheil business."

"With this kind of sensational case, I'm surprised the other information hasn't leaked," Eriq replied.

"In the body of one of the stories, the writer referred to the killer as the 'Brain Snatcher.' The other story referred to him as the 'Brain Cleaver.' Don't they know you have to cleave before you can snatch?" she asked, falling back into the folds of the couch.

"Cahil had similar news accounts on him when he was brought in. He claims it's the reason he contacted you."

"Another reason, you mean? He decided the heat was too much for him."

"He claims he's innocent of all charges. That he's not the Digger. That is, when he's not speaking from other personalities."

"Yet he's got a piece of someone's brain at home in the freezer."

"There's something you ought to know about his 1990 doings, Jess."

"Shoot."

"When Cahil was first put away, he copped to using the newspaper obits to select his victims. You find any newspapers accumulating at his residence?"

"Some, you could say," she facetiously answered.

"Too bad you didn't find a bone saw. That's what he used in '90."

"Yeah, he sounds good for the Skull-digger, Eriq."

"Corroborated now by his own website and that piece of flesh you brought in. I'm hoping for the death penalty this time around."

"Yeah, he can do an elocution for us," she replied. "Hopefully, he'll tell the whole story, beginning with his Richmond victim." *If I tell him what he wants to hear, I can get some sleep,* she thought.

He blew out a long breath of air, his Cuban features darker than ever. "Morristown was good for our side. We match this tissue you found at his place with any of the victims, and we put an end to it."

"I'm banking on Cahil, too, Eriq. Still . . . some things don't add up." *Can't help yourself, can you?* she reproached herself.

"Ah, you mean the estimated weight on a shoe print in Georgia that may or may not have been made by Cahil? Not to worry. You have human tissue found in his Morristown home."

"What more evidence do we need?" she asked, a mock smile coming over her along with a mock sense of relief. "All the same, we need to check his shoes against the prints taken in Georgia, along with his tire treads, if we ever find his van. As for now, Boss, I gotta get a little sleep."

But Eriq was keyed up, not listening to her. "Since he's been incarcerated, no one else has been murdered in his trademark fashion. Like I said, the new killings started up after—*after his release*—and he's well aware that this time he may go into the general population rather than a safe, private padded room."

She closed her eyes and lay her head on a pillow.

"Well, I can see you're fatigued. Get some rest. I'll check back in an hour."

"Make it two. And thanks, Eriq." Jessica had curled up in the fetal position on the couch. Eriq smoothed the blanket over her to encompass her shoeless feet. Then he left, closing the door behind him.

She was grateful she'd remembered to unplug the phone on her desk.

A stream of thoughts bombarding its way over rocks of doubt ran through Jessica's restless sleep there in her office. The river of reflection came full circle back to the lunatic Cahil. And the Skull-digger's career had begun only *after* Cahil had been released. Maybe there was a perfect connection between the two maniacs of 1990 and 2003, the perfect connection being that they were one and the same man— possibly another manifestation of Cahil's multiple-personality syndrome. Spots never change, she told herself.

Yet her unconscious mind hit a snag on its way to executing Cahil, as her sleep self considered the disparity between a killer's lusting after a dead victim and a *live* one. World of difference, she told herself.

Deitze whooshed into her dream state and said, *Children are closer to something Daryl calls the eternal cosmic mind residing in us all; said he had tapped into it through his Rheil thing.* Dr. Deitze glanced toward the refrigerator in Cahil's house.

Jessica's dream self asked, *So, you think Cahil is at it again? No . . . never. I cured him.*

He's just twisted his formula, cooked it differently, said Max Strand, forcing his way into the conversation.

His prey are now live young female victims to find oneness and wholeness with his warped idea of the universe and how it works? her unconscious asked in a tone of disbelief.

It's a very real possibility that one of his personalities has branched out, Dr. Coran, added a gray, ashen-looking Max Strand. *It's him, all right. I'd stake my career on it. Daryl is the Digger.*

NINE

Later that morning

"DOESN'T want to talk to anyone, including a lawyer. Just wants you, Jess," said Eriq, who had awakened her at 11 A.M., allowing her two and a half hours' sleep. They'd come down to the interrogation room together.

"I know my rights!" shouted Daryl Cahil into the one-way mirror from inside the interrogation room, where he paced like a caged animal. "You can't do this to me. I'm not the Skull guy! Get me Dr. Coran. I want to talk to Coran. Get me Coran."

"So, he's not exactly confessing?" asked Jessica, standing on the other side of the mirror as two FBI interrogators were fast becoming frustrated with Cahil and getting nowhere.

"Goes back and forth. One moment he's confessing, the other he's denying. But he doesn't know enough details about the crimes, the MO," explained Eriq. "At least that's the game he's playing."

The intercom picked him up loud and clear now. "Don't listen to this idiot or his crotchety bitch, Cessie. She lied to you about me. I'm clean. Been cured of all that sickness that once drove me."

"Sounds like another voice," said Dr. Albert Coulongua, an African-born FBI criminal psychiatrist who'd been called down by Eriq to study the suspect's reactions. "He's manifesting different personalities, I'm afraid, and I don't know which one you ought to be interrogating."

"Maybe it would be helpful if you were in there with us, Dr. Coulongua," suggested Eriq. "Kinda as a . . . a . . ."

"Referee?"

"Translator."

"Problem is, one of his manifestations has really objected to my being on hand."

"Then stay close for consult if we need it, all right?"

"Absolutely."

Jessica studied the man through the mirror. The rattle of chains came so loudly through the intercom that it pierced her ears painfully. Cahil's hands and feet struggled with the shackles. His body appeared a sad, awkward, gaunt skeletal shell. Suffering from malnourishment, he seemed a man almost without shadow. In fact, Jessica found herself having to search for his shadow as he made his way back to a chair and sat dejected at the interrogation table.

Eriq pulled the interrogation team, leaving Daryl alone for the moment.

Cahil's head appeared out of sync with the rest of his body. His head dwarfed his shoulders, threatened to pull from its moorings and roll from his bony frame at any given moment. His forehead creased with veins that looked ready to explode. Emaciated and pale, he appeared too frail to overpower anyone, much less a string of victims in a matter of six weeks. His intense green eyes, massive forehead and balding scalp dominated his appearance, making him look like a mad scientist escaped from a bad science-fiction film.

Mulling over his obvious physical limitations, Jessica imagined that prison life for his foul cemetery acts had taken its toll. She also had trouble squaring his height and weight with that of the shadowy figure who'd left such deep impressions in the Georgia soil at the death scene there.

She looked at Dr. Coulongua. "Any suggestions?"

"I think your plan to use the Rheil tissue you recovered is good. Shock him . . . shake him up. His other selves are a bit too onstage and outraged right now. Knock them off and who knows? The real Daryl may appear. Then work on gaining his trust."

Jessica was unhappy about all the multiple-personality talk. "We don't want to set him up for another stint in a hospital, Eriq. We want the real man to stand trial for the real crimes he's committed."

"As does Daryl, or so he has been saying," said Coulongua.

"Blame it on someone else who possesses him. Nice dodge," said Jessica.

"Play back the tape from where I had you dub it, Agent Hanson," countered Coulongua. Hanson had been called in to guard the prisoner.

On the videotape, Jessica and Eriq heard a confession. "I'm responsible for those four murders. I did it, and I should be punished to the fullest extent of the law."

On the videotape, Jessica and Eriq saw that it was Cahil, but he had transformed into another person altogether. Every nuance, every inflection and intonation different, yet all emanating from one man.

"So . . . if we already have Cahil's confession . . ." said Jessica.

"That confession is from the personality isolated as the star of his own show. He is strong, dominating, but he refers to himself as 'Keyhoe' and he really only seems to want the notoriety of being the Skull-digger, taking responsibility for the killings for the spotlight of it all. His core personality is extremely fragmented, but only the real Daryl seems to know right from wrong in a legal sense."

"So he wants to confess, but not really?"

"Other sides of him won't allow it."

"Thank you, Dr. Coulongua."

Eriq squinted and nodded. "And if we can say that the confessor is the dominant, true personality—the real Cahil—then that's going to help our case, right?"

"We've got to be doubly careful now, Eriq, to verify everything he cops to," cautioned Jessica. "He's got to have prior knowledge of the cross found in the victims' skulls, and whose DNA is inside this vial." She held up the brain tissue sample that had been returned to her by Jere, who'd taken enough for the DNA analysis. Seeing the item for the first time, Dr. Coulongua's black face took on an ashen hue.

ON entering the interrogation room, Jessica found Cahil's stare unnerving. He eyed her suspiciously and studied her silently—now and then a glow of amazement lit up his face. She imagined these strange, dark, penetrating eyes pinning his victims.

"You came . . . you finally came, Dr. Coran. All the way here just to talk to me? I didn't think you would. Will you tell these idiots they've got the wrong man?"

"I can only determine that after we've had a chance to chat, Mr. Cahil."

After several hours of what began to feel like useless interrogation of a lunatic talking in circles as frustrating as any professor of philosophy Jessica had ever had the misfortune of meeting, Jessica displayed the vial bursting full with the brain tissue. "Familiar, Mr. Cahil? We found this in your freezer in Morristown."

His eyes widened and his skin shivered like a ripple of fear manifesting itself along every inch of his epidermis. "I knew I should've eaten it. But Keyhoe wanted to keep it for this day."

Eriq and Jessica exchanged a look. "Why didn't you consume it?" asked Eriq.

"Like I said: Keyhoe. He hurts me if I don't do what he says."

"Keyhoe wanted it for a special occasion like this, huh?" asked Jessica. "Well, Daryl, would you care to tell us who it belonged to at one time?"

"I don't know. I really don't. Do you?"

Jessica, determined to corner the elusive Cahil, lied now. "DNA tests tell us it belonged to the Gleason woman, Anna Gleason, killed in Richmond."

"I'm no fool. It takes weeks, months sometimes, to get DNA test results back."

"Preliminary reports are back, and my lab people've hazarded a guess as to how long this beauty has been on ice. The time frame puts it *close* to the Gleason slaying. Now, do you want to dispute that?"

"*He* sent it to me. The Seeker killed her and sent it to me. I've never lied about that. Defied Keyhoe when I put the fact on my website."

"The Seeker? And who is that? One of your multiples?" asked Eriq.

"The Seeker isn't me; I am not the Seeker. He did this, not me."

"Someone else, somebody outside your head sent it to you?" Eriq pressed. "Do you expect us to believe that, Daryl?"

"No. I mean yes, a guy who contacts me on the Web, calls himself the Seeker."

"It's always somebody else's doing, isn't it, Cahil?" Eriq shouted.

Jessica dovetailed this with, "Dr. Deitze ever point that out to you, Cahil? That you can't seem to take responsibility for any of your actions?"

"I served my time for what I did, but I'm not the Digger any more than you are, and I do not advocate murder on my website."

Jessica went on the attack with a subtle, calm voice. "But you advocate eating a portion of the brain, the Island of Rheil, and—"

"You know I do, but it's different now."

"—there's no way to get that nourishment, Cahil, without cutting open somebody's head for it."

"Read my site, Doctor. With Dr. Deitze's help, I've worked out a solution, a spiritual solution that doesn't rely on ingesting the actual thing. You make replicas of the brain and the Island of Rheil with clay, with pasta hidden inside, and you feed *symbolically*, you see. Like . . . like the body of the host, the blood of the host, all that. *Same difference*."

Jessica had told Eriq of the strange practice and the clay brains found by Strand in the basement at Cahil's home. "Are you telling me that if I dug around in one of your clay brains, I'd find a pasta replication of the Island of Rheil?"

"That's right. I've been producing them for people. They order them through my Web page."

"Isn't that just swell and hunky-dory," said Eriq. "That way nobody gets hurt. But people have been hurt—four women murdered now, Cahil, and *you* killed them!"

"No, I tell you! I didn't do it. And I'm not talking to you! I'm talking to Dr. Coran."

"Killed them for that part of their brains you believe

houses their souls," continued Eriq. "So you could have power over their souls in this life and the afterlife, right? Right?"

Cahil cringed and physically went into himself, turtle fashion. Jessica feared they were about to lose him.

"Isn't that right, Daryl! Isn't it!"

"Chief! Chief Santiva!" Jessica shouted Eriq down. "Can we talk outside?" She picked up the vial containing the oddly shaped frozen scrap of gray matter, fearful Cahil or one of his personalities would throw it down his throat if he got hold of it. She dropped the vial into her lab coat pocket. "While we're outside, Mr. Cahil, I want you to look closely at this." She laid out a sketch of the cross left etched at the posterior of Amanda Manning's skull in Florida. "And I want to know what it means to you."

"That's my symbol for the Island of Rheil." His words stopped the FBI agents from leaving. "It's the same basic shape you see, that is if you look at it in the right attitude."

"Where on the victim's body did you mark this symbol for us to find, Daryl?"

"Where on the body? I haven't any idea what you mean. How could I? Since I did not kill those girls. I would only be *guessing*."

"Exactly where *near* or *on* the bodies of the victims?" Jessica pressed.

"I'm sure I wouldn't know." His voice had become so proper and correct now.

The two FBI people now glared at one another for a moment before Eriq stepped outside and she followed. With the door closed, Jessica said, "Your angry tone of voice and your provoking him will only shut him down, Eriq."

"I can't stand this creep."

"We can't succeed at getting information out of him if he shuts down. It's as good as if he were to lawyer up."

Coulongua added, "Chief Santiva, he must be handled with a certain compassion and tolerance if—"

"Compassion and tolerance? Listen to this guy, Jess!" The Skull-digger needs our understanding."

Jessica took a deep breath. "We have to go carefully here, Eriq."

Coulongua added, "He may well have contacted you, Dr. Coran, to give himself up not because he's guilty, but only to remind the world of his existence, wanting to grab the headlines for himself, while someone else—someone who actually committed the murders—goes free."

"My sentiments, exactly," added Jessica.

Eriq said, "Of course, I understand that but—"

"But HQ wants results yesterday, I know," she said. "And I know that you're on edge. All right. I'm here. Let me talk again to the Ghoul."

She and a more-subdued Eriq returned to the interrogation room. Jessica found herself again engaged in another round-robin session with Cahil, who kept changing like a chameleon with every other question.

"Tell me more about this symbol of yours, Cahil."

He took on the mannerisms of a woman before their eyes, and he explained in a distinctly female voice, "The cross represents the eternal within us all, the holy trinity of man, horizon and godhood achieved through contact with the eternal cosmic mind."

The female voice sounded familiar to Jessica. She put it together with the phone call she'd received in Jacksonville. "Can you guess where I first saw this representation, Cahil?" She wanted him to hang himself. Only the killer would know the answer to this question.

"Likely took it off Cahil's Web page," the female voice replied.

"No, the very first time I would have encountered it. You left it for me to find, remember?"

His head shook slowly from side to side. "Don't know what you're talking about."

"All right . . . all right, but maybe Cahil does?"

"Nothing Cahil knows is worth your time," continued the female persona.

"OK . . . Listen . . . What's your name?"

"Cesillia. Name is Cesillia, but he insists on calling me Cessie—when he's not being vulgar."

Jessica's tilted her eyes and chin toward the ceiling in exaggerated fashion. "You're the woman who first contacted me, tipping me off to Cahil's being the Skull-digger. Aren't you?"

"I'm his wife. Got a problem with that? Wife . . . naughty wife, that's me. I did it as a prank, you know." She got up, the chains rattling, and she seductively made her way toward Jessica. "You like women in chains, Dr. Jessica?" she asked. "We could be so good together."

"Sit down!" shouted Eriq, threatening to take Cahil in hand.

Cesillia looked at him with disdain but did as told. She then continued, "We married the *second* year of his imprisonment. Surely, Deitze told you about me? I waited for the bastard all this time—*a damn decade*. But now . . . now that he's free, I just can't deal with all his shit. Hell, I've run away before but always came back, but this . . . this *fear* that he could be the Skull-digger—the one you're all after— it . . . it terrifies me." Now she was simply being over-dramatic. She didn't sound terrified but rather mocking.

"How did you get my number?"

"He gave it to me. Dared me to call you and tell his secrets. He ought to've known I would."

"OK, how did he—Cahil—get the number?"

She paused to dry tears on her sleeve, rattling chains as

she did. "I left it with a note begging him to give himself up."

"No, how did he originally come by the number?"

She shrugged in a feminine show of confusion, rising again from her seat and placing her shackled wrists on the table, snaking them toward Jessica. "He's grown bored with me. He wants you, Dr. Coran. He wants to give himself up *and over* to you."

"And is that what you're doing? Giving yourself up?"

She recoiled, the chain rattling anew. "No! Not me! I could never hurt anyone, including Daryl."

"Then why did you call me?"

"To clear my name."

"Cesillia's name?"

"It's damned crowded living in here," she replied, pressing a palm against her head. "And in this crowd, it's every woman for herself."

Another blinking of his eyes and a slight shake of the head, and Cahil transformed back to his core personality. A masculine voice replaced Cesillia's. "I want you to catch this guy so I can be cleared. I can help you."

Eriq shook his head and scratched behind his left ear. "Tell us about the cosmic mind, Daryl. How if you eat enough of these brain pieces, you will build your own soul exponentially."

"I tell you I'm past that stuff. I preach that it be done only in the *symbolic* sense."

"Just which one of your personalities is the Skull-digger, Mr. Cahil?" asked Jessica.

"I believe the Digger is someone who's plugged in to my website, someone who doesn't care for the symbolic but must have the real thing . . . the Island of Rheil. The thing you had in your little plastic jar, that came to my address wrapped in tinfoil. It came from the killer: UPS."

"Your fridge, Mr. Cahil, was filled with animal brains, as well. All wrapped in tinfoil and newspaper," Jessica countered.

Impatient, Santiva stormed at Cahil, shouting, "We have scientific ways of determining your guilt, sir. You left your tire and shoe prints in the mud in Georgia when you killed Winona Miller. You left this representation of your fucking Rheil prize"—he jabbed a finger onto the drawing—"on all your victims."

Jessica gritted her teeth and muttered to Eriq, "I wanted him to say that, not you, Eriq."

Cahil lifted his right foot to show off his jailhouse booties. "They stripped me of my shoes. Are they testing my soles?" he asked with a grimacing smile. "Good, because then you'll know it was me. You've got enough to convict me ten times over, so why the hell're we dancing around here?" He ended by screaming. His face had contorted into another personality. "I really liked that one in Georgia. Winona . . . Her name was Winona, and she was a tasty young morsel."

"To whom am I talking?" asked Jessica.

"Keyhoe . . . I'm Keyhoe, aka the Skull-digger."

"If you're the killer, where on the bodies did you leave this mark?" she again pressed the picture of the cross with her index finger.

"On what was left of their heads."

"Can you be more precise?"

"I could be, but I won't. You people bore me."

"Again, do you want to tell us the truth about whose brain tissue was found in your freezer?" asked Eriq, his voice evenly controlled now.

Keyhoe replied, "Anna Gleason."

Jessica realized that Cahil was now simply mimicking what they had already provided him to work with.

"All the victims had nothing in common, the newspapers said. Said you guys didn't have a clue to connect them. I can tell you what connects them. They all logged on to my website at one time or another. And the killer, me . . . I fucking hunted them down through cyberspace."

It was startling to hear this, and Jessica wondered if there could be any truth in it—a theory they had contemplated earlier. That the victims were among the hundreds of thousands who'd logged on out of curiosity over the years. And that Cahil had made physical contact with them.

"Keyhoe's telling you lies," said Cahil suddenly. "Look, I'm sure I have likely contributed to this killer's thinking, that perhaps he's a disciple who's gone off the deep end. My website attracts a lot of strange people, weirdos, but *I* didn't kill anyone—not in 1990 and not now. Somebody's framed me, maybe Keyhoe, and you're too stupid to know that!"

"Which is it, Cahil? You did it or you didn't?" asked Eriq, tiring of the game.

"If you're telling us the truth now, Daryl, which of your many cyber disciples do you suspect is the Skull-digger. Who do you believe sent you the brain tissue to frame you?"

"Maybe the Seeker. He's the one I suspected sent me the Rheil. I said so on the site, in the caption I put on the photo of it."

Jessica recalled the notation.

"He's the most outspoken against me, against what I stand for, a symbolic method of glimpsing the eternal mind."

"I'm sure of it," said Eriq sarcastically. "Why don't you let us talk to this Seeker character. Come on, bring him on."

"Why *didn't* you eat it?" asked Jessica. "The Rheil in your possession?"

"I told you. I only do the symbolic thing now."

"Then who would carve your symbol on the victims?"

"I told you already, the Seeker."

"Why didn't you just eat the evidence?" she pressed again.

"I saved it for you, as evidence. I read that you were investigating the case, the FBI's most famous." He paused to study the reaction he'd gotten from them both. Eriq had remained stolid and silent for a moment but now he stood and said, "We're going to book you for all four murders, Cahil! What do you have to say to that?"

"You've got the right man, but you've also got the wrong man."

"Take this piece of human waste back to holding," Eriq said into the two-way mirror.

Hanson came in and escorted Cahil out, Daryl protesting his innocence while Keyhoe asked for the death penalty.

AGAIN they had ended where they had begun, and the day's long interrogation had come to a grinding halt.

"Listen, Eriq, we have to match the DNA we took from the brain tissue to one victim's DNA. That single test alone may be enough to bury Cahil if it's a match. And I think we should follow up on what he said about all the victims having made contact with his site. Another nail in his coffin. And we need to look at this guy he calls Seeker that—"

"This Seeker guy is likely another of his personalities. But you're right about checking on the computer habits of the victims."

"Lorena Combs is doing just that from her jurisdiction. She's got the cooperation of the Manning family and the Miller family. I'll call and ask how it's going with her. Meanwhile, I'll ask the Cyber Squad to do the same from here as soon as J.T. gets back with Cahil's computer. But I have to tell you, I have reservations about Daryl being our guy. I pictured a larger man with more strength."

"How much strength does it take to pump a syringe of Demoral into a woman's arm?"

"I just don't want us jumping the gun on this, Eriq. We lock down on this guy as the Skull-digger, and maybe the real guy goes free and starts up someplace else—the West Coast or another country even."

"You mean this phantom *Seeker* that Daryl just made up? Jess, we need the Digger in custody, and we need it now."

"You have *someone* in custody. Patience, Eriq. Give us time at least to develop the evidence we have against Cahil."

"I guarantee you, as long as we hold him, Jess, the killings will end. I can promise you that much."

"Hold him on the animal-cruelty charges. That will keep him in limbo for weeks if not months."

"Animal cruelty. The press will laugh in our faces."

"You go ahead and charge him as the Digger then, Eriq. Go right ahead. I suspect that's what's going to happen whatever I say or do."

"I want you to back me on this, Jess."

"I have to exhaust all leads, Eriq, and I have my doubts about this guy being the Digger. You're a gambler by nature, Eriq, always have been. You want to gamble that at least one of his personalities is guilty, but suppose you're wrong?"

"One of his personalities *did* it, Jess."

"My instincts are screaming otherwise."

"I need your backing on this, Jess."

"And you'll have it, as soon as I can give it in good conscience."

He stormed away from her, obviously as frustrated as she over the direction the case had taken. Cahil had not been shaken by the Rheil tissue in their possession, confusing enough, but he also had given them no real indication he knew where on the bodies the mark had been left by the killer.

"We both want the same thing, Eriq," Jessica shouted after his fleeting figure, "to put an end to—" but he was gone.

A gut-gnawing intuition told her that Daryl simply didn't complete the picture, that he was possibly part of it, but not the whole. Cahil had shown little surprise when they put the sketch in front of him. And, if he truly wanted to confess, why didn't he take full advantage and divulge where on the skull the symbol was left. Why hadn't he known the location? Aside from this, his physical size was wrong. The shoe prints hadn't matched, and no weapon or van had been located. She knew she'd have to put all this in a formal report, and that by tomorrow Eriq would have to sober up and get off this addiction he had for Cahil as the Digger.

ALTHOUGH, she harbored doubts from the moment she'd met him, Jessica had not completely given up on Cahil as a serious contender for the Digger. She reserved judgment, and after Eriq had left the interrogation area, she went back at Daryl later in the day and again asked him tough and uncompromising questions. After this, in spite of Eriq's lust for Daryl as the killer and what they had found in Morristown, she felt even more certain that if Cahil were involved it was *not* as the Digger but as an accomplice of some sort. Perhaps he arranged to set the victims up. She went over everything Cahil had said, and what he'd *failed* to say about the details of the killings. He had been unable to get the calendar straight, which victim came first, second, third and fourth. Dates were confused. Nothing added up.

She left headquarters for home, picking up a takeout meal

from a Quantico restaurant called Mia's Place. Arriving at her silent house, she placed the food on hold and put in a call to Richard. They had a long conversation, both keeping to light subjects. When he brought up the case she was working on, she changed the subject to his own mission there in China. Everything was going well, he told her and changed the subject to a sporting event he was scheduled to see there. After exchanging words of love, they said good-bye.

She then called Lorena Combs, asking if she had any news on the computer habits of the Georgia and Florida victims. "Examine the E-mails for this E-address," suggested Jessica, giving her Cahil's website address. "See if they ever logged on to the site."

"So, you're still fixed on the New Jersey Ghoul?" Lorena asked.

"Not a hundred percent, but if we can make a connection with one of his victims having been in contact, we might more easily get a federal warrant to open and scrutinize all the subscribers to Cahil's site."

"I'll see what comes of it," Combs replied and then said good night.

Jessica next located J.T. by phone. He finally had gotten back from New Jersey with Cahil's computer. She updated him on their interrogations of Daryl. "I doubt he's our primary target, and I'm beginning to doubt if he's involved at all, other than as a ready patsy."

"Funny, Eriq says it went well and that you guys nailed his ass to the wall."

"When did you talk to Eriq?"

"Got a call from him while on the plane back."

"Cahil claims that all the victims had at one time or another logged on to his website."

"I assure, you, Jess," he replied, "Cahil could not know

that unless the individuals chose to reveal themselves to him by name. He's likely blowing smoke."

"Still, there's the possibility, right? Given the sheer numbers logging on, I must assume some foolish people find his computer persona somehow charismatic."

"Fact is, anyone can project a charismatic image over the Net. Still, it's unlikely he'd leave word in his correspondence with a victim's actual name for us to find. And like I said, he'd have to convince them to give him personal information, address, meeting place. We'll do best to get our cyber experts to help out here, Jess."

"And as for this Seeker guy?"

"Well, code names can only be traced with help from the server, unless our experts can find a way to hack into the guy's computer."

"How likely is that?"

"Fifty-fifty, depending on what kind of firewalls he's put up."

"Give it a try."

"Could be this Seeker is just another of Cahil's other selves, you know. If he's as multiple as Eriq says he is, he likely has more than one computer persona as well."

"You *have* been talking to Eriq."

"Yeah, I have."

"All right, get the computer search underway. Let me know where it leads," she said.

"Like Max Strand said, there'll be roadblocks."

"Who knows, maybe the server will be cooperative."

"Like they were after Nine-Eleven?" J.T. facetiously asked.

"Maybe they've learned something since then."

"I won't hold my breath, Jess. This company in particular guards its subscriber list with a vengeance."

They said their goodbyes and Jessica sat upright in bed

and ate. While using the remote, flipping through TV land, she picked at her meal. She then took a shower to the sound of argument and laughter on the late-night TV talk show *Real Time with Bill Maher.* The soothing hot shower eased the tense muscles in her neck and shoulders, and she trusted this would help her to sleep soundly.

Donning a terry-cloth robe, she returned to the bed, where a second plate, filled with vegetables and fruits, awaited her. Suddenly the TV chatter turned to the Digger. Bill Maher made a grim joke about the Digger, asking why the Skull-digger hadn't gone after the Dolphins in Discovery Cove if he wanted brains. "What's so brainy about the average American woman?" he asked the audience, garnering a wave of groans instead of laughs. Everyone on the show was critical of how the police was handling the case. The public had learned many of the shocking details, except those withheld by authorities. Everyone feared it was the beginning of a long nightmare. "News of FBI involvement," according to Maher, "has not calmed anyone's brain."

Jessica lay her head down and in a moment the TV talk show was replaced by the interrogation room, but it had clouds all around its periphery. She was again grilling Daryl, who wore a Cheshire cat's grin during the entire interview.

"What's this we found in your house in Newark, Daryl?" she demanded, holding out a small bag filled with seeds.

"Birdseed," Cahil announced. "I feed the birds out back of the house."

"Other than the house in Morristown, Daryl, is there someplace else you spend time?" asked Jessica.

"One place else, yes."

"And where is it located?"

Cahil pointed to his head.

Jessica gritted her teeth, feeling horribly uncomfortable

in such proximity to the man. She felt his horrible hot breath on her.

"Any other physical place outside your head, that we might search?" she pressed.

He looked absolutely befuddled by this, losing the grin, concentrating on her words to the point she thought his head would explode.

"Do you reside anywhere else, say in a van, for instance?" asked Jessica.

"Nah, no other space or place. This is it. . . ."

Jessica studied the man's off-center features and his black-bean pupils to determine if he were lying or not. But there was no life in his eyes, so no reading them. She watched his hands for signs of clenching or cutting himself with his nails. She watched his breathing and his movements for any sign of telltale lying. But there was nothing to read in this man, nothing in his body language, eyes, tone or stance. The system had taught him well. He was as zombielike in this dream as he had been in the actual interrogation.

"I was very popular when I was in prison," Daryl said. "Three women wanted to marry me."

"Really?"

"Started out as pen pals. They all proposed marriage. They wanted me to impregnate them, to have my child."

I can see why, Jessica thought. "Daryl, have you been in contact with any of these women since leaving prison?"

"Of course, the ones who're alive." His grin proved satanically grim.

"One of them died in Richmond, one in Winston-Salem, the third in Jacksonville, Florida."

Jessica started in her sleep, her body involuntarily tensing and releasing, waking her in the process. She knew on awakening that her every instinct insisted that Cahil's confessions—both in *real* time and in *dream* time—were lies. Cahil was indeed *not* the Skull-digger. Some part of him *wanted* to be the Skull-digger, but that hardly qualified him as the killer.

That left one of his Web-page visitors, one who had forwarded the brain piece to Daryl. His contributors literally numbered in the hundreds of thousands over a decade. It would be a grueling and time-consuming search, necessitating cooperation among hundreds of agents and from Cahil's Internet server.

If Combs could find a link between the Manning girl from her computer in Florida to Cahil's website, Jessica felt hopeful that they could get a court order to open up the Internet server's records. Short of that, as J.T. said, they'd have to rely on the hacking skills of their Cyber Squad. She tried to fall back asleep on that hopeful thought, but a phone call awakened her.

"Dr. Coran . . . Agent Owens in Morristown."

"Agent, what is it?" She glanced at the clock which read 11:43 P.M.

"Thought you'd like to hear it from us first."

"Don't tell me. They found a woman's body at Cahil's place?"

"No . . . sorry . . . bad news about Max Strand."

"What? What's that?"

"Max was . . . he was killed sometime yesterday in a park a few blocks from Cahil's house. He . . . he was bludgeoned to death by a pair of homeless guys in the park. They're in custody, ratting each other out."

"Oh, my God."

"But Max did something strange just before he died. Thought you ought to know about it."

"What's that?"

"He made off with one of the cat brains from Cahil's freezer."

"Made off with it? What the hell do you mean? Made off with it?"

"Took it with him . . . to the park. He cut it open there and kinda . . . kinda, I don't know, threw it around. All of the brain pieces were scattered, as if . . ."

Jessica tried to picture it. "As if he were searching for something?"

"Yeah . . . yeah, that's what it looked like. Strange as hell."

Searching for something like the Island of Rheil in humans? she wondered.

Jessica further wondered what this might mean. How many people are to be infected in one manner or another with Cahil's dangerous notions? She thanked Owens and said good night, and somehow the aloneness and the night became larger tenfold.

TEN

I am dying of thirst by the side of the fountain.

—CHARLES D'ORLEANS, 1391–1465

JOHN Thorpe had tried to relax on his flight back to Quantico, Virginia. He had made mental notes on what he'd found on Cahil's website. He thought that many of the E-mail visitors to the Cahil Web page sounded like teens and preteens at play, getting a kick out of the zaniness of it all. But then many others sounded truly psychotic. Teenybopper or psychotic—a hard distinction to make in real life much less in cyberspace. He chuckled.

J.T. knew Jessica would want him to create a watch list from the countless numbers on the page's history, but that could take a month or more of full-time work to compile, and even when finished, it would only be a list of coded names. He wondered how they could get at the truly *disturbed* among all the hits. He had no way of telling from this end if any of the Digger's actual victims had logged on; nor had he any way of learning who the Seeker was without help from the online server, a difficult thing to get.

His flight back to Quantico with the computer safely stowed away had given him time to rest and contemplate how to best handle the niggling problem. He decided he would have to split the task among a small army of computer adepts who could weed out the actual crazoids from the youngsters at play, given certain key words to use as cross references.

To date, however, he was unsure what those words might be, but he knew the expert linguists with the bureau could help out there. They knew the jargon of the day and what kids would be speaking as opposed to a disturbed adult. J.T. had already looked closely at those Web contacts who strongly agreed or disagreed with Cahil's bizarre notions. Anyone doing so vehemently either way might well prove fixated on the strange arguments Cahil routinely put forth. He had also noted that anyone fixated would likely pump out reams to argue for or against Cahil's beliefs. The sheer length and breadth of the messages on the bulletin boards and in the chat rooms by the same user must prove a useful guide as well. The Seeker had a great deal to say, and he sounded somewhat sophisticated by comparison to others J.T. had looked at, but he was by no means the only Web visitor who looked like a candidate. In fact, there were many, and Thorpe had only scratched the surface.

He wanted to get the process underway as quickly as possible even before he'd spoken to Jessica. To that end, he had contacted Eriq to get him back to Quantico as fast as possible. J.T. had met the private jet at the Morristown airport, and they had wheeled Cahil's computer on board. Then en route to headquarters, he got a phone call from Santiva saying they were certain that Cahil was the Digger. After that, Thorpe had relaxed the idea of working so hard to crack the computer problems facing him. He started breathing a bit easier.

"You know what strikes me, Eriq?" asked J.T. over the phone from the plane.

"What's that?"

"The numbers—the sheer numbers of people in the world so bored as to want to spend time with Cahil's rant-ings."

"Manson had the same kind of worldwide following on his site. And all his reams of news to his constituents was one long stream of consciousness, all of which read as lunatic rantings. Still they came."

"If you write it, they will come?"

Santiva laughed in response.

"So, how did Cahil react when you guys put that brain tissue in front of him? Did he freak out?"

"Hardly phased him. He says it was sent to him by a fan on his website. Says he held on to it for us, as evidence against the guy, but we think the 'other guy' is another of his identities. He's got this schizo routine down pat."

"I will need computer experts to help dissect the hard drive."

"As much as we can spare or dig up. Don't worry, some-thing will be done. I want you to bury this freak, John."

J.T. said goodbye and then dozed off. He awakened in what seemed minutes when the plane touched down at Quantico. He had barely gotten settled in at the lab with the confiscated computer when Jessica telephoned. He was amazed at the disparity in how each of the two—Chief San-tiva and Jessica—had characterized the Cahil interrogation, and obviously, they were going off in separate directions. He worried about getting caught in the crossfire that would likely result. Both of them were more than colleagues, they were friends.

And now his friends were clearly at odds over just what was gained from today's interrogations.

He knew from experience that when the lead investiga-tors saw everything so differently as this, the momentum of the case would suffer. *Keep your head down*, he told himself as he got off the line with Jessica.

Valdosta, Georgia
Late that same night

GRANT Kenyon cruised the deserted streets of late-night Valdosta, finding nothing of interest to Phillip. He had stopped at a hotel earlier and had used their computer to make contact with Cahil's website, but for some unaccountable reason he could not get through. He wondered if anything had happened to Cahil. He wondered if he dared try to get through on his own laptop, fearful it could be traced if authorities had apprehended Cahil and his computer.

Now he drove around the too-small city of 42,000. He felt exposed here; everybody in this town must be a local. Still, Phillip wanted him to persist, and so he did. Cruising on. Looking for an opportunity. He had failed with a local Valdosta girl with whom he'd made contact through Cahil's website. She had failed to show up. Not uncommon in the computer-dating scene, as evidenced by several occasions when he had been stood up.

As he drove, Grant Kenyon thought of his days in medical school, which had fed his fascination for the brain. He thought of how Professor Dobson had spoken so reverently of the mind and brain. The man's words still resonated in Grant's brain.

"Lying below the exterior folds of the cerebral cortex, deep within the cerebral hemispheres, at the border of the brain stem, you will find the limbic system—five hundred million years old. It controls the instincts to flee or fight, to eat or drink. It represents the first swelling of the spinal cord to create the primitive brain, which also controls the emotional areas with senses of pleasure and displeasure."

"And Cahil wants to suggest that this primitive center is the home of the soul. Foolish idea, indeed," Kenyon said aloud to the empty cab of his van as he drove onward to his next destination. He had turned from the Carolinas for Valdosta, heading south.

As he cruised in search of a victim for Phillip, Dr. Grant Kenyon thought of his past life at Mt. Holyoke Memorial Hospital in the New Jersey suburb of Holyoke. He thought of how back in 1990 he had become obsessed with the Cahil case as it appeared in the papers month after month; and how after the trial, pretending to be a reporter, he had bribed a court bailiff and paid dearly for a copy of the trial transcripts to learn every detail, including precisely what Cahil had confessed.

He got in touch with Cahil by writing him, using a PO box for replies. He had learned of Daryl's website early on, becoming one of its most frequent visitors.

He soon lost interest in all else.

He thought now of how he had lost his job back in Holyoke. The resident pathologist, he had often been called upon by local law enforcement to perform routine autopsies to determine cause of death in suspicious or unknown circumstances. He had been involved in such a matter when he convinced a young intern, Dr. Mitchell Erdman, that he could finish the job himself. With the rotation of interns Kenyon worked with, he'd had no problem in the past with removing the brains of such victims and stuffing the craniums with gauze and cotton. He had gotten away with two years of such brain feedings, and the evidence was—so to speak—well buried. Kenyon had enjoyed feeding on the brains of freshly dead victims brought to his morgue.

But one night, while in the process of re-stuffing the head and replacing the forehead bone, Kenyon was surprised when Dr. Erdman returned unexpectedly. Pushing through the door at a wild, energetic pace, Erdman found Kenyon stuffing a dead man's head with anything but the earlier-removed gray matter. The brain itself lay on the weighing scale, registering at three and a half pounds.

"Dr. Kenyon? What're you . . . what're you doing with Mr. Allandale?"

Caught in the act, Kenyon stuttered, "I need more time with the brain, have more tests to run . . . more than I can possibly complete in the time allotted. Family wants the body like yesterday. No way they'll know the brain isn't intact, and we're not going to tell them, Dr. Erdman. Do you understand?"

"Ahhh . . . I suppose, so long as it's in the protocol as part of the necessary procedures. Still . . . it seems highly unusual, Doctor."

"We don't want to alarm the family, but we must know the truth. It's our duty to find the exact cause of death, and as yet, we have only suppositions and unknowns."

"Still, it seems highly—"

"It's not! I mean, it's not so unusual as you might think. Happens at times, Erdman. Here, in my files, I'll show you another case where exactly the same thing happened six or seven months ago."

Kenyon worked hard to find the file he had mentioned, and he went to a lab table with it. "Here . . . have a look."

Dr. Erdman read it over; indeed the procedure involved holding on to a woman's brain after the rest of her had been sewed up, returned to the family and cremated. "What did you eventually do with what was left of the woman's brain?" asked Erdman.

"Went out with all the other medical waste."

"I hope it helped you to understand why she died."

"Tumor was found, yes. It's all there."

Erdman read on. "Buried so deep that none of the technology could locate it?"

"Deep in the fissures. Took slice after slice to locate it. Changed death from unknown source to undetected brain tumor. Made a great deal of difference to the family in the long run. Medical claim was settled for quite a tidy sum."

Erdman examined the autopsy file for a Mrs. Georgia Bhrett and nodded. "And you have the same feeling about Allandale?"

"Exactly. Now do you understand?"

"Why not lay it out for the family; get them to wait?"

"I'm not a medical examiner or coroner, Doctor," countered Kenyon. "I don't have the kind of muscle to require the family to submit to my wishes on the matter. We're just small city hospital pathologists here."

"Gotcha, yeah . . . Look, I just wanted to know if you'd like to go to a ball game."

"Football game?"

"I've got two tickets and can't make it, and I know you like the game, so . . ."

"That's decent of you, Erdman, but it won't win any brownie points when your quarter review comes up."

Erdman had nervously laughed at this. "I only meant . . . I mean, I didn't mean for you to read anything like that into . . . It's just a simple—"

"Just kidding Erdman . . . just kidding, my friend. Thanks for the tickets. Just leave them on the table there. They're much appreciated."

Erdman looked from the table to the scale for a final glance at Allandale's brain. "Amazing thing, the brain," he said.

"Yes, very extraordinary . . ."

"What's the next step for Allandale's?"

"On ice, of course. Have to freeze it before I can cut into slices for the microscope."

"Yes, of course. Well, I'm off. Have to catch up with Sandy."

Kenyon gave his intern a perfunctory wave. "I'm almost finished here myself. Have a good night."

Kenyon thought he'd covered himself well, but weeks later, he was called to the administrative office, where he faced the chief of staff and the chief of surgery. Both Whitehead and Bondesen went ballistic over Erdman's allegation that Dr. Kenyon was practicing some unspeakable act on Allandale's brain. They wanted to know what he had done with the brain, and they had protocol files on both Allandale and the female patient, Georgia Bhrett, that Erdman had snuck out from the morgue. The story regarding insurance claims for both proved bogus. Never one capable of thinking fast on his feet, Kenyon told his superiors that with Halloween approaching, he had made off with the brain to use at a local YMCA haunted house, and that it had proved extremely successful. "So successful in fact that someone stole it."

This made his superiors wince.

"That still leaves the woman's brain," said Bondesen. "That was around Easter. You didn't take it to the Y for Easter, did you?"

"All right . . . all right . . . I've been doing some research on the side. I'm on the verge of isolating cells I believe that might have something to do with the Lupus disease."

A red-faced Whitehead replied, "Do you have any idea at what risk you have placed this hospital, Dr. Kenyon? And for what? Whether a Halloween prank or secretive research projects, you put us at great jeopardy indeed.

Kenyon pleaded, "It was the only way I could get more

hands-on experience with the brain. I have long wanted to specialize in the brain." It was an explanation they at least accepted as less outrageous than the ones coming before.

Kenyon, placed on low-level scut work usually reserved for internists, could perform no autopsies until the matter was reviewed. Two weeks later, a review board found Kenyon's medical ethics and conduct in question. None of them knew exactly what Kenyon was guilty of, but they didn't like the ideas and assumptions that sprang to mind. They didn't like the idea of unnecessary surgery, even on a dead man. Still, in the end, they gave Kenyon the benefit of doubt, that he was, as he'd said, attempting to learn more. All the same, they couldn't condone such behavior. He was quietly removed and found himself unemployed.

He could not explain to his wife how it had come about. He could tell no one what had happened to old Mr. Allandale's brain, because he didn't fully know himself. Only one person knew the complete story, the voice inside his head, Phillip, who had fed on previous corpses for their brains for a long time. To cover himself, Kenyon had created the false autopsy protocol for Mrs. Georgia Bhrett in the event someone like Erdman should stumble onto Phillip's activities.

Unable to continue in his normal life, with no one to speak to about such matters, he turned once again to the computer website that encouraged his bizarre cravings. It was only there that he could feel at ease.

And now even that was cut off to Grant and Phillip. Had he been re-arrested? This time as the Skull-digger? If so, and the authorities believed him guilty—and that they'd put an end to the terror—there was no one now to contact. No one to send any more treasures to, as he had with the island of tissue dug out of his first victim in Richmond—a present to Cahil, one that would incriminate him. Apparently, it had worked.

Grant knew now that he should end his career as the Skull-digger. Disappear and let Cahil take the rap for the four murders he himself had committed. At the same time, he wondered how Phillip would react to such a conclusion. He knew the answer: His other self—*Phillip*—would not allow it to end. Not for long. Not for anything.

Valdosta was closed up, silent. Nothing and no one about the darkened streets. He thought of going back to the hotel but then thought better of it. He needed to get out of the Georgia-Florida area and onto new ground. If Phillip were to strike again, it must be in another region.

He drove on, out of Valdosta, southwesterly for I-10.

One week later

A week had passed and in that time no new victims of the Digger had surfaced, leading many in the bureau to believe that Daryl Thomas Cahil had perpetrated the murders. Lorena Combs in Jacksonville had determined that Amanda Manning indeed had been in contact with Cahil's website, a significant hit. FBI field operatives continued to work with the families of the other victims to determine if there were similar connections among the other victims.

Eriq was elated over the news, believing it the final nail in Cahil's coffin, but Jessica's doubts had only grown larger in her mind.

She knew time was running out, that the mechanisms to put Cahil away for the rest of his natural life were in motion. The cases across the southeast *wanted* closing. Jessica had pleaded for Eriq to at least keep news of Cahil's being charged as the Skull-digger out of the press. Eriq did so, despite the pressure on him to bring the case to a close and to speak to the press.

Meanwhile, a twenty-four-hour watch had been placed on Cahil's website. Those manning it were paying close attention to any new visits from the Seeker in particular, and getting none, which further solidified official thinking that Daryl Cahil was their killer.

In the meantime, Eriq and Jessica continued to interrogate Cahil, attempting to pry loose any additional information. J.T. did a little more digging at her insistence. He learned that the clock on Cahil's computer had not been tampered with, so the dates were indeed accurate, and they showed him at home and responding to E-mail at the time of the Winston-Salem and Florida murders. Not so with the Richmond killing or the Georgia one. It was frustrating as they all knew that Cahil could have responded to his own E-mail from any terminal.

"We need more time, Eriq," Jessica continued to plead.

"All right. We'll hold him on the animal-cruelty charges and hold off announcing that he is the Digger," agreed Eriq. "For now we make him out to be someone who surfaced as eating animal brains. But the clock is ticking on this, people."

Jessica knew he was annoyed with her, but she imagined Cahil would be far more annoyed when he learned he was being booked for animal-cruelty charges for the time being, rather than as the now-infamous Skull-digger.

Jessica knew that if news of Daryl Cahil's arrest for the killings went public—making Cahil guilty by default— then the real killer could easily fade away, *unless he could not control his urge to kill and eat.* Meanwhile, Jessica learned that Cahil himself was trying to get the word out that he was the Skull-digger. Cahil was enjoying the idea of celebrity nowadays—standing in for the most-wanted man in America. She imagined he would plaster his cell at the asylum with news accounts of his horrid deeds once the story on *him* broke.

Eriq had phoned her about Daryl's latest episode. "Through his lawyer, Cahil is fighting to obtain one of his plaster-cast brains and a supply of noodles, claiming his *need* as a religious ritual that he should be allowed while incarcerated."

"Give him all of his goddamn toys. I'm done with him, Eriq."

With Eriq holding back the will of the agency against her, with nowhere to turn, she had enlisted others to her cause, beginning with J.T. Together they poured over the computer history of log ons. They dismissed single hits and concentrated on repeated hits, isolating the larger numbers in hope that the computer server would soon be made to turn over records. Primary among their targets was the Seeker who was logged on near two of the crime scenes just before or after the kills were discovered. He communicated through public-access computers, all of which were within 150 to 160 miles of the kills.

From all the log-on names and E-mail addresses, they created their list of possible suspects. It numbered in the thousands and had to be refined down.

AOC, America On Cyberedge, was the Internet server, but getting such a fringe Internet server to cooperate by allowing the FBI access to so many files proved useless without a special search warrant that named the suspect or suspects in question. It was as Strand had predicted, a catch-22. Even the federal judges Jessica had spoken to and pleaded with wouldn't go near it—right to privacy—unless the FBI could prove a state of *imminent danger* to substantial numbers of people existed. And with word getting around law-enforcement circles that Cahil was in custody, it had proven impossible to find a judge who believed any danger still existed.

The search-warrant request had to be amended to make a case for the FBI's need of a watch list being created from Cahil's website for *future* possible crimes against humanity. One old federal judge went so far as to tell Jessica, "Sorry, but I can't justify opening private records of hundreds of thousands of citizens to FBI scrutiny on the basis of a single victim in Florida having logged on to this man's website. Nor on the supposition of future possible criminal suspects. Especially since, as I understand it, you have this man in custody for the murders anyway."

"But, Your Honor—" Jessica began to protest.

"Not on the basis of one person using this site, can I open everyone's lives to your agency. We have trampled on enough civil liberties for a decade in allowing you people access to combat terrorism. Now you want the same latitude for murder cases?"

Finally, news of her failed attempts had gotten back to Eriq who marched into Jessica's ready room, where a row of computer experts worked on Daryl's website, while others worked phones and files. The walls were plastered with photos of the victims, names, dates, times and places. Maps with pins in them spoke of the geography of the crimes.

"I'm shutting you down, Dr. Coran," Eriq announced to her and all the assembled people. "It's time you cease and desist from any further investigation of this case. We're going with Cahil as the Digger. He'll be indicted this afternoon."

Jessica shook her head. "You've got to give us more time."

"It's over, Jess. I've taken hell from everyone above because it's taken this long to indict Cahil on more than dog-and-pony crimes."

Then the phone rang. It was from the FBI field office in Mobile, Alabama, an agent named Ben Lowery. There authorities had found a floater in the water with her head cut open and her brain removed.

As she listened to the words, Jessica's insides fell. She had known this call was coming; she had braced for it. She knew it would prove her right, but she felt horrible in the bargain.

She turned on the speakerphone here in the task-force ready room, and she asked, "Agent Lowery, would you mind repeating what you just said to my team?"

Lowery did so to a solemn audience.

"Keep the scene intact until my team arrives. Don't disturb a thing. We'll be there as soon as possible." She then hung up and stared at the small group that had been left to pursue the case.

"Well, so much for Cahil as the Digger," said J.T., summing up everyone's initial reaction.

"A hollow victory." Jessica's gaze immediately met Eriq Santiva's.

Eriq looked as stricken as anyone. "Be out of here to Mobile within the hour. I'll make arrangements."

Shortly after, Jessica and John Thorpe were on their way to an FBI jet bound for Mobile, where Jessica recalled Santiva's words to her, "If it does indeed prove the work of the same killer, with Cahil behind bars, I promise you one thing. I will personally go back to the federal court system for the warrant to get AOC to open its goddamn files to us."

JESSICA and J.T. settled into the small special transport Cessna six-seater. They taxied to the runway and, having immediate clearance, were soon racing toward the sky. Jessica loved the exhilaration of takeoff.

"If this is our guy and not some copycat, Jess," said J.T.

with an upraised hand, "then he's moved considerably west."

"Yeah . . . you're right. He worked along the east coast, now maybe he's heading southwest, changing his hunting grounds."

"If it's him."

"After all the faulty, misfit evidence, J.T., you don't honestly believe that Cahil is guilty."

"I believe that Cahil is insanely nuts."

"Agreed, which makes him an easy target to set up. I just feel it."

"Instincts?"

"Call it what you will."

"If the Manning girl was in touch with Cahil, it could mean that his other victims were as well. They could have accessed through computers other than those at home." J.T. had left the capable team of computer experts to monitor Cahil's website and continue checking on those possibilities.

"The libraries I traced the Seeker to won't allow us access either, not without a court order. Public policy."

"Yeah, I recall they pulled the same argument following the Nine-Eleven attacks."

"Might as well try to relax and get some rest," he suggested, handing her a cup of tea brewed for them.

"Thanks, and you're right." She stared out at the darkness of the never-ending sky.

GRANT Kenyon had wrestled with himself for a month before he had killed again. He knew that taking another life would risk *their* capture, his and Phillip's, a sure end to any future. But Phillip had become *insatiable*. It made no difference to him. Like a junky, all he wanted was the stuff to end his craving, and if it meant throwing away a well-orchestrated plan to implicate Daryl Cahil, then so be it, according to Phillip.

He knew all the good reasoning in the world would not stop Phillip. The geography of his brain had been divided from the day of his birth, he supposed now as he sat in a restaurant drinking coffee. It was a Cajun place in a rural town in Mississippi and they had brains and eggs on the menu as the specialty of the house. He had ordered them.

"What kind of brains are in those eggs?" he asked the rough-looking, matronly waitress, who appeared to do all the work. No one else remained in the place. It was nearly 10 A.M. and the breakfast crowd had come and gone.

"What kinda brains you looking for?" she replied.

"It says the house specialty."

"Pork brains, mister."

He nodded. "Pig brains."

"Hog brains. That OK?"

"Hogs'd mean they were full grown, adult?"

"Yes, that's right."

"OK, thank you, I'll have some. Wouldn't sit right, my eating little baby piglet brains."

"I reckon you're some kind of animal activist type, huh?"

"Actually, yes." He lied to appease the woman, who went off for his order. She seemed almost happy, he believed, because she thought she had so *penetrated* his mystique.

He laughed at the woman.

WHEN they arrived in Mobile, Jessica and J.T. rushed from the airport to the crime scene, a patch of desolate sand and weed beneath a bridge straddling Mobile Bay, where the body had washed ashore. They were met by Police Chief Randall Boyd, a short, stout man whose uniform buttons looked to be near exploding against his barrel stomach.

Apologizing for Agent Lowery's absence, Special Agent Harry Douglas of the local FBI also greeted them, informing them that a member of Boyd's deputies had been able to ID the victim already.

"Deputy Joy Kirchner," said Chief Boyd, "did some good work. She hauled in a homeless guy she saw rifling through a trunk in an alleyway near the Greyhound station. She took it for stolen. It had a picture ID in one of the flaps, and it matches our victim here, along with a library card from Linville, Tennessee. Name's Sharon Ashley." He pointed to the prone figure beneath the sheet below the bridge.

"Her ticket has her arriving from Nashville at 8:45 P.M. last night," said Agent Douglas. "She was spotted here by a fisherman at 6 A.M. this morning. My men have contacted her parents in Tennessee. She's . . . she was a runaway."

Jessica gave a moment of thought to the reason or reasons the girl might have run away and straight into the waiting hands of the Skull-digger. She wondered if some of the girls had been lured to their deaths via the Internet, or if the killer routinely staked out bus stations for his prey.

"She was from a rural town fifty or sixty miles from Nashville, where she caught the bus to Mobile," Boyd informed them. "Word is, she had no relatives in Mobile, so no one knows who she met at the station—if anyone."

"Authorities up in Nashville," began Agent Douglas, "say she spent all her free time at the library in her hometown of Linville, but the damned library will not give the authorities a look at the girl's E-mails. They'll only do it if ordered by a court."

"Then let's get one!" shouted Jessica, frustrated by the dead ends.

"It's in the works," replied Douglas.

J.T. and Jessica now stepped closer to the covered body

and Agent Douglas said, "She's just a kid, younger than the other victims."

Boyd said, "Parents are driving down."

Agent Douglas then said, "Most awful sight I've seen in my thirty years with the bureau." With that he removed the sheet covering the corpse. Staring down at yet another mask of mutilation, Jessica felt a wave of weary sadness envelop her. She turned away for a moment, gathering her courage, wondering anew how anyone could so brutalize another human being.

J.T., meanwhile, gritted his teeth and clenched his jaw and fists. Jessica, shaking off her emotions as best she could, went to work. J.T. followed her stoic lead.

She pulled out a tape recorder and spoke into it as she examined the body. After reciting the date, locale, name, race and approximate age of the victim, Jessica added, "Again a young woman, this time still in her teens, staring back, vacant-eyed, vacant of forehead, vacant one brain." Overhead noise from a number of fighter jets reminded them of how close the Pensacola Naval Air Station stood.

"Maybe some creep from the base," said Boyd.

The bridge overhead lay down a dense shadow over the body, like a thick paint stroke. Jessica took out her penlight and shone it into the open cavity of the cranium, searching for the symbol at the back of the skull.

"Is it there?" whispered J.T.

She breathed deeply, her forehead creased with confusion. "No . . . no it's not."

"Then it may not be him. It could be—"

Boyd supported J.T.'s stance. "Maybe it's some lunatic on shore leave from one of those gunboats out there." He pointed out at the huge, horizontal buildings along the other shore—naval ships, battleships.

J.T. whispered, "Maybe it's a copycat killing, Jess."

She disagreed. "No, it's him, all right, the same hand at work. Microscopic analysis of the bone cutting will tell us for certain, but I just *feel* it's him."

"But the fact there's no mark inside the skull . . ."

"Other than that, it's exactly him. He wants us to *think* it's a copycat killing, by leaving something crucial out. He couldn't help himself. Don't you see, John?"

"It's just another way to throw us off, make us think he's not at work here, you think?" replied J.T. "But if he wanted to do that, why precision cut the brain out? Why not use a goddamn ax?"

"Something tells me if we look microscopically at the lines and cuts, we will find the identical hand at work here, identical saw striations against the bone, J.T." She took a rag and a solution from her bag and wiped the wounds of blood. "Now look, here and here," she added, pointing at the red marker lines about the cut bone. "Same emphasis to the left."

"Without lab confirmation, you can't know that it's the same hand at work here, not for certain, Jess."

"I know it in my bones, J.T."

"Take your bones to a courtroom. Look, what're you going to tell Eriq? About the missing signature mark on the inside base of the skull?"

She failed to answer J.T. directly. "Look at her—the victim's wounds are identical in every other measure. Down to the binding marks at the hands, feet, throat and head. It's the work of the same man, using the same equipment. I'd stake my professional reputation on it."

"But Santiva will want to know about the mark inside the cavity. If it's there or not, before he issues that warrant request. What are you going to tell him?"

"That it's the work of the same man."

"That's risky, Jess. You're putting your—or should I say *our* careers on the line, lying to a superior."

"Regardless, John, it's our chance to get the federal order we need against AOC. Look, you've got nothing to do with this decision. It's all mine. As far as you know, I told you the mark was found."

Police Chief Randall Boyd and Agent Douglas had stepped off and were conferring together. Boyd now sauntered in his bowlegged fashion back over to their conversation, asking, "Well? Is it the work of the same guy as over in Jacksonville and Savannah?"

"It is," Jessica firmly replied. "Victim number five."

Boyd eased off and now Agent Douglas joined them, saying, "I took the liberty of contacting Jacksonville, courtesy you know—let them know we have another brain snatching."

Boyd pulled out a sketch of the suspected killer, a composite made up of two possible witnesses now, the Fayetteville woman and the street beggar. "The sketch looks nothing like that creep you have locked up in Virginia, that Cahil guy," said Boyd.

"How do you know what Cahil looks like?" she asked Boyd.

"Douglas here had a likeness of him."

"Is that true, Agent Douglas?" she asked the field agent.

"There was an old press picture of him from his first trial. Everyone's assumed he's the Skull-digger, so our office had the pictures made up."

"For what possible reason?"

"Public relations, to show that the FBI got their man, but now it appears it isn't so."

"Yeah, I'd say any case against Cahil has been blown out of the water with poor Sharon here," she replied.

"So, Dr. Coran, what advice do you have to offer?" asked Boyd.

"He has never struck in the same place twice, so he's likely on the move already, most likely heading due west, on I-10. I'd like you to alert all law enforcement due west that the Skull-digger may be in their jurisdictions in the coming days, maybe hours."

"Unless he's reversed himself," suggested Boyd.

She ignored this, adding, "Forward this suggestion with the artist sketch and description of the van he uses. And please don't confuse the witness sketch with Cahil's photo."

"Sounds like a good idea."

Jessica then got on her cell phone and contacted Eriq. "It's his work, Eriq. I'd stake my career on it."

"Then a renewed request for a federal warrant to get AOC to open up Cahil's lists is on its way."

"We'll need more manpower to make contact with all of the John Doe's contacting that Web page of Cahil's. Can you get us the help we need?"

"OK . . . you told me so. I'm heading to court, and I'm keeping your team together. That's the best I can do right now. I've got personnel stretched to the limit on other cases, and there's been another bomb explosion on a college campus that we're tracking down."

"I need more manpower, Boss."

"I can give you half of your Behavioral Science Unit on a part-time rotation, but I can't promise any more . . . not at this time."

"I have an idea. What if we just seek a warrant for this guy calling himself the Seeker, Eriq?"

"Gamble on the say-so of Cahil?"

"If it's him, the Skull-digger, then it will have paid off."

"And if it isn't? You might speed up the process to a dead end."

"Scale the warrant down to this guy alone, and maybe we'll get some cooperation," she countered.

"But if we're wrong about the Seeker, what are our chances of getting another warrant for all the other people on the list?"

She breathed deeply. "You're right. It's a gamble either way. We push for one breach by AOC for one individual, or we continue to push to open them all in a massive search for their whereabouts and send agents to every suspicious address."

She hung up to find J.T. in her face. "Well . . . I hope this doesn't backfire in our faces, Jess. Lying to the chief . . ."

"I didn't exactly lie. He didn't specifically ask about the symbol inside the head."

"So a lie of omission."

"I believe I'm right on this, John."

"All right," he relented. "So . . . what do we do now?"

"One thing we don't do is sit it out here until another victim surfaces. It's time we stalked this guy before he stalks and kills another young woman."

"Then it's back to Quantico and the computer trail."

"We'll turn this crime scene over to Douglas with strict instructions that the red marker and bone cuts be microscopically filmed and sent to us in Quantico immediately."

"Think Douglas will go for that?"

"You ever meet a field op who wasn't eager to have it his way?"

J.T. nodded knowingly. "Then let's explain it to him and get back to the E-trail connection."

ELEVEN

They flee from me, that sometime did me seek
With naked foot, stalking in my chamber.

—SIR THOMAS WYATT, 1503–1543

Hardscrabble, Mississippi
July 21, 2003

GRANT Kenyon lingered over breakfast, finding it not half bad with the hot coffee. He again thought of his last contact made with Cahil's website. He'd gotten through to the website, but something was up. Cahil was backed up, not answering. Perhaps Phillip's plan, as the Seeker, to implicate Cahil was actually unfolding. Maybe Daryl and his website had been busted, and he was in custody for the murders Phillip had committed with Grant's assistance. It was for this reason that Grant had argued with Phillip to stop killing, so that Cahil would be brought to trial for the deaths, and then Grant could go back to his old life in New Jersey.

However, Phillip wasn't accepting any of it, and so Grant could not help himself, or rather, he could not *stop* himself, or rather, he could not stop Phillip. And so, Phillip had again killed for the brain matter he craved, this time a young woman named Sharon. This time, he decided to throw authorities off, not marking the victim with the Rheil symbol as he had before, wanting to confuse them into thinking it a new killer, a copycat.

After the kill in Mobile, Alabama, Grant knew that Phillip had lessened his chances of ever returning to a normal life. The authorities were probably closing in, as indicated by Cahil's absence. While he'd seen nothing about an arrest, he knew Cahil never left his computer for long, and it had been a week without an update from him.

Before the killing in Mobile, Grant had tried desperately to explain to Phillip that they should not strike again until they had gone as far west as they could go, across the continent to California. But no, Phillip couldn't wait that long. They'd driven from Valdosta, Georgia, but had only gotten as far west as Mobile, Alabama, off I-10 when Phillip had demanded to be fed again.

From there they'd made their way to a Biloxi, Mississippi, area hotel in a crossroads patch of buildings in a place called Hardscrabble. While there, Grant arranged to have the van painted green, as he tried to plan for a future that didn't include getting caught or killed. As Grant worked out a plan—since Grant could not prevent Phillip from killing—Phillip slept.

From California, he planned to go north after perhaps three or four feedings. As he moved north, Phillip could continue feeding. Once he got to Washington, he'd turn east and go back across the continent on a northerly track, again taking some time off from feeding to throw authorities off. He would continue to move and Phillip could feed as they went.

Still sitting at the table in the restaurant, his brains and eggs long finished, he opened a single sheet of paper with the names and addresses of people who had confided in him their real-time addresses, people he had chatted with on Cahil's website. Four of the names had been marked off, and now he marked off a fifth. He had rendezvoused with only two of them, three others had refused to meet, but he had learned of their addresses because they trusted him. He told them he would help them get a fresh start. Each one was in a troubled relationship or was having difficulties at home with parents. He sent them bus tickets and timetables where to meet him. He told them his name was Phillip. There was always the chance that one of them would use the tickets he'd forwarded. He'd also struck up an online friendship with males, and one lived just north of New Orleans. Grant had chatted online with this fellow for more than a year, knowing him only as Mr. SquealsLoud on the computer, but he had given Grant his real name and address. Now Grant and Phillip knew him as Dr. Jervis Swantor and they knew he lived at a marina outside New Orleans. Swantor had said he'd be in Florida sometime this month as well, but Grant and Phillip had found themselves too busy and they'd missed the agreed upon date, and when Grant had checked at the marina in Jacksonville, it had been crawling with cops.

As Grant continued to kill time in Hardscrabble, Mississippi, waiting for the paint to dry next door, he gave thought to Swantor.

Dr. Swantor had claimed to be in complete agreement with Grant against Cahil's notions on how to properly go about finding the cosmic eternal mind. After a while, Grant felt comfortable with Swantor, that they were of a like-mindedness he felt with no one else. Missing him in Florida had been disappointing, but Swantor had also said he'd be returning to New Orleans immediately after. Perhaps Grant and Phillip should look the man up.

Still, Grant wasn't certain he could trust Swantor or anyone else, for that matter, with the dark secrets he and Phillip shared.

Grant put Swantor out of his mind for now. He instead focused on the garage owner. He had promised to pay the elderly man twice what the man asked for in an effort to keep him quiet about the van and Grant ever having been there.

He next returned to thoughts about his plans for California. It was a grand scheme his mind had devised and fixed upon, but already it was undermined by Phillip. Still, there was no dissuading Phillip, not anymore, not once he set his mind—their mind—to feeding.

All night long, Grant had lain in a state of dormancy, like a moth, sleeping as if cocooned up. Still, while his body had shut down, his mind raced headlong, planning his next move, wondering if Biloxi had a Greyhound station or a train station, certain it must have one or the other or both most likely with all its gambling casinos, advertised on every other billboard sign along I-10 in this and adjoining states.

Grant had found Sharon, Phillip's latest victim, at a bus station. Runaways. They made easy targets, but the kills would have been impossible without his van. If he hadn't had his van in Mobile, he wondered how he could possibly have handled the girl. He had expected everything to go smoothly, since he had assurances from a *Bolinda* that *she* was on her way. She lived close to Mobile, only a short bus ride away, she had confided. They had first met in Cahil's chat room and subsequently she had given up her E-mail address to him. She had been intrigued by him, she'd said on more than one occasion.

It turned into a long wait.

She wasn't on the bus she'd said she would be on. He waited for the next one. He had spent a suspicious hour in and around the Greyhound station, when finally a young woman got off a bus coming in from Nashville.

No one at the station hailed her or went near her, as others found their loved ones. This one stood apart, alone and vulnerable, like the last gazelle at a watering hole.

She looked the part he had planned for her: young, naïve, frightened and hungry. No one paid any heed when he went up to her and said, "Bolinda? Is that you?"

The young woman glared at him, not surprisingly. "No, my name's not Bolinda. You're looking for someone else."

"It's me, Seeker." He didn't flinch. Instead, he offered her a meal and a place to stay for the night, along with any drugs she might like.

She stared back at him, her eyes wide. "I'm not Bolinda, and no, I don't think so."

"Well, whoever you are, you can't stay on the streets. A pretty girl like you? You'd be dead by morning."

"Get away from me, you creep," she said, the words echoing about the room.

He looked up and raised his shoulders to anyone who might be staring, mimicking a lover's quarrel.

"I only want to help you."

"What're you? The local pimp?"

Grant thought of how he pimped for Phillip. "I'd only do that for you if you chose to, if you wanted to make money. I wouldn't force you into it."

"You've got some nerve. You've got to be kidding," she replied.

"Just stay the night. There's other girls you can get to know. They'll tell you I never hurt so much as a fly, and that I only want what's best for them."

"I'm sure you have them all well trained."

"Well fed and well trained, and they get whatever they want."

She stared at him, studying his features.

"Just stay the one night, and by morning, you can make your decision."

"You say you've got some drugs?"

"I do."

"What kind?"

"Any kind, anything you want, sweetheart, for the taking . . . for now. Here, let me carry your bag. I'm parked just around the corner outside."

She sheepishly followed. He confidently walked ahead of her, taking charge, asking, "If you're *not* Bolinda, what is your name, sweetheart?"

"Sharon."

"Nice name. Nice."

"Who's Bolinda?"

"Someone who stood me up."

In a moment, they stood at the rear of his van, and he placed her bag on the curb. He opened the rear door on the black interior while she stood beside him, gauging the wisdom of her decision. He could feel her thinking, it was like a pulsing beam coming off her cranium. She was young and filled with a powerful energy, he decided. It was an energy Phillip craved.

As he opened the door with one hand, he grabbed and shoved her head into the metal with the other, knocking her into submission and jamming the needle into her arm. She slumped into his arms.

"Everything OK here?" asked a Latino street beggar with his hand out.

Grant hefted the girl inside, lifted her bag and told the street man that he could have it and its contents. This gesture both stunned and pleased the beggar, who marched off quickly with the girl's things.

Grant then secured Sharon's extremities and head. He wisely locked the rear doors and climbed into the driver's seat, going for the secluded place beneath the bridge that he had earlier scouted for the work. Phillip later told Grant that he believed Sharon was sent to them, and that she had more soul in her head than Bolinda would ever achieve.

Reliving it here over coffee and the remnants of his late breakfast, Grant tried to recall the moment of touching that cosmic universal soul that Phillip had so guaranteed him. Phillip described it in beatific terms and was filled with excruciating happiness over it, but Grant had to be told about it, as by then he was no longer in the van. The operation was Dr. Grant Kenyon's doing, but the feeding and subsequent feelings of power and ecstasy belonged to Phillip.

BEFORE leaving Mobile, Jessica had been assured by Agent Douglas that an alert on their killer there would go out. Unfortunately, the description of the van he used was a match for millions like it. Still, Douglas assured her that he would ask cities and towns dotting the map along I-10 west of Mobile, Alabama, to be on heightened alert for anything looking suspicious.

She and J.T. had talked about their next strategy during the plane trip back to Quantico.

"Listen, J.T., before Daryl Thomas Cahil was labeled the Skull-digger, the FBI had amassed 6,511 tips from the public as to the identity and whereabouts of the Skull-digger." Jessica spoke over the hum of the plane.

J.T. nodded. "Several of those tips pointed to Daryl. We had an army of agents across the nation looking into each tip, but since word Cahil got out . . . sorry, but all such tips were put in a holding pattern."

"According to Jere Anderson we now have a positive

DNA match between Daryl's delicacy found in Morristown and Anna Gleanson from Richmond." Jessica had checked in with the Quantico lab just before boarding.

"Which implicates Daryl even more than ever. This fact alone will be enough to cement the case against Cahil in most minds."

"Most minds haven't seen what we've seen in Mobile, Alabama. We never had the Skull-digger in custody, John. He's still at large, a lunatic who likely took cues from Cahil."

"So what's next?"

"We concentrate on the civilian tips," she told J. T.

"That's a lot of tips," replied J. T. "We'll need a miracle to jump-start this case."

Every instinct and desire was to close a case, and once closed, minds shut down as well. No one back at Quantico would welcome the news that the FBI still had no clue as to the identity of the Digger.

"I think Cahil's records—his database—are still very useful. We have to proceed under the assumption that whoever sent him that small portion of Anna Gleason is our killer. Daryl believes it to be the man who logs on as Seeker."

"I ran it through VICAP as a possible alias, Jess. Got nowhere."

"Then we run all the code names we've culled as possible leads through VICAP. See if it spits any back at us."

"We can do that, sure . . . good idea."

"I was thinking that we can do the same against all the crime tips that have gone uninvestigated because the FBI grapevine had the case, quote: 'winding to a close.' "

"Great idea . . . we'll run cross-checks on both lists."

In fact, the tips that still remained in an uninvestigated status numbered well over five thousand, with more coming in every day. Most of these unchecked tips would prove a waste of time, but somewhere in the slush pile of tips, some-one somewhere may have information vital to locating the real Skull-digger.

"Earlier we asked VICAP for *similar* crimes. This time we go back to the unsolicited tips, pursuing each only in the event of matching key words and phrases that we'll pro-gram the computer to locate, such as 'doctor,' 'brain re-moval,' 'cannibalism' and 'Rheil.' "

Jessica telephoned Eriq and, after greetings, she said, "We need to divert all the tips on the Digger case from every field office electronically to our Quantico computer."

"To consolidate them all in one place. Should've been done a long time ago, I agree."

Jessica suggested to Eriq, "We can then cross-reference them with other lists, like VICAP."

"It will take you months to run down every one of them," he countered.

"I have an idea that might save us months."

"Really?"

"Once we finally get AOC to release information on the users on Cahil's website, we cross-reference them with names provided by VICAP and the tipsters."

"That's not bad . . . not bad at all, if we can get the AOC to release the goddamn subscriber names, make a three-way match, the list can't be so long."

Jessica was speaking over him. "Then we look very closely at any three-way matchups, and—"

"We take only those crisscrossing people, and we inves-tigate each thoroughly." Eriq had a knack for making any good idea sound like his own. "Set it up. Let's do it."

Now the jet carrying them back to Quantico was circling for a landing, and Jessica could see the airport tower and the buildings of Quantico in the near distance. She saw the pleasant small town of Quantico, the comings and goings of cars in and out of store lots, people busy with their lives, the marching training cadets in the FBI compound, the place looking like a cross between a military barracks and a college campus.

The sight always reminded her of the first time she'd come to Quantico as a cadet, recruited from her medical examiner job in Washington, D.C.

THE little stopover at the Mississippi grill had reminded Grant Kenyon of his childhood, devoid of color or charm, when his name had been Corey Lyttle. He had legally changed his name when he'd gone off to college, never seeing or speaking to his parents again. Growing up as the son of a farmer in rural upstate New York, his life had been filled with the raising and slaughtering of animals—chickens, sheep, goats, hogs and cattle, and the seasonal deer kill. The slaughters were always detailed and time-consuming, involving getting at the intestines and organs—the *vitals and vittles* as his father had called them. The process involved salvaging every item of the carcass, from hoof to head, including the brain.

He had grown up watching and learning and taking part in those slaughters, *so as to become a man*, as his father had put it. He recalled his callous and heavy-handed father's wielding of an ax to open the skulls of slaughtered cows, and his equally callous words: "Waste nothing from an animal, boy."

His father had had no finesse when it came to going into the cranium for the brains of the animals. He simply shoved his gloveless hands inside the cavity created by two strokes of the ax, and then he wrenched the brain free. Inside the old house, his mother chopped the animal brains into mince-meat to be used like hamburger.

When they slaughtered an animal for their own use, they fed on its every part, including the brains. His mother had recipes for cornbread and brains, brain potatoes, brain soup, brains and eggs, brain brownies even. It had started young Corey Lyttle on a lifelong taste for brains. How many times did his father repeat the words, "Listen close, boy. Them animal brains'll make you smart, and we both know you need all the smarts you can rustle up. Besides, they fill you up when nothing else will."

Now Grant had gotten back on the road, heading west, going toward New Orleans on I-10. He recalled how, as a child, he had become sick to death of brains, and once he left home he had vowed to never touch them again. He held on to that promise for many years, until he learned of the crimes committed by Daryl Thomas Cahil, and his motive for committing those grave robbings. That was the first time he'd ever heard of a physical connection between brain and soul, and it brought about the growth, development and metamorphosis of Phillip the Seeker.

He'd left home with two overwhelming urges: to become his father's opposite, and to feed his thirst for knowledge, which would keep him from ever having to return to Stark, New York. He finished high school at the top of his class and earned a scholarship to college at NYU in New York City. Far from endearing himself to his mother and father, his education only worked to further their estrangement.

Traffic now buzzed by and around Grant, while the sameness of the divided highway all around him induced boredom. A look into the rearview mirror reminded him how similar in features he was, at middle age, to his father. The same large brow, the same wrinkles in exactly the same places, along his jaw, about the neck, the same ears, eyes, nose even. It felt like staring at a ghost.

"Some things you can't escape from, Corey," said Phillip, the voice in his head.

"What the hell do you want?" he replied.

"What do I always want?"

He drove on.

He next thought of his wife and child, left in New Jersey to fend for themselves. Their family had been doing well up to a point, while Grant had kept his demons at bay. He'd purchased a nice house in Holyoke, a subdivision just outside Newark, and he and Emily were happy for a time, and when Hildy was born, it appeared all would be heaven and peace. He hadn't practiced any sort of brain-feeding for several years, keeping that powerful, gnawing craving at bay. On learning of Cahil in the papers, he began to follow the case, and he fulfilled his cravings vicariously for a long time by going online with Cahil's website, a secret fascination. He had even, for a time, practiced Cahil's prescription for his so-called *legal brain-feeding*. But ultimately, his urges took over, and he began to practice Cahil's first notion of eating the brains of dead people, in ready supply at the hospital morgue where he worked.

Phillip had slowly emerged and had pushed Grant to sample and feed on the bodies he would autopsy at the morgue. So he had, on occasion, sampled human brain tissue. Then he slipped up badly during the Allandale autopsy the night his problems began with Erdman and the hospital.

That night he had devoured the brain in his office, washing it down with wine.

"No doubt, Emily's put out a missing-person's report on you by now," suggested Phillip, causing Grant to jump in his seat and swerve.

"I should've faced Emmie; should've told her I needed some time alone."

Phillip sanguinely said, *"Little Hildy will soon be having another birthday."*

Grant had always felt estranged from others. His entire life had been spent in a kind of numb dullness that kept him an emotional cripple, and he felt certain that it all had to do with his mother and father, not just the upbringing but something in the poisonous gene pool they had together created. A passing road sign read:

> New Orleans—59

Today, he had climbed from bed determined to control Phillip's insatiable appetite for killing and consuming the gray matter of his victims. Now he felt the urge at every turn, as with accepting the stand-in at the bus stop in Mobile. In fact, wherever he looked nowadays, he saw a possible feeding. Phillip wasn't as choosy as he had once been.

Each new encounter now—a maid, a waitress, a clerk—any passing soul, save the decrepit and aged, would do. "What happened to your standards, your list?" he asked Phillip.

"I sense our time is running out. We've had to lower standards. That ought not to be hard for you, Grant."

"Stop calling me that."

"Shall I call you by your father's name?"

"No!"

"Huh, should I call you 'Phil'?"

"You sonofabitch," cursed Grant.

"Even if I did disguise my voice and tone, boy, you're still somewhere inside this head, boy. You had to know it was me, Corey, son."

"Shut up! Shut up! You damn demented old bastard." To drown out Phillip, he snatched on the radio and turned it to its highest level, nearly blowing a speaker.

The old couple running the restaurant had looked too much like his parents, and the old woman kept eyeballing him, as if she knew everything about him. The phone on the wall hadn't rung, and growing impatient, he had asked the old woman, "How damn much longer's your husband going to take with my van?"

She'd replied, "Saw the old man finishing up, but he's got no phone in the garage. We can only afford the one line."

"I gotta go out there and check on him, you mean?"

She nodded. "Need me a nap," muttered the old woman, a phrase she had repeated ad nauseam. She then asked him, "Just where you heading, young man?"

He had seen too much interest paid him at Lou and Lew's motel, restaurant and body shop, this mom-and-pop operation in the middle of nowhere. Using a small snub-nosed .38 Smith & Wesson, one he always kept tucked away, he leapt up and terrified the old woman. He led her to the register, opened it and tore out the larger bills.

Her arms flailing like wings, she cried out, begging, "Please, mister, take whatever you want, but please not our lives! Please!"

"Shut up," he'd shouted, a fistful of her hair now a towline as he forced her out back to visit her husband in the shop. Chickens scrambled to get out of the way, raising noise, so that the old man saw them coming. Obviously, the woman hadn't lied about the phones. He had no way of contacting help, except for his CB radio. With a shotgun in one hand, he tried to hail someone on the CB.

Unable to get anyone on the radio, the old man in overalls and paint bravely came at him with the huge shotgun, but

Grant gave him a choice. "She gets a bullet through the head if you don't drop that damned thing."

"You give her up to me, then!"

"Deal." Grant viciously pushed the old woman into him, and the old man grabbed hold of her as both went down to the earthen floor.

He forced them onto their knees, snatched all the money in a second register here, and said, "Now, you two sweethearts can take a long nap." He then put a single bullet through each head.

"It'll look like a robbery murder. Keep the locals busy," he said to the dead and to Phillip, "if we leave their goddamn brains intact."

Phillip didn't argue this time. *"Old brains carry too much disease,"* he muttered.

Grant took time to open and pour paint all over the garage and the bodies. He emptied some twelve to thirteen gallons of different colors, creating a rainbow of the place. He believed this would confuse anyone wondering about the killer of Lou and Lew's *pigsty*.

He then climbed into his now dark green rather than blue van and tore from the body shop. A lone red pickup with an old man in it was just pulling into the restaurant's gravel lot.

That had been less than two hours before, and now he saw the steeple-top skyscrapers of New Orleans coming into view on the horizon. He'd be safe here for a while, he told himself, if he could control Phillip.

Quantico, Virginia
July 23, 2003

OVER the next few days, Jessica, J.T. and their team began taking portions of the tips by state and encrypting them onto the ACC program—the Automated Cross-Check software developed specifically for such a massive search.

They began the painstaking effort of searching for common names on VICAP and other lists of known offenders against the thousands of uninvestigated tips, hoping something would shake out from the mix. Adding to the cauldron what little they knew of the killer's approximate height, weight, race and vehicle, they further reduced the possible suspects.

The process proved tedious and time-consuming, as many of the field agents worked on their own clock; the process was also hardly cost-effective as it took a great deal of time to download all the reports coming in from across the nation. In the meantime, Jessica had grown increasingly impatient for the court order to open Cahil's enormous list of patrons. The delay had everyone on edge.

Amassing the information that Jessica wanted—more than five thousand unanswered tips in the Skull-digger case—proved daunting. They were scattered over hundreds of field offices, some as far away as Oregon. However, the first dividing up was done geographically, whittling the list down from the massive pile sent in from each field operative. Naturally the southeastern states, where the killings had begun, were by far the largest in number of tips.

After working all afternoon, Jessica and J.T. took a moment's break in her office, and she began to talk about her frustrations, all of which he shared. Then the conversation turned to Cahil's patrons.

"Tell me, J.T., what is it inside people that make them so curious about cannibalism and brain eating, about grave-robbing gray matter from dead children, about a monster like Cahil?"

He sipped at a cup of cold coffee and replied, "What prompts otherwise intelligent people to open that gruesome

Web page and spend hours there? Some dark corner of the human psyche, I suppose."

She raised her own cup, drank from it, and said, "As much as we've seen over the years, I suppose we ought to be used to seeing the worst in people."

"We ought to, yes."

"But this . . . this . . . It makes me think of the scam artists who, days after the World Trade Center attacks, began bottling and boxing up dirt and debris from the rubble of thousands of lives to sell at whatever price they could get."

"A slap in the face to all decency and humanity otherwise displayed at Ground Zero."

They had embarked on a long journey, the first step in reinvigorating the investigation. They were only hours into it, knowing it would take days and a great deal of luck. And while Cahil remained in custody, and would likely stay put for some time, the real murderer remained at large. And since no other victims had been found since Mobile, a low-level buzz among the people working overtime on the case had begun. Everyone wondered if Mobile had not been a copycat killing after all.

Eriq Santiva suddenly entered the room, followed by the head of the FBI, Director Thomas Hinze. Santiva remained silent while Hinze blasted away. "I just got a copy of your DNA analysis on the brain tissue found at Cahil's residence, and it matches the Gleason woman killed in Richmond. Given the date, I'd like to know why it took so long to get to me? That's strong evidence linking Cahil to her murder, wouldn't you say, Dr. Coran?"

"Yes, it is but—"

"And I have a copy of your protocol sent to Santiva here on the last victim located in Mobile, Alabama. She didn't have the mark of this Island of Rheil thing on the backside of her skull or anywhere else. Chief Santiva here tells me that you had informed him that the killing in Alabama was the exact same MO—identical. Says he has only now learned it wasn't. What kind of games are you two playing, Dr. Coran, Dr. Thorpe?"

"Director . . . Chief, it's my report, not J.T.'s," she said, standing now to keep from cowering beneath them.

"Aren't we all on the same team here, people?" asked Hinze.

J.T. said, "I'm as much to blame as Jessica, sir. I kept silent about it, too."

"Only at my request," she countered J.T. and turned to Eriq. "Look, I know in my gut that one of Cahil's Web buddies set him up." Her tone matched her look of defiance. "You know my instincts about this kind of thing are good. That I'm good at what I do. Just let me do my job."

Santiva said, "Jess, I think you two made a grave error in Mobile."

"How so?"

With an upraised hand, Hinze stopped Santiva from answering. "This just isn't panning out, Dr. Coran. Thorpe here has monitored the Web page to no avail. We've got hundreds of agents working overtime on a *hunch*. We need to cut our losses, indict this Cahil person, and get on."

"We're in too deep for that," she countered.

"We've wasted too much time on this case, and I think it's time you came to the same conclusion, Dr. Coran."

"We're not halfway through the tips yet, Director."

"If the Skull-digger were still out there, he'd have struck again. We'd know about it conclusively. This murder in Mobile was a copycat."

"I don't think so. Our profile all along said that the Digger could not control his urge after a few days, remember?"

"Unless he's become more disciplined," suggested Hinze. "And incarceration has that effect!"

Jessica added, "What if the latest body just hasn't surfaced yet?"

"Do you two have any idea how much hot air's breathing down my neck right now?" asked Hinze. "Besides, suppose for a moment you're wrong, Dr. Coran, and you and I know you've been wrong before—"

She thought of mistakes made in Chicago that had gotten her friend and mentor, Otto Boutine, killed. She thought of mistakes she'd made in tracking Mad Matthew Matisak, and the trail of bodies he had left in his wake, and how she had almost gotten herself killed on more than one occasion.

Hinze, a tall, imposing figure, continued talking over her thoughts. "Suppose the woman in Mobile . . . that her killer goes free, this *Citizen X*—because we decide it's the work of the Skull-digger. And instead, it's just some guy using the same MO to cover his tracks!"

It had been known to happen more often than officials cared to inform the public. How many murders were tacked on to a serial killer list might even surprise a criminal judge.

"We're set on this course, Director. We are investigating another theory, that the Digger is one of Cahil's website junkies. We know his online name—the Seeker."

The director paced the room. "All right. Chief Santiva tells me you have a thing for this guy that Cahil pointed out early on. But he also tells me Cahil's page has not heard anything from the Seeker. Isn't that right? And there's a theory that the Seeker and Cahil may be one and the same. Santiva is beginning to think so, aren't you, Eriq? Tell her."

Eriq cleared his throat and replied, "That thought has been discussed, yes, but I have to stand with Dr. Coran's assessment. We need to keep the investigation open until we can follow the leads we've uncovered to a conclusion we can all live with, sir."

"We're still hopeful that we'll hear from this Seeker character when he checks in again with Cahil's page," added J.T.

"The guy who calls himself the Seeker argues that Cahil has no special knowledge of where the soul resides in the brain, argues against the Island of Rheil being of any consequence. And Cahil claims this person sent the brain tissue from Anna Gleason to him."

"Through field ops, we raided a Richmond PO box this Seeker guy used for surface correspondence, but the guy used phony identification."

J.T. then hefted a computer printout in his hands. "I did locate an interesting old letter from the Seeker to Cahil. It's about the Seeker's childhood, all about slaughtering animals on a farm, but it includes slaughtering them for their brains. He doesn't give any details as to time or place or his identity except for a first name—"

"Which is?"

"Corey," J.T. replied. "You might find it interesting if gruesome reading."

Jessica added, "I think maybe we ought to go after a discovery warrant on this guy alone, take our chances with the roll of the dice."

"Too late for that," said Santiva. "I wrote the order for full disclosure of every user." Eriq and the director now stood over Jessica's shoulder and scanned the data J.T. had handed her.

"Still we can put him at the top of the list." Jessica pushed back in her chair and tried to calm her nerves. It had appeared for so long now that no one stood with her save J.T., but she realized now that Eriq firmly backed her as well, despite his earlier doubts.

Eric and the director left, and J.T. soon followed their

lead. Left alone, Jessica stared down at the collected E-mail letters from the Seeker. She had mumbled a goodbye to J.T. but her eyes and mind were focused on the letter describing the Seeker's upbringing. "I know you're out there, whatever you care to call yourself—Seeker, Corey, Satan."

JESSICA Coran stood over a team of men and women sifting through the computers in the computer analysis section of the FBI at Quantico. She nervously paced, holding on to reams of information coming out of their new investigation. She remained anxious to get word from a judge that AOC had been made to comply with the FBI request to open up the subscriber lists visiting Cahil's website. But so far, nothing forthcoming. Everyone on the team felt stymied.

Daryl Cahil's name had come up so far as the only three-way match among the civilian tips, the VICAP program and, of course, on his own website. He remained the only known user still, and would so long as AOC continued its fight with the FBI. The court battle had brought out curious reporters, and AOC, happy with the publicity it was now garnering, wanted nothing more than to fight for the rights of their customers—to drag the publicity out. This also dragged into the light the whole story of Cahil's arrest, his website and the AOC controversy and what it had to do with the Skull-digger case. This only caused a flood of hits on Cahil's website, causing more problems for the team's monitoring efforts—adding to the nightmare.

Meanwhile, all the other users logging on remained unknowns. Cross-referencing with Cahil's website log-on code names proved useless. But they had learned that the Seeker and a handful of others had faithfully logged on for years, and that in fact, the Seeker was among the first to contact Cahil while he remained in jail.

Santiva relentlessly pursued the federal court judge to get AOC to open its files on the E-mail addressees. The result had been a long, anxiety-ridden delay. In its arguments, AOC cited that many of the log ons came from hotels and libraries, as well as private homes, and that what the FBI wanted was tantamount to invasion of privacy and against the public's right to assume they had privacy as upheld by the AOC's contract with the public.

The bad news from AOC was called in from a female representative of the company, a spokesperson. Jessica had immediately asked the AOC representative if she would at least pinpoint which users had logged on from libraries and hotels in Richmond, Winston-Salem, Jacksonville, Savannah and Mobile on specific days and nights. The representative stood firm, spouting policy, adding, "Only in the event of a terrorist attack can we lay aside the principle of privacy to our customers."

"There is a serial killer on the loose, looking for his sixth victim!"

The phone clicked dead.

Jessica had even contacted Dr. Jack Deitze, Cahil's keeper while imprisoned, and pleaded for information on anyone contacting Cahil via U.S. mail or phone before he began his website. Neither Dr. Deitze nor anyone else at the facility could help her, as records kept on U.S. mail addresses coming into the prison were not kept beyond ten years. They'd been destroyed two years before. Phone logs likewise.

FBI code-breakers continued to work on Cahil's hard drive. Meanwhile, several hundred other names had also made a two-way match-up between VICAP and civilian tips, and this formed the long list Jessica now held in her hands. She pulled a chair alongside Dana Morrill, a bright young computer aide, and she said, "Using these two-way matches as your starting point, cross the list with the words

'island,' 'isle,' 'soul,' 'brain,' 'mind,' 'doctor' and 'R-h-e-
i-l,' " she said, spelling out the last word. As an after-
thought, she added the word "butcher." She recalled that in
Cahil's pitiful little biography he had once been a butcher.

J.T. had been on a well-earned break, but now he reen-
tered the unit and saw that Jessica appeared as much in hot
pursuit of the leads as before. He came near and whispered,
"Jess, we just got a report out of a place called Hardscrabble,
Mississippi, of an elderly couple murdered at a body shop—
a freshly painted van was involved. You said we should be
on the lookout for an escalation in violent and erratic behavior."

"Where's this place located?"

"Some seventy or so miles from New Orleans. A crossroads between Biloxi and New Orleans, right off I-10. Police
are suspicious it could be our guy, since there's evidence of
a freshly redone van. Like I said, it occurred at a shop run
by this elderly couple—both shot to death. A dark green
van was seen leaving the place."

Jessica studied the report J.T. held out. "Location is
right. Could be him driving a freshly painted van since this
involves a body shop. Do we have anyone to ID the killer?"

"Negative. Witness only saw the van peeling off, headed
toward New Orleans. Word is, the guy just executed these
two—bullet to the back of each head."

"May be our guy, maybe not. He's got to be feeling us
on his heels. Look at this." She extended the computer's hits
from the keywords she'd asked for earlier. "Sixty matches."

"Wow, that many doctors on a violent-crime list and on
civilian tips at the same time? That's kind of scary."

"Wonder how many visited Cahil's chat room? Damned
AOC gets their way, we may never know."

"Eriq's back at the courthouse now, trying to get us what
we want," J.T. assured her.

Jessica turned to the computer aide. "Bring up any photos we have of our gallery of rogue doctors and butchers—see if we find any Sweeny Todds. I want to see if any of them vaguely resemble the work of the two sketch artists in Fayetteville and Mobile."

"All sixty of them?" Dana Morrill looked at her watch. It read 5:47 P.M.

THEY worked throughout the evening hours on Jessica's notion, but in every case the level of violence was ruled as entirely out of keeping with the violence done victims of the Skull-digger. Still, since there were two-way match-ups between "doctors" and "butchers," each conceivably possessing the tools and skills to remove a human brain, Jessica dispatched the information to respective field offices to investigate these doctors.

One agent complained, "We're already canvassing a list you gave us that's three times as long."

"Drop the long list. Use the short list for now. They've been identified as doctors and butchers taken from the long list. One of them might be the Skull-digger." One of them might be the Seeker, she thought.

"So, the man being detained is not the Digger?" asked an agent in New Orleans.

"Jesus. That's for the press. Official thinking, right now, is what you're pursuing, Agent."

"Damn, and we thought it was over," replied the field agent. "You know, a little more cooperation and information sharing, and a little please and thank-you, Dr. Coran, might help."

"Yeah, please and thanks." Jessica's level of frustration felt at an all-time high. She feared that anytime now the

Digger would strike again, and still no one knew his identity or whereabouts.

She called Eriq on his cell phone. No answer. She tried again. When he finally came on, he said he'd had to leave the courtroom to take the call.

"How's it going with FBI vs. AOC?" she asked.

"We're going to win this thing, but they're putting up a stubborn fight."

"We suspect the real Digger is in and around New Orleans with a newly painted van. Dark green in color. I believe we should put New Orleans on a heightened-alert status."

"How sure are you, Jess?"

"Fairly sure."

"Then consider it done."

"And how soon are we going to win the order against AOC?"

"Like I said, still in the pipeline, but I think it's finally going our way."

She replied, "Something has to."

TWELVE

I will make you shorter by the head.

—QUEEN ELIZABETH I

Downtown New Orleans
9:20 P.M.

OFFICERS Tony Labruto and Collin Doyle sat idling in their cruiser at Plymouth and Juniper, drinking coffee and eating burgers for their late dinner, when the FBI dispatch came over the radio. They had heard the news once before, at the debriefing before going out onto the streets of New Orleans. Labruto had even joked about it earlier. "Be on the look out for a newly painted dark green van. And, get this, license plate unknown—with a suspicious-looking character in the driver's seat. Suspected of killing two people in Hardscrabble, Mississippi. Oh, and suspect may possibly be the Skull-digger, but the people killed in Hardscrabble didn't lose their brains and were shot with a .38 millimeter."

"What more do you need to go on, Tony?"

"Oh, nothing I s'pose."

The cab filled with the crackle of the police radio, a pleasant feminine dispatcher's voice calling out a ten-10, disturbance at a downtown address, skirting Bourbon Street in the French Quarter. Something to do with a fight between two men over a woman.

"Hi-ho, Dispatch, this is Unit 112. We're on it," said Labruto into the mic.

"So much for dinner." Doyle moaned. "Hit it."

The lights began to spin and the siren wailed as the cruiser sped for the nearby destination. Labruto thought of his six years in New Orleans. He felt it was the finest force he had ever worked with, barring the military unit he had belonged to during Desert Storm. He liked New Orleans, the home of Cajun passions, great food, Mardi Gras, jazz and the Saints. The city had a throbbing fascination with life and lust, which suited the single cop just fine.

Doyle, on the other hand, was a family man with several children, and he missed his native home, Chicago. He was continually going on about being stuck in New Orleans. He had come here for higher rank and pay. Tony liked Collin's sense of humor and his skill with a gun, but he'd grown weary of the man's constant comparisons of how much better life in Chicago was than in New Orleans. He exaggerated his idyllic Back-of-the-Yards community and home and how wonderful everything in Chicago had been, from the food to his beloved Blackhawks, Bears, and the White Sox ad nauseam. Still, they managed to get along, and even visited the firing range together, where they competed with each shot.

As they barreled toward the scene of the incident, siren and lights roaring, Tony complained, "The city ought not to have moved Precinct Ten out of the French Quarter. We needed that presence there at all times, not just in peak seasons."

"You'll get no argument here," agreed Doyle. "Can't figure NOPD sometimes. Not like you can the Chicago police force. Even if you dislike a decision, you still understand it there, even if it is crooked politics behind it."

As Labruto approached the intersection where he intended to turn, a large van came around a corner. Taking it wide, the man's headlights and grill came face-to-face with the squad car, heading straight for them.

"Sonofabitch!" shouted Doyle.

Labruto held his breath and stirred. The weaving, shambling van, dark green in color, its headlights waving like two madmen with flashlights, almost rammed them. But at the last minute, it pulled *right* to Tony's pulling *left*. The two vehicles missed each other by inches, and Labruto joked, "Did you feel that, partner? Missed by an eyelash!"

"That was a green van, Tony!"

"Did you hear the metal constrict on my side? I didn't miss that guy, our unit dodged that last hair all on its own."

"No, Tony, that wasn't the car metal constricting to avoid a hit. The noise you heard was my stomach dodging the rest of my organs to jump out my goddamn mouth. Nothing supernatural about it."

"Same unit that saved my life three years ago, in that shootout at Nelson's Boatworks."

"Have it your way, but right now, tell me just what the hell was that flying by us?"

Dispatch came back on, calling out, "Ten-10 now a possible kidnapping. Perpetrator is on the move, heading east on Grandview, away from the Quarter in a van, no plate ID."

"Kidnapping?" asked Doyle, now on the radio. "Dispatch, this is 112. Does the kidnapping involve a green van?"

"Man on the line says *yes*. The vehicle is a Chrysler, dark green, possibly a '96 or '97 model." The dispatch officer added, "Be advised 112. The perp has a hostage and is considered to be violent, possibly armed."

Doyle reminded Labruto, "Remember the alert put out

on the Skull-digger being in a dark green van?"

"Course I do. You think it could be the guy the FBI's after?"

"It'd make us heroes. Turn this can around."

Labruto called in their location and added, "We've made visual with the van. We're in pursuit. Request backup." He added for Doyle, "We'll just see what this *can* can do."

Labruto violently twisted the wheel, turning the squad car completely around, sending up a scream of burning rubber to give chase, but as they sped up, they could see nothing. The pachyderm of a van had disappeared.

They peered down side streets as they slowed, searching for anything that resembled their prey, but it was gone. They cruised slowly for several more blocks. "How can he just disappear like that?" asked Doyle, a growing frustration coming over him.

They continued on in silence until Labruto asked, "What the fuck?"

Labruto finally said, "He's got to be heading for a safe location."

"No cheap hotels around here except for the Plaza."

"If he is the Digger, he's going to kill her in the van. Isn't that the word on the guy? How he operates?"

"That's right."

"Then he'll be looking for a remote location to dump the body."

"Old Harbor walkway, along the Miss. That's the closest deserted rat hole I can think of."

Turning off the siren and the overhead lights, Labruto eased the car around and headed back toward the river and where they had lost the van down any number of small streets and alleyways. New Orleans was dotted with small arteries, most one-way. The guy in the van could have turned down any one of them, but aside from a few vacant lots and construction sites, the broken-down Old Harbor walkway was a good guess.

They drove through the once-thriving business area, now a den of ghost saloons for long-gone and long-dead bikers. Isolated like an island amid the city palaces and pinnacles around it, the old place bordered an access street to the interstate. If the van had slipped onto the interstate, there would be no catching him without the help of the highway patrol, but they had no license plate number.

"Can't believe we lost the fucker," said Labruto.

"The interstate would be the smartest move for the guy," replied Doyle, pointing to a sign that led to the exchange.

"Who said the creep was smart?"

"If it's this brain whack-job, then he's evaded officials in what, six states already?"

Scanning ahead as they neared the interstate, they saw no one on-ramping in the grim area.

"Take the ramp! Take the ramp!" shouted Doyle.

Labruto instead pulled beneath the interstate, winding through a bevy of pylons with bridge overpasses high above, following the ancient, cracked blacktop to its end, and onto a pitted, weedy path toward the river and the old warehouse district and the wharves. Doyle, realizing that Labruto was familiar with the area, lightly joked, "So, this is where you take your dates?"

"Area's too creepy now, but yeah, in the old days."

A light silver drizzle dappled the windshield. Lights off, the cruiser rolled almost silently toward its destination, both men squinting in the darkness for their prey.

SELESE Montoya felt cold and clammy, her skin bristling, and she could not think straight. She felt helplessly tossed about like an object inside a bottle, but she felt no pain, only a dull ache against her left wrist. She felt disoriented, confused. *What is it?* she wondered. Something to do with her head, she imagined. Yes, her head, which felt like a spongy dull pumpkin. And while, from time to time, she felt a cold, weighted piece of steel against her left wrist and she heard the sound of a chain rattling, she did not connect it to the tug on her left wrist. Instead, she tried to think clearly about who she was and where she was and what had happened to her.

Her eyes—as if independent of her will—blinked, opening and closing on images passing the windshield. Images that went from dark to light, reflecting signs, telephone poles, bridges, buildings and an array of wide, staring windows.

"I wanna go home." She moaned, unsure if her words had traveled any distance beyond her tongue. In fact, the words seemed imprisoned in her head.

She only recalled having said good night to her employer at Farley's Whiskey Hole and walking out of the bar where she kept the records. She didn't serve or hustle drinks, not even from behind the bar; she didn't sell anything. She didn't sing in the band, and she didn't do floor shows. She maintained her own hours, working when she wanted on Farley's books, and she pet the cat from time to time.

She had plans to save enough money to move to California, tired of New Orleans and its tourists-crowded streets. In California, she meant to find a quiet place to live, far from any crowds.

She was alone and glad of it. Carl had proven a great disappointment in the end, and she hadn't any desire to get involved with another man, so she had kept herself immune to any overtures men made toward her. Ironically, since she had sworn off the opposite sex, they turned up everywhere.

Farley had waved good night to her from the bar, and a few of the regular stiffs shouted her name as she left. She had a small dog at home to see to. Maybe she'd pick up a treat for him on the way, along with her much-needed cigarettes and gum. *That's right. I was on my way home when something happened.*

As she'd walked the familiar streets of the French Quarter, going toward the quieter apartment area to the north, she ran through her mind for anything else she might need at the little corner store near her house. She also thought about her sister in Texas who should be having that baby soon, her third. Selese wondered if she would ever have kids. She wanted to, but not now. Not the way things were.

Her mind had wandered. She needed to concentrate on the grocery store. Something had happened at the grocery store. But she didn't know what had happened. Her senses were not communicating with her. A broom flashed back and forth in her mind's unfocused eye. Something to do with a fight, and she had been in the midst of it. How unlikely. It had to be the rantings of her dream state.

Then she saw the broom flash across her mind's eye again, but it faded with every thought, as she settled into a blank, featureless sleep of *nots*: *not* hearing the siren behind them anymore, *not* feeling any tug on her wrist anymore and *not* feeling the pounding of the van as it yo-yoed into narrow spaces. *Not* caring who sat alongside her, *not* understanding the depth of her own terror as the death van bumped and maneuvered over potholes.

GRANT still had the young woman secured in the back of the van where he had parked it behind and between dilapidated old buildings along a weed-infested backwater section of the Mississippi in the center of New Orleans. A large, verdant levy loomed over the van like a giant, sleeping dragon. He could hear boat whistles blaring in the near distance.

It had been a close encounter with authorities, too close. He thought them still in hot pursuit when he approached the interstate ramp. He had two ways to go, the interstate or the old wharf area. If they'd picked up the plate on his van, he could be spotted by other radio cars. If he drove into the backstreet area along the wharf, he would be dead-ended. It was a gamble either way. He stared ahead at the interstate ramp, but instead of taking it, he tore into the remote area that he had planned to use all along.

Things had become quiet after that. The siren that had been chasing him was silent now. He felt relatively safe that he had outfoxed his pursuers. Still, he sat for some time, listening to his drugged victim's heavy breathing, and staring out his rearview. Deciding that no one was following, he felt reasonably safe to continue with his work.

When he had first arrived in New Orleans, he had hoped to meet with a woman named Franklin, one of the contacts he'd made on the Internet, but Saundra Franklin, aka Sweet-touch had moved out, according to the landlord. Frustrated, Grant had begun cruising the old lamp-lit, famous French Quarter for a victim. When he saw the young woman who stepped from a Bourbon Street bar alone, he pulled into a side-street parking space and made his way on foot beneath the city lights to a corner store she had stepped into. Inside, he arranged to inch up to her side, and he whispered in her ear, "Hello there. My name's Phillip. I'm a professional photographer."

"Is that supposed to interest me?"

"She's perfect," Phillip said deep within Grant. *"We must have her."*

"I take shots for a new magazine called *Slinky*." He sported an expensive camera about his neck, a ruse he'd successfully used before. He handed her a card specifically created for such occasions.

"*Slinky*? Never heard of it, but the name sounds appropriate for you. What is it? Another Viagra-endorsed male hormone magazine? Is *that* supposed to interest me?"

"When I see a beautiful woman"—he tipped his Nikon at her—"naturally I think she must know the best local hot spots. That's what I'd like to photograph, the best local hot spots—and you, of course."

"I'm not interested, and I'm not that beautiful."

"Oh, but you are beautiful."

"You men. Do you really think lying is a turn on?"

"Look, I'd pay you well."

"I have a job."

"Working for minimum wage?"

"That's none of your business."

"Look, I'm new in the city and—"

"Do you ever need a new line."

"—and I don't know where to begin to find someone to show me around, to party, you know? I can see you know your way around." He dared not tell her he'd been watching her since she stepped out of the bar on Bourbon Street.

"I am not that someone," she firmly told him.

"Of course, as I said, I can pay you well."

She hesitated a moment. "So you said, but I am not interested." She was interested, if the pay helped her get out of New Orleans, but she didn't want him to think her over-eager.

"When I say party, I mean with some good stuff, sweetheart."

"Oh? Really?" She showed a moment's interest, purchased her things, conversed with the grocer who had been staring at the two of them, listening to their talk.

Grant followed her out the door and onto the street, where she finally acquiesced. "I might like to make a purchase from you, but that is all."

"A purchase, sure . . ."

"And that is all. We exchange goods, and you say goodbye."

"Of course, I could arrange that. But not here on the street. You'll have to come with me to my van."

She followed him to the side street, far from Bourbon Street where all the pedestrian traffic herded together like cattle. At the van, she insisted, "I will not get inside this thing with you. I don't know you."

"Then just climb into the passenger seat. You can leave the door ajar."

"Not the seat, not getting in. No way am I going into your van."

He argued, "I'm not conducting illegal business on the street, my dear, now come along."

"I am not, I repeat, going anywhere with you."

From her dress and manner, he imagined she lived nearby, that she was a native to the city.

"Your place then? How far is it?"

She had second thoughts. He was too pushy for her liking. "Just give me two packets of your best weed."

"Not out in the open like this."

They continued to argue, and as it heated up, the grocer came out and, with a broom in hand, began to shoo him away as if he were a fly. Frustrated at the man's interference and the woman's determination, Phillip caused Grant to lash out and grab the broom, and he and the grocer began a tug of war for it. The broom flashed wildly before Selese's eyes. A handful of onlookers from windows overhead and a few children straddling bikes on the street looked on from a safe distance, some laughing when the broom slipped from the grocer's hand and hit the woman in the temple, causing her to shout, "You stupid bastard!"

Grant heedlessly grabbed her and forced her into the van at that point, handcuffing her to the seat. Her cries for help were cut off when he slammed the door shut. As he did so, the grocer tried to stop him, but Grant knocked him down, and the older man's head slammed into a metal pipe railing. More laughter erupted from the boys on the bikes.

That's when Grant heard sirens. Some meddling person had called the police. He quickly leapt into the van and tore away from the place, knowing it was time to change his license plate for the one he had stolen in a hotel lot in North Carolina.

He looked out his windshield to see a police car approaching, lights and siren going. His immediate thought was to race by it, but Phillip said, *"Calm down, pull over like a good citizen."* Just as the thought came to mind, however, the woman reached over and bit him in the neck, tearing wildly with her teeth, causing him to weave and almost hit the patrol car. He elbowed her in the gut, knocking the wind out of her, and she doubled over while he regained control of the van, missing the squad car by mere inches.

Now he found himself in a police chase. "Fucking stupid, Phillip!" he shouted. "Look what you've got us into now!"

Rounding a corner, he instantly wheeled the van into a dark little alleyway where he pulled in behind a large trash container. He next heard the approaching siren, and then saw the single set of flashing lights as the New Orleans police car raced by, missing him. She yelled out, but he covered her mouth and with his free hand, he stabbed her with the syringe and put her under with the Demoral.

He again cursed. "Phillip, you sonofabitch, look what

you've gotten us into!" He tried to breathe but found his air coming up short. He knew he could not remain there, that he had to find a safer place, the place along the levy that he'd scouted out earlier. He looked at the features of the woman as she began to doze off. Taking her purse from her, he found her ID.

"Well, Selese, that's a pretty name, Miss Montoya."

He recalled how absolutely disinterested in him she had been, and he knew early on that he should have stepped away, apologized even. "Instead, I draw a fucking crowd and knock a man into a pipe. He's likely in a damned coma. Cops are all over my ass. Your fault, Phillip, your damned fault!"

"My fault? How so?"

"Bloody fool. You're getting so arrogant, so reckless that you don't care what happens to me."

And now here they sat parked in a dead-end box canyon of a place within sight of the Super Dome with a victim, the tools that would mark him as the Skull-digger, and the police in pursuit. He thought his heart would burst.

"Calm down," Phillip told him. *"Calm down and get to work."*

Grant replied, "You fool! You almost got us caught back there."

"Shhh . . . think I hear something."

Grant listened intently. He heard it, too. A slow rumble over gravel and potholes, followed by silence; then the sound of a door squeaking ever so inaudibly open but not quite silent, followed by an even noisier second door squeak. A look in his rearview mirror told him the situation. "The cops. They're here."

"We've talked about when and if this day ever came, Grant. It's going to be OK. Just remember how to play it."

He uncuffed the girl and quietly opened her door, telling

her to run, that she was free. She moved like a zombie, but she did fall out and get up, attempting to escape in her heavily sedated state, creating the diversion Phillip knew she would.

Meanwhile, he reached for the shotgun attached to the sidewall, and gingerly crept back toward the rear. He'd secured the shotgun when he'd first outfitted the van for just such a moment. He called out that he was giving himself up and unlocking the door.

"We put in your location and the license plate," said Doyle to whoever was in the van. "You did call it in, didn't you, Tony?" he whispered to Labruto.

"Yeah, but that was back a ways, when we were in Jackson Heights."

"Maybe you'd better call it in again—now!"

Labruto inched back toward the unit, but like Doyle, he watched the door latch jiggle and then came a thunderous *pop*, telling them the driver had suddenly unlocked it from the inside. Yet the doors remained closed. And the two officers remained anxious, their weapons pointed.

"Open it up and come out with your hands on your head!" ordered Labruto.

Collin Doyle thought he heard a sound from the side of the van, and even as he shouted, "May be two of them, Tony!" his eyes darted from the rear door to the direction of the sound of clumsy footfalls. Labruto glanced for a moment, and, seeing a woman stumble into view, shouted, "Hold your fire, Doyle. It's the woman." Just as Labruto said this, Grant viciously kicked open the rear doors, resulting in an explosion of noise as he sprayed both officers with one round each of buckshot to face and upper torso. Both Labruto and Doyle fell to the sodden earth and weeds, even as Grant reloaded both barrels. The crackle of the buckshot wafted out over the river and toward the Super Dome.

Silence followed the two explosions. Seeing no movement, hearing not so much as a moan from either policeman, Grant believed the shotgun blasts at such close range had killed both men.

No doubt they had called in the plate, learning it was stolen. No doubt backup was on the way.

He grabbed Selese Montoya and shoved her unceremoniously into the rear of the van, leapt in and secured her completely—ankles, wrists, head. He then grabbed the new license plate and quickly changed it out. Tossing the old plate into the van, he closed the doors and went to check on the two cops.

Labruto had worked his way up to a sitting position, bloodied, dazed and attempting to steady his gun to fire. The noise he made against the gravel surface alerted Grant who turned from Doyle's silent body to find himself staring at Labruto's gun. Grant could not understand why the policeman did not fire, but it was written in his eyes. He hadn't the strength to pull the trigger.

Labruto fought to get the words out, bluffing. "Don't maa-kee me ffff."

Grant grabbed up the shotgun and fired again, instantly killing Labruto this time. Doyle had not moved an inch since the first round. Grant let it be, rushing back to the driver's seat and tearing away from this place. To do so, he had to back over Labruto's body to get out of the dead end he found himself in.

He wound his way back toward the interstate ramp, hearing sirens on the way. He sped onto the ramp and blended in with a stream of dense traffic on the interstate.

Quantico
The same hour

EVERYONE on Jessica's team was asked to pull a double shift, and no one balked. They had gotten word that AOC had lost the final and deciding round in their battle. Still, AOC found ways to delay, and so Jessica had asked all her people to stay on board. Phone calls to home were made, cots were set up, a catering service was called in for food, drink and coffee urns.

The doctor list was still being closely examined against what little they knew of the Skull-digger. A doctor named Simon Wells looked like a good candidate from his picture and a history of violent episodes that had lost him his career. Several others appeared good leads, including a domestic disturbance arrest against Dr. Jervis Swantor. Jessica immediately recalled the man from the yacht in Florida, and J.T. reminded her of both his suspicious behavior at the crime scene, which Combs had told them about, and his having attended the Jacksonville victim's funeral. They had cleared him as a serious candidate when Lorena Combs had done a complete background check on him. They hadn't taken Swantor as a serious candidate then, and he didn't look any better now. No other suggestions that he was violent had been reported to law enforcement since his wife's complaint months before. There was no coincidence in his coming up on VICAP; it was the same report Combs had flagged earlier. "Still, if and whenever we get access to Cahil's vistors online, I'd like you to check for Swantor's name."

One after the other doctor on the list fell to the wayside as alibis, time and geography cleared them. But Simon Wells still appeared worth a look, as his case was so curious.

Eriq Santiva's Cuban features looked particularly weary when he entered the task force unit. Everyone cheered on seeing him, knowing he had fought and won against AOC.

"Yeah . . . finally . . ." he replied to them all, a bit embarrassed at the show of gratitude. "We finally have a victory over those damned AOC lawyers. The important thing is that we now have access to their database."

This was met with mutterings and shakes of the head.

Eriq stared at Jessica and then J.T. "Don't tell me you're still waiting to hear from them?" asked Eriq. "The order was given over an hour ago." He looked at his watch, which read 9:05 P.M.

"Yeah, they're still stalling," replied Jessica. "Now it's some nonsense about technical difficulties."

"The judge's order was plain enough." Eriq found a chair and fell into it. "Tell me Jess, John, tell me that you've had *some* progress, that you've got something in the works."

"We've got a curious fellow here," said Jessica, holding a readout of the information she had amassed on Simon Wells. "A tip from the ex-wife of a Dr. Simon Wells looks of interest. Wells was listed as a juvenile offender in VICAP—J.T.'s idea to check it. Anyway, Wells came under scrutiny when a high school student. He was put on a minor watch list for possible serial killer tendencies due to his cruelty to animals."

"Fits the profile," commented J.T. "Not unlike Cahil."

"Really. Of course, the juvenile-offender program of violent criminal activity. Why didn't we go there sooner?"

"It doesn't come up on its own with VICAP requests. You have to key it in separately," said J.T.

"Oversight," said Jessica.

"Perhaps it wouldn't have been if I'd been able to get you more help down here."

"In 1984, at the age of sixteen, he was at the American Academy for Young Men in Lauralie, Massachusetts, when that private boys' school had something of a scandal involving the ingesting of cooked cat brains. Some other students in the dorm objected to the odors coming from Wells's room, where he often cooked on a hot plate. While the American Academy downplayed the incident, the state wasn't so willing to sweep the incident under the official rug. Still, after some initial moves against Wells to try him in juvenile court, it was dropped. However, the DA contacted the closest FBI field office and reported the incident, which was placed in our files more than a year after the incident. The man who sent in a report, an agent named Alvin Degrasso, interviewed the kid."

"What did this Degrasso find?"

"He found that Wells roamed the campus and town of Lauralie for its stray cats, offered them a home and soon they disappeared."

"Another cat eater like Cahil, huh?"

"When confronted with it, the young man had confessed to the headmaster to killing the cats, skinning and cooking their flesh and eating them. This included eating their brains. He admitted to doing the same with a dog as well."

Eriq asked, "Why wasn't he expelled and sent packing?"

"He was—for one term. Wells later went on to medical school at Northwestern, concentrating on pathology and forensics."

"He got into med school?" asked J.T.

"Must have somehow gotten his record expunged, and like I said, it never went to court."

"But Degrasso made sure," added Eriq, "that VICAP had his number."

"Degrasso hounded Wells for a time. In later years, discovering that Wells was marrying, Degrasso made it his business to inform his fiancée of Wells's earlier habits. The young bride stood by her man at the time, and she and hubby threatened a lawsuit against the agent for harassment.

Degrasso was reprimanded and soon retired from the bureau. Urged to do so," Jessica added, "I imagine. The wife left Wells soon after."

"You've done some digging," said Eriq. "So, where's Wells now? Do we have him in our sights?"

Wells's case had intrigued Jessica more than the others on the list because so many serial killers began their careers as children who harmed animals. "He's a general practitioner in Elixir, Mississippi, but he hasn't been practicing for a year. He was brought up on some ethics charge involving a scam on Medicare patients. He was out on bail when he disappeared. The wife divorced him seven years ago. At the moment, we don't know his whereabouts, which is another reason we're looking so hard at him for the Digger killings."

"Anything else?" asked Eriq.

"Every new lead and a lot of old ones are being followed. Agents across the nation are questioning suspects, and we've urged them to ask our targets if they have ever logged on to Cahil's Isle of Brainsite, to see what the reaction might be. At the same time, we realize that the Digger is a moving target, not likely a homebody."

"Why are we still waiting on AOC?" asked Eriq, pacing the computer-analysis room now. Stating the obvious, angry. "What kind of technical difficulties are they saying?"

"Something lame about a problem with getting all the IDs to us on a continuous flow. They thought it best for us that way. . . ."

"Thinking kindly of us now that we've killed their sorry asses before a federal court?" Eriq sarcastically replied.

J.T. said, "We know this Wells character owns a Dodge van, and that he may have relocated to the D.C. area, which would give him quick access to Richmond and the other early kill sites."

"Wait a moment . . . hold on," Jessica suddenly interrupted.

"What it is, Jess?" asked Eriq.

"We've been going at this all wrong . . . *backward*. Suppose we have a doctor who comes up on the tip list but *not* on the violent criminals file?"

"I thought the idea was to cross-reference the three lists, VICAP, civilian tips and AOC, and if not, the two lists." Eriq scrunched features displayed his confusion.

"Yeah, that's been the plan, but suppose this Seeker guy has absolutely *no* record of any sort? *Nothing* on file?"

"A killer like this Digger . . . He has to have had some run-in with the law somewhere," said Eriq.

"Not if he's been careful and lucky. Just suppose it's possible . . . that he's avoided and eluded everyone around him . . . then . . ."

"Then he wouldn't be on the list we just developed," said J.T.

Jessica went to the computer technician, Dana, and said, "I know this is redundant, but I need a list taken from the civilian tips *only* to be crossed with the words we've been matching."

"I saved that list already when creating the crossover list," she replied. "No problem." Dana stroked a few keys and in a moment the printer erupted and the list from all the civilian tips with their key words encrypted was complete. "Here you are," finished Dana.

Jessica lifted the list. Only those on the civilian tips who were doctors and butchers in which the tip used the words, "brain," "mind," "soul" "isle" or "island." The list was hefty at forty plus names, but it was quickly reduced as Jessica, with J.T.'s help, began comparing it with the ones on the VICAP list as well. J.T. called out the names from his list, and Jessica pencil stroked them off her list.

"This seems counterproductive," said Eriq. "Subtracting the men who made the VICAP list."

Jessica asked for his patience. "Once more," she added.

Simon Wells, along with most of the others on the original list, were now hand stricken from the new list. Simon Wells had been put into VICAP by Degrasso years ago, and now he had come in as a tip from his ex-wife, who had hounded a field agent in Mississippi to take her tip to the highest authorities involved with the Skull-digger case. This had him on two lists. Jervis Swantor was also on two lists. Such names then were stricken.

Jessica hesitated over Swantor's name for only a moment, seeing his boat marina address in Grand Isle, Louisiana. She wondered how close his tie-up was to New Orleans. Still, having met the man, she decided the civilian tip and the VICAP registry had come from the same source—Swantor's ex-wife. She wanted only those *not* on the violent criminal program.

"We want only those names gleaned from a tip alone," Jessica said, finishing the list with J.T. "Anyone *without* a criminal history."

J.T. said, "Swantor and Wells aren't carrying what you'd call a long criminal history, Jess."

"All right, we'll keep them on a secondary list. For now, let's be strict on ourselves."

As a result, a number of new names appeared that had previously been eliminated because they'd not been placed on VICAP, as Swantor and Wells had. Those doctors and butchers who were never listed with VICAP, some twenty-six in all, accounted for a significant reduction of suspects, if Jessica's theory held up.

The remaining names were then broken down into two lists according to profession. Jessica handed the lists to Eriq.

"Here's some that almost got by us," she said, "the doctors on the tips list who have no previous record."

"Bring up the actual files on each tip, please, Dana," asked Eriq.

The tips appeared in all cases but one to be feeble. The best tip, in everyone's estimation, had come from another physician. A Dr. Mitchell Erdman who claimed that he had worked with a Dr. Grant Kenyon at Mt. Holyoke Memorial Hospital in New Jersey, where he witnessed the disappearance of brains from cadavers.

"This could lead to something," muttered Jessica, hopeful it was so.

"Bingo time, if you ask me!" J.T. added.

"Like Daryl, stealing brains from dead people," said Eriq.

"Another coincidence, New Jersey's home for this guy. Not far from Morristown. Cahil's stomping grounds," said Jessica.

"Place must breed brain-eaters," replied J.T.

Jessica held her breath and read on. Erdman claimed that Kenyon lost his position at the hospital in mid-May. That's pretty close to when the first killing took place back in June. "Traumatic event like being fired could have triggered latent violent aggressiveness."

They attempted to locate and speak to Erdman, but the hospital said that he had left with no forwarding address. Jessica identified herself as an FBI agent and pressed the operator to put her on with the senior most person at the hospital. After some confusion and several transfers, a Dr. Bondesen came on, saying that he could speak for Mt. Holyoke Hospital. She questioned him about Erdman's allegations against Dr. Kenyon. The man began stammering before he could say, "Neither of these gentlemen work here any longer and—"

"Doctor, I want to know exactly what went on there. We

are hunting a brain-stealing killer you know in the press as the Skull-digger. We need your complete and honest co-operation, sir."

Bondesen cleared his throat and said, "Erdman found it difficult to work in the morgue where Dr. Kenyon had previously worked. Nightmares, you know, over what he *allegedly* saw."

" 'Allegedly'? Did you or did you not fire Grant Kenyon over these allegations?"

"We did fire him, but not due to Erdman's wild accusations. More to the point, he was fired because he was exhibiting shoddy work. His mind never seemed on the job at hand, you see."

"Didn't anyone there, aside from Erdman, think that Kenyon's behavior might be connected to the Skull-digger case?"

"But you have someone in custody for those awful murders."

"There may be accomplices," she gave the standard reply.

"But you see, we . . . we sealed all information on the allegations against Kenyon as a courtesy to Dr. Kenyon, and we gave Grant's position to Dr. Erdman—all this in return for both men remaining silent."

"To protect the integrity of the hospital."

"And the families involved."

Eriq picked up another phone and came on the line, bursting into the conversation, introducing himself and adding, "Well, now, Dr. Bondesen, you can expect all that was sealed regarding this case open to scrutiny by the FBI, the press and the world if you fail to cooperate now. I will have a field representative sent within the hour to take charge of both Kenyon's file and Erdman's. Is that clear?"

"Ahhh, yes, quite clear."

"And I want social security numbers on both Kenyon and

Erdman. Can you give them to me now please?" Eriq requested.

After hanging up, with the numbers in hand, Eriq turned to Dana, "Get us a location fix on a Dr. Mitchell Erdman. Also get a location on this guy Kenyon."

Dana stroked in Erdman's number and began the search. "He's out of the country on a passport. Philippines, it appears."

J.T. said, "I'll see what I can do to get in touch with him."

Dana then attempted to locate Kenyon.

Eriq was on the phone with the closest FBI field office to Holyoke, New Jersey. He informed the agent there to immediately get to the hospital, speak to Bondesen only, and take charge of the two personnel files in question.

Jessica watched as Dana's screen instantly filled with information on Kenyon, down to a map of precisely where he lived in Holyoke, New Jersey. His telephone number was also listed.

Jessica returned to the phone and dialed the number. A woman answered.

After Jessica introduced herself, Mrs. Kenyon gasped into the phone and pleaded, "Have you found Grant? Have you? Is he alive . . . please tell me he's alive!"

"Are you saying he is not currently at this residence, Mrs. Kenyon?"

"I reported him missing months ago! I thought that's what you were calling about."

"This is the FBI ma'am. Do you know a Dr. Erdman, Mrs. Kenyon, a man who once worked with your husband?"

"He was my husband's assistant, yes."

"And there was some unpleasantness between them to cause Dr. Kenyon to leave his position."

"Yes, but . . ."

"And then Dr. Kenyon simply disappeared?"

"Yes . . . yes, that's about it, yes."

"Can you give me any details about what happened at the hospital between your husband and Dr. Erdman?"

"Erdman stole Grant's job. That's what he told me. Said Erdman had backstabbed him. I only know that he lied about Grant."

"About the brains you mean? Taking them from the morgue?"

"Nothing mysterious, really. He was conducting a series of experiments. So he needed the . . . needed them for study."

"What sort of study?"

"Something to do with some sort of bacterial infection and any number of debilitating diseases, like Lupus, Alzheimer's. Grant told me that men had within their skulls three brains, not one: the mammalian brain, the reptilian brain and the human brain. And that many brain disorders mimicked animal disorders, and he was out to find a cure."

"I see." Jessica realized the woman was in denial.

"Mrs. Kenyon, what kind of vehicle does your husband drive?"

"He left me the car. He took the van."

"I'll need the license plate number, make and model of the van, and any distinguishing marks. A scratch, a dent or missing fender. And we'll need any credit card numbers you have that are his."

"What is this all about?"

"We want to find your missing husband, Mrs. Kenyon, and we can do that if he uses a credit card. And if he contacts you, we want to know. Call me immediately at either of these numbers," Jessica relayed her cell phone number and her office number. "And I'd like to send agents to your house to—"

"My God . . . You people think he's the Skull-digger, don't you?"

"Have you had such thoughts, Mrs. Kenyon?"

"Is he a suspect?"

Jessica decided to be direct with her. "He's a suspect, yes."

"I thought so. It's that awful Dr. Erdman at work again. He's trying to ruin Grant. I know it. If anyone's a killer, it's Erdman."

"We suspect that your husband made numerous contacts via E-mail to a man named Cahil, a man we have in custody in connection with the murders, Mrs. Kenyon."

"Cahil? The man who robbed children's graves?"

"How did you know?"

"Ten years ago, it was all over the news. Grant was fascinated with the case."

"Mrs. Kenyon, exactly when did your husband disappear?"

"Two days after losing his job, May eighteenth."

Jessica thought, How perfect . . . two weeks before the discovery of the first victim. More and more, Jessica believed she had found the Seeker. "Mrs. Kenyon, do you have a computer in the house that your husband would have used? And do you know his password? Is he using the name Seeker when he logs on?"

"I . . . no, he has a laptop, but he doesn't let me near it. Says all his research is in there, and no, he would never tell me his password or call name."

"We believe your husband is dangerous, Mrs. Kenyon, and we fear he will strike again. He already has in fact."

"That's sheer nonsense." Mrs. Kenyon began weeping. She groaned. "I'm certain you people are wrong. I know

Erdman must have lied to you, too. Grant would never harm anyone, ever. I'd stake my life on it."

Jessica heard a child crying in the background. "And your child's life, Mrs. Kenyon? Would you take that risk?"

Mrs. Kenyon's tears erupted. Jessica had to calm her. "As long as he's out there, Mrs. Kenyon, he poses a danger to himself and others. We need your help and cooperation if he's to be safely brought in and questioned." Even as she said it, Jessica knew that she'd rather see Kenyon killed in the field than get the kind of treatment Daryl had gotten at the taxpayers' expense.

"We would like to post FBI men at your house, and put a tracer on your phone, in case he should call."

"All right, whatever you think is best, but in all this time, he hasn't bothered to contact us."

Who knows. He may get homesick, Jessica thought but did not say. "I'm going to put you on with my associate, Dana. She's going to take down all the information I asked for on your husband. And can you find a recent photograph of your husband?"

"I'm sure I can."

"Hand it over to the agent who comes to your door. He'll get it to us. And thank you, Mrs. Kenyon."

She handed the phone to Dana, took a deep breath and wondered if she dared believe that they finally had something tangible to go on. Could Kenyon be the Seeker and the Seeker be the Skull-digger? Mrs. Kenyon had said her husband had been fascinated with Cahil's case; it would then figure that he would be a frequent visitor to the website.

THIRTEEN

I who am in the night, will move into today.

—GIORDANO BRUNO, 1548–1600

The same night
11:45 P.M.

JESSICA and her skeletal team were working around the clock now that the AOC files were available to them. The photo of Kenyon, provided by Mrs. Emily Kenyon, cooperating with local FBI in New Jersey, was immediately used to place features on the phantom, and now he looked out from the FBI's Most Wanted website. By tomorrow morning, his image would be duplicated and sent out across the country, putting his likeness on every TV and newsstand and post office as a suspect in the Skull-digger murders.

Jessica stared into the screen image of Dr. Grant Kenyon in suit and tie. For all the world, he looked normal and healthy, certainly far from a mad killer. There were no stones for eyes, no overhanging brow, no scars or misshapen features. In fact, he was handsome in his three-piece suit. Quite urbane, she thought. No one would guess him to be a brain cannibal. Nonetheless, everything pointed to Kenyon as the real Digger, who'd led them on this horrific chase.

Armed with the photograph of Kenyon and the make,

model and the by-now-discarded license plate number of the van belonging to the missing doctor, Jessica believed for the first time that they actually had a bead on the right man, the real brain thief.

Among the names found on Cahil's subscribers according to AOC files was Grant Kenyon, using the handle of "Seeker." His most recent online correspondences, some arguing with Cahil over statements and beliefs Daryl professed, some chatting with young people, had been from library terminals, making his contacts as he moved. These E-mails corresponded by time and place in or around the cities that the Skull-digger had visited and left victims. All indications pointed toward Kenyon.

A telephone call came through to the task force ready room. It was from authorities in New Orleans. Jessica put it on the speakerphone for all to hear. Two police officers had been shotgunned to death after giving chase to a dark green Chrysler '96 or '97 with a kidnap victim named Selese Montoya inside.

The report came two hours after the incident, from Field Agent Michael Sorrento, placed on conference call. Jessica informed Sorrento of their new suspect and that he need only go to the Most Wanted Web page. "You can toss that lousy sketch we've been using. It was way off."

"Did anyone get the license plate?" asked J.T., joining Jessica at the wall map, which they used to trace the killer's known movements.

"One of the lost officers called in a partial number on a Georgia plate. Likely stolen during his time in Savannah," replied Sorrento.

A look at the map showed how close New Orleans was to Mobile. J.T. said, "He's most likely switched out the plate with another one. His original plate is New Jersey 14H-555."

"After shooting down two police officers, he's got to be feeling the heat," replied Jessica. "He's got to find a hole to hide in."

Sorrento in New Orleans said, "He has every cop in the city dedicated to one thing—locating that van and putting an end to his sorry ass. But he's got the hostage; abducted the woman right off the street."

"He's got to dispose of the van or disguise it again," said Jessica.

Sorrento informed them that he had alerted local authorities along the I-10 corridor west of New Orleans with the description and last-known partial license number. "I'll get word out on the photo. We're canvassing all body shops in the manhunt for a van fitting the description."

"He's most likely to feed on his latest victim and dump the body before he attempts to rid himself of the van," Jessica predicted. "He may dump the van with the body this time."

"We're on highest alert status," Sorrento assured her. "Thanks for forwarding this creep's likeness. Have it up on my computer now. Too bad Labruto and Doyle didn't have more to go on. Maybe if they had . . . who knows . . ."

"I'm coming there, Agent Sorrento," said Jessica. "I'll want to examine the bodies and be on hand when you apprehend this creep. He can't get far now."

"We'll get him," Sorrento assured her.

She hung up and stared from Eriq to J.T. "John, find out whatever else you can about Grant Kenyon." She then turned to Eriq and added, "And I want full support from our field office down there. Not like the last time I went to New Orleans on a case."

"You'll get full cooperation, Jess. And my apologies. You were right about this all along."

Jessica was on her way out the door when J.T. shouted,

"Hold on, Jess!" He pointed to Cahil's website on the computer screen, which he'd been monitoring for activity. The screen had come alive with a digitized image, that of a man struggling for consciousness, but not just any man. It was Grant Kenyon's live image being e-mailed to them. J.T. stammered. "It's him . . . I believe it's Grant Kenyon."

"The Seeker is finally checking in?" she asked, rushing to J.T.'s side. Eriq joined them. They were treated to a glimpse of Kenyon, out cold, lying against a bloodstained pillow in a sparse room with only a bed and a nightstand, possibly a hotel room. It appeared the camera was moving, all the angles going from side to side, up and down—sometimes jarringly so.

"He looks as if he's on something," said J.T.

"Bloodstains on the pillow."

"Who's photographing him?" asked J.T.

"He's trying to say something," added Eriq. "His lips are moving."

Then the image was gone. Jessica said, "What's going on? Where's it coming from? Is he sending the image?"

"No, it's another subscriber, calls himself SquealsLoud," replied J.T.

"Run him down, J.T. We've got to know who that is."

J.T. ran the image back. Eriq asked, "Could this have been on a delay, a timer? He's fucking with us."

"No . . . no, that was live, happening now," J.T. informed him.

Eriq asked, "You supposing this other Cahil groupie has Kenyon and what? He's holding out for some sort of reward?"

"He's got to contact us again. Meanwhile, we'll be tracing him," replied J.T..

"Whoever has him seems nervous. Couldn't hold the camera steady," said Jessica.

"Yeah, it was shaky."

"Replay it," said Eriq.

By now everyone in the room had gathered around J.T.'s seat, craning for a look at Kenyon.

J.T. replayed the incoming message. They watched the short clip again.

Eriq said, "He's not doing anything but lying there, muttering to himself."

"I'm sure I can hack back to this guy, and if he's in the AOC files we've downloaded, we'll get him," said J.T.

"OK," said Jessica. "Run a geographic list for anyone on our final list who lives in or around New Orleans. Right now, we only know of two—this Wells guy and Swantor. Get someone in Mississippi to visit Elixir, and someone in Louisiana to pay a call to this Grand Isle to check in with Swantor's residence. See if all is kosher there."

"But neither Swantor nor Wells are on our single-complaint list," countered Eriq, holding it up.

"At the moment, they're the only two we know of with residences in or near New Orleans."

Eriq said, "Wouldn't it be just poetic to learn that his latest abductee is shooting the footage?"

"Too good to be true," she replied.

"More likely, he's hooked up with another psycho user on Daryl's loony website, and judging from the blood, they didn't quite get along," added J.T.

"Perhaps a like-minded psycho," replied Jessica. "We know how many have gravitated to Cahil's website. It's like a fulcrum for fanatics."

Eriq said, "The two witnesses to this guy's crimes have said he acted alone. So maybe he did hook up with another Cahil nutcase, and they had a falling out."

J.T. added, "I've seen some E-mails between this

SquealsLoud character and the Seeker, and so if he is in the Orleans area . . . "

"We need to check for *anyone* who got cozy with Kenyon in the chat rooms, who happens to live in and around New Orleans," said Jessica.

"Damned AOC," said Eriq. "We might've shut this guy down *before* he killed again if they'd cooperated with us."

Midnight

GRANT Kenyon awoke feeling groggy, disoriented, drugged even . . . like one of his own victims. He awoke to the nightmare he had gotten himself into. He awoke to the realization of being shackled by one ankle to the wall of a cabin on a boat that, presumably, was traveling along the stretch of islands and canals that made inroads to the Mississippi Peninsula.

He worked to recall what had happened to him. He had driven to and searched for his destination, one he had counted on should things get too complicated or hair-raising. Killing two NOPD cops certainly qualified, so he had located a quiet cemetery, parked and found his laptop computer. He hadn't used it in a long time, and he had subscribed to another server on it, wanting to keep his Internet tracks as blurred as possible. He now used it to make contact with Dr. Jervis Swantor.

He had been lucky. Swantor even joked in his reply:

SQUEALSLOUD: I was expecting you sooner. Come to the address on the screen. You will find I live on my yacht.

SEEKER: A *yacht*? You said you lived on a *boat*.

SQUEALSLOUD: Only thing I got from the divorce. She got
                the rest.

After signing off, Phillip insisted they feed on the girl
first and dump the body in the graveyard.

Grant put his foot down. "No! This van's too damned
hot. We've got to find safe shelter and devise a plan to get
rid of the van, the woman and us—you and me."

He tried to remember more . . . what had happened.
How he had become a captive himself, and what had happened to Selese Montoya. But the drugs wore him down and
he again fell into a deep slumber. Phillip tried to rouse him,
but nothing could, not now.

He had a vague sense that someone was nearby, but he
had seen no one. He also had a vague sense that the camera
mounted high above, across the room, was running, captur-
ing his image. He had a vague sense he was in some pain
and bleeding from a head wound. But all his vague fears
were overwhelmed by the drugs in his system.

WHILE Jessica was on an FBI Cessna headed for New Orleans, back at Quantico headquarters, J.T. began the daunting task of tracking Dr. Grant Kenyon—the Seeker—
through time and cyberspace, thanks to AOC's now-
downloaded files. He kept a list of the men and women that
Kenyon had shown an interest in and they in him. J.T. was
amazed when he came across the name of Anna Gleason,
first victim of the Digger.

He instantly asked Dana to track the user list sent by
AOC to quickly determine if any other victim—other than
Gleason—had used Cahil's list, while he himself searched
on for information on SquealsLoud.

Dana announced that a second victim came up, the

Winston-Salem woman, Miriam McCloud. He instantly contacted Eriq and then Jessica with the news. They had discussed the possibility before, that the killer could be enticing his victims via the Web. Victim families had been asked questions designed to determine this, but here was the definitive proof that at least two of his victims had accessed Cahil's website.

J.T. continued to search for contacts Kenyon had made in and around New Orleans. It appeared that the mad doctor made friends easily and frequently over the Net. While his other victims' names did not appear on the list, he had made contacts with women and men in all the areas he'd visited.

Over the phone, J.T. now told Jessica, "This fellow calls himself Mr. SquealsLoud. Registered to a PO box in a place called Steeple Top, Louisiana, fifty miles from New Orleans. Name is Mark Sweet. Sure is easier to locate information now. We'll have to wake up the postmaster in Steeple Top. Get an address on this PO box for Sweet."

"Get back to me when you have it."

On the plane, Jessica tried to get some sleep. Her thoughts drifted like a ghost ship over a foggy ocean until she fixed on a single boat named *Uneven Odds*. That was the boat Amanda Manning's body had turned up on. Then she envisioned another, far more spectacular boat, a yacht with beautiful running lights named *Lands End*. She thought of how persistent Jervis Swantor been about visiting the body. She pictured the man's large yacht in Jacksonville, thought again of his inordinate interest in the case and recalled how the live computer image of Dr. Grant Kenyon had been *bobbing*.

He's on a boat . . . perhaps Swantor's boat! she suddenly realized. Swantor had listed his home address as Grande *Isle*, Louisiana. Cahil's website was *Isle* of Brain. Could it be coincidence or more than that? Could Kenyon be a prisoner on Swantor's boat?

She immediately telephoned Lorena Combs in Jacksonville, waking her at home. "I need to know what Swantor listed on his manifest as his next port of call after leaving Jacksonville."

"Neighbors and the harbormaster told me he was off to Cancun. I can check it for you. What's up?"

She informed Combs about the live feed and her hunch that it had originated aboard a boat.

Combs replied, "The man made my skin crawl, but he checked out clean."

"I got bad vibes off him, too, if you remember."

"I'll get over to the marina, check it out firsthand. I'll get back to you if anything's changed."

GRANT Kenyon, trying to shake off the latest drugs injected into his arm by SquealsLoud Swantor, tried desperately to piece together how he had been so blind to his captor's mad plan. On meeting Jervis Swantor in the flesh, Kenyon had quickly sized him up. The other man's size and weight, his skin color, the same blue color of eyes and brown hair as his own—it all played out beautifully until Grant got careless.

Soon after shotgunning to death those two cops, Grant's likeness had unaccountably gone out to the world, radio announcers giving details of his appearance down to a mole on his upper lip. Undoubtedly, the TV news would also have his likeness. By tomorrow morning, his picture would be on everyone's kitchen table. On seeing Swantor's general resemblance Kenyon believed he could use Swantor as a body double, should he have to fake his own death—at least long enough to throw off authorities when the time arose, and that time had come. He needed only a little sleight of hand to put such a plan to work. Anyone discovering a pair of torched dead and hopefully long-decayed bodies in his van, one at the wheel, one chained in the rear, might easily be led to the conclusion that he had discovered the body of the Digger and his last victim. Phillip liked the plan. Grant even thought of sending the fiery van over the side of a cliff and into the Mississippi River.

He had had ideas of taking Swantor's yacht before moving on. So he had followed Swantor's directions down to the parking lot at the marina, and next found his way to the Windjammer yacht of Jervis Swantor, his marina address and the name of his boat, *Lands End*.

Grant had hesitated, for a moment fearful of Swantor's reception, wondering if it was a setup. He had circled for an hour, dangerously so, desperately anxious about the police patrols that were surely looking for him and his van. In the rear, he still held his victim shackled and drugged, but he had had no time to feed on her. Phillip would have to wait.

He went up to the yacht and rang the bell and the cabin door quickly opened. Jervis Swantor beamed with a wide smile and told him to come inside. "So, you are the Seeker. I'm delighted you've come. *Mi casa es su casa*, and all that, as they say. Anyone with the chutzpah to do what you've done, imagine it. The Skull-digger here with me."

"What do you mean? I'm not the Digger."

"Your face is plastered all over the tube, Kenyon. Yes, they've got your name, too."

"Jeez-us!"

"It's wrong to worry about *me*, my friend," Swantor assured him. "If I only had your guts, I'd be doing the same thing. I tell you, I'm so . . . *touched* that you've come to me for help and shelter. I'd hoped we'd have met before now. I just can't tell you." He took Grant's hand and patted him on the back and insisted, "Sit down, relax, your secret's safe on *Lands' End*. Have a drink, relax. I waited for you in Florida, but you didn't show up."

"You really feel this way?"

"Absolutely. I admire you." Swantor smiled wide, his eyes beaming as if meeting his hero.

"In that case, I need you to help me outside to . . . to ditch the van. It's hot."

"Yeah, nightly news is going on about how two cops were shot tonight."

"I need to stow the van," he repeated.

"I'll take care of it entirely. You come inside and find your bed. It's got to have been a trying night for you, and it's getting rather late."

Grant then sized up Swantor, finding him a bit larger than himself, beefier. He thought of how he needed to find the right moment to gain control over Swantor. He wondered if the fire would remove the fingerprints. In the middle of his back, he carried the gun, but he wanted Swantor's death to appear to be the Skull-digger's suicide. However, he might have to improvise and modify his plans as he went. Aside from the gun, he had a ready needle with Demoral in his pants pocket, should it go that way. Should he have to overpower the larger man. But first he needed him to step out to the van.

He awaited the exact right moment to attack Swantor.

"I've closely watched your development, Grant," Jervis said to him, "and I guessed you to be the Digger given your sudden absence from the website, along with those girls you were always flirting with, some of whom also disappeared abruptly from the Net. You were busy with the real thing. . . . Or should I say the 'Rheil' thing. Nifty how you sent that Island of Rheil tissue to Cahil to implicate him. You do know they've had him in custody for the killings, right? You really should have laid low after that, but not you . . . you're something else."

"Yes, I guessed as much about Cahil even before the public knew."

"An educated assumption." Jervis had ushered him belowdecks, and he now pushed open a door and pointed, saying, "This cabin is yours, if you want it, for as long as you want it. We'll set off tonight, Cancun perhaps. Get you out of the country. Put some distance between you and New Orleans at least. Whataya say?"

"And in return?"

"Showing is better than telling. Come with me." Swantor turned his back and led the way to the midsection of the yacht where a large living-room space abounded with state-of-the-art computer equipment, several screens sending forth images at once. "It's my control room, you might say."

"This is fantastic. Incredible." Grant and Phillip already thought of it as their own—as soon as they ridded themselves of Swantor.

"I have the capability of beaming all over the world any words or images I choose, and I can do it from international waters. I've got a stop tracer on my hard drive that's stupendous. I've bought myself a new identity, and I'm ready to start my own Web page, and you, sir, are my star—*America's Most Wanted*."

"Star? What exactly do you expect of me?" Grant walked about, staring at the electronics, awed by the display of power, but confused by the man.

"All I ask is that you share with me and my audience, what it's like."

"What it's like?"

"To be the Skull-digger! Feeding on human brain tissue. In fact, I'd like to film you in the act."

"Film me?"

"Doing the operation, yes, and feeding. I'll provide you with the means."

Grant had swallowed hard at that point. This guy's crazier than Phillip, he thought. "It's a deal, but I need your help with—"

"The woman you abducted from the city? She's still alive? Perfect."

"She's in the van, along with my tools."

"Yes, you will need a *costar*. Don't worry. I'll assist you in discarding the van, and I'll arrange for you to feed on your latest victim, so long as I can film it, you see. By the way, what's her name? I think viewers will want to know her name."

"Selese."

"Lovely . . . yes. I think we should get her situated in here first"—he opened a door opposite the room offered to Grant—"and then we can get your tools inside, and then I'll take care of the van."

"I think we should take care of the van as soon as possible," Grant replied.

"Of course, agreed. We can do the filming later."

Grant immediately replied, "Of course, you're right. We transport the girl here, and then get rid of the van." Grant frowned and decided that Phillip had to have the Montoya woman aboard the boat, and that authorities would be left with Swantor's body alone. Phillip wasn't about to give up Selese until his hunger was satisfied.

Amendment one to Grant's well thought out plan.

Jervis Swantor and he had then gone to the van and, careful to see there were no witnesses, they took hold of the still-drowsy Selese and led her, dragging her heels, to the yacht.

"How're we going to keep her from escaping?" asked Grant.

"I'm prepared for that, too," Swantor replied. He led the girl into what was to be her cabin. There he chained her hands to the metal-framed bed. As he worked the handcuffs, he asked Grant to help him with her ankles.

While Grant worked the bonds, he let his guard down around Jervis for a moment as the other man stood and went to the door, saying, "I know of a road that will take us to a backwash of the river, a perfect place to ditch the van."

"*And you,*" Phillip said only to Grant.

It was then that Grant and Phillip felt a crushing blow to the back of their shared head, and all turned to black.

FOURTEEN

*Another iron door, on which was writ, be not too
bold.*

—EDMUND SPENSER, 1552–1599

*In a back bay in the confluence of the Mississippi
Peninsula Island area*
3 A.M.

THE effort of having fought his way to wakefulness caused
a searing pain to throb throughout his brain.

When Grant Kenyon had fully awakened, he'd found
himself shackled to a wall and lying in a bed in a room
opposite Selese Montoya's accommodations. He fought to a
sitting position and discovered his left ankle was bound by
an enormous chain, each link the size of a crab. The girl was
nowhere to be seen. He fought with the chain on his ankle,
a futile effort. It had been securely bolted to the cabin wall.
He then suddenly remembered his hidden gun and the needle in his pocket, all meant for Swantor.

He reached for the gun, not surprised to find it gone. He
patted for the syringe, also gone, along with his wallet and
keys.

He imagined Swantor would be turning him over to the
police now, but then why the elaborate hoax? Why hadn't
he simply had the cops waiting in the bushes? How much

time had elapsed since taking the blow to the head? he wondered. Then he felt the rhythmic movement of the boat and realized they were on the water en route somewhere known only to Swantor.

He screamed out, "Swantor! You bastard! What're you pulling here?"

He got no answer.

He tore at the chain, bruising himself in the process.

He sat on the edge of the bed now, his head in his hands.

He looked up to the ceiling corner to watch that damned camera eye moving from side to side, watching him.

Muttering to himself, he realized that Swantor meant to do exactly what he'd said he would, film the Skull-digger at work on his latest victim and put it on the Internet. "Not if I kill him first . . ."

Phillip told him, *"I'm angry as hell. Angry enough to tell you this, Grant. I'm hungry to the point that this creep's brain will do as well as any."*

"He's a bigger psycho than you, Phillip."

He recalled now how Swantor had earlier entered the room with a gun—Grant's gun—and the Demoral-filled needle. "I insist you inject yourself now. I'm going to attend to your van, and when I return, we'll leave New Orleans together, the three of us."

"But we're on the water, already set sail."

"Just took us off a bit. I don't want anyone showing up at the marina to find the three of us. That won't do."

"But the van?"

"I'm on it." He pointed the gun and held out the needle. "Puncture yourself with this now! Or die now!"

"That would spoil your plans for a good show."

"But it would make me a hero—saving the girl, killing you! Shoot up or be shot."

Grant now recalled how it had all come down to this, having to administer the Demoral into his own arm.

AFTER securing both hostages in the yacht, Jervis Swantor had moved his home to a private marina covered with low-hanging willows, a place no longer in use on the other side of the river. He then took a dingy and returned to the van, all the while a timer on the computer photographed his two hostages and sent out a few minutes of each directly to Cahil's website in cyberspace.

He expected little trouble ditching the van, but on closer inspection from behind the wheel, Swantor cursed the fact that it was a stick shift. He sat grinding gears trying to find reverse, sending up a cat cry to the marina residence and the moon. When finally the thing lurched backward, Swantor drove off calmly, heading for the back bayou road he had surveyed a day earlier for this purpose.

Oblong black objects—buzzards—slept on the branches of trees garlanded with eerie moss. "Witch hair," he muttered, recalling what he had heard Spanish moss called in his youth.

Off in the distance behind him, he heard the wail of a siren. He knew the danger of being caught within a hundred yards of the van, much less in the driver's seat, but he didn't want it located smack in front of his marina address, either, should some enterprising cop locate it.

He wound through the thicket and finally came up on the bluff overlooking the Mississippi, a granite cap. Swantor first opened the driver's side door should he need to jump. He then shifted into first, holding the brake hard against the machine's desire to go forward. Tires rotated madly now as he held firm to the brake. He then shifted and rolled from the cab as the monster van screeched and squealed headlong into the air, diving nose first into the great river.

Swantor got up, mud-encrusted, feeling his heart pounding as he did so. His heart had been racing along with the van's tires. He went to the edge of the bluff to stare down at his handiwork by the half moon, crouching on his knees in the soft drizzle. Only the rear of the van showed, and if the river swelled, it would be washed downstream and perhaps consumed altogether.

Swantor made up his mind to leave and worry no more about the van. He had a long walk back to where he had left the dingy. He stood from the crouching position he'd taken, thinking of the fantastic computer film he planned on making, when suddenly his shoe slipped on the gleaming, flattened mud, where the van's tires had turned it into a slick spot of earth winking wet-eyed back at the moon.

Swantor wound up on his knees again, but this time backward, his feet and lower legs extending over the cliff in mid air. He tried to move, but each movement sent him slipping ever so slightly back toward the air and the river. He imagined if he did fall, he might well land dead atop of the van's back doors. Ironic enough, he thought.

He looked about for anything to grab hold of. Useless hanging tree moss presented itself as if to taunt him. There was nothing, no saving branch, no vine, no swinging rope. He realized how crucial this moment was. He pictured this as one of those moments that came in stark black and white, when the eye pinpointed on the fact that one's life could end or resume based upon something as slight as a single choice. No room for mistake. From somewhere overhead, he heard an owl cooing its eternal question, and he imagined what he must look like to the bird. A man in the position of prayer, teetering on the edge.

He gave a thought to his two guests back on the yacht,

thought of how eventually they would be found shackled there. He wondered what authorities would make of it should he die here like this, while Kenyon and the woman were discovered on his yacht.

He could do nothing and remain here on his knees, or leap up from the kneeling position and find solid ground or find himself on his way to the bottom.

He took action, using his knees as springboard. One knee did well, but the other slid beneath him like a tire stuck in mud, landing him on his stomach. But he had managed to gain a bit more land. From there he pulled and clawed himself to safety.

He ushered the strength and breath to crawl and next to stand. The dark, empty woods around him heard his delighted laughter, but seemed not to care, and the owl had taken wing, disappearing out over the great and silent river.

Dr. Jervis Swantor had made his way back to the yacht by 3:40 A.M. He was mud-caked and so he threw his filthy clothes overboard. He then showered and looked at Grant via the monitor. The other man still lay prone on the bed in the other room, muttering to himself. He turned the volume up to listen.

The infamous Skull-digger is cursing me! he thought with delight.

Swantor would send no words or photos out on the Internet that might lead to him. He knew the FBI and other authorities had sophisticated ways of locating a computer's whereabouts, but his machine scrambled such information in hundreds of different directions, thanks to his Anon program.

For the second time tonight, he spliced the tape to the section he wanted and uploaded it and sent it out to Cahil's website. "Now I'm in your face," he said to the invisible person manning Cahil's website. He then forwarded the picture to countless other sites, after which he went to the yacht's controls and started downriver.

After a long couple of hours, he had put some distance between New Orleans and himself, meandering about the canals and anchoring the yacht in a cotton grove. He then retired to his master bedroom for sleep, glad that he had repainted her trim, and now he pulled off the stencils that changed the call numbers and name to a smaller ship kept registered and harbored elsewhere under the name of a dead uncle named Sweet.

He heard a faint crying out, but it was not a woman's voice. He only dully heard Kenyon's voice from the other end of the boat. A distant tugboat whistle wafted over the water, drifting down from upriver. He closed his eyes on the sound, feeling he had done a good night's job.

CAPTAIN Emil Hammerski had plied his trade as a tugboat captain for sixteen years along the Mississippi. In the darkness the water and the waterway, the tree-lined, fog-bound earth and sky often played tricks on a man's eyes; but traveling during the early morning hours meant less traffic and fewer problems, if you knew how to avoid the snags and continually developing sandbars. What he stared at now was no sandbar or snag, but it seemed a real enough threat—a huge black square up ahead where it *oughtn't* be.

Captain Hammerski knew every inch of the river from Minnesota to the Gulf of Mexico. "I tell you, this here is something foreign to the shoals along Three Forks Bend," he told his first mate, handing over the night-vision binoculars.

"You sure have an eye for obstacles, Captain," replied his

first mate. "You think we ought to invest time in it or run round it?"

Busy at the moment, the captain reminded himself. His tug was pushing a barge filled with metal and wood structures for homes being built in Mobile. He was on the clock, and already running behind schedule. Slowing to look over something he could not identify would mean explanations when he showed up even later at the other end. The company's insurance would go up. He'd be to blame. The crew working the barge wouldn't care for the delay either.

He decided to ignore it, go on by. "Whatever it is . . . UFO maybe . . . maybe a government secret of some sort . . . some things aren't meant to be seen," he muttered.

His first mate, young Bryan Carsen listened to the old man closely. He had learned all he knew of the river from the captain. He stood just outside on the bow, trying to get a closer look at what the old man had discovered. It was not a natural formation, that much was for sure.

Shrouded in fog and cold, Carsen spoke to Hammerski through the window. "Whataya think it is, Captain?"

"I just told you, not sure I want to know."

"Looks like a black refrigerator. Folks use this poor old river for all kinds of junk, like's as if it were a great big garbage disposal."

"Likely somebody's junk, all right, that thing," replied Hammerski, puffing on his pipe.

As they neared, the captain asked for the binoculars again and peered through to the strange object. "Damn if it don't look like a huge trunk."

The other man took the binoculars from the captain for a closer look. After a long moment of study, Carsen said, "Oh, my God. It's worse than we thought."

"What is it, Carsen?"

"I think it's the backside of a van that's somehow gotten into the river."

"See anyone around it? Any survivors?"

"No . . . and no telling how long it's been stuck there facedown." Young Carsen looked as if he might be readying to dive into the water, but they were still a hundred yards from it, and the captain reminded Carsen, "We got a two thousand ton barge drifting under our direction."

Carsen looked to be considering this.

The captain also reminded Bryan, "Remember our first responsibility is to the cargo, Bryan. We can't do anything anyway. No survivors. Possibly only an empty truck. We'll call it in to New Orleans police."

"Hell, yeah, we are close to New Orleans. Hell, Captain, radio's been buzzing about how the cops there're looking for a van they think might be linked to the Skull-digger case."

"Yes, I heard something about that. Do you think this is connected?"

"We gotta call it in, Captain."

"Yes . . . Will you do it, Bryan? You're much better explaining things over the radio than I am."

The first mate went back inside and immediately got on the radio to call the NOPD. The conversation was long and confusing on both ends, but finally, Bryan got his message across. He explained who he was, about the barge and that they could not stop until after they were miles past the van crash site. He identified the location of the van as Three Forks Bend. Finally, he got off the radio, saying, "They're on their way. The guy assured me that if we have seen no one in or around the van, then we are free to continue on."

The same morning

AN FBI vehicle met Jessica at the airport, and a young agent introducing himself as Michael Sorrento pumped her hand and told her how much he had admired her work over the years. "I've read every word you've ever published, Dr. Coran. Real fan."

She thanked him and asked if he'd had an opportunity to check out Dr. Swantor's Grand Isle address. "I have," he replied, "but it's an all clear. He's not there according to the local sheriff, a man named Potter."

"Did he go out to the address?"

"Said he did."

Sorrento was going to drive her to the NOPD laboratory and medical examiner's office. Sorrento told her about the ditched van located *in* the Mississippi River by a tugboat crew.

"Get me straight there then."

"No . . . it'll take the wrecking crew they have out there hours to haul it out. May as well go on with your plan to look over the bodies of those two officers."

"I brought tire and footprint impression photos. I'd like to compare them to anything that may've been found at the scene."

"The only prints found, due to the rain last night, were those across Labruto's clothes and his chest. Coroner says one tire ripped open his uniform, the other tattooed his chest pretty good."

As they made their way to the morgue, Jessica's cell phone rang. She took the call from J.T. He apologetically said, "Jess, sorry to inform you but that SquealsLoud guy's PO box in Steeple Top that's registered to a Mark Sweet? Turns out to be a literal dead end, all information on file proving fictitious, the Mark Sweet in question being a dead man."

"Damn it." She told Sorrento the news, and the agent took it calmly.

"But we have reason to believe a Saundra Franklin, living in New Orleans, may be worth looking into. She and the Seeker were tight, e-mailing back and forth."

"What's the address?" She jotted it down. "Let's get a couple of agents over to check this out," she suggested to Sorrento.

"We can do it ourselves. It's on the way."

She liked this agent. "All right. Let's do it."

They drove to the address. Sorrento quickly located the landlord, asking after the Franklin woman, and they were told she'd relocated in a rush, leaving no forwarding address.

"How long ago?" Jessica asked.

"Three days ago, and now suddenly she's real popular."

"Whataya mean 'popular'?" asked Sorrento.

The pudgy little man replied, "A middle-aged guy, too old for her, come looking for her last night."

"At what time?"

"About tenish. I was watching the news."

Jessica flashed a copy of Kenyon's photo. "Was this the man?"

He studied it. "Yeah . . . yeah, that's him, but he looks different: long hair, unshaven, dirty."

They journeyed on to the NOPD medical examiner's office. "We're close," said Sorrento. "I can feel it, Dr. Coran."

In the car, she got Lorena Combs's call back and the Florida sheriff verified that Swantor had supposedly left Florida for a trip to Cancun. Nothing had come of it or the Wells connection in Elixir, Mississippi. Agents there could only locate the wife.

With no other pressing leads, Jessica reasoned that going first to the M.E.'s office made sense. They soon reached the NOPD headquarters and the coroner's office. As they located the elevator from the underground garage, Jessica asked, "How far is this place, Grand Isle?"

"It'd take some getting to. Most of your daylight hours. But like I said, he's not been spotted there." Jessica thought young Sorrento an ambitious man. She liked his enthusiasm for the hunt. "Look, if you say he's operating off a boat, then maybe the marina near where we found the van is where we ought to start. There're more boats in Louisiana than there are people," he exaggerated with a smile.

They arrived on the necessary floor, and Sorrento escorted her to where the two dead policemen lay under scrutiny while doctors performed simultaneous autopsies. During the autopsies, Jessica stepped into the room where doctors worked over Labruto. They had taken blowup shots of the tire treads imprinted across his uniform. Jessica held up a large file she'd taken from a briefcase, while a white-templed, heavyset man in his late fifties, Dr. Alan Mays, objected.

"You can't burst into an autopsy, young lady, without proper clothing, gloves, mask! Do you have any idea how many bacteriologic hazards can be floating around in here?"

Sorrento stepped in, saying, "She ought to know, Doc. She's the M.E. from D.C."

"Quantico, Virginia, actually. FBI . . . Dr. Jessica Coran."

The man stepped back and examined her, nodding. "Still, you should know better."

"I wanted to catch you before you disappeared. I urge you to compare the tire marks left at the kill scene in Georgia with the tire marks left on Labruto's body."

"Of course, that can be done, but it will take time."

"What time? Just compare the photos."

"We don't have a tire expert on staff. Lost him months ago. We'd have to call someone in from outside."

Jessica replied, "I'm just looking for an eyeball confirmation at the moment, something I can do on my own. The experts can verify it later. For that, it's just a matter of putting them side by side below a magnifying glass. I've done it many times."

"You're a tire tread analyst?"

"I've worked closely with the best. Look, we just want to know if it's even close, if we are on the trail of the same man here. There's a possibility we have a second killer mimicking the Digger."

"I see."

"When we get the van itself out of the Mississippi, then we'll have a three-way comparison. At that point, we can turn it all over to the experts."

"All right." Dr. Mays relented, turned to his assistant with the camera and instructed him to go with Dr. Coran and "appease" her.

The young male assistant gave her a half smile and said, "Come with me then, Dr. Coran."

Dr. Mays's assistant took Jessica and the camera down a long corridor. "I'll rush developing, and we'll see if this will help," the eager-to-please assistant said.

A half hour later they placed the tire treads side by side beneath a high-powered microscope. While Labruto's marks were far smaller and less defined, curving away with the contour of his body, Jessica found significant markers to indicate the tread writing was from the same tires. "Now a real expert can go to work identifying the tires to manufacturer and lot number and serial number."

After this, she and Sorrento drove past the Federal Bureau of Investigation offices in New Orleans. The NOPD and local bureau offices were in close proximity, and everyone in the city who wore a badge of any sort seemed bound together by this manhunt. By now everyone had learned that a tugboat crew pushing a huge barge had reported seeing a van trapped in the river. She had brought a laptop computer with her, wishing to remain in direct contact with J.T. for any further developments at Quantico, but also wishing to have the capability of logging on to Cahil's website for any new digital film of her prey.

The unmarked FBI car now bounced along on a back road of dirt and sand that followed the contours of the Mississippi—a winding, twisting path that was at once treacherous and beautiful and strangely fog-laden under a dull gray sky. It was ten in the morning. She imagined how dangerous it must be along the narrow road at night. The rains of the night before had pitted the dirt road, and each turn of the tires threw up mud as they neared the site of the van crash.

"Harbormaster at the marina where Swantor *may* have been says a guy named Swift, booked through the week and disappeared overnight without leaving a manifest," said Sorrento. "He may be your Dr. Swantor."

"Wait a minute. You've already been to this marina?"

"Like I said, it was down from where the van was found. And you mentioned Swantor to us, and that he might have a marina address, remember?"

"Yeah, right. Look, the boat didn't happen to be named *Lands End*, did it?"

"You got it."

Jessica again recalled how the computer video of Grant Kenyon had bounced, as if on a boat sitting atop choppy water. "It's time I told you something, Michael."

"I knew there was something you're holding back. What is it?"

She informed him of the computer images sent to Cahil's site back at Quantico. "It's why I've brought my laptop, in case he contacts us again."

"We've got the Coast Guard looking for his call numbers,

and they've tried to hail him on the maritime frequencies, but no response. Here I was thinking that Kenyon clubbed the guy, buried him with the van, and took his boat."

"He's either harboring Kenyon, or he's holding him hostage for reasons only he knows. Either way, Kenyon has been drugged."

They sped along the river road, sirens wailing.

"Interesting . . . brain-eater meets wanna-be. They have a falling out, and it looks like Swantor has the upper hand, but where is Selese Montoya?" Sorrento wondered aloud.

"She's likely going to be found, that is most of her, in the van."

"Guess we'll all know more when we dredge up that green monster from the muck."

They drove on and Sorrento asked, "Have you ever visited New Orleans for fun? Not the job?"

"A convention once, two murder cases now. No, I guess not."

"You don't remember me, do you?" asked Sorrento.

"No . . . I mean, maybe. You do look somewhat familiar," she lied.

"You don't have to spare my feelings, Dr. Coran."

"I just mean that I speak at countless bureau functions and teaching situations involving hundreds if not thousands of would-be law-enforcement people in and out of the bureau each year. Maybe we met briefly at—"

"I met you your last visit to the city, Dr. Coran." He swerved the car and for a second, she thought he meant to kill them both. "Sorry . . . a turtle in the road."

"You're taking me back a few years, when I cornered and killed Mad Matthew Matisak here."

He lifted an index finger and replied, "And helped end the career of the Queen of Hearts killer as well! Don't sell yourself short. I was on the Hearts case but then so was every eager young agent in the bureau," he reminded her. "Just relocated from Iowa at the time. So I was pretty far down the totem pole, certainly not in the spotlight like you. Not sure I ever want to be."

"You're in it now with this case," she countered.

A voice came over his radio, hailing him. He lifted the microphone and said, "This is Sorrento. Go, Dispatch."

"Patching Lieutenant Besant through, sir."

"Nick Besant's the NOPD officer in charge out at the scene," he told Jessica. "We have a presence there, too."

Besant's voice buzzed from the radio. "Work crew's finally got a secure hold on the van, and it's being hauled up from the river. We're pretty sure it's Kenyon's. Dark green Chrysler, maybe a '97. Has a stolen plate on it that doesn't match the one Labruto and Doyle called in, but we suspect he changed it out."

"Seconds away, Nick. I have a forensics expert with me from D.C., Dr. Coran. She's been on the case since the get-go."

"The crew has the van's nose over the water now. Don't worry. We have Dr. Brunner and his team on hand. They'll do a thorough job, but you'll also have time with the van and its contents."

Sorrento grit his teeth, but he calmly said, "Thanks for the cooperation, Nick."

"Don't mention it, Mike."

He turned to Jessica and said, "Two dead cops and a missing woman in one night has helped a little to raise the spirit of cooperation, but not by much. Every cop in the city wants to John Wayne this thing." He then pointed at the masts of ships at a marina they sped by. Two squad cars were parked among some unmarked vehicles. "That's where *Lands End* disappeared from last night. We have men interviewing neighbors and the harbormaster for any additional information, maybe get up a sketch of Swantor."

"Coast guard should be able to locate the boat from the call numbers kept in harbor records," suggested Jessica.

"And the fact it's a white Evenrude Windjammer 2000, capable of moving at great speed through the Gulf waters. It should stand out."

"Let's hope so, before he reaches Mexico."

THEY arrived at the van site where the wrecking crew sent up a screeching sound followed by a thunderous belch, and then the dripping van settled on its four tires beside the road. The day had remained dismal and overcast, imprisoning a dense, low-lying fog in the gullies along the river. Shrubbery and dead branches added to the morbid feel of the place. It obviously had been a gargantuan effort to remove the mud-caked van from the muck and mire along this stretch of river. And they had done it in thick fog. The work crew looked like pencil sketches of gray ghosts, Civil War ghosts, each caked with mud.

"Get your mud boots on, Dr. Coran."

" 'Fraid I didn't pack any."

He pointed his key holder and an electronic *blip* indicated that he had popped the trunk. "I have an extra pair."

They quickly donned heavy Wellington boots. Everything was covered with slippery mud from the evening rains and the water, spilling geyserlike, from every crevice of the Chrysler van. "It's definitely the make and model," said Jessica as they approached.

"And the color Labruto and Doyle had radioed in. I gotta wonder how the bastard ever got from the French Quarter to here without being detected?"

"Luck of the devil," she said.

"I suspect you know all about that, Dr. Coran. I read

about that weird case in London, and that strange business in Philly."

Jessica bit her lower lip and nodded. "Unfortunately, yes, I've danced with the devil a time or two."

Jessica rushed ahead toward the back of the van, where she saw a field of debris—destroyed paper, cloth, maps, packs of gum, a comb, a toothbrush, coins and small bills—that'd been dumped out. Someone had already opened the back doors and inspected for the Montoya woman's body, yet no one was talking. Rather, everyone stood stone silent as if in mourning. "Have you found the dead girl or not?" she asked a man who introduced himself as Assistant M.E. Brunner.

"Dr. Coran . . . heard about you from downtown. The van's empty except for a lot of soaked rags and trash. We're having it towed to a place where we can thoroughly work it," he said in a nasally voice. Fighting a cold, he sneezed into a handkerchief, knocking his glasses down his nose.

"We found nothing. Apparently, the perpetrator saw no reason to lock his doors," said a voice in her ear. She turned to stare at the fiery blue eyes of a determined man. "Lt. Besant, NOPD, Dr. Coran," said the tall, thin man with a mustache who now stood between her and Brunner. Brunner had chosen to back off. "You should first let us determine if there're any water moccasins or other poisonous snakes inside. We're still removing water and—"

"Yes, I can see you've removed quite a lot," she indicated the debris at the foot of the van doors, seeing a license plate swim by, wondering what else had floated out. "Thanks for your concern, Lieutenant, but please, out of my way."

After donning gloves, Jessica climbed in the van, where the water was still ankle deep. The officer in the front shouted, "The rest of the water'll come out when we hoist it again. Then we can tow it."

Jessica pulled a penlight from her pocket and scanned the rear of the van. She felt Sorrento before she saw him climb in behind her. "Whata we got, Doctor?"

Her light showed the leather viselike head shackle peeking out from beneath the water. She estimated where the hands would have been held, and she found thick blood-crusted chains attached to both seats. Her light telegraphed this fact to Sorrento. He then located the ankle shackles lying beneath the water, heavy and slick like a string of mollusks.

Jessica announced, "It's his killing ground all right."

"We've got men in the water, searching," said Besant. "They are black water divers, capable of locating anyone who might be down there."

"Did you find any tools? The damned bone cutter, a scalpel, anything along those lines?" asked Jessica.

Besant shook his head and rubbed the back of his neck. "Cutting tools, no. But we did fetch a shotgun, a completely ruined laptop computer and some audiotapes and a tape machine, all soaked, but with FBI help perhaps we can restore the tapes, and get something out of that computer."

"We have that capability here in New Orleans, right, Michael?" Jessica asked.

"That's right," replied Sorrento.

Besant turned the laptop and the tapes over, exactly five, the number of known victims. They were labeled by number, not name. "This could be a good sign," Jessica suggested. "If he has a tape for each victim, and he failed to make one for Selese Montoya, she may still be alive."

"You think she's on *Lands End*, too?" asked Sorrento in a conspiratorial whisper.

"I'm thinking aloud. If he didn't have time to make a tape, he may not have had time to feed on her, and if Swantor's incapacitated him, she may still be alive."

"And you think Swantor's taken her with them."

"And if the two of them are kindred spirits . . . Swantor may be as dangerous as Kenyon," said Jessica as she and Sorrento climbed from the death van.

"Taken her where?" asked Nick Besant who'd listened to their conversation.

"We're not sure, but we have a Coast Guard cutter and a helicopter searching the river for any suspicious-looking watercraft."

"Suspicious how?"

Sorrento updated Besant.

Jessica heard only snatches of what Agent Sorrento told Besant, but she heard enough to know that he had made it a simple abduction theory, that Kenyon had commandeered the boat and taken its owner hostage along with the girl. She did hear Sorrento add, "It's a long shot, but one we thought worth pursuing."

"I'll see about getting some NOPD water cops out there to help the Coast Guard," Besant replied.

"That's the scene, Nick," lied Sorrento, the look in his eyes told Jessica to play along. Jessica wanted no part of the petty games played between these two, so she instead turned away and returned to Mike's still open trunk to remove the boots and climb back into the car. Once settled in her seat, she opened her laptop to check Cahil's Web page to see if any additional images of Kenyon had been put up on the board.

Sitting amid the mud, shrouded in a fog that chilled her to the bone, Jessica keystroked in the necessary dot-com.

Jessica was startled to find a woman cuffed to a bed in what appeared the same room where she'd seen Kenyon in earlier. The camera motion was the same, too, swaying . . . bobbing.

The woman on the screen appeared exhausted from long

hours of tears and crying. She only whined now, unable it seemed to shout. Her eyes appeared glazed and dull. She looked as if drugged.

Jessica stared at the struggling young woman, presumably Selese Montoya. She felt the helplessness of the poor woman's situation from where she sat in Sorrento's car, unable to affect anything. The victim was likely miles and miles away, and here Jessica sat hopelessly mired in the gloom of a place called Turtle Fork Bend.

She could save Besant and his divers any trouble now. They would not find the body in the river, at least not yet. Selese was being held somewhere, likely Swantor's boat.

"That's her! I've seen her picture," said Sorrento, looking in on Jessica. "That's the Montoya woman."

"And this is being fed to us live."

Sorrento had tossed his boots in the trunk, and he'd climbed in beside her. No one else saw the images being fed them. Now the image of the woman in chains was replaced by Kenyon, pacing like an animal. His ankle chain rattling and visible in the shot. He paced. He shouted into the camera, presumably at Swantor, but the words were edited, and at times nothing came out of his open mouth.

"We've got to locate Swantor and fast. I don't know what his plans are for the next installment, but I can imagine it's not going to get any prettier."

"We'll get him," promised Sorrento. "He belongs to the FBI, not the NOPD. We take him, he's ours. Besant gets to him first, we lose him. It's as simple as that. They'll put him up on charges of murdering Labruto and—"

"We've got to tell them the Montoya woman's not down there in the river," Jessica said.

"No, that's valuable lead time that we need, so we can make the grab, Dr. Coran. Trust me, NOPD just wants to blow this guy away as a cop killer."

"Michael, we have an obligation to cooperate with these guys."

"Do you want this guy to stand trial for the string of murders of *all* his victims in a federal court or not? Louisiana's got some jurisdictional loopholes a homegrown lawyer could run a twenty-ton elephant through. Unless we pick him up, they could spend a year prosecuting him here for cop killing, he goes away to Angora to serve time. I want him the fuck executed. How about you?"

She mulled over Sorrento's logic. It made a certain sense, although she knew the state had the death penalty. Still, she didn't know Besant, but she had gotten the distinct impression that he wanted Kenyon every bit as badly as she did.

"Just buy us a little time. They were going to do the search here anyway. If we hadn't seen that video . . ." He backed the car up into an embankment, cut hard to the left and turned the car around, heading back toward the marina.

As they drove away, Jessica had mulled over the names, SquealsLoud, Sweet, Swantor in her mind. Were they all the same man? "All right," she finally agreed. "We do it *our* way."

FIFTEEN

*Your eyes are so sharp that you cannot only look
through a millstone, but clean through the mind.*

—JOHN LYLY, 1554–1606

Downriver
Later that night

JERVIS Swantor awoke to the sound of a boat whistle, someone hailing his ship, he feared. It was far too soon to be
caught and stopped.

He looked out the porthole above his bed and could see
absolutely nothing. Just as predicted by the weatherman,
the Mississippi was awash in a thick, gray fog, a soup that
blotted out sight.

He grabbed his night-vision binoculars and saw that it
was a southbound barge, pushed by a tugboat, and it came
within feet of his yacht. Barges were plied up and down the
river like silent dinosaurs, but he could not believe these
fools were still running under such conditions. If they saw
his lights at all, they must think the same of him. He feared
anyone seeing him out in this would report his position,
thinking him in danger.

The swells from the barge also indicated just how close
they'd come to swamping Swantor's yacht, as they caused it

to bob like a giant cork, stirring his two guests to shouts and pleadings.

He picked up the tool kit belonging to Kenyon, and went to the woman's room to look in. She pleaded with him to save her from a madman. "I've got your madman next door, opposite you." He pulled forth the brain saw and held it up to the camera, which could only catch his upraised hand and the saw. "I've got his tool kit. For now, you needn't worry, my dear." He had turned the audio off for now to lessen his need to edit out his voice and any references to himself.

He straddled the two rooms and pushed open the door, which allowed him to see both Kenyon and the woman at the same time.

"You stinking, lousy bastard, Swantor!" shouted Kenyon, getting up from his bed and rushing Swantor, but the chain stopped him a few feet from Swantor, like a collared dog.

"Well now, everyone's awake. Likely hungry, aren't you?"

"I'll kill you, Swantor."

"Make nice, Mr. Kenyon. I intend on feeding you." He held the saw out to Kenyon. "Take it."

"What's going on?" pleaded the woman.

Kenyon took firm hold of the bone cutter. His eyes locked with Swantor's. "What're you planning?"

"I'm going down to the galley to fix you a bite, my dear! No one should die on an empty stomach," Swantor said to the woman. "Be right back."

Swantor smiled as he closed each door and left. He'd gotten it all on film. His next installment. Before his last installment for this episodic adventure, he would first prepare a hearty meal for the lady.

Swantor glanced at the monitor screens for each room. The woman looked weak, vulnerable in her chained position. By comparison, Kenyon was enervated by the bone cutter, huddling over it, rocking, and once or twice he placed it to his temple, but he didn't turn it on. Instead he held it at arm's distance and studied it in his fist. He looked as if he were revisiting each of his kills, savoring each moment, his jaw hanging open, his eyes fixed.

He then applied the bone cutter to his ankle chain, creating sparks. Swantor turned off the tape and turned on the intercom, warning Kenyon that he would not eat if he broke the blade. "The chain is made of titanium steel. You're wasting your time and the blade on it."

"If I get my hands on you, Swantor, I'll kill you."

"They're going to say you were crazy, Dr. Kenyon, and I must agree. I've heard some of your conversation with your friend, what's his name? Phillip. Yes, they're going to call you crazy, but they're going to say I was even crazier."

Kenyon stopped the horrid scream of the bone cutter, and as its whirring ended, he heard the woman's screams. "Music to all our ears, Dr. Kenyon, Phillip," Swantor said and turned toward the galley. "Must now fatten the calf, as they say."

INFORMATION about Swantor at the marina proved scarce. According to everyone they spoke to, the man was a loner. He had come off a bitter divorce battle and had been living on his boat for several months. It hardly sounded like the know-it-all, nosy Swantor of Florida, and here he was known as Jacob Swift. Except for these few details, their time canvassing the marina had proved useless. Besant had joined them there, filled with questions. Sorrento asked the frustrated Besant to place his men on a boat-to-boat search for the Montoya woman. This done, they drove off for a small nearby airport where Sorrento chartered a small helicopter. The pilot agreed to get them to a Coast Guard cutter but that was all. "Bad weather and poor visibility'll make any river search for a single craft impossible until conditions improve. Weather report says that could be twenty-four hours."

They accepted the ride to the cutter.

Jessica and Sorrento soon stood on the deck of *Triumph*, the Coast Guard cutter, plying through the water at a good clip, considering the weather, in search of Swantor's yacht. Sorrento had called for the cutter to pick them up at a designated rendezvous point thirty miles south of where the van had been found. They assumed Mexico to be Swantor's destination. Still, to be certain to cover any escape, they also sent a cutter north along the river.

Jessica felt good being on the ship, felt good at being in pursuit.

Every port city and town along both banks of the Mississippi River was alerted to the description, call numbers and the name of the yacht, and asked to report any sighting.

Using her laptop, Jessica found a countertop where she could work on the cutter. Since Swantor was not responding to the Coast Guard via the radio, she wanted to try reaching him using what she suspected was his SquealsLoud E-mail address, which she had gotten from J.T. She taunted him, saying she knew that he was both Swift and Sweet as well as Swantor. She sent him a warning that he was being pursued, and that he should give himself up to authorities. She said if he cooperated, they would go lightly on him. That they wanted Selese Montoya released unharmed, and that they wanted Kenyon. She also wrote in their coordinates and added:

We're right behind you on the river. So far, you've just impeded our investigation. Don't make it any worse, Mr. Swantor.

The only response was a series of moving digital images. She and Sorrento watched this series of images displayed, images of a helpless woman chained to a bed by hand and foot, followed by a shot of a handheld bone cutter, the sort used in autopsies. It was held to the camera in a man's hand, the woman now in the background. There was only a muted audio, but the woman's screams were raised in volume.

This was followed by a new scene of Kenyon, one which displayed him shouting and racing toward someone—presumably Swantor—stopped only by the ankle chain. The prisoner was then shown the same bone saw as had been displayed to the woman. Again, the audio was silent save for Kenyon's shouts and screams, carefully edited, screening out any reference to Swantor, and not once did she hear the man's own voice.

Jessica replayed the tape, studying every detail, and her eyes went to the anguished eyes of the victim. It disturbed Jessica to know that this image was beaming across the globe, and to know that some people would copy it and replay it over and over, even enjoy it with popcorn.

Usually, Jessica dealt with the dead, but here lay the near dead, the soon-to-be dead, the *soon-to-be-separated-from-her-brain* dead. The anguish she felt, the helplessness of it all, ripped at Jessica's heart. "This . . . this is awful. He intends something awful for her."

This was followed by a text message from SquealsLoud that read:

A brain is a terrible thing to waste. . . . If he consumes six, then I consume him, I have the reward of seven, but if he consumes ten and I him, then I am rewarded by eleven.

Following this came reams of information on the brain, the brain's functions, and the relationship between mind and body, soul and brain. The history and evolution of the brain.

Jessica again imagined how many people were receiving these words and images throughout cyberspace at that moment. Swantor meant to take both Kenyon's and Cahil's places in a big way.

She then saw that she had an incoming message from John Thorpe at Quantico. J.T. had arranged for a private chat room for himself and Jessica on the website. J.T.'s message from Quantico was brief:

> Open up to the Web page. Cahil's site is getting more images of the hostage and Kenyon. We've got another true Cahil disciple here, I think. And I fear this new message is all too horrifying to contemplate.

Jessica wrote back that they had just seen what Swantor had forwarded, telling J.T. of the latest developments in the case and how they were now on a chase to locate Dr. Swantor. She added:

> Remember the shaky camera? It wasn't the camera shaking, it was the guy's yacht. From what I gather, watching the graphics, he intends on throwing the female hostage and the bone cutter to Kenyon. Then he plans to film the entire event. After that, I don't know what he may or may not do. He may attempt to bring Kenyon more people to feed on, so he can go on filming the cannibalism.

Jessica logged off. "We've got to locate that fucking yacht," Jessica told Sorrento.

"They've got every available boat in the Guard looking for it, along with the NOPD water police by now, I'm sure," he replied. "Doctor, if it's out there, we'll find it."

"Why aren't we getting any aerial help from Coast Guard

choppers, Captain?" she asked Captain Jon Quarels. "They're used to such conditions."

"Bad weather-related problems south in the Gulf. Everything's been diverted there for rescue operations. Looks like a hurricane on the way."

She stepped away from Quarels and huddled with Sorrento. "Something doesn't feel right. Swantor's too smart for this," she said. "He's got to be planning some sort of getaway that involves another vehicle. He's got to know how hot that boat is right now."

"Yeah, I've thought about that possibility myself," replied Mike Sorrento. "But I don't think he'll abandon ship until he's finished his sick little game."

"Unless," she replied.

He saw that her eyes had grown large. "Unless what?"

"Unless he intends to go down with the ship."

"A double-murder and suicide. Not until after his last installment . . ." Sorrento softly said.

"Can't we get any more speed out of this thing?" she asked the captain. "A woman's life is at stake."

"We're surveying the shore and every rock and island in the river, Dr. Coran. We don't want to miss anything," replied the captain. "Nor do we want to run aground."

"What about that helicopter?"

"They're trying to find us one, but I can make no promises."

"What kind of an outfit is this?" Jessica shouted. "Should I request one from the Army, the Navy?"

"Take it easy, Jess," cautioned Sorrento. "Let's go below, have a cup of coffee to settle our nerves," he suggested, guiding her outside and on deck.

Jessica relented, knowing she needed settling. "Damn it, he's going to feed her to that mad dog if we don't locate him and stop him."

"Why . . . What's Swantor getting out of all this?" he asked as they went down a flight of stairs.

"I'd be guessing but . . . it seems like he's gone into competition with Kenyon, to outdo Kenyon's horror with his own."

"And to die at the top of his form?"

"All this spawned from the mind of Daryl Thomas Cahil and his Internet lunacy."

JERVIS Swantor had pushed his craft to its limit and had burrowed in at the swamps that would eventually spill out near Grand Isle. To evade capture, he had used one of the old canals cut during the Civil War by black regiments for U. S. Grant. Few people knew of the canal and even fewer knew how to maneuver in the swamps. He had fed the woman and spent the rest of the evening racing from authorities and hiding. There were a thousand directions and waterways and islands in the swamp, but one place in particular where he could find refuge—his former home at Grand Isle, the boathouse there—and then he could introduce Kenyon to his ex-wife, Lara.

But for now it was time to feed Kenyon.

Darkness had descended over the swamp, along with another beautiful blue fog saying a long hello to Swantor where he stood on deck. He opened a small hatchway and looked down at Kenyon, who lay on his bed, his fists pounding at his sides. The camera never left Kenyon, and he had to know that by now.

Swantor opened a second small hatch and stared down at the woman named Selese. She had tried to work on his sympathies, giving him her name, where she lived, names of relatives, even her dog's name, Ronnie, but he had only listened dispassionately, never stepping before the cameras.

His face and presence would only be felt after the great event was filmed. This was mere rehearsal, he kept telling Selese. Lara would be the real show.

Swantor went below and shut down the filming in Kenyon's room. He then entered with a key to Kenyon's shackle, tossing it to Kenyon. All the while, he held the gun on the other man, telling him, "Pick up your bone cutter and tool kit and go into the other room for your mind meal, Grant."

"You don't have to keep me chained up," Kenyon pleaded. "We ought to be able to trust one another."

"You'd kill me at the first opportunity. I have no illusions about that, Grant."

"But I wouldn't."

"Shut up and do as I say!" Swantor indicated the gun in his hand. "You must be starved. Aren't you hungry?"

"I am . . . that I am."

"Go then, feed."

Swantor locked Kenyon and Selese Montoya in the cabin together. As he made his way toward the living area, Swantor heard the woman's uncontrolled screams. Selese continued to scream hysterically as Swantor watched the viewing screen and set up the computer to send to Cahil's website. A part of him grew fascinated, and he slowed to watch it all unfold as he filmed it. He keyed in the necessary strokes and beamed it directly to the world. He added a special message to the screen for the FBI woman who had contacted him:

You and the rest of the world are going to enjoy this.

He imagined all the people who would see the film, duplicate it and forward it on to others. It represented a kind of immortality for Swantor.

Swantor had given Kenyon no Demoral to work with,

but Phillip didn't care. In order to make her hold still, he knocked her unconscious. Then the Digger had gone immediately to work, shaving the woman's head, marking her fore scalp with bold red lines and lifting his scalpel over her closed eyes. With his left hand, Kenyon worked deftly, cutting down to bone. With the first bloody incision, Selese awoke and immediately screamed, and realized what Kenyon was telling her: "I only want your brain." Knowing now what he was doing to her, she pleaded for help from anyone on the other side of the camera lens.

From his seat at the controls, watching, Swantor smiled and said, "I beseech thee! I beseech thee!"

He then watched Selese swoon before fainting altogether from blood loss.

Swantor could not have been happier with the results. His camera had caught every blood spatter, every deft movement of the doctor's hands. And Swantor, now the Webmaster, zoomed in to display a close-up of the disfigured forehead. Now the camera recorded as Kenyon's bone saw came to life. Its mechanical *whirr* created a terrifying sound in this context, and an even more horrifying noise as it made its screaming, grinding path through the skull—*shattered shards of glass ground in a mixer.*

"I give you the Skull-digger," said Swantor, recording his master of ceremonies voice. "Finally, the star of his own show . . ."

"I hope you're enjoying this, Swantor!" Kenyon shouted as he placed the bone cutter to Selese's forehead *again*, making the final, methodical cut in his medically delicate manner. The computer had been told to blip any mention of Jervis's name. His own fifteen minutes of fame would come at his own choosing, in time.

The computer camera next captured Kenyon plucking the cut window of flesh and bone from the forehead and discarding it. The camera then showed him lifting his surgical tongs, opening them, plunging them into the window he'd created, and plucking forth the brain. He held it up to the camera eye. Like sweetmeats prised from a crustacean.

"Is this what you want, you bastard? Is it?" He bit into the brain matter, tearing away a portion, devouring it half chewed. He repeated this again and again, his hands slick with blood and brain fluid.

Swantor reveled in what he filmed, clicking off the audio and saying through the intercom, "Perfect . . . perfectly executed, Dr. Kenyon. This will make us both great men!"

Kenyon as Phillip devoured the last of Selese's brain. As he did so, Swantor said over the intercom, "I'll have another for you soon."

The camera left the bloody mouth of the killer and focused on the body of Selese Montoya, slowly making its way from her toes, along her legs, to torso, neck, lower face and then to the black rectangle created in the empty skull.

"This is going out live, Kenyon, to the world. Take a bow."

Grant cried out, his mouth still bloody, raging at the camera. "Let me out of here now, Swantor! Let me out!"

"Audio's off, Dr. Kenyon. No one can hear you."

THE captain of the cutter, on which Jessica and Sorrento traveled, stood looking out over the broad expanse of the river. A cruise ship made up to look like an old-time paddle-wheeling riverboat passed them by, tourists waving from every deck and chair, a gleaming diamond-colored chandelier winking at them from the windowed restaurant aboard. The gaiety of the riverboat stood in stark contrast to the work at hand aboard the Coast Guard cutter. "Imagine the guy's insurance premium if that damn floating restaurant should go down out here in this fog," he said to Joseph Konrath, his first mate.

Jessica and Sorrento returned to the bridge, and the captain greeted them and then said, "I've checked in again and again with boats downriver and no one's seen him. But I have an idea."

"What's that, Captain?" asked Sorrento.

"Reports from here to Pilottown—end of the river—say that no one has spotted this yacht. That's just too unbelievable, unless he's taken another tack."

"What tack? North, you mean?" asked Jessica.

"Well, he may have used one of the old canals to cut from the river to a bay area."

"The canals? What canals?" asked Jessica.

Quarels took them to a nautical map on the wall. "We are about here, the canal I have in mind is right here," he said, pointing just ahead. "Leads west into the bay and some swamplands."

"Isn't that the fastest way to get to the Grand Isle area?" asked Sorrento. This guy has some real estate there and most animals do run back to their lairs when chased."

"Show me where Grand Isle is, Captain," asked Jessica.

Quarels pointed it out, a small dot on the map to the southwest of their position. "It's just a hunch, but when Sorrento asked about Grand Isle before, I recalled the canal up ahead. Just a hunch, but I think it may be the reason why no one's seen our man."

Jessica turned to Sorrento and said, "Grand Isle, of course. He's got to be heading there, Mike." She then said to Quarels, "We had a local lawman check there yesterday, and he found no sign of Swantor in the area, but all that's changed now."

"Follow the course of the canal, Captain," said Sorrento.

"All right. We'll do just that, but the storm's going to

pound us in there, and we have a skeleton crew."

"Back in Florida, Swantor made some passing remark that his wife got the house, and he got the boat. Perhaps the house in question is on this Grand Isle," said Jessica.

"Mansions, high living," said the captain. "That's Grand Isle."

"Combs's background check on Swantor had the house in contention."

Sorrento rubbed his chin. "Swantor's ex-wife, maybe she still resides there on the island."

"His ex." They all fell silent.

"You thinking what I'm thinking?" Sorrento asked.

"That he intends on feeding his ex to Kenyon?"

"If so, what's he need Selese for?"

"I don't know, maybe to . . . to keep Kenyon in line?"

"My God."

Jessica wondered at the curious irony, if her long, circuitous chase after the Skull-digger should end on an island.

"Under normal circumstances, I'd radio for assistance, bring up another cutter to go around the boot at Pilottown, surround the island," suggested Captain Quarels. "But reports are bad all along the coast at the Gulf, and I can't get any help, not at the moment."

"We'll keep trying," said Konrath. "But reports of flooding problems south of us are keeping all crews busy."

"Rains preceding Hurricane Alice," said Quarels.

"What about helicopters?" asked Jessica.

"Sorry, they tell me that all our helicopters in this sector've been diverted to the coast until they know what's going to happen there. It's a category four, with several waterspouts. Already had a ship in the Gulf swamped by this thing, so they're expecting additional rescue efforts will be necessary."

It was getting stormy here, as well. When Jessica and Sorrento had made their way back up to the pilothouse, the wind had whistled down the length of the boat, swirling and eddying about them, threatening to send them overboard. The western horizon had been ablaze with beautiful colors at dusk, but now it'd become late, and darkness had suddenly come on with the stormfront, clouds blotting out moon and stars.

Jessica drew an imaginary line on Quarels's Mississippi River map with her index finger the distance to Grand Isle. "How many hours?" she asked Quarels.

"Three perhaps in good weather. Can't say in this." He nodded to the black windows ahead of them.

They drank coffee under the light of the pilothouse and watched as a deluge of rain began pouring over them. The powerful winds made the ship shiver.

Jessica said, "He's facing worse weather if he is south of us. We have to make better time, and hope he's had to slow down."

"When we get into the center of the canal, we'll open her up," Quarels promised. Then he invited them to look on at the sonar and radar screens. According to the equipment aboard, the cutter began a wide turn into a sharply cut canal, its banks like walls sketched in thin green lines. Jessica tried to imagine them by day.

Now they headed into deep backwater swamp. "I wonder how much your fugitive is relying on the weather," Quarels said to them. "Normally, in a dry season, some of these canals might not be deep enough in sections. Lot of boaters get hung up on sandbars in them. But if he's been monitoring the weather . . . well, he's planned this thing out, that's certain."

The canal took them west first through a back bay area that Captain Quarels had pinpointed on the map. He showed them how it would sharply turn again south. Jessica and Sorrento were studying the nautical map of the area when Jessica's phone rang.

She stepped away, taking the call. "Jess, it's me, John."

"What's is it, J.T.? Any good news? I could use some good news."

"Unfortunately, SquealsLoud has gone through with it, Jess. The Montoya woman was handed over to Kenyon, and the other madman filmed the entire thing. It's a horror movie beyond anything I've ever seen."

"And it's playing on Cahil's website?"

"As we speak, and God knows where else. You can access it if you want to, but I'd leave it alone, Jess."

She looked across at Sorrento and the captain. "He's already killed his captive. We're too late to help her."

Sorrento wrapped his arms about himself and rocked. The captain took in a deep breath of air and bit his lower lip, shaking his head.

"It's on the computer as a graphic film. The entire event, according to my partner in Quantico."

"Are you going to open it? Take a look at it?" asked Sorrento.

"I hate giving the bastard the satisfaction, but we might draw some clues from it," she replied angrily. She went to her laptop, opened it and logged on to the Internet. She found his E-mail waiting.

Sorrento stood beside her, placed an arm on her shoulder and said, "Steady yourself."

"I'd like to see what kind of a maniac we're chasing as well," added Quarels.

Jessica opened the media E-mail, and the three of them watched the scene unfold in stark dread. From the wheel, First Mate Joe Konrath watched his controls but intermittently looked over his shoulder at the computer screen as well. When the bone cutting began, Jessica looked away. The men remained fixed on the sight, disbelieving it at the same time that they witnessed it.

"My God in Heaven," said Quarels.

"Poor woman," added Sorrento. "We've got to nail these two bastards."

In all her years with the FBI, Jessica had never seen anyone actually executed before her eyes. She had never even gone to a federal or state prison to watch an execution. This murder brought about by Swantor was meant to shock, and it did.

"If he reaches Grand Isle and finds his wife, he'll do the same to her," Jessica projected. "We need to contact police there. Have someone get the ex–Mrs. Swantor out of there if she's on the island."

She shut down Swantor's horror show. She then asked Sorrento to contact this man Potter at Grand Isle and attempt to get word that Swantor was on his way there, ending with, "And warn Mrs. Swantor to leave at once."

Sorrento explained that the island was police free, but that it was serviced by a Sheriff Danby Potter, a one-man police force from a small town on the mainland, Lewistown. "Station house is the size of a phone booth. The isle gets mail service from Lewistown, too."

"Just summerhouses, recently developed land," said Quarels.

Jessica said, "We've got to get the wife's phone number. Warn her he's coming for her."

Sorrento got on his phone and contacted Lewistown police, reminding Sheriff Danby Potter of who he was and asking, "Is Mrs. Swantor on the island?"

"She is . . . or was when I went out there yesterday, yes."

"We're chasing the Skull-digger, Sheriff."

"My Lord . . ."

"And we fear Mr. Swantor is involved. I need the phone number to the house on Grand Isle."

"I always said that Jervis Swantor was some kind of puddinghead. I'll get that number for you."

Sorrento heard Potter ferreting through paper for the number. "I got the number!" He read it off to Sorrento and quickly added, "I'm damn confused by you people. I checked out the place early this morning, a second time. Mrs. Swantor was there, so far as I could tell alone, no sign of that Dr. Swantor or his yacht. You asked me to ascertain his whereabouts, but the missus, she claims not to know or care so long as her check's on time."

"We believe he is on his way there now, Sheriff, and to say that she may be in danger is an understatement."

"So you fellas suspect Swantor's the Skull-digger now. I can't believe it, but you know, I can at the same time."

"Please, listen, Sheriff. It's a little more complicated than—"

"I know what he looks like. Used to come into town for groceries and the hardware. Maybe I should go back out there to the island and sit with Mrs. Swantor till you—"

"No, don't go out there alone, Potter. We think she has time to get out, and we're going to call her to warn her from here. We're on a Coast Guard cutter only a few hours away."

After he hung up, Sorrento telephoned the number Potter had provided for the Swantor summer home, but only an answering machine responded. He left his name and number for Mrs. Lara Swantor to get back to him as soon as possible—a matter of life and death.

Jessica took Sorrento aside, saying, "Perhaps we ought to ask the sheriff to organize a few deputies and go out there to the house, cover Mrs. Swantor until we *can* get there."

"She's not answering her phone," he replied. "Let me give it another shot." Still no answer. "She must not be there."

"Or she may be unable to answer her phone."

He nodded. "OK, I'll call the sheriff back." He did so, only to get a recording stating that Potter was out and would return within an hour. The tape gave them another number in case of emergency.

"Damn, I hope that old fool hasn't gone out there alone. He doesn't know what he's dealing with."

"Try the other number," Jessica suggested.

Sorrento dialed this number, getting the sheriff on his cell phone, the sound of rain splattering a hard surface like static in Sorrento's ear. "Sheriff Potter, it's Agent Sorrento again. You're not to go out to the house alone. If you must go, do so with a team of men."

"Ahhh, yeah, I'm getting a posse together right now."

"Good . . . good. There's more danger than you realize. Let me set the stage for you."

Real static obliterated anything Sorrento might have said. He turned to Jessica. "He's on his way out there. Claims to have gotten help."

"Claims or did?"

"I'm not sure."

The cutter made its way deeper into the black shaft of the canal.

7:00 P.M.

INSIDE the expansive house on Grand Isle, Mrs. Lara Swantor and her newfound lover, James Harris, drank wine and played with massive bubbles in the large, oval bath. They played with one another as well, fondling and kissing, when the phone rang. "Now, who knows I'm here? Who could be calling?" she slurred her words while glancing at a clock that read 7 P.M. Outside the storm shook the house, and its intensity frightened Lara, but James, a psychiatrist, said the best way to overcome such a fear was to enjoy oneself in the midst of adversity. It sounded good, but what he really meant was that he wanted to bathe with her.

Besides, the latest newscasts had the brunt of the hurricane heading toward Mobile now. All the same, each lightning strike shook her to the bones. Only James's attentions took her mind off the storm.

When the phone rang, James had said, "Let the machine get it," as he held on to her, caressing her in the way she could not resist.

"All right . . . good thinking," she replied. "Hmmm . . . baby."

She heard the sound of someone she didn't recognize leaving a message she could not make out. "What did the man say?" she asked James who, being younger, must surely have better hearing, she thought.

"Didn't catch it. Likely a neighbor worried about the storm."

"Old Mrs. Philbin, I suppose."

They continued with their bathing of one another. A second time the phone rang, and James got up and walked naked and bubbly to the phone, but it quit ringing—no message this time. He lifted it off the hook and put an end to it.

"Get back in here, you!" she called out to him.

"On my way!" he called back. "Just going to get us another bottle of wine from the pantry. Are you hungry?"

SIXTEEN

*He cometh to you with a tale that holds children
from play, and old men from the chimney corner.*

—Sir Philip Sidney, 1554–1586

Even in the darkness and the storm, Jervis Swantor had easily maneuvered his yacht, equipped with the best radar and sonar instruments in the land, through the treacherous canal. He had more trouble locating and docking the yacht in the boathouse than he had with the river and the canal. Down below, he'd re-chained Kenyon in his cabin, placing his tools just out of the man's reach. Now all he had to do was find Lara, whose small transport craft was tied to the dock. Once he found her, he would introduce her to his new friends Grant and Philip.

Knowing that the authorities were extremely close, and that they likely already knew of his final destination, he must act fast. Once the boat was secured, he climbed off and onto the boathouse landing. From there, he could see the house. A light was on in the master bedroom. From all appearances, Lara was home despite her ignoring the phone. Any servants would have gotten off the island by nightfall, especially with such a storm brewing.

Fighting the driving rain, Swantor made his way up the long flight of cedar steps to the house, lit by the occasional lightning bolt. Soaked, wild-eyed, he stared up at the bedroom light again. Some shadow moved across the room. Lara, he decided, unable to sleep. She had always hated storms.

Swantor meant to make his way around toward the back of the house. He had kept a key to the rear door.

"Now, sweetheart, time for judgment day."

Her dog, a Jack Russell terrier named Opal, began barking from her doghouse. He went to the dog and strangled it with his bare hands, silencing it. "Never liked that dog," he muttered to the corpse.

SHERIFF Danby Potter, fifty-nine, approached the house via the river directly across from the mainland, knowing the dock area well. His uniform covered by a yellow rain slicker, he warmed his insides with the moonshine liquor he sipped at. From what he had gathered over the phone with Sorrento, it appeared that Dr. Jervis Swantor was the butcher that the FBI was in search of. He knew Swantor on sight, and he knew the man's boat. He didn't need any pimply-faced young squirt of an FBI cop telling him how to proceed, and when he saw that there was no other boat at Mrs. Swantor's place other than her own, he knew he'd arrived in time.

He'd tried to telephone her from his cell phone, but he'd been unable to get through, getting a busy signal instead. He had pictured the worse, that Swantor was already inside the house, that he'd taken the receiver off the hook. This worried Potter.

He put in beside Mrs. Swantor's transport. He'd seen her car parked on the mainland at the marina. Grand Isle was a no-cars-allowed island, serviced by water boats for mail delivery and medical emergencies, and sometimes a medevac chopper was called in from upstate.

He wanted to believe that she had taken the phone off the hook herself, perhaps wanting to get some sleep. If so, she'd not gotten the warning from the FBI people. He hoped to find her simply asleep with the phone off the hook.

Potter had heard the rumors of just how nasty her divorce from Swantor had gone, and that she was in a bad way. He now tied his launch to the wharf, got out onto the slippery deck and hitched up his britches and gun belt. As he did so, he thought he saw movement in the shadows up at the house, just going around back, followed by barking and then silence. He turned and secured his boat better against the wind and storm. It was a night no one should be out in, he told himself, but then he was the only law for a good fifty miles. He stared up at the house and studied it for any further sign of movement and checked his watch which read 7:05 P.M.

Must've been the dog, he told himself. Then he heard something odd on the wind, something like muffled shouting. Was it coming down from the house? No, his ear told him it was emanating from the boathouse.

He stepped inside to find the enormous yacht the Coast Guard was looking for. *Dr. Swantor is here!*

He slipped back out into the rain and telephoned the house again. Still no answer.

Again he heard a voice coming from the interior of the yacht inside the boathouse. It sounded as if someone were hurt somewhere in the bowels of the big boat. He wondered if the sounds might not be Swantor's hostage, the woman he'd heard about, abducted in New Orleans.

Potter climbed aboard, and made his way into the depths of the luxurious boat when his cellular phone rang, his emergency line. He cursed it for having frightened him, and he shut it down. No one could have a greater emergency than he had right here on his hands, he told himself.

*   *   *

NAKED, James Harris had kept going down the hallway, despite Lara's objections for him to not leave her alone in the storm. He shouted back over his shoulder that he was hungry, and that they needed more wine, and that she had to confront her fears. He dripped water and bubbles the length of the hallway and down the stairs and out into the kitchen. Stark naked, he began rifling the refrigerator when he thought he heard a key turning in a lock.

Looking across the darkened room and through a window on the back porch, James saw someone letting himself in. James grabbed hold of a bottle of wine and positioned himself crouching behind the kitchen cabinets where he felt himself shaking, fearful.

As he held that frozen pose, James Harris heard the door open and close, heard the footsteps as they neared him, and watched, unable to move or act, as the large man wandered through the kitchen and out to the stairwell, going up, going toward Lara. James didn't recognize the man but guessed that it was the ex. Lara had complained that he had harassed her throughout the divorce proceedings, and here he was, the bastard.

Then he saw the silhouette of a gun in the man's hand. James silently cursed, wondering what he should do, what he could do, but he was without an answer. *One pretends to know what one will do in such a crisis, but one can't really know what one will do until one is in such a crisis,* his mind said. *Fuck that,* he told himself, *what do I fucking do?*

He'd never imagined that such a crisis, if it were to come up, would catch him nude, but even if he had clothes on, he suspected he'd be just as paralyzed.

He held back, trying to muster his courage. Hadn't Lara said the guy had strange and bizarre ideas about getting even with her? *What would he do to me?* the new lover wondered.

When he stood up, James gazed out at the storm and down at his naked body. The only way off the island was Lara's transport, and that would strand her, but he could say he was going for help. He imagined sneaking about Lewistown in his birthday suit.

He took a deep breath of air and turned back to the interior of the house, still clutching the bottle of wine. Not much of a weapon, he thought. What the hell do I do after I hit him over the head with the bottle?

Then he began searching the kitchen for something to defend Lara and himself with. As he quietly searched for a knife, he lifted the telephone off the wall in the kitchen as well, dialing 9-1-1, but the line was dead.

SHERIFF Danby Potter moved toward the sound of a man in anguish. As he did so, he passed through the living area on the boat, amazed at what he found. Computer screens displayed a room with a woman who had been butchered, lying chained to a bed, the sight making Potter ill, a healthy fear of the monster he was now chasing coming over him. On another screen, in another room, paced a man chained by one ankle.

Potter recalled the phantom figure he'd seen up at the house. The man on the screen, alive and in pain, was not Jervis Swantor. Potter had seen Swantor at such places as the Piggly Wiggly grocery store on the mainland on more than one occasion. He had heard rumors that Mrs. Swantor had taken a lover, and he had seen a man slip from sight when he had visited Mrs. Swantor the day before to ask after her husband's whereabouts. Potter now wondered if the man chained on the boat might not be Mrs. Swantor's lover, and the bloody figure in the other room with half a face, poor Mrs. Swantor.

He realized now he had stepped into a horror house, and he needed backup. He saw that the call he'd cut off had been from the FBI on the Coast Guard cutter who had called for Mrs. Swantor's number. He hit return dial to reach them. Meanwhile, breathless, he'd made his way toward the cabin to help the man there, stopping at the door when he got through to Sorrento.

He told Sorrento where he was and what he had found. "I need you people to get here as fast as you can. I think Swantor's inside the house. Phone line to the house is dead now. Think I'll be safe till you get here. It's too late for his wife. Located her mangled, disfigured body on the yacht, and he's chained her lover here, too. Can you get here before daybreak?"

Sorrento shouted back, "No, I mean yes, we can, but Potter, you need to get off that boat and to a safe distance. And whatever you do, don't touch anything on that boat or release—"

"He's already killed his wife! Cut her head open here on the boat."

"No, that's not the wife, and the chained man—"

But Potter wasn't listening. "And he's got some poor guy locked in a room down here. I'm going to get him free. Get him to the mainland, and we'll wait to hear from you there."

"No, no, Potter, don't go near the other man! That's—"

But Potter had cut Sorrento off. He pushed open the door and said, "Don't worry, son. I'm going to get you out of here."

"The leg iron," said Kenyon. "This maniac plans to cut me up like he did the woman. There's a key. *Find* the key."

Potter rushed back to the living room area, frantic and searching everywhere for the key. He finally located it in a drawer below the computer, and looking up, he again saw the mutilated body on the screen but he could not look too closely at the horror. He grimaced and then rushed back to Kenyon. His phone began ringing again, but he ignored it for the moment.

"Swantor's a madman," said Potter.

"Hurry! He could come back at any moment," said Kenyon. "That maniac wants me to suffer before he kills me," he continued as Potter worked the ankle bracelet off Kenyon.

"My name's Potter. Sheriff from over on the mainland," he said, still stooping, tossing the ankle chain away when he grabbed for his ringing phone. As he opened the line, Potter's phone was drowned out by the sound and pain of the bone cutter that split open the back of his skull, the thing sinking its teeth into the old sheriff's brain.

Potter went down like a stone statue, his every fiber stiff, his eyes thrown wide open.

Kenyon said to the dead man, "Thanks old-timer. Now, where's that motherfucking Swantor?"

Kenyon soon stood on the boat deck staring up at the mansion with its lone light. Bone cutter in hand, his angry features were lit up when a lightning bolt streaked across the sky overhead. "Swantor," he muttered, staring up the long flight of stairs that spiraled their way up the hillside and to the house.

He began his long walk up the steps, thinking of what Swantor had done to him, how the man had ruined his plans, how the man had exposed him and used him. The bastard had displayed Kenyon cutting open a woman and feeding on her still-warm brain. Grant had had no control to stop Phillip at that moment, and certainly Phillip had had no control over himself once Swantor provided the venue to feed after withholding Selese from him for so long. By then, the hunger had again taken over, and the Seeker had no resistance once she was within his grasp.

By now the murder video was being beamed worldwide. Even if he could escape the FBI, he could not hide anywhere in the world, thanks to Swantor.

He had only one thought now. He wanted to kill Swantor and feed on his brain as his last act before being apprehended. Until then, he would remain here on this island to await the inevitable end.

JESSICA impatiently paced the pilothouse as Captain Quarels's ship moved against the storm, the small crew pushing the cutter to its limits. Every man aboard had heard the news of what had happened on the computer screen, and a healthy hatred of their prey—both Kenyon and Swantor—had welled up inside them all.

Sorrento's phone call had determined that indeed Sheriff Potter had gone out to Swantor's island home, and that he'd found Swantor's missing yacht. But Sorrento's final call to Potter returned an ugly sound, the sound of the bone saw.

They had long since left the canal behind them and were now in the safer waters of Grand Isle Bay.

"How close are we?" she asked the captain.

"Quite close, a matter of twenty minutes perhaps. I'll have a launch ready for you and Agent Sorrento to board. I can't risk the cutter in this weather, and I don't think you want us taking time to make depth soundings. It can get extremely shallow along the banks."

"Where do we board?" asked Sorrento, turning from watching the storm.

"Belowdecks. My first mate, Mr. Konrath, will guide you and take you ashore with two of my best men."

A tall, uniformed officer with a boyish face, Konrath stepped forward, handing them each a rain slicker and saying, "This way, please." Like the FBI agents, Konrath was armed and prepared to use deadly force.

Jessica and Sorrento followed him out into the storm, down the steps and past a bulkhead, and finally through a hatch and down into the ship. While topside, they had seen men working to lower a boat over the side. Konrath now directed them to an interior hatchway. On the other side of this door, they heard the pounding water and the *thud* of the lowered lifeboat.

Konrath checked his watch, went to a nearby phone and called up to the captain. "We're in position, Captain."

"Stand by," Quarels said. "The island has come into sight. Searching for the right house and dock."

"We'll stand by."

Moments passed like hours as the storm slammed the lifeboat into the side of the hull and they waited for the go sign.

Finally, the captain rang their position. "Konrath, we've located the dock—a police boat is tied there. It's directly off our starboard bow."

"We're on our way then, sir."

"Good luck and be careful. Keep in radio contact. . . . Out."

The two armed guards stood nearby. Konrath indicated the hatchway door, and one of the Coast Guard men turned the wheel on the hatch, and in a moment it was pushed open. Rain and wind stormed through the hatch, making it difficult to see, and just below the hatch, the lifeboat swung wildly in and out against the side of the cutter. Overhead, crewmen worked to hold tow cables firm to keep the boat from thrashing about wildly, but the cable was being given a battle by the wind and water.

Joe Konrath went first, leaping across the sometimes short and sometimes gaping space between the large cutter and the small lifeboat. Jessica was then helped across by Konrath onboard the smaller craft and Sorrento from behind. Finally, Sorrento joined them, along with the two armed crewmen. The only light Jessica could see at this vantage point was that coming from the hatchway they'd exited. A moment later even that small beacon was shut off when a crewman, struggling with the door, finally closed it from the inside.

The tow cables came off the boat and rattled upward and disappeared like angry snakes. The smaller craft bobbed and whirled uncontrollably at first, but in a moment the crewmen, under Konrath's orders, had manned the oars and stabilized the boat. Though they had an engine on the boat, Konrath suggested they go in as quietly as possible. The cutter overhead of them had long since shut down its lights.

When they pulled silently into the now-crowded dock, Konrath ordered the line secured. The nose of the craft nestled into the front of the dock and they disembarked from there. First Mate Joseph Konrath shouted over the wind, ordering his two men to follow his lead. He said to Sorrento and Jessica, "I'm taking my men with me up those stairs and to the house."

"Wait here until we've had a chance to check out the yacht," said Sorrento, urging Jessica into the boathouse. The two of them climbed aboard Swantor's craft.

"We've got to locate Potter. If he's still alive, we can get him medical assistance on the cutter," she said.

"And if he's dead, it's my damned fault. If only I could've gotten him to listen to me!" complained Sorrento.

"Yeah, if the old fool had only listened to you."

Sorrento insisted on leading the way down into the yacht. The rainwater dripping from their slickers puddled and ran down the steps ahead of them.

His gun in the ready position, Sorrento lost his footing,

going to his back and sliding down the final stair and into the living room area. Jessica was blocked by his body. If someone should come from the control room the other side of the stairs, Sorrento was a dead man. She leapt over him and turned, her gun pointed into the control room.

"Nobody here," she told Sorrento.

Mike made it to his feet, his gun still held firm. Jessica looked about the room they stood in, filled with computer equipment and two screens she remembered well from Florida. Splashed across one screen were the remains of the Skull-digger's second-to-last victim, Selese Montoya. Jessica gasped anew at the sight and shut the screen off.

"Oh, Christ . . . look at this," said Sorrento, staring at the second screen.

Jessica gazed at the prone body in a yellow rain slicker with the letters that spelled out SHERIFF in black. The man's head was smeared with blood and bone that had caked his hair. Potter lay on his stomach, the back of his head splayed open, the wound obviously the work of the Skull-digger's bone cutter. "Sonofabitch," Jessica muttered.

"Was the old fool deaf? Why didn't he listen to me? Why'd he go near Kenyon?"

Sorrento went deeper into the bowels of the ship, kicking open each cabin door, his gun pointed and ready. Jessica sensed that no one but the dead were aboard. She held back, waiting for Sorrento.

When he was satisfied that there was no one else aboard, Mike relaxed his grip on the gun, put it away and returned to her.

"Both Swantor and Kenyon must be up at the house. Potter must have helped Kenyon to get free, and that"— he indicated the screen displaying Potter's body—"that's what Potter got for his trouble. Damned old man. Why didn't he stop talking long enough to listen to reason?"

"Shut it off," Jessica said of the screen, but Mike continued to stare at Potter's body.

"It's not your fault, Mike." Jessica cut off the image on the second screen.

"Tell that to my priest."

"You couldn't have predicted this. All you asked of the man was to give you a phone number. He wanted to play hero, get her off the island. You begged him to wait until we got here, and you tried to tell him to stay away from Kenyon."

"Let's get up to the house before these butchers kill someone else."

"Shoot to kill," she told him.

He took a deep breath and nodded. "Count on it."

Jessica and Sorrento made their way topside and off the death ship. Stepping out of the boathouse, Jessica and Sorrento found themselves in a renewed, vigorous downpour and alone. Konrath had taken his men up toward the house.

They rushed up the rain-slicked cypress boards of the stairs leading to the mansion. Jessica stared up at the house as she went. The place was cloaked in a kind of ethereal green darkness from all the ivy on its walls and the foliage all around the structure. All the lights were out except for one that appeared on the third floor. Ahead of them, they saw the cautious Coast Guard men inching ever closer to the house.

"Wish we knew the lay of this place," said Jessica, near breathless. She slipped but caught the handrail and continued. Sorrento had gotten twenty yards ahead of her. He stopped and turned, asking if she were OK.

"Keep moving. I'm fine," she called back softly.

"Looks like G.I. Joe Konrath intends a frontal assault on the place."

"He should've waited for us like we asked."

"Everyone wants to be a hero, bring down the Skull-digger."

SEVENTEEN

And then it started like a guilty thing
Upon a fearful summons.

—SHAKESPEARE

INSIDE the house, Jervis Swantor inched his way toward the master bedroom and bath, and looking into the bathroom, he found Lara, her head on a satin pillow and her eyes closed in a bubble-filled tub. "How's the water, sweetheart?" he asked in a chillingly calm voice.

"Jervis, my God!" she replied, her eyes coming open in shock. "I . . . I didn't expect to see you here tonight." She recalled yesterday's visit from Sheriff Potter, asking after Jervis's whereabouts, and she'd thought then of vacating the place, but then she had James to protect her. "What do you fucking want, Jervis? What are you doing in my house?"

"I have someone I want you to meet. We're all going for a nice cruise to Cancun."

"You're mad."

"I know. Now get up and come with me." He jabbed her cheek with the barrel of his gun. "I said get up from there, you cunt!" he ordered.

She took in a deep breath of air, wondering if he'd harmed James and left him bleeding somewhere in the house. "Jervis, what the hell are you doing? What more can you possibly want from me?"

"Only a little more, sweetheart. Now stand up and step out of there!"

She stood before him, clothed only in tumbling bubbles, still wondering what condition James might be in. She gasped again at the sight of the gun.

Outside the wind howled about, and she could feel a scream welling up from inside her, but she controlled it.

"I'm surprised to find you alone. I thought you'd have had another man by now."

"What nonsense are you planning, Jervis? I always knew you were insane, but killing me? Everyone is going to know you were behind it."

"At this point, Lara dear, I really don't care who fucking knows that I had you killed. It's the way in which you're going to die that interests me."

She reached for a towel and wrapped it about her body. "Don't tell me, you're going to make good on all those times you threatened to feed me to the alligators."

"Better . . . much better than that. I have a guest on the yacht I'd like you to meet."

"A guest . . . the yacht?" She unconsciously clutched at the towel she'd wrapped herself in. He yanked it off.

"Down at the boathouse. We're going to go down there, you and me, just as we are. My guest won't mind."

"I mind! It's cold and wet out, and—"

He slapped her hard across the face, sending her to her knees, pushing the gun against the nape of her neck. "You never could follow simple orders, Lara. Do you want to die here, like this? Now, just do as I say!"

While on her knees, she saw a shadow of movement near the darkened doorway leading out into the hallway. She dared believe that James had come back to save her. But now Swantor pulled her to a standing position and ushered her ahead of him, the gun held to her back, coldly kissing it here and there. As they exited the bathroom, and went through the bedroom, she sensed it was true, that the shadow must mean that James was nearby.

"I'm sure you've heard of the now infamous Skull-digger, sweetheart, haven't you? The serial killer who carves out people's brains and consumes them?"

"What's that got to do with me?"

"I told you . . . I have someone down at the boat who wants badly to meet you, sugar."

"What are you saying, Jervis?"

He urged her forward. "I intend feeding you to him, darling, and filming it when he carves open your head for that useless brain of yours. I'm going to film it, so that I can watch it over and over again."

"You are insane!"

They entered the hallway where she saw the silent phone off the hook, not even a dial tone. She recalled the two phone calls she'd not taken and momentarily wondered if either one of them had been from Potter over on the mainland, to warn her. "The sheriff was here only an hour ago, Jervis," she lied, "wanting to know your whereabouts. They'll know it was you, Jervis."

"Old Potter! That's a laugh!"

When they arrived at the stairwell, a shaky hand came out of the shadows. Wielding a butcher knife, James Harris slashed wildly, cutting deeply into Jervis Swantor's forearm and wrist, causing him to drop the gun, which bounded down the stairwell. Swantor wheeled to his left, blood from his wrist spurting in all directions, coloring the walls. At the same time, dazed, his weight went forward and against Lara. She lost her footing and screamed, her body following the gun, tumbling down the stairs.

While Swantor fought off the naked man who'd leapt out at him, he heard Lara's scream and the sound of her thumping down a half-flight of stairs. She lay halfway between the third and second floor landings as the two men continued to struggle. Swantor held firmly to James's wrists, seeing that the other man had a knife in one hand and a bottle of Swantor's wine in the other.

Incensed at this development, Swantor growled and sent his knee into the other man's testicles. Using all his strength, he brought James Harris up over the top of him and the railing, sending the other man out into thin air. The wine bottle hit the bottom first, followed by Harris's naked form, which had spiraled down to the marble foyer below, his head plopping open like the sound of a ripe melon. He'd held on longer to the knife, but it too had followed Harris down, and it had come to rest in his chest.

"Sonofabitch," Swantor cursed, rushing for his ex-wife, praying she hadn't been killed, while ignoring his bleeding arm and wrist. When he got to her, he found her breathing. "Oh, thank God. I *so* want you to meet the Skull-digger *alive* not dead, dear thing."

He looked about for the gun, but it wasn't anywhere near her. It must be on the second-story landing. He hefted Lara into his arms and began the trek downstairs, looking for the gun. Outside, he could hear the winds gusting far stronger and louder than before. Lara started to come around, her eyes blinking. "Now, let's go see Dr. Kenyon . . . See if he appreciates you, Lara, as much as I do."

She screamed again.

"Go ahead, scream all you want. There's no one to hear you. Your boyfriend is dead, and it's off season, sweetums. No one on the island but us. It's as if God himself has ordained it all."

"Jervis . . . don't . . . don't do this," she pleaded as he carried her down. "You can't do this."

"A little late for any further negotiations, dear Lara."

*   *   *

A rain-soaked, dripping Grant Kenyon stood staring at the dead man lying in blood on the marble floor of the foyer where he had watched the man's flight from above. In the dark, he'd heard a struggle and screams, followed by the explosion of the wine bottle at his feet, splashing him with wine. The body and the knife followed instantaneously.

Obviously, Swantor had an unwelcome guest. Grant's pants legs and shoes were splattered with the mix of wine and blood.

He stared up into the darkness but could only see movement of shadows on the stairwell. In a moment, he overheard Swantor talking to the woman, referring to Kenyon. He caught only snatches of words, but he could hear her pleading with him.

Looking back at the nude dead man, Kenyon reasoned that had been the boyfriend.

Swantor was a dangerous man indeed.

He wondered if he should lie in wait, ambush the man and kill him outright with the bone cutter he'd brought with him—risk being shot—or just make his escape from this asylum. He wondered how much the authorities had been able to piece together about his and Swantor's connection, and decided they likely knew everything by now since SquealsLoud had shown them Kenyon on tape killing the New Orleans woman.

Now Swantor wanted to repeat the process with his ex-wife as victim. Grant—and especially Phillip—didn't like being used by Swantor for his malicious ends. Phillip had said it best: *"We are not going to be remembered as someone else's puppet, Grant. That's what Swantor will have authorities believing, that he was in control of my—our—actions all along."*

"The video will go a long way to prove that. Now that

it's done, how can we change it?" Grant had asked Phillip.

"We kill the bastard, so he can't spread his lies anymore. He can't be left alive after we're gone. Imprisoned, he would only have a forum to continue his lies about us."

Grant was then startled to hear someone shouting, the sound coming in from the storm outside. *"In the house, this is the Coast Guard! Open up! Show yourselves!"*

Kenyon backed into the shadows. Swantor had arrived at the foot of the stairs, forcing Lara to her feet, holding out the gun he'd recovered. Mrs. Swantor stood frozen over the body at her feet, repeating the name "James" over several times before she screamed again.

"Shut up!" ordered Swantor, tugging at her and pushing her out toward the rear of the house. Kenyon quietly followed them, going toward the kitchen and the rear exit where he had earlier found the unlocked door and entered. It appeared that Swantor meant to make his getaway there.

"But there's no escaping me, Swantor," he whispered to himself as he held firm to the bone cutter. Time was running out; the authorities were at the door. If Grant and Phillip were to kill Swantor, it had to be now and quickly.

Again the strong voice at the front door shouted. "U.S. Coast Guard! We're coming in!"

Thanks to Swantor, Grant Kenyon had enemies to the front of him and enemies to his back now. A flood of desperation, like an unchecked raging river, inundated Grant's and Phillip's every sensibility.

WITH one man standing at the rear of the house, Konrath and his other man marched up onto the front porch as they heard screams erupt from within. He had again ordered the door to be opened. No one responded to his second order accompanying with his pounding fist.

The doors were ornamented with beautiful stain-glass windows. "We're going in, so break the glass. Break it in, O'Hurley," Konrath ordered his hefty guard.

It took the butt of O'Hurley's rifle to break the glass and scatter the metal parts wide enough open for O'Hurley to reach his meaty fist inside and maneuver the lock. They then rushed in, fearful of what they might find and stopped cold as both stared at the naked dead man with the knife through his chest, lying akimbo like some oversize rag doll on the bloodstained marble foyer.

"Is it Swantor or Kenyon?" Joe Konrath wondered aloud, his voice echoing up the stairwell.

"I think we should stay together, Mr. Konrath, sir," said O'Hurley.

"Yeah . . . yeah, right. It's obvious this man's body came from up there," replied Konrath, pointing.

"Someone did a hell of a number on this guy, sir. Stabbed him through the chest and threw him headfirst," said O'Hurley, his gun pointed as he wheeled about the room.

Konrath radioed to his man around back. "Watch yourself, LaPlante! We have a dead man on the inside. You see anything your location?"

LaPlante and O'Hurley had been chosen for this mission due to their marksmanship. The guardsman replied, "Found a dead dog, sir, but otherwise it's an all clear, sir. Nothing but the wind and rain."

"Keep your eyes open, LaPlante. We've definitely got a murderer running around here someplace. Possibly has taken a female hostage."

"I heard screams, sir. I'm on the alert."

"Hold your position." Konrath stepped back to the front door and saw the two agents coming up from below, Sorrento and Coran.

"Maybe we ought to get more men up here, Mr. Konrath, so we can canvas each floor methodically," suggested O'Hurley.

"Help's on the way. Those two agents are right behind us, which means both front and back exits are covered."

"Then we concentrate on the lighted rooms upstairs."

"Turning on lights as we go."

They started up the stairwell, guns in ready position.

SWANTOR held his ex-wife in the shadows, his hand over her mouth in the kitchen, listening to the intruders. When he heard them going upstairs, he ushered Lara toward the back door, keeping his hand tightly over her mouth. Still bleeding from his wrist, Swantor forced Lara through the door, and seeing someone in a yellow rain slicker with a rifle outside, he shoved Lara out into the storm.

The guardsman rushed to save the nude woman, relaxing his carbine rifle in order to tear off his yellow rain slicker, placing it over her shoulders. The guard failed to see Swantor, who opened fire and killed him just as he placed the raincoat over the woman's shoulders. The single shot sent the man to his knees where he momentarily clung to Mrs. Swantor before going to his belly. This sent an array of shrill cries up from Lara Swantor, enough to overcome the wind.

Swantor then raced out to her, grabbed her and covered her mouth with a palm still covered in blood that had spilled from his wrist.

"That bastard boyfriend of yours cut me good," he said into her ear, feeling faint from the blood loss. "Now let's get to the boathouse. Mr. Kenyon's waiting on us. Don't want him to grow impatient."

Just as he said this, he heard a new roar in the wind and

instantly felt something bite into the back of his skull. He turned to come eye-to-eye with Grant/Phillip Kenyon, realizing as he fell dead that somehow Kenyon had gotten free. His last thought was of not finishing his film.

"Oh, thank God you've stopped him!" cried out Lara Swantor, whose eyes only now met Kenyon's. She saw a strange lust in the man's pupils, and she saw the still *whirring* bone saw. Instinctively, she pulled away. "You're Kenyon. You're the Skull-digger!" She turned and ran in the slippery mud, fleeing him.

Kenyon grabbed up Swantor's gun when a shot rang out, and he felt the bullet bite off a piece of his ear. He rushed at Mrs. Swantor as she attempted to get away, still wearing the open yellow raincoat. He caught her, grabbed her by the arm, and dragged her toward a steep drop-off at the rear of the house. Kenyon then shoved her down the gully and watched as the yellow raincoat made an easy visible target.

From below in the gully, Lara Swantor felt a cold desperation infiltrate her mind along with the chill to her body—and, as she rolled down into the depths of the black swampy area in this backwater ravine, she recalled how often Jervis had warned her of alligators on the prowl all along here. How he meant to feed her to them one day. Apparently, he had found a human alligator to do the job for him.

Grant dropped into the ravine as well, a second bullet from an upstairs window whistling directly at him, striking his right forearm and sending him rolling down the gully after Mrs. Swantor.

The second bullet had gone clean through him, leaving pain but little blood.

He picked himself up and rushed after Mrs. Swantor, his bone cutter in hand. *"One last meal before they kill me,"* Phillip said to Grant.

But Mrs. Swantor had had a sudden burst of energy fueled by fear, and she was getting away. He saw the yellow color darting in and out of trees and brush. Behind him, he saw lights approaching and heard the others chasing him.

EIGHTEEN

All evils are equal when they are extreme.

—PIERRE CORNEILLE, 1606–1684

JESSICA and Sorrento had heard the shouting from above, Konrath's voice; the tone meant he was delivering orders or demands. They had seen him at the front door, and they'd seen O'Hurley break in the glass and tear the door open. Something had happened. But by the time Jessica and Sorrento arrived at the front door, Konrath and O'Hurley had vanished. Jessica announced their arrival, calling for Konrath as they bounded up the porch and into the foyer.

They'd been instantly hit with the sight of the dead man lying in the foyer, obviously having fallen from above. Jessica knelt for a moment, trying to identify him as Swantor or Kenyon. It was neither man. "Someone in the wrong place at the wrong time."

"Looks like overkill."

"Or Kenyon's work."

"Konrath!" shouted Sorrento. "O'Hurley!"

They heard a gunshot coming from the rear of the house. This was followed by two additional gunshots originating from upstairs. They heard O'Hurley shout, "I think I got the bastard! LaPlante's down!"

"The rear!" shouted Jessica, going for the back of the

house. Sorrento slipped on the dead man's blood; not slowing, Jessica raced ahead of him, gun pointed.

When Jessica made it to the back door off the kitchen, she saw the two dead men lying out in the rain. She rushed out to where the two men lay in the blood-soaked grass. Jessica saw the youthful face of the man in the Coast Guard uniform, his nametag proclaiming him LaPlante, dead of a clean gunshot wound through the heart. The other man was tall and hefty, and the back of his skull was grinning with a gaping wound like the one they had seen on Sheriff Potter, but this wound to the back of the skull had been washed clean by the rain.

Sorrento was beside her now, doing his own assessment of the situation. With Mike's help, she turned the body and stared into the face of Jervis Swantor. "One down, one to go," she said through gritted teeth. "It's Swantor."

Sorrento and Jessica crouched over the bodies in the storm, their weapons pointed, but they had no target, and they were exposed. The two agents scoured the landscape for any sign of Kenyon and Mrs. Swantor. They saw no one.

Konrath came racing from the house, going to his knees over the young guardsman, LaPlante. "Oh, Christ! No, no!"

O'Hurley followed, saying, "He's got the woman! I got two shots off from the upstairs window. I'm sure I hit him."

Konrath bellowed, "O'Hurley, which way did the bastard go?"

"They went straight down, just as if they were swallowed up by the earth," said O'Hurley. "There's got to be a steep drop-off right out there, maybe sixty yards. She's wearing LaPlante's raincoat. The man's wearing dark clothing."

"Let's get this bastard before he feeds again," said Jessica, her teeth set. She grabbed her flashlight and beamed it toward the area O'Hurley's own light sought out. The men followed suit, and they spread out along the drop off, shining their lights at the dark hole into which Kenyon had crawled, taking his prey with him, like some beast out of the scriptures.

They tentatively made their way in the slippery undergrowth for about ten minutes before Jessica's flash picked up a slight movement and the color yellow in the far distance. "There! There she is. Come on!"

They carefully negotiated the incline, when a shot rang out, a bullet whistling past them. This made O'Hurley fall and tumble, sending up a bevy of frightened quail and shattering his ankle on impact against a tree. "Sonofabitch." He moaned.

First Mate Konrath ordered everyone to discard their slickers, realizing they presented too much of a target. Konrath then tended to O'Hurley while Jessica and Sorrento went toward the yellow marker, where they hoped to find the woman.

They fought tough, jagged underbrush, palmetto bush and gnarled branches that cut their hands and faces just to win a foothold on the riverbank where the yellow coat winked again and again at them like a lure.

Jessica whispered in Sorrento's ear, "Do you see it, the raincoat?"

"Could be there to decoy us in, a trap," he replied.

"What do you suggest?"

"I walk into the trap . . . you cover me," he told her.

"No, I walk in, you cover me."

"Not in this life."

"Then we go in *together*."

"We don't have that option," he insisted.

"Look, if he hasn't killed her already, this may be our only chance of flushing him out before he does."

They then heard a flurry of crashing noises in the water, and the yellow raincoat suddenly went in and out of sight.

Jessica instinctively rushed toward the sound, ahead of Sorrento.

"Wait . . . wait up! We go in together!" he shouted, rushing in behind her.

The sound of a struggle ahead in the fog-laden bayou beckoned her on. So far, they had been unable to save any of the Skull-digger's victims. Jessica, acutely aware of their utter failure in this regard, meant to change that here and now. Then a deafening silence fell over the place, and Jessica again spotted the yellow cloth. It began to move and thrash about in the black water, and then she heard the sound of the bone cutter's deadly *whirr*.

"Jesus, he's killing her right now!" Jessica rushed toward the flagging yellow marker in the dense forest ahead. They had come perhaps a hundred yards from where they'd left Konrath and O'Hurley. Her flashlight shone crazily, hitting the tops of trees now as she brought up her 9-mm semiautomatic to bear on the scene.

As she came into a clearing of caked mud and ooze, she fell and her body was trapped up to her hips in a sucking muck. She'd fallen prey to the swamp. Just ahead of her, from her prone position in the sucking mud, she saw the last of the color yellow go down the gullet of a feeding alligator that was pulling back into the river. Then she realized that Kenyon had leapt onto the monster, that he was actually wrestling with the alligator, using his bone saw now on the creature, cutting wide swaths of tough skin from its head, attempting to kill it. She knew instinctively that this was no act of heroism on Kenyon's part, but rather a rage against the beast and an attempt to regain Mrs. Swantor—*or rather her brain*—for himself.

Jessica, staring at this sight, froze, curious and amazed.

From behind her, Sorrento shouted as he broke through the brush, almost joining Jessica in the quagmire. Balancing himself, he came to a standstill and stared out at the water where the battle raged. "Shoot . . . shoot him," Jessica shouted at Sorrento.

While Mike hesitated, Jessica managed to bring up her gun, readying to fire at Kenyon when she saw that he'd vanished. All had gone silent in the water as if there had never been a disturbance. Nothing left of the battle but ripples on the surface.

Sorrento cursed himself for having hesitated firing. He imagined either the gator had sunk its teeth into Kenyon, or the madman had slipped away. He could be making his way to shore, given that the alligator was busy with Swantor's wife. She pictured Kenyon wading from the water and crawling onto shore somewhere on the island, still holding firm to his bone cutter.

"Can you get me out of this muck?"

Sorrento worked his way to solid ground as close to her as possible, trying to reach her. He perilously reached a hand out to her, nearly falling in beside her. "Sonofabitch is getting away," he complained, unable to reach her.

"No, he slipped off to the left. I saw him," countered Konrath who'd come up on the clearing from another direction. "He's still out there."

"Will you two please get me the hell out of here?" asked Jessica. "We've got to follow the riverbank. Try to keep up with Kenyon."

Konrath located a strong branch, and with Sorrento's help, they towed Jessica to safety.

"We have to split up." Jessica told them. "Kenyon could crawl ashore anywhere on the island, maybe down by the boathouse, make a clean escape. I swear I won't have that, gentlemen."

Konrath helped her to her feet. "I say we call in for help and wait until daybreak before one of us gets killed."

"You do what you think's right, Mr. Konrath," said Jessica. "I'm going after the bastard." She stood mud-soaked before them, her eyes determined.

Sorrento suggested, "Why don't you radio for everyone aboard the cutter to form a search party, Mr. Konrath? By time they get here, it will *be* daybreak."

"I'd do that but I lost my radio someplace out here, and the only other one is back with LaPlante's body."

Sorrento then turned to Jessica, but she was gone, moving swiftly along the bank and out of sight.

"Damn that impetuous woman," said Sorrento, before going after her.

KENYON had felt terror rip through him as the alligator plunged below the surface, turned topsy-turvy, spinning and going for the bottom while holding on to Mrs. Swantor, a little of her coat still extended from its jaws. Kenyon's own ability to hold on became a question of losing either the gun or his bone cutter, something he couldn't allow. So he'd lost the gun in the struggle. In the end, it had been a futile attempt when the alligator dove into the depths, dragging Mrs. Swantor with it.

He imagined her brain deep inside its gullet on its way to the stomach, and awaiting digestion.

He cursed those chasing him; he'd had to give up the fight when they appeared. He had swum away, trying to keep the bone cutter from taking on any more water than it already had.

He tried to catch his breath as he swam, hearing the authorities in the distance. He quietly made for the bank, disorientated and wondering where he was in relation to the house and the boat dock.

Then he saw the gator coming for *him*, weakened but coming on, its eyes filled with an eternity, its mouth still filled with small parts of Mrs. Swantor's raincoat.

Horrified now, Kenyon hurled the bone cutter ahead of him, hoping it would make shore, and then he swam faster and noisier in the same direction. The creature was right on his heels, snapping and trying to grab hold of Kenyon.

Kenyon had weakened it considerably with the damage he'd done the monster's head, yet it came on like a demonic force. Kenyon now pulled himself to land, and tugging at the exposed roots of trees, he threw himself onshore, tearing at the earth and pulling himself as far from the bank as he could. When he looked back, he saw the thing had somehow climbed ashore as well.

"Fuck, the damn thing's fixated on you, Phillip," Grant reasoned. "Something in it has to *have* Phillip—to feed on Phillip's cosmic mind."

But Grant didn't want to die, not like this. He clawed his way farther along, mustered his strength and got to his feet. He ran.

HAVING heard Kenyon's struggle from the water and the thrashing alligator, Jessica positioned herself as close to the battle as possible. She had grabbed a vine in the underbrush where she saw Kenyon attempting to escape the alligator, and she pulled the sturdy vine taut just as Kenyon raced toward her, unaware of her presence. Jessica had waited for the exact moment to rip at the hanging vine that cut across Kenyon's path. The vine stiffened at an angle, cutting him viciously across the face.

This sent him down on his back, a bruise across his forehead like one of the lines he'd so often drawn on his prey.

Seeing Kenyon immobilized, the alligator now took one last, powerful leap, and with its front feet firmly set, its bottom jaw scooped beneath Kenyon's skull and the massive upper jaw awaited its lower counterpart. The consequent *crack, snap* and *pop* through bone sounded like small gunfire at a distance, muffled as it was by the monster's closed jaws. The massive teeth met directly at Kenyon's forehead. Again the monster chomped, and Jessica heard the subsequent sound of crackling bone until she imagined the man's brain was spiked. She wondered if he were yet alive in this position.

Grant Kenyon, the man she had chased halfway across the continent now, *writhed*, his body stiffening and his every fiber feeling the pain, not unlike the pain that he had inflicted on his victims. He was still very much alive. As the gator thrashed, so did Kenyon's body.

Finally, Jessica listened to the horrible sound of bubbles and air escaping Kenyon in a long, painful agony of last rites.

She held out her firearm, preparing to put an end to it, but she questioned such an action. Kenyon had shown not the slightest mercy to his many victims, victims he presumed to rob of their souls while they suffered a live torment.

Her gun pointed at Kenyon, she saw that his body was still now, dead at last.

"Now, you sonofabitch, you've got a taste of nature's bone cutter," Jessica shouted, her eyes firmly held by the sight, when a final spasm of the man's body made the alligator chomp-swallow on him once again.

The beast then tried to pull Kenyon's dead weight back toward the water, tugging at its prey, and shaking its tail to move in reverse.

"Jessica! We can't let that gator get away!" shouted Mike Sorrento from behind her. "We've got to recover both bodies, Kenyon's and Mrs. Swantor if we can."

Jessica fully agreed. She both wanted to recover Mrs.

Swantor's body from the bowels of the beast, and to hold on to Kenyon's body, so that no one could ever question whether the Skull-digger was killed this day or not. She wanted no ambiguity remaining.

Since she didn't want to lose the alligator a second time, Jessica aimed and fired into its brain. A second shot from Sorrento rang out, hitting the beast as well. Right as it made the riverbank, the creature expired like a balloon losing air, dead of wounds earlier inflicted by Kenyon and now their combined gunfire.

She turned to Sorrento, his gun smoking. How long had he been there? How much of her behavior he had witnessed, she did not know.

The rains had softened and the sky along with it, a hint of daybreak showing through in the east.

Mike Sorrento stepped before her, and he stared at the scene: All but Kenyon's head extended from the alligator's mouth, his brain crushed inside the monstrous jaws. "Makes for a fitting metaphor for the man's life."

"Going to make one hell of a forensic photo, too," she replied, standing over the scene.

"Yeah . . . yeah, one hell of a shot. Good of you to put Kenyon out of his misery."

"I shot the gator, not Kenyon."

"No, I shot the gator," he disagreed.

"Then we both shot the thing."

"How long did Kenyon suffer?"

"All of his life, I'd say."

They stared for a moment at one another, each keeping silent. Jessica again wondered how much Mike Sorrento had seen, and how much his remarks were meant to elicit from her. In the distance, they heard Konrath calling out, trying to locate their position.

"I don't want anyone thinking we just sat here and let the alligator do our job for us," she said.

"I can't imagine anyone thinking that, Dr. Coran."

"I stopped him with a vine strung across his path. The moment he fell, the gator grabbed him. There was no pulling him to safety."

"I know . . . and you didn't have time to react. I saw the whole thing," he concurred. "And if it becomes necessary, Jessica, I'll back you up."

It wasn't lost on her that this was the first time he'd called her Jessica. Now that they shared a secret, he presumed them closer, she imagined.

Konrath came through the underbrush and stared at the scene. "Jesus," he said. "Terrible way to go."

"No more so than his victims," Sorrento replied.

Jessica knew that even dead, the gator's digestive juices would only continue to eat away at Lara Swantor's flesh. "Look around for that brain saw. It's got to be around here someplace."

The two men did so, and Sorrento complained, "It's likely in the water, six feet under."

"No, here it is!" shouted Konrath holding it up.

"Let me have it." Jessica examined the machine and expertly started it. "Good, it's still functioning."

"What're you going to do?" asked Sorrento.

"I'm getting what's left of that woman out of that beast, OK? Now, first thing we need to do is pry open the gator's mouth and get Kenyon's weight off. Then I want you two to help me roll that damned beast on its back. I'm going to cut it open."

"Don't you want to wait? Get a CSI team in here, photos, the whole nine yards?" asked Sorrento. "Cover our asses, so to speak?"

"Some things can't wait. We couldn't save this woman in life, least we can do is help her in death."

"How much of the woman do you hope to recover?" asked Konrath.

"Gators swallow whole chunks, like sharks. *Most* of her will be intact."

O'Hurley came through the brush on a makeshift splint. He gaped at the scene, and Konrath brought him up to date. Together, the three men pried Kenyon from the monster's jaws. Jessica and the others grimaced at the sight of the crushed skull and oozing gray matter. They then rolled the gator onto its back. In a moment, the alligator's bulk quit shimmying under the blue light of dawn, and it lay now on its back, its green-to-white stomach shimmering like glowing mildew.

Jessica revved up the bone cutter again and began the incision, unconcerned about precision as the cutter sailed through the tough underbelly of the twelve-foot-long monster.

Sorrento in a failed attempt to ease the tension said, "Some cesarean section you've got going here, Doc."

After the difficult work of the center cut, a visible, odious gas flume expelled from the stomach, sending Jessica backpeddling, the odor too much to bear. When it was safe to return, she cut two flap wings at top and bottom of the original cut.

With no other instruments to work with, she worked in butcher fashion to open the stomach lining. More gas fumes erupted, and Jessica said, "Think there's something here." She grabbed hold of a gooey yellow swath of clothing and pulled at it. A large portion of the raincoat. She was finding nothing in the way of flesh and bone.

Working on, without gloves, she used her blood-smeared hands to pull back the tough, unyielding skin once more.

Sorrento lent a hand, holding back one of the massive flaps, the odor of the insides threatening to make him ill when Jessica declared, "There's no Mrs. Swantor here. She's got to be out there somewhere."

"In the woods?"

"In the river?"

"Someplace other than the gator."

"She may've drowned."

"Maybe the gator has a hole someplace below the water where he stashes food."

"She could be in shock, wandering about in a daze."

The theories came fast and furious.

They began calling her name, their voices wafting through the thickets and out over the river. No answer.

"We'll get some help from the cutter, do a thorough search of the entire area," suggested Konrath.

Jessica searched for her cellular phone but realized it must be in the Mississippi muck that Konrath and Sorrento had pulled her from. "All right," she said, relenting. Looking down at herself, she saw that she was covered in animal blood and tissue, caked in with mud. Ignoring this, she began to spout orders. "Yeah, we need reinforcements. You're right."

"We have some black-water divers aboard the cutter. We'll get them out here, too. We'll find Mrs. Swantor," Konrath assured her.

Jessica breathed deeply and rubbed the back of her aching neck. "We've got to grid the house, the backyard and the yacht as well as three additional crime scenes. There's a total of six bodies, seven if Mrs. Swantor is found dead. And we need to confiscate the tapes that Swantor made aboard his—"

"Jess, I think you need some rest and—" began Sorrento. "Rest?"

"—to step back. Let others handle things from here on," he suggested.

"You're cold and shivering, Dr. Coran," added Konrath. "We could all use some hot food, nourishment, coffee. It's been a rough night."

Sorrento took her by the shoulders and firmly said, "I'll stay behind, keep any animals from getting at the bodies until *you* send in a team, Doctor."

"Good news is we've put an end to the Skull-digger. I'll let them know back at headquarters, get the word out."

"Come on, O'Hurley," said Konrath. "You need that ankle taken care of."

Jessica again thanked Sorrento for all he'd done, and then she thanked the Coast Guard men. Looking up at the top of the rise, she saw sunlight up there above this backwater hole.

"Yeah, you're right, Mike. I'll be able to coordinate everything from the ship a lot more efficiently than from here."

"Exactly."

Along with Konrath and O'Hurley, Jessica made her way up the incline, climbing for the light.

Sorrento watched all the others leave. When he felt certain he was alone, he stepped around to Grant Kenyon's shattered head. He easily plucked away large pieces of shattered bone from the skullcap created by the powerful jaws of the dead gator lying nearby. He squatted over the man's exposed gray matter, removing more and more of the fractured pieces from around it. He then, curious, proceeded to dig with his hands, and he liked the texture and feel of the cortical matter on his fingertips. Finally, Sorrento dared taste Kenyon's smashed brain.

The head was fractured wide, part of the skull easily

picked apart like an eggshell. He found pieces, shards, whole chunks easy to prize out, just like feeding on a large walnut. Other parts had to be ripped with some difficulty from the crushed skull. Sorrento was convinced that this man's brain held power after he had cannibalized so many, and that if he now consumed Kenyon's brain, he might quite possibly have a glimpse at this "cosmic mind" he had read so much about on his computer since he had first logged on to the website run by Cahil, after a high-school kid up in Chimera, Louisiana, had first contacted him about it. Something about Cahil's suggestions were hypnotic, as radical as they sounded. But he had never entertained the idea that Cahil was the real Skull-digger. But rather that Cahil had influenced the Skull-digger.

Peering in through the cracks of Kenyon's demolished skull, he saw there was more inside he could not get at because his hand was too large to reach inside. He saw the bone saw lying where Jessica had left it, but dared not use it. That would tip his hand. Instead, he grabbed up a rock and smashed it against the cranium, opening the already existing fissures wider still. Using his Swiss Army knife, he managed to dig out more of the brain. He fed on it, not caring for the taste, but devouring it nonetheless for its magical power.

The situation, the location, it was all so perfect for his needs. No one need ever know. Everyone would simply believe the alligator got at Kenyon's brain before it died. Jessica had been too busy worrying over the woman's remains to pay close attention to the condition of Kenyon's brain.

No one would be the wiser . . . no one but Michael Sorrento.

Just then he heard a twig snap, and turning, the raw gray matter of what was left of Kenyon's brain in his hand, he saw a naked, shivering woman staring at him, but her eyes didn't register a thing. It was Mrs. Swantor, and she was in complete shock.

He stood and smiled, stepped toward her and said, "Mrs. Swantor . . . I'm FBI Agent Mike Sorrento. I've been looking for you everywhere."

She could not speak—showing only fear and looking like a deer caught in headlights. Frozen. Still, she might bolt. She stared past him at the bodies of the gator and Kenyon. Sorrento wondered how long she'd been standing here, staring; how much she had seen.

A Coast Guard helicopter began whirring overhead, a deafening sound. Sorrento guided the woman beneath a thicket of trees. "Stay right here, Mrs. Swantor, until I come back." He went for the bone cutter. The sound it would make was no longer a concern.

EPILOGUE

And keeps the palace of the soul.

—EDMUND WALTER, 1606–1687

Several months later

D ARYL Thomas Cahil was being held on charges that his website instigated a murder spree, and he was being held for observation at the same facility where he had spent thirteen years under the care of Dr. Jack Deitze. A case was being put together that Daryl was a danger to himself and others. Still, Jessica felt certain that charges brought against Daryl would never stick unless a direct link could be drawn between his text and graphics and the two killers, Kenyon and Swantor. The freedom of speech issue regarding dangerous and inflammatory materials spread across the Web would protect Cahil and others like him. Still, the legal team set against him asked for and got full cooperation from Jessica, J.T. and the FBI Cyber Squad. They cooperated in showing how the website had influenced first the kill spree and then the madness unique to Swantor. The trial was set for next month in a federal courthouse in Richmond, Virginia.

In the meantime, Daryl had become despondent since he was denied the fame of the Skull-digger—and access to a computer.

Still, Jessica feared, the *U.S. vs. Cahil* would end with his release, unless federal prosecutors could prove conclusively he had *intended* to incite behavior such as Kenyon's kill spree and Swantor's act committed against Selese Montoya, James Harris, and his ex wife. They must prove beyond reasonable doubt that Daryl's warped ideas were tantamount to criminal intent, that he meant—like a cyber prophet, a modern-day Charlie Manson—to bring about the death of others. Kenyon's audiotapes represented exhibits one through four; Swantor's computer video of Selese Montoya's death number five. Kenyon had killed Sheriff Danby Potter and Jervis Swantor as well, and presumably Mrs. Swantor, whose body had never surfaced. The prosecutors would back their arguments with Swantor's horrible actions, citing that Daryl's website had had a domino effect.

Daryl might be his own worst enemy at his trial, however, since the stronger the prosecution's case for intent and influence grew, the happier he became with his growing, newfound notoriety. When he heard about Swantor's having filmed Kenyon's last murder, sending it into cyberspace, he became giddy with his power over the two men. Jessica hoped his smugness would hang him in the courtroom.

It had grown late in the day when John Thorpe entered Jessica's office at Quantico carrying a stack of binders. "Here're the autopsy reports from Grand Isle, all six of them."

She indicated a cleared spot to her left. "Right there."

He placed the thick bundle of reports in a pile on her desk. "You really need more reading?" he joked.

Jessica had not looked at the death scenes involving so many at the Swantor estate on Grand Isle. She had decided, once she had returned to the comfort and warmth of the Coast Guard cutter that horrible morning, that she didn't want any more to do with the Skull-digger case. She stayed on long enough to monitor the massive manhunt launched from the air, the ground and underwater for Mrs. Lara Swantor. The woman was never found, dead or alive. After that failed attempt, Jessica had chosen to step back, allowing others to clean up the mess left in Kenyon's and Swantor's wake. With so much devastation, so many lives lost in a single night on the island, six autopsies—seven if she were to count the postmortem on the alligator—it had taken all this time to entirely complete the forensic work, so that every murder scene from the yacht to the house, and Kenyon's end, could be understood down to the smallest detail. Except for the official reports, only the nightmares created by the work of the Skull-digger lingered on.

"Everything's in order, Jess," J.T. assured her. "Damned fitting that alligator should chomp down Kenyon's brain, too."

"I thought it a fitting justice," she agreed.

"No chance for a Jack Deitze to turn him into a pet project. As for the protocols, trust me, Jess . . . you can rest assured the CSI and M.E. teams sent to Grand Isle did a first-rate analysis of all three crime scenes—the yacht, the house and the backyard—as well as the site where Kenyon was killed."

"I'm sure they did a thorough job of it, John. All the same, you know how I operate."

He frowned and nodded, going for the coffeepot. "I know . . . I know . . . bound to review it."

"I'll just give it a quick going over."

J.T. poured himself the last of the coffee, sat down across from her and watched her go to work on the files, one for each victim and the two perpetrators. "Like I said," Thorpe spoke between sips of the acrid coffee. "The team New Orleans put together paints a clear picture of how each died, and by whose hand each had met his or her end."

"You know, John, you don't have to go over them again with me."

J.T. smiled. "I'll just hang for a little while, in case you need me to go over any of the fine points with you." He finished with a yawn.

She sat back in her chair and drummed a pencil on her desk as she continued to read.

"You ought to get home to Richard. Leave this for to-morrow, and get that drumming habit fixed."

"I'm not planning to review every item and detail to-night. Mostly interested in the Kenyon and Swantor reports, see if there's anything in either or both that might strengthen the case against that other freak, Cahil."

She *wanted* to rush home to Richard. They had made plans for the evening. But looking over the protocol made by the attending FBI medical examiner from field to lab at Grand Island and in New Orleans worried her for some reason. All appeared exactly as Jessica recalled it, and the photos brought back graphic memories of the event, but she felt an obligation to at least peruse the final reports.

Something caught her eye, and she leaned forward in her chair, causing it to squeal. This got J.T.'s attention. "What is it now?" he asked.

"What's this about the bone cutter going missing, J.T.?"

"It was never recovered, so far as I could tell from my reading of it."

"But it was *there*. I used it on the damned alligator."

"I guess someone must've thought it'd make a hell of a souvenir."

"That'd figure. Damn, you want something done right, you've got to do it yourself."

"Ain't it the truth."

"I knew I shoulda kept control of the damn scene, John.

You know as well as I do that that's no ordinary bone saw. It could speak volumes to a jury."

"Kenyon's not on trial, Cahil is. It's unlikely the bone saw would get in, Jess."

"We'll never know now, will we?"

"Jess, they have a strong case against Cahil."

"All because I couldn't take any more. Thanks to my turning every goddamn thing over to—"

"Stop it. Damn it, Jess. We've been over this. You won't be viewed as weak because you stepped away. You chased this guy across what, six, seven states. You'd been through enough hell for three agents down there, and it was time to turn over the reins, that's all."

"Who told you that?"

"Who told me what?"

"That it was time to turn over the reins, that I was exhausted beyond my limit."

"Well . . . no one put it in those terms."

"Who put it in any terms?"

"Your friend Mike Sorrento for one, that Captain Quarels of the Coast Guard cutter for another."

"I see . . ."

"Jess, you're only human. You did your job, and you did it well."

"Yeah . . . I did my job. I rushed back here when I should have remained at least as a consult on the postmortems."

"You've already had this talk with Eriq. No one's holding it against you."

The medical team that had taken over consisted of a small army of men and women who had to autopsy six bodies: Selese Montoya, Sheriff Danby Potter, Petty Officer Nicholas LaPlante, Dr. James Harris, Dr. Jervis Swantor and Dr. Grant Kenyon.

"The team, by all accounts, appears to have done a thorough job," J.T. added. He got to his feet and bid her good night. "Got a couple of loose ends to tie up in my office before I turn off the light there."

"Just want to get away from my bitchin', right?"

"That too."

After J.T. had left, people began to disappear from the building, until soon the place appeared deserted, a ghost town eeriness coming over the offices. She brewed a fresh pot of coffee and gave each of the various reports a cursory look, and then she turned over the file relative to Grant Kenyon. Sipping at her coffee and reading, she stumbled onto something that made her sit up a second time tonight. The words lifted off the page and filled her mind with question and worry.

The attending M.E. at the FBI lab in New Orleans had written:

Parts of Kenyon's skullcap and all of his brain matter *missing*. Presumed ingested in the alligator carcass discarded at the scene.

"All of it? This doesn't make sense," she said to the empty room.

Jessica rifled through the accounts, looking for any mention of this by anyone else. There was nothing else mentioned, but she clearly recalled finding nothing of the kind in the alligator she had turned inside out in her search of Mrs. Swantor.

She stared at the words about the missing brain matter. She recalled seeing some of Kenyon's brain oozing out when they had pried him from the alligator's death grip. She distinctly recalled that while his skull was significantly crushed, there was no reason the brain would not be encased in the mangled outer shell. It just seemed so odd, so strange, so like . . . like the contagion of Cahil's madness, infecting someone new, as it had with Max Strand.

She recalled the moment when she, Konrath and O'Hurley had parted from Sorrento, leaving him alone with the body. To her knowledge, he was the only one left alone with Kenyon's remains and the missing bone saw. In the interim, a part of Kenyon's remains had vanished, and so had the deadly saw.

She could hardly believe her thoughts. Mike Sorrento? Why? She recalled Max Strand's strange end, and how even Dr. Deitze had fallen into a fascination with Cahil, and she thought of the hundreds of thousands who logged on to Cahil's website.

She buzzed J.T., catching him still in his office.

"Jess're you still here?"

"That computer list of AOC subscribers to Cahil's online brain show . . ."

"Yeah, what about it?"

"Do you have it nearby?"

"I've got a copy, yes. Prosecutors have the original."

"Log ons before and *after* Daryl's arrest?"

"Yes. I have 'em, why?"

"Pull it for me, will you?"

"Jess, what's this about?"

"I'm not sure just yet."

Thorpe located and pulled the list, laying it pound for pound on his desk. He got back on the line. "What now?"

"Look down the list to the S's."

He rifled through to the S's. "You want to revisit Swantor?"

"See if you have the name Sorrento listed."

"Sorrento? As in *Michael* Sorrento?"

"Just do it, John."

In a moment, a breathless John Thorpe said, "No, Sorrento's not on the list."

She felt a wave of relief wash over her. "Good . . . that's good."

"Of course, he could be using another subscriber other than AOC."

"Of course . . ."

"Actually, all our field offices use PQ Uninet. If he were say investigating the case, researching, he might log in via Uninet."

"Who's got Cahil's computer now, our Cyber Squad?"

"Watching it like hawks, yeah."

"OK, I'll talk to Dana in the morning about this."

"About what?"

"Ahhh, it may be nothing . . . and unless I have more to go on, I think I'll keep it to myself, John."

"More than one agent in a field office logged on while we were monitoring, Jess, out of curiosity, you know. You know how the FBI grapevine works. We also had a few field agents warning us about this dangerous website from tips they'd received. Mike Sorrento may've been among them."

"Forget about it tonight, John, and thanks."

The following day, Jessica pursued it with Dana Morill, and the computer expert left a written message in an envelope by the end of business day. It read:

Yes, Agent M. Sorrento, New Orleans Field Office, logged on August 12, seeking information. Was he researching the case? His inquiries look like a fishing expedition. They date back to just before we confiscated the computer. He never logged on again.

Perhaps he had been fascinated with the case and was researching it against the day that he could contribute to it, but it seemed odd that he had said nothing to her about logging on to the weird website.

When she again looked at the crime-scene files, she looked closely at the photos of Kenyon's body, and the close-ups of his cranial wounds inflicted by the gator. She called J.T. into her office and pushed one of the photos at him. "What do you see?"

He stared for a moment. "A dead man I recognize as Grant Kenyon with his head crushed."

"Look closely at the negative space, all darkness inside, like Kenyon's victims. There's no brain inside that head."

"As I recall, they said the gator got his brains."

"And what, sucked them out through the cracks?"

"What're you suggesting, Jess?"

"When I left Kenyon's body, all of it was intact. Someone at that scene . . . before this picture was taken, before Dr. Alan Mays, M.E. for New Orleans, made his initial report . . . someone stole and possibly consumed the brain of the Skull-digger."

"This is a hell of an accusation, Jess. This have to do with your questions about Sorrento the other night?"

"Maybe."

"But you can't prove it."

She bit her lower lip. "I guess I can't. No one can verify it, other than the man who did it."

"Suppose Mrs. Swantor somehow got at the body."

"Sorrento said he'd guard against *any* animals getting at it. He volunteered."

"You know I trust your instincts, Jess, but this . . . It's pretty wild."

"I'll have to write up my suspicions. Someone's got to keep an eye on Agent Sorrento. And meantime . . . hope we don't hear of any more brain-snatching murders erupting someplace."

"As in New Orleans?"

Jessica sighed heavily, and in a moment the silence was shattered by the phone. "Yeah, this is Jessica Coran," she said.

"Dr. Coran, it's me, Mike Sorrento."

"Sorrento . . . how . . . how are you?"

"You're not going to believe this."

"I don't know. Try me."

"We got something weird going down in my city."

She took a deep breath. "Go on."

"Looks like some bastard's taking up where Kenyon left off. Victim was left without a brain."

"Dear God no."

"Thought you might like to join us down here on the manhunt. We certainly could use your brain power."

"My God . . . I-I thought we'd seen the last of such horror."

"Wish it were so."

"When did it occur?"

"Last night, a college kid named Samantha Poole from Tulane. Head cut is different, but same kind of tool used, a bone cutter—"

The one never found—Kenyon's cutter, she guessed but did not say.

He continued, adding, "This guy just cuts around the entire head, back to front, Dr. Mays tells me. Lifts off the skullcap entirely and appears to eat out of the bowl of the head. Like I said, *different* but *alike.* Guess it shouldn't come as such a surprise, not to *us,* huh?"

She was stunned to hear him say this. He was either guileless or he had taken on Kenyon's sense of arrogant power. "Guess we shouldn't be surprised? What do you mean?"

He repeated it. "We shouldn't be surprised, knowing that damned cyber video of Swantor's was beamed across the whole damn planet."

"Yeah, agreed . . . see what you mean now."

"Will you come and help us out on this one?"

"Absolutely," she said, thinking: *Along with an arrest warrant for you!* She needed to get her facts together, organize her thinking on this. She needed to inform Eriq of her suspicions, have a discreet background check done on Sorrento, and talk directly to Dr. Brunner and Dr. Mays. She'd get a blowup done of the photos, contact O'Hurley and Joe Konrath for their testimony, and she'd pull the record of Sorrento's visit to Cahil's site. It wasn't conclusive evidence, but when she went to New Orleans, it would be in the company of two U.S. marshals to calmly, quietly arrest the new Skull-digger.